ROBIN'S RESOLVE

BREANNE LEFTWICH

For my husband, my biggest supporter who never stopped believing in me. Thank you for all your love and encouragement. You believed in me before I believed in myself, and for that, I'm eternally grateful.

A special thank you to my sister, Cheyenne. You are seriously my number one fan, pumping me up at every turn. I think you're more excited for these books than I am . . . *Almost!* Thank you for everything you've contributed to my stories—especially a certain sarcastic character I love so much.

CHAPTER ONE

Ben . . . my Ben . . . was lying in a hospital bed, hooked up to a ventilator. Paralyzed from the waist down and in a coma, the doctors said he'd never wake up. They told his family to prepare themselves because Ben . . . my Ben . . . was going to die.

"You have to let me bring a healer to him!" I yelled, everything in me prepared to fight the council.

Yesterday, after Claire landed her blow, we immediately summoned an emergency meeting of the Keepers of Balance. I'd been in shock and cried during most of the interaction as my parents and Matthew begged them to let us bring a healer to Ben. But today, I was fired up. I wouldn't let them stand in my way of saving Ben. Not when he could be healed so easily. I wouldn't sit around knowing his death could've been prevented. I wouldn't let him die.

"Robin, the council has discussed it in length," a younger earth element named Luna told me, "and though we're split right down the middle on the situation, we decided we can't allow you to do that. Keeping Garridan secret is of the utmost importance and—"

"Do you think I care about that?" I cut her off. "Someone I love is *dying*, and we have the ability to save him! You can't expect me to just sit back and be okay with not doing anything because you're scared!"

"We aren't scared," Peter spoke up, and I glared at him. He'd always been my least favorite person in this room, and I had no problem turning my wrath on him. "We just value our people's safety."

"If you value our people's safety so much, why were you perfectly okay with sending *me* to spend months with the Cyfrin?" I asked, folding my arms over my chest. "You knew it was dangerous, but you didn't care. At all."

"That was a very unique circumstance," he answered coldly, his beady eyes and pointy nose playing into his sinister character. "Giving them you kept everyone else safe."

"So, what you really mean to say is that you're okay with doing what protects *you*."

"You listen here little girl—" he started with malice in his voice.

"Enough, Peter," Chang inserted, raising his hand to silence him as he watched me. "Let her speak her peace."

He nodded his bald head towards me, and I took a deep breath, knowing I had to try to reason with them. Yelling wouldn't get anything accomplished. I needed to appeal to them in a different way.

"I've known about Garridan for a year now and in that time, I've only spent about six months here," I started. "Despite that short time frame, I've already sacrificed *so* much for it. My mom and sister were killed. I had to leave the only place I ever called home and with it my school, my friends, my boyfriend.

"Then I chose to go to the Cyfrin to protect this place I barely knew. I went through hell and back while I was there, but it was worth it because I helped take them down for good. I've given everything for this place. *Everything*. And now that I ask for *one* favor in return, you can't give it to me? Even after everything I've done for you? For your world? For *your* loved ones?"

The Keepers of Balance were exchanging looks, most of them guilty, and I knew my heartfelt plea had been heard better than my sleepless tirade. But was it enough?

"I hope you know how much we appreciate everything you've done for our home, Robin," Darby finally spoke up, pushing a stray strand of hair out of her tired face. "And we're well aware of the trials that have been forced on you since you found out about us."

"But that doesn't change the fact that the council already voted," Chang finished, his wrinkling, dark eyes full of sympathy.

His words were like a knife in my heart as I realized what he was saying.

They're going to let Ben die.

I frantically looked towards Mom as I began to hyperventilate. Matthew and Claire came up on either side of me, ready to catch me if I fell apart, and I grabbed onto their arms for support.

"What if we bring the boy here?" a voice asked as someone came through the door.

I glanced over my shoulder to see Akio walking towards the middle of the room.

"Preposterous!" Peter exclaimed.

"It would allow us to do our work without fear of being caught," Akio continued. "Garridan's secret would remain safe and so would the boy."

"Outsiders aren't allowed here," Peter told him angrily.

"He already knows about Garridan though," Dad spoke up, "and he's kept it a secret. I don't think we'd have to worry about him. He's not a threat to us."

I could see some of their faces beginning to change, and hope filled me as I squeezed Matthew's arm tighter.

"You can't honestly be considering this?" Peter asked the room. "We have our own problems to attend to! Some of our brothers and sisters died, and it's of utmost importance we find replacements for them so the council is balanced."

"Bringing Ben here wouldn't delay any of our other duties," Mom said. "Voting in new Keepers of Balance will still be a priority. We're very well adept in multitasking our responsibilities. You know this."

"But the boy isn't our problem," Peter griped as conversation broke out. He seemed to have no other reason to deny our request, so he sat back in his chair with his arms crossed.

After a couple moments of loud chatter Luna said, "I think we should take another vote. I'll start . . . With a yes."

"Yes," Chang agreed.

"Yes," Darby echoed, and tears filled my eyes as they went around the room with all but two voting the same.

"Thank you," I whispered as a tear escaped down my cheek. "Thank you!"

"It's the least we can do," Chang said with a thin smile. He sounded as if he was pleased to have gotten around their own rules.

I turned to Akio as my parents and Malachi came up to us. "Thank you. Thank you so much," I told him.

"Of course," he replied.

"When can we go?" I asked Malachi.

"I can have a plane ready in thirty minutes," he said, and I nodded eagerly, so he walked away with Akio at his heels.

The sooner the better.

"I'm going to stay here with your friends," Dad said, "but I'll be at the hospital waiting when you get back with Ben."

"Okay," I replied, giving him a quick hug before turning to Mom. "Are you coming?"

"Of course," she responded. "As I'm sure Matthew is."

"He's my friend too," Matthew said. "I'm going."

"I need to run by the house before we go. Do you two want to come?" Mom asked, and I shook my head. "I'll swing back by to pick you up in twenty minutes then."

"We'll wait on the steps," Matthew replied before she and Dad left.

A thought popped into my head, and I grabbed Matthew by the front of his shirt in a panic. "What if his parents take him off the vent before we get there?"

Matthew tried to loosen my vice like grip and said, "They won't."

"You don't know that!"

Claire took hold of both my shoulders. "Hey. Calm down." I took a deep breath and pushed it out slowly, trying to get my bearings. She looked me over then said, "I have an idea. Come on."

Matthew and I followed her to one of the back offices on the first floor, where a high school girl wearing all black was lounging in a chair.

"Wendy, I need a favor," Claire told her as we came into the room.

"What's up?" the pink haired girl acknowledged.

"I need you to communicate with someone on the outside," Claire requested, and Wendy instantly looked a little less willing.

"You know that's against the rules," she said.

"When have you ever been one to follow the rules?"

"Since I've been on major probation. My dad would kill me if he found out."

"Then we'll do it quick. Please. It's for a good cause."

Wendy hesitated, her black lined eyes full of consideration. "Fine. Close the door."

"What do you mean 'communicate?'" I asked as Matthew did as she requested.

"Wendy is a telepath," Claire explained. "A really skilled one at that. She can break through the barrier around Garridan and get a message to Ben's family."

"Not Ben's family," Matthew inserted. "Felicity. She already knows about Garridan too. If you tell her the message is from me and Robin, she'll believe it. She won't think she's going crazy hearing a voice in her head."

"Okay, Felicity it is," Claire agreed.

"Do you have a picture of her?" Wendy asked. "I need a clear visualization so I can sense her presence."

"Not with me," I answered dejectedly, but Matthew pulled out his wallet and slid a small photo into his hand. It was one of him and Felicity. I gave him a disapproving look, and he shrugged sheepishly.

"I keep forgetting to take it out," he said, and I arched one brow, not believing him.

"Claire, can you help me out?" Wendy requested. "Tell me where she is. Exactly."

Claire closed her eyes, and I watched them moving behind her eyelids as she began seeing what Felicity was seeing. "She's in the hospital. She's sitting in the waiting room with two kids."

"Dakota and Mahka," I murmured, my heart being pulled apart as I thought of how they were holding up.

"I got her," Wendy said, her own eyes closed. "What do you want me to say?"

"Tell her you're a friend of Matthew and Robin's and to nod her head if she hears you," Claire instructed. After a moment of silence she said, "Alright, she heard us. Tell her Matthew and Robin are coming. Tell her they'll be there by the end of the day and to not let Ben's parents pull the plug on him."

I watched as both of them did their own thing. Their abilities were so different, but they were using them in unison to do something remarkable. I was, once again, amazed by my people's powers.

"Okay," Claire finally said. "She's going to talk to Ben's parents now."

I nodded, breathing easier. "Thank you. Both of you."

"You're welcome," Wendy responded before sitting back down and rubbing her temples.

"You good?" Claire asked.

"Yeah, just a migraine. Getting through the barrier takes a lot of work."

Claire hung back, making sure she was okay, while Matthew and I headed to the front doors.

"Are you alright?" he asked.

"Do I look alright?" I asked in return, meaning it rhetorically.

"Not at all," he replied, always ready to tell the hard truths. "You look horrible actually."

"Wow. Thanks," I grumbled, but he stopped and turned me towards the far wall that was lined with a mirror.

"I'm serious, Robin. Look at yourself."

I gazed upon the face I knew so well but didn't recognize at all. My mouth fell open a little as I looked at the heavy bags under my lifeless eyes. My cheeks were pale and pasty, and my lips were chapped and peeling. He was right—I looked horrible. I looked *sick*.

"I know how worried you are about Ben. I am too. But I'm also worried about you, and you should be too. It's not your fault you haven't slept much the last week and a half, but it's taking a really heavy toll on your body. It can't handle any more stress."

"I'm fine," I told him, turning away from the mirror.

"Why are you so stubborn?" Matthew growled.

"The somnokinesis effects are almost gone. In a couple days, I'll be able to sleep again, and I won't look like the grim reaper is about to snatch my soul."

"The what?"

I rolled my eyes before saying, "I'm fine, okay? Or, at least, I will be after we get Ben here. Stop worrying."

"Impossible," he remarked quietly as we sat on the stairs.

I leaned my head against his shoulder, my eyes drooping shut. I knew the lack of sleep was affecting me negatively. I was irritable, snappy, and extremely unpleasant to be around. My attitude was out of control, and I couldn't seem to find any reason to be happy.

Not to mention, every single motion was becoming harder to perform. Sometimes I wasn't sure I was really awake because my body seemed to be on autopilot as it tried to get things done. But there was nothing I could do about it. Until I could sleep, I just had to try to survive. I had to outlast the voices that were getting fainter and fainter every day.

Saving Ben, though, that was something I could do. My time to heal would come. For now, all I cared about was him.

CHAPTER TWO

Mom and Matthew walked on either side of me as the hospital doors opened for us, and Akio followed behind silently. The atmosphere was calm, almost peaceful, but I wasn't fooled. I knew the tragedies that unfolded in the rooms hidden down the halls. My tongue was dry against the roof of my mouth and my heart raced as my nose was attacked by the intense smells that came with the hospital setting. Matthew must've sensed my rising panic because he put his arm around my shoulders as we stepped up to the front desk.

"We're here to see Benjamin Toves," Mom told the receptionist, who nodded and turned towards her computer screen.

"Robin?"

I turned around just as Felicity's arms pulled me to her. She squeezed me tightly as she sobbed into my shoulder, but my arms hung weakly at my sides. When she pulled back, she ran her nose over her sleeve and gave us a shaky smile.

"I'm so glad you're here," she said, her bloodshot eyes continuing to spill tears.

"How is he?" I asked.

"No change," she replied sadly. "His doctors said his parents need to make a decision soon."

Over my dead body.

"Where is he?" I questioned, the need to see him overwhelming.

"Come on." She grabbed mine and Matthew's hands.

She led us to the other side of the hospital, where Ben's dad was sitting with Dakota and Mahka.

"Jeremiah," I said, and he glanced up.

A sad smile covered his face as he stood to greet me. "It's good to see you, Robin," he said as he wrapped me in a warm embrace. He stuck out his arm to shake Matthew's hand over my head. "You too, Matthew."

"I wish it was under better circumstances, sir," Matthew responded as Akio took a seat across from the boys.

"I do as well," Jeremiah said, rubbing his hand over his drooping face.

"How did it happen?" Matthew asked as I leaned down to hug Ben's brothers.

"We were on a ski trip with the basketball teams," Felicity answered, her voice quivering. "Some of our parents sponsored the trip so everyone could go. The guys wanted to go down the black diamond trail, and Tom kept calling the girls sissies for saying no. Jill and I wanted to prove him wrong, so we followed.

"Amara tried to stop us, but you know how stubborn we can be so w-we kept going and once I started . . . It-it was too much for me. Ben saw me losing control and he reached out to pull me away from the cliff I was heading towards." She buried her face in her hands as her voice broke. "The momentum must've thrown him off balance because he ended up falling and . . ."

"And?" I pressed, my voice thick as the image formed in my mind.

"And he rolled off the cliff," Jeremiah finished.

My breath caught in my throat as the scene finished playing out behind my closed eyes. When they opened again, everyone was watching me, but I stared coldly at Felicity as heat rose in my core. I glared at her, my jaw clenched and my hands turning to fists by my side.

"This is all *your* fault," I whispered as the fire inside threatened to come pouring out.

Felicity's eyes widened, the grief in them now mixed with shock. "W-what?"

"You did this."

"Robin!" Mom exclaimed, her voice layered in warning.

"You've always been a horrible skier," I continued, ignoring the looks being thrown my way. "Why would you think you could do a black diamond trail? You shouldn't have been anywhere near that! Why would you be so stupid? You could've gotten hurt!" I scoffed. "But, even worse, you got someone else hurt. And for what? To impress some jerk you don't even like? Was Ben dying really worth that?!"

"Robin," Matthew snapped as Felicity turned and ran away from us, her pounding feet echoing in the wide space.

My rationality was battling to be placed over the anger, knowing Felicity wasn't really to blame, but my usual sensibility was washed far away. It was lost under the emoti-ons that were intensified by my sleeplessness. Ben had gotten hurt saving her. Ben was lying in a hospital bed on the brink of death because he had to save her. It was her fault.

"Deep breath," Matthew told me.

"What?" I questioned as my mom started telling Jeremiah how sleep deprived I was. I guess my cruel outburst needed some sort of explanation.

"Deep breath and count to twenty," he instructed.

"But the voices aren't here," I responded, not understanding why he wanted me to use my coping strategy for the somnokinesis withdrawal.

"I don't care. You need to calm down so I can knock some sense into you. You're not really mad at Felicity. You're just tired. You're not thinking straight. So deep breath and count to twenty," he repeated, but this time he crossed his arms and stared me down with narrowed eyes.

I let out a sigh thick with attitude but did as he said, washing my lungs with fresh air and expelling the old air as I silently counted. As I got closer to twenty, the tension in my body began to dissipate, and shame replaced the anger I'd been feeling.

"What have I done?" I asked quietly, misery washing over me. "I need to go find her but . . ."

"Go see Ben first," Matthew said. "I'll find Felicity and explain that you aren't yourself right now. You can apologize before we leave."

"Do you think she'll forgive me?"

"Of course she will. You're her best friend."

I nodded but found little comfort in his words. He walked away as I turned towards Jeremiah. "I'm so sorry. I didn't mean . . . you're going through enough without me causing a scene."

"We've all had our moments of being angry," he replied, the tone in his voice making me wonder if he'd blamed Felicity at one point as well.

"Can she see him now?" Mom asked. "I think it would do her some good."

"Sure," Jeremiah agreed. "Follow me."

Mom sat down next to Akio as Jeremiah and I walked through the ICU doors. I knew she'd send Akio in after I had a minute alone with Ben, then we'd have to convince his parents to let us take him. Jeremiah stopped in front of the third room and peered in sadly as Kiona sauntered out.

"Oh, Robin," she said when she saw me, burying her face in my shoulder.

I held onto her, waiting until she loosened her grip before I dropped my arms away. She placed her hands on my cheeks as she assessed me.

"Honey, you look awful," she told me with concern.

"I just haven't been sleeping well," I replied. I didn't know how she could possibly have any room to think about my well-being with what she was going through.

She nodded sadly and said, "I understand. But you have to take care of yourself. What would Ben say if he saw you like this?"

I peered down at my scuffed-up shoes, unable to answer. He'd be more unbearable than Matthew. Instead I asked, "Can I see him?"

"Of course. We'll go sit with the boys. Give you some time alone with him before . . . Before . . ." She exhaled sharply then turned away from me as she leaned into her husband for support. As they walked away, her shoulders shook, and I knew she was crying.

We had to save Ben. Not just for me, but for everyone who'd be affected if he died.

I took a deep breath then stepped into Ben's room. The window was wide open, letting in a cool breeze just like he would want. Flowers took up most of the available space, and they almost allowed the feeling of happiness. Almost. My eyes finally landed on the thing they most wanted to see, and I let out an inaudible gasp.

Ben was lying in the bed with a tube running out of his mouth. I could hear the steady hum of the machine that was breathing for him and could barely see his chest rising and falling under the hospital gown. I stepped closer and saw healing cuts on his pale face. It was a strange color on his usually dark complexion, and it made him look sickly.

I sat down in a chair that was pulled next to the bed and hesitantly grabbed his hand in both of mine. It was abnormally cold, and I wondered if his circulation was starting to suffer. I gently ran my fingers down his cheek as my chin began to quiver.

"You're gonna be okay," I told him quietly. "I'm not going to let you die. You're gonna come back home with me, and we'll get you all fixed up." One side of my lips turned up in a smile as I played with his hair. "Then you'll get to meet my new friends and see where I live. You'll love it. I know you will. Maybe you'll even want to stay."

I closed my eyes as tears spilled down my face. He wouldn't want that. His whole life was here. His family and tribe were something he would never give up. Plus, he was graduating high school in a couple months and would be off to college. The only thing Garridan would have to offer him is me, but that was next to nothing compared to everything else. Especially since he had a new girlfriend.

I'm not enough.

A sob tore through my chest as I leaned my head against his arm. Seeing him again reopened the wounds I'd been trying so hard to heal. Mom was right—not being allowed to see him was a good thing. Having him completely ripped out of my life was the only way I'd be able to move on. Which meant this *had* to be the last time I was around him. After he was healed and sent back home, I couldn't see him again. We had to be over. Completely. It's what was best.

I sniffled as I placed his hand under my cheek. Every part of me ached to have him closer while I could. My eyes drooped closed, and I let out a loud yawn. Maybe I could take a quick cat nap. I started to drift off, soothed by Ben's presence. Just as I was falling into a deeper sleep, the door was pulled open, and my head shot up in a panic.

"Sorry, hon," a nurse said as she walked towards Ben. "I have to check his vitals."

"It's okay," I murmured, trying to rub the sleep from my eyes. "I'll get out of your way."

I sluggishly made my way down the hall to the waiting room. When Mom saw me, she jumped up and asked, "Is everything okay?"

"Yeah. A nurse had to check his vitals and stuff, so I was just trying to get out of the way."

"How's he seem?"

I snorted. "Kinda a stupid question, don't you think?" The second I said it, my hands flew over my mouth as my eyes widened. "I'm sorry, Mom. I didn't mean that."

"Yes, you did," she replied, her voice gentle. "And it's okay. It was kinda a stupid question."

"I didn't mean to be so rude though." I sighed and rubbed my hand over my face. "It just seems to keep slipping out."

"You have a very good reason for it." She placed her arm around me, and I leaned my head into hers. "Once you finally get a good night's sleep, though, we'll all be a little less tolerant of your outbursts."

"Once I finally get a good night's sleep, I won't *have* any more outbursts."

"Something to look forward to."

I glanced up at her sheepishly. "Have I really been that bad?"

"You're my daughter, and I love you," she replied before releasing me, "but yes. You've been a real pain to deal with these last couple weeks."

"I appreciate the honesty," I muttered sarcastically, and she laughed. I looked over her shoulder, watching Ben's family as they held onto one another. They all looked so broken. "We should talk to Jeremiah and Kiona."

"I can't imagine they're going to take our request very well," Mom said, and I shook my head.

"No, probably not." We shared a knowing look then made our way to where they sat. I cleared my throat then quietly asked, "Can we talk to you for a minute?"

"Of course," Jeremiah answered. "What's up? What's happening? What's the down low?"

"Dad, stop," Mahka told him with a roll of his eyes. "You're not funny and you're definitely not cool."

"Just trying to lighten the mood," Jeremiah said with a shrug.

"Like that's possible," Dakota mumbled, crossing his arms and turning away from us all.

"*Anyway,*" Kiona said pointedly. The look she gave her husband was enough for him not to try to crack another joke. "What do you need, Robin?"

I opened my mouth then shut it again as I glanced at Mom.

How do I even go about this?

She nodded encouragingly, so I tried to shut down my nerves as I decided straightforward was the best way to go.

"I'm fully aware how crazy this is going to sound, but we need to take Ben back home with us," I said.

"What?" Kiona asked, sounding almost horrified at the thought.

"Garridan has some very advanced medicine," Mom spoke up. "Medicines that aren't accessible to most. We can help your son. We can save him."

"I don't understand," Jeremiah said. "The doctors said he's brain dead. There's no cure for that."

"There is in Garridan," Akio responded, finally standing and drawing attention to himself. "I'm a heal- I mean, *doctor* there. We can fix your son's ailments. All of them."

Jeremiah and Kiona stared at one another incredulously. "I don't understand," Jeremiah repeated.

"I know how scared you are," I said softly. "I know the grief you're feeling. Believe me, I do. And I know how ridiculous this sounds but it's *true*. Ben doesn't have to die."

"It really is true," Felicity added, trying to be another trusting source as she and Matthew walked up behind us.

I glanced over at her, but she wouldn't meet my gaze.

"You can save my brother?" Mahka asked Akio with scrutiny in his eyes.

"Yes. I can."

Mahka observed him for a moment, his hard eyes thoughtful, then turned to his parents. "Let them take him. Please."

"We can't just take him from the hospital," Jeremiah said. "They'd never let us."

"We'll cause a distraction and take him out the window," Mom told him.

"Is that even legal?"

"In your world or mine?"

"What?"

"Nothing." Mom waved her hand to dismiss her previous comment.

"Would we be coming with you?"

"No. I'm afraid he has to come alone."

"This is absurd," Kiona said, shaking her head. "No. No! Absolutely not."

"Kiona." I stepped in front of her and reached for her hands. "You know me. You know how much I love your son, and you know I would *never* do anything to hurt him. So, please. Just trust me. Let us take him."

She pressed her lips together tightly and looked to Jeremiah. A tense minute of silence passed before she whispered, "No. He'll die if you move him."

"I hate to be so blunt, but he'll die if we don't move him," Akio responded. "Those doctors will remove his air vent, and he'll pass away. After that, there will be no hope for him. He'll be dead."

Mom placed her hand on his arm to silence him as Kiona narrowed her eyes.

"If you let us take him," Mom said, "he'll have a fighting chance. He'll have an opportunity to get well. I know it's hard to imagine because the science you know is telling you there's only one option, but it simply isn't true. You don't have to lose your son. We can help."

Kiona clung to her husband, looking ready to collapse, and he supported her weight as he sat her back down in the chair she'd gotten up from.

"I think we need some time to discuss this," he told us. "It's a very complicated situation."

"Yes, absolutely," Mom agreed fervently. "We'll leave you alone while you come to a decision."

Mom and Akio made their way past me to the opposite end of the waiting room, but I lingered for a moment. I licked my lips then quietly said, "He doesn't have to die. If you can trust me . . . He doesn't have to die."

I stepped away, turning to face Felicity and Matthew. "Hey," I greeted them, holding my arms behind my back as I tried to figure out what to say.

Felicity glanced up then averted her gaze just as quick but replied, "Hey."

"Talk," Matthew commanded. "I'll be with Akio and Adriana if you need me."

I cleared my throat, waiting for Felicity to say something. When she didn't, I threw my hands up, suddenly feeling exasperated. "I don't know what you want me to say."

That got her attention. She narrowed her eyes and scowled. "Seriously? You don't think you owe me an apology?"

"Of course I do!" I snapped back.

"Then?"

"Then what?"

"Apologize!" She placed her hands on her hips, but the tears in her eyes didn't match her hostile attitude. She was hurting just like the rest of us.

I closed my eyes and slowly counted to twenty. Why was I being so rude to her? I wanted to apologize, so why was I getting so agitated? It was two very simple words: I'm sorry. She deserved to hear them, and I had no reason to react so aggressively right now.

I breathed in deeply, blowing out the air through my tight lips as slowly as possible. When I finally opened my eyes again, I felt much calmer than I had before. Felicity watched me with her brows knitted tightly together, and I could hear the unspoken questions she was thinking. I grabbed her hand and pulled her forward.

"Follow me," I said.

She didn't object as I led us back into Ben's hospital room. I sat down in the chair again and ran my fingers over his arm, immediately feeling a second wave of calm. I inwardly sighed then turned towards Felicity, who had her hand on Ben's ankle.

"Felicity, I am *so* sorry," I told her, my gaze intent as I watched her chin quiver. "I had absolutely no right to say all that to you."

She pressed her lips together and pushed a stray hair into her messy bun. "Thank you."

"I don't really deserve it, but can you forgive me?"

She gritted her teeth together, and silence raged between us as I waited for an answer. Just when I thought she wasn't going to say anything at all, she spoke.

"What you said really hurt me."

"I know," I replied softly, self-loathing filling me.

"Can you imagine what it's like?" she asked, her voice thick. "Being the person everyone blames for someone dying?"

"No one blames you."

"Everyone blames me!" she yelled, her voice cracking. "The basketball teams, his parents, you! And they should. This wouldn't have happened if I'd just not been so stupid. It *is* my fault. I know that! But do you think I want to actually hear it? Especially from the person who's supposed to be my best friend?"

She fell onto the foot of Ben's bed, sobbing into her hands. I stood and wrapped her in a hug as she shook from the violent cries that left her.

"I don't think I could live with myself if he dies. Can you imagine what it's like to be the reason someone is dead?"

I swallowed around the lump in my throat as images of my mom and sister dashed through my head then whispered, "Yeah . . . I can." I let her cry for another minute then pushed her away from me so I could look at her splotchy red face. "But you're never going to know that feeling because Ben isn't going to die. We're going to save him, Felicity, I swear. You won't ever have to live with that kind of guilt. Okay?"

She nodded slightly then ran her arm over her face. "Okay."

"And I really am sorry."

"I know you are. And I forgive you."

"You do?"

She nodded again then blew her nose before saying, "I'm still really hurt and a little mad, but after Matthew told me everything going on with you, I knew I couldn't hold it against you."

"What exactly did he tell you?" I asked suspiciously.

"Everything."

"He told you *everything?*" I questioned, feeling completely exposed as my nightmares with the Cyfrin were revealed to someone I never wanted to tell.

"Well, just a broad overview, but I can imagine how bad it was." She smacked my arm, her lips turned down in a scowl. "Don't *ever* volunteer for a suicide mission again!"

I smiled wryly and quietly said, "Yes ma'am."

"I'm worried about you."

"Don't be."

"Matthew is, which means I am too."

"It'll be better in a couple days."

"Because you'll be able to sleep again?"

I nodded. "Because I'll be able to sleep again," I confirmed. "When we bring Ben back, you'll see for your-self. I'll be back to my old self and this angry, unlikeable version of me will be long gone."

"Hallelujah," Felicity murmured, and I couldn't help but laugh.

I really must be a nightmare from hell right now, and I knew I'd have a lot of apologizing to do when I could think straight.

"He's really going to be okay?" she asked, her eyes filling with hope as she stared down at him.

"Yes. He's really going to be okay," I assured her.

"What if his parents don't let you take him?"

"You'll provide a distraction, and we'll kidnap him."

"Wait, what?" She gawked at me in a panic.

"I'm kidding," I said. "Kind of."

"Robin—"

Beep. Beep. Beep. Beep.

My head shot towards the machine that was now going crazy. Feet pounded against the ground as a group of nurses rushed in just as the monitor slowed to a single, continuous sound.

"He's in cardiac arrest," one of them said as another pull-ed Felicity and I away from the bed.

"What's happening?" I asked, despite what they just said.

"Get them out of here," a doctor instructed as he entered the room. A nurse tried to usher us out, but I didn't move as the man continue. "Asystole. Push one of epi."

"What's happening?" I repeated, panic rising in me.

"You need to step out so we can do our jobs," the lady in front of me demanded.

I let her push me out of the room but stayed in front of the door as I desperately pled for them to do something. My cheeks were hot, and it took everything in me not to throw up as my own heart threatened to stop beating. Felicity's vice like grip on my arm began to hurt, but I didn't care. All the color was drained from her face, and she looked as close to throwing up as I felt.

The nurse injected something into Ben's arm. They all stopped to watch the monitor, and after a gut-wrenching pause, his heart began to beat again. I wept into Felicity's shoulder as relief washed through me. He was okay.

After checking his vitals, the doctor gave the nurses in-structions before walking out the door. I stepped in front of him and asked, "What happened?"

"Are you family?" he questioned, and I shook my head. "I'm sorry but I can only give information to immediate family."

"They're in the waiting room."

"Then follow me," he said. We stayed on his heels as he walked through the ICU doors, then pointed out Ben's par-ents to him. As we approached, they stood with wide eyes, and I grasped onto my mom's hand as Felicity held onto the other. "Your son's heart stopped again. We were able to get him back, but it's going to keep happening. His body is shutting down. I'm afraid we may not be able to resuscitate him the next time it happens."

Kiona buried her face in her hands as Dakota clung to her waist. Mahka continued to sit in a chair, his face stoic as he stared straight ahead. Jeremiah cleared his throat, blinking rapidly.

"You need to say your goodbyes," the doctor told them, his lips turned down as he left us alone.

Anguish overcame all my senses at hearing those words. I knew we were going to heal him, but the reality of how close he truly was to dying shook me to the core. Kiona encased Dakota in her arms as he cried, and I rubbed my lips together, knowing the suffering they were experiencing.

"I hate to push but now we really need an answer," Akio said. "There's a certain point that even I won't be able to fix his ailments, and we're getting dangerously close to it."

Ben's parents exchanged a look and I said, "Let us help him. You'll regret it if you don't."

"Robin," Mom murmured with a shake of her head.

"I don't mean it disrespectfully," I replied. "I just mean, if you don't say yes, you'll always wonder if things could've ended up differently. At least this way you'll know you did everything you could for him."

"Listen to them, Dad," Mahka spoke up, his quiet voice full of unusual authoritativeness. "Just take a leap of faith here. Believe in something bigger than what you may be able to see." He peered over at me, the faintest hint of a smile playing at his lips. "Robin wouldn't suggest this unless she knew it was the right thing to do."

Did he know the truth about Garridan? I opened my mouth to question what he was insinuating but decided against it. This wasn't the time.

"I'm afraid we need an answer," Mom told them gently, and they stared at one another, assessing the other's feelings.

Finally, Kiona nodded. "Okay. Take him."

A weight lifted off my shoulders at the words, and I let out the breath I'd been holding. "Thank you," I said as I wrapped her in a tight embrace. "He's going to be fine. I promise."

"Go say goodbye," Mom instructed. "We need to leave quickly if we're going to get him back home in time."

The Toves family, while still looking apprehensive, did as they were told. Mom and Akio followed, but I stayed behind to say bye to Felicity. Matthew squeezed her shoulder in a farewell gesture before leaving us alone. I lunged forward, pulling her into a hug, and she threw her arms around me in response.

"I'll see you soon?" she asked.

"Yes," I replied, already giddy at the thought of seeing her under better circumstances. "But until then, look out for Ben's family for me."

"I will."

"And, hey, I really am sorry for earlier."

"Don't mention it," she replied quickly. "Seriously. Please don't ever mention it again."

I nodded as guilt swept over me, knowing she was still hurting from my words. I backed away from her with a single wave then sauntered back to Ben's room. When I came in, Akio and Mom had already begun unhooking Ben from all his wires. I noticed Akio running his hands along Ben's body and knew he'd already begun to heal him so he would survive being taken off the vent. But to the outside eye, it looked like he was just removing the blankets that held him down.

"We're ready when you are," Mom told Ben's parents.

Kiona ran her hand over Ben's cheek and murmured, "My boy . . . Please take care of him."

"We will. You'll see him again before you know it," Mom replied with a reassuring smile.

Mahka came up to me and leaned in close, watching my face intently as Dakota gave his eldest brother one more hug.

"He's gonna be okay," I told Mahka.

"I know he is." He ducked down so his lips were by my ear. "That dude's going to heal him with magic, right?"

I drew back, my eyes wide. "W-what?"

"Don't act dumb. I already know."

"Ben told you?" I asked.

"Not technically. I overheard him talking to Felicity a while back," he explained. "You can control water, right?"

I glanced around the room, making sure no one else heard him. "Mahka, you can't tell anyone. Ever."

"I know. I won't, I swear," he assured me. "I just want to know if that guy is healing him with magic."

I hesitated. I shouldn't confirm his suspicions. He wasn't supposed to know, But, then again, what harm could it do at this point?

I nodded my head ever so slightly. "Yes. He is."

"Wicked," he said with a wide grin. "I always knew you were a badass."

I held back my own grin and pulled him into a headlock, which wasn't an easy task considering he towered above me in height.

"Stop eavesdropping."

"Never!" He managed to pull away then slung his arm around my shoulders. "Can you show me your magic some-time?"

"It's called a power, not magic," I said with a roll of my eyes. "But yeah. I will. If I can."

"I have so many questions!"

"I'm sure you do."

"Mahka," Jeremiah called out. "Let's go."

Mahka squeezed my arm and said, "I expect answers later," before following his family into the hall.

His comments in the waiting room made sense now. No wonder he was so vocal to his parents about letting us take him—he knew what we were. I still couldn't believe they'd agreed to it without knowing the truth, but it warmed my heart a little knowing how much trust they must have in me.

"We aren't really lugging him out the window, are we?" Matthew asked as Mom opened it.

"Of course not," Mom replied. She peered out, then waved somebody over. "Why do you think we brought Charles? He's been waiting outside to teleport us all back to the plane."

An older man hoisted himself into the room and let out an exaggerated sigh. "I'm getting too old for this, Adriana."

"Oh, no you aren't," she said, swiping at his arm. "Think you can get us all in one sweep?"

Charles counted us up then nodded. "I'll be cranky for days, but I can do it. Everyone grab a hold of one another."

We did as we were told, circling around him and grasping each other's hands. Akio and I each kept a hand on Ben, and Charles closed his eyes as he began to whisper something to himself. The room around us blur like I suddenly needed glasses, then it mixed with the images of a different scenery. The two warped around one another, making me dizzy, until only one remained—the wide terrain where we left the plane.

"Whoa!" I exclaimed with a smile lighting up my face.

Charles chuckled and asked, "Haven't ever been teleported?"

"This would be the first," I answered.

"Amazing, isn't it?"

"I'd say so," I agreed as he placed his hand on Matthew for support. It must've taken a lot out of him.

We loaded into the plane, and I stood next to Ben as Akio started working on him. Matthew came up behind me and grabbed my hand.

"We did it, Robin," he said, sounding as surprised as I felt. "We really did it."

"I thought you knew we would," I replied.

"I actually wasn't so sure. I didn't think his parents would agree so easily, and I didn't know if he would even hold out until we got here. But I couldn't let you know that. Someone had to settle you down."

I rested my head against his arm as I watched Ben's peaceful face. "Do you watch out for me so much because you promised Ben you would?"

"Partly."

"And the other part?"

"Because you're family, and I love you."

A smile crept onto my face. "I love you too."

CHAPTER THREE

Akio worked on Ben the entire flight home. At a certain point, my pacing became too much for everyone to handle. So Matthew petrified my feet to the floor of the plane, and I seethed silently in the seat I'd been grounded to. When we arrived in Garridan, Akio's ashen skin looked ready to drop off his face. Matthew helped him off the plane, and two other healers waited for an update so they could take over where Akio stopped.

"He's going to be okay, though, right?" I asked Akio when he was done explaining the situation to the healers.

"It's very touch and go at the moment," he replied. "The brain isn't an easy organ to repair when it's in such a state."

"But he's going to be okay, though, right?" I repeated.

"It's a very delicate situation," he responded. "We still have a lot of work to do before I can give you an answer to that."

"But I promised his family he'd be okay. I promised Felicity." I was on the brink of hysteria, and Mom placed her hand on my shoulder.

"That wasn't your promise to make," Akio said, not harshly, but I could see his growing frustration with me.

"The healers are going to do everything they can," Mom assured me. "How about we go home and get some rest while they take him to the hospital?"

"What's the point?" I asked. "We all know I won't be able to sleep. I'd rather go to the hospital. I want to know what's happening with Ben."

"Okay," she relented, "but you're going straight to the cafeteria when we get there. I haven't seen you eat all day, and I'm not going to let you be sleep deprived *and* malnourished."

"Deal," I agreed, relieved she wasn't going to force me to go home.

When we walked into the hospital, the healers wheeled Ben down one of the hallways. I stepped forward to follow, but Mom shook her head and said, "Let them do their jobs. They'll update us as they can."

"Fine," I replied.

"Let's get you some food, then I'll call your father to see where he is."

"I'll join you," Matthew said as he came up beside us. "Akio is sleeping in one of the patient rooms. He wore himself out."

"I'm not surprised," Mom replied as we walked. "The type of healing he was performing is very intricate. Not a lot of our people can work on the brain like that and certainly not for as long as he did. I'm sure he'll be asleep for a while."

"Someone remind me to thank him when this is all over," I murmured. "He's the only reason we even got permission to bring Ben here, but all I've done is harass him about how Ben's doing."

"I'm sure he understands," Matthew said.

"And I don't think you'll need a reminder to thank him when the time comes," Mom added. "You may be a pain in the butt right now, but you'll still be overjoyed when you hear Ben is safe. The gratitude will come naturally."

"I'm not so sure about that," I muttered, thinking back to all my other inappropriate responses to things lately.

Mom led me to a table in the wide room as Matthew walked around the different stations. He placed two trays with a bunch of different foods on the table then imme-diately shoveled some fries into his mouth. Mom said some-thing about finding Dad, excusing herself before standing, and I stared at the food as my stomach protested the smell of it wafting into my nose.

"You need to eat," Matthew said.

"I really don't think I can," I replied, pressing my lips together as I swallowed back a baby barf.

"Your body is going to give out on you if you keep this up."

"At least I'd get some sleep that way."

He scowled. "That isn't funny."

"It wasn't meant to be." I rubbed my hands over my face then leaned into them so I was surrounded by darkness.

The chatter around me faded into the background, and a small calm washed over me as my body relaxed. I inhaled deeply, thinking I might fall asleep again, when a faint voice drifted into my head.

I'm dying because of you, Ben said. *Are you happy now? Being with Alexander wasn't enough, you had to kill me too?*

I slammed my palms into my temples, gritting my teeth as I did it again so pain could replace the voice. "Leave me alone!" I yelled.

Matthew grabbed my hands and firmly said, "Deep breaths, Robin. Count to twenty."

"No!" I shot up, knocking the chair out from under me. People glanced my way, but I ignored them, not caring that I made a scene. "No more counting! No more voices! I can't handle this anymore."

"Robin—"

"Let her go," I heard Mom instruct him as I walked away.

I headed back down the way we'd come, venturing through the doors to the hall where they'd taken Ben. My eyes skipped over each small, glass cutout in the doors I passed. Most were empty, but a few were occupied by a team of healers helping some unlucky guest.

Near the end of the hall, I finally found what I was looking for. Ben was lying on the gurney, eyes closed and skin still pale. He didn't look any better than when we'd been in the hospital in Milton. Two healers were deeply concentrated near his head, working on reviving his brain, while another three ran their hands over the length of his body.

"This is just a mess," the black-haired healer near his head sighed.

"Will you be able to fix it?" a younger girl at his leg asked.

"I hope so."

"Me too. Otherwise the rest of this hard work is for nothing."

I pressed my back against the wall by the door as my breaths came in shallow gasps. Her callous comment sent all my fears into overdrive. Had we been too late after all? I knew Ben was far gone, but were they saying there was less chance at healing him than I'd thought?

I slowly dragged myself away from the wall, each step harder than the last. As I trudged away from the operating room, my pace picked up into a walk then a jog until it became a sprint. Before I knew it, I was outside running with no clear destination in mind. All I knew was I couldn't be in that building for another minute.

* * *

I sat on the highest ledge atop the courthouse, dangling my legs over the side as I stared at the furthest edges of town. The sun was slowly rising, lighting up the buildings with its golden glow, and I realized I'd been here all night. I wondered if it was illegal to climb the building then decided I didn't care enough to get down. I didn't care about anything. My mind was too focused on Ben.

I felt like a coward running away from the hospital, but I just couldn't stay. Knowing he might be dying not far from where I helplessly sat was too much to bear. If his heart stopped beating, I couldn't be in the same building when it happened. I couldn't be around the people who'd let his life slip away from them. I couldn't listen to anyone trying to comfort me. I knew I'd lash out and do something I'd regret.

A sneer twisted over my face as I realized I'd done the same thing when I was told my mom and sister perished in a car accident—I'd ran away.

My hands balled into fists, hitting the ground angrily. I'd already lost two of the most important people in my life. How was I so close to losing another?

It's not right. It's not fair!

I punched the ground over and over, letting the physical pain match the emotional turmoil raging inside. My knuckles split open, and blood seeped over my fingers, but still I slammed them down.

I let out a strangled, frustrated scream that sounded foreign to my ears. My head pounded against my skull, and I paused as my stomach roiled around. It knotted violently as I began to dry heave, the motion making my nose run incessantly, then I emptied the only thing currently rooming in my abdomen—bile.

My breath came raggedly as I ran my arm across my mouth. I fell back against my butt, grabbing water from the air to push against the puke on the roof. The calming sensation my powers usually brought was nonexistent. Instead, I had to use every ounce of effort for the simple task, and my whole body began to shake.

Is this what people consider rock bottom? Am I finally breaking?

Maybe I am. Maybe this is my last straw. Maybe this is the thing I don't come back from.

I eyed the ground, gauging how high I was. A fall from this height could break a couple bones or be fatal depending on how you landed. All it would take was a jump . . .

A shaky sob escaped me, and I placed my hands over my face as I fought the urge to let the bad thoughts win. They seemed so easy to give into, but I knew I couldn't. There was still a chance Ben would be okay. If he died, there'd be no reason not to let them take over but, for now, I had just enough hope to hold on. Ben could still live.

"Robin, what did you do?" Matthew asked, his head peeking over the roof as he climbed the last of the stairs. The concern in his voice tugged at the last bit of composure I had, and my chin started to quiver again. He ran over to me and gently pulled my hands up to examine them. "Let's get you to a healer."

"No," I mumbled.

"I'm pretty sure your left hand is broken. You need to get it fixed."

"What's the point?"

His brows pulled together tightly. "What do you mean 'what's the point?' You're in pain. They can help."

"They can't fix the pain I'm in."

Matthew opened his mouth then shut it again as his eyes traveled over me, taking in my broken demeanor. He glanced at my legs as they hung over the ledge, and his eyes widened slightly.

"What were you doing up here?" he asked, his voice sounding strangled. When I didn't answer, he cupped my face in his hands so I'd look at him. "Were you going to jump?"

"No!" I replied harshly, then I swallowed and whispered, "I don't think so."

"Robin . . ." he trailed off, looking away as he blinked quickly. I thought I could see the lightest reflection of liquid covering his eyes, but I wasn't sure. When he glanced back at me, his jaw was set and his expression gentle but firm. "Let me help you. Okay?"

I nodded, and he sighed in relief before grabbing onto my upper arms and helping me to my feet. He purposely placed himself between me and the side of the building, guiding me towards the stairs to what he probably now considered safety.

"I don't think I can climb down," I admitted as the pain in my hands began to radiate up through my wrists and forearm.

Matthew wasted no time in pulling out his rarely used cellphone. Within a matter of minutes, Charles appeared beside us.

"To the hospital?" he asked, and Matthew nodded. The view of our town dissipated, soon replaced by one of the front entrance to the hospital.

"Thank you," Matthew told him.

"My pleasure," he replied before disappearing again.

"Do people who teleport ever walk anywhere?" I asked as Matthew led me into the building.

"Only if they have to."

"Lucky them."

"Mhmm."

"Robin, what happened?" Dad asked as he and Mom ran up to us.

I noticed Peter, Chang, and Darby standing behind them. "Just a clumsy moment," I replied with a wry smile.

Matthew shot me a look but didn't speak his version of events, which I was grateful for. "Nothing serious," he told them. "She should be in and out fairly quickly."

"Oh, good," Mom said, the relief showing in her face.

Guilt ate into my gut as I realized what they'd go through if they lost me. I knew that feeling all too well and knew I could never do that to them. I looked down at my feet, trying to hide the shame I was suddenly overwhelmed with.

"I'll take her back," Matthew offered. "It looks like you were in the middle of something."

"Nothing too important," Dad said. "They just wanted to check on Ben."

I snorted. "Peter didn't come here to check on Ben."

"No, he came to check on the 'situation' as he put it," Mom replied, rolling her eyes.

The action seemed misplaced on her, and I grinned. Peter wasn't anyone's favorite person around here.

"Speaking of which," I hinted, unable to form the words to ask.

"We haven't received an update in a while," Dad replied. "Last we heard, Akio was joining them again, and things were looking good."

"You wouldn't say that just to avoid giving me bad news, would you?"

"Maybe, but it happens to be true, regardless," he said, and I nodded absently.

"Go get your hands fixed, honey," Mom said. "We have some good news for you when you're done."

What could I possibly care about if it wasn't Ben?

"Okay," I replied, no energy to even be snarky.

As the healer worked on my hands, the warm feeling of rejuvenation filled the rest of my body. It didn't take away the exhaustion entirely, but it gave me enough energy to feel semi normal, which was a nice change. Matthew watched the process, his face becoming more and more withdrawn as mine became lighter.

"I feel so good," I said as I stood and stretched. Matthew nodded, flexing his crossed arms tensely. "What's wrong?"

"We need to talk," he replied, his hard gaze cutting through me.

"About?"

"You know what about."

I pulled at my fingers as I stared at my hands. "The roof?"

"Yes."

"Do we have to?"

"Yes."

"Why?"

"Because I don't think you realize what you were considering doing up there."

"I didn't go up there with that in mind," I said quietly as my tangly hair fell into my face. "I swear. After a while, my mind just kinda wandered in that direction."

"You wanted to jump," he clarified. I nodded and he hissed in a breath.

"Don't be angry at me," I whispered.

"I'm not angry at you. I'm concerned." His Adams apple bobbed up and down as he swallowed. "And, honestly, I'm a little scared now."

"I'm sorry," I offered up weakly.

"That's not something you have to apologize for. I just—" he stopped and swallowed again. "I feel like I failed you. I've been trying so hard to help you through this, but clearly it hasn't been enough."

I watched him as my lips turned down. "This isn't about you. It has nothing to do with you at all actually."

"I didn't mean—"

I held up a hand to stop him. "I know what you meant. I do. But you should never try to make someone else's suffering about you. Do you even realize how much worse that makes me feel?"

"No," he admitted.

I walked up to him and grabbed his hand.

"Matthew, I appreciate everything you've done for me. You've been there literally twenty-four seven since I've come back home, and even before that you always looked out for me. You're one of the most important people in my life." I smiled, but he averted his gaze. "But you can't save me from everything—especially not myself. My life is *not* your responsibility. Okay?"

"Okay," he mumbled, and I couldn't tell if he was upset or just uncomfortable with the conversation.

"But, for the record, I'm not suicidal. If I wasn't so tired, those kinds of thoughts never would've crossed my mind at all."

"You sure?"

"I'm sure."

"Good," he stated, squeezing my hand, "because there's a lot of people who'd be worse off with you gone. You know that, right?"

"I know," I replied softly. "I feel like I should go give my parents a hug."

"I'm sure they'd be very happy if you did." He gave me one more quick look over then said, "Come on. Let's go find them."

We made our way back to the waiting room, where Emery was sitting next to my mom and dad. I waltzed up to them and bent over to give them each a long hug.

"What's that for, kiddo?" Dad asked.

"Just because I love you," I replied with a shrug.

"You look better," Mom noted, and I nodded.

"A happy side effect of having something healed."

Dad chuckled. "If only we could use that healing power to end your suffering entirely."

"I wish," I replied, deeply meaning it.

"Well, this will only help your good mood," Mom said, the side of her eyes crinkling as she smiled.

She waved to someone behind me, and I turned to see Akio strutting towards us. He looked much more alive than he had yesterday, and the look in his eyes had my heart beating quicker.

"Ben?" I asked hopefully.

"After a very extensive healing session—one that took three highly skilled brain experts I might add—we were finally able to heal Ben's most serious ailment." The look of pride that flashed on his face reminded me of a young kid ready for praise. "He's no longer brain dead."

"So, he'll be okay?" Matthew asked, wanting the words spelt out just like I did.

"Yes," Akio confirmed. "He's going to be just fine."

I reached up and gave him a tight hug, thanking him profusely as the relief radiated off me. I hadn't realized the amount of grief I'd already been harboring at just the thought of Ben dying, but now with it gone, I felt ten times lighter. Ben was alive and that wasn't going to change anytime soon. I only wished I could contact his family and tell them.

I wiped the wetness off my cheeks as Matthew shook Akio's hand. Mom and Dad stood, each with big smiles on their faces, and Emery smirked lightly as she leaned into her chair. When the excitement died down, Akio excused himself, and I let out a slow breath.

"I can't believe this is real," I said as pure glee radiated from every pore.

"We're so happy this had a positive outcome," Mom said. "The council will be too."

"Except Peter maybe," Dad inserted.

I rolled my eyes and shrugged one shoulder. "He can get over it." I glanced at Emery, finally realizing two people were missing. "Where's Kodi and Andre?"

"Upstairs with Mateo and Toby," she replied as a grin crept onto her face. "They're both awake."

"They are?" I exclaimed, and she nodded. "Why didn't anyone tell me sooner?"

"You were a little preoccupied," she said.

"Too wrapped up in my own misery," I murmured with a shake of my head.

When did I become the person who was so self-interested that people couldn't tell me things?

"Yeah, basically," she replied unapologetically, and Matthew nudged her with his elbow. "What? It's true."

"She had good reason to be," Dad said, giving me a comforting smile, and I returned it halfheartedly.

"Why aren't you up there with them?" I asked Emery.

"I was for a while. But the crying became too much for me."

"Crying?"

"Yep. Happy tears, sad tears, frustrated tears, angry tears. We've been all over the spectrum since they were caught up on everything."

"I'm guessing they didn't take learning what will happen if they want to leave too well."

"Not well at all. Mateo is pretty upset. More upset than Toby, surprisingly enough."

I wasn't surprised by that though. Toby would be sad about Kodi, Mateo, and possibly Andre wanting to leave, but at least he'd be here with his memories intact and a new family. He was starting a new future with us, so he had much less reasons to be upset than the others.

"Did you go meet them?" I asked my parents, and Dad shook his head.

"We didn't think we should meet our new son without our entire family there," he said.

I smiled at that and said, "Let's not make him wait any longer then. Let's go say hello."

"Are you sure you're up for it?" Mom asked.

"Definitely," I replied, meaning it wholeheartedly. "It'll do me some good to see them, and I really can't wait for you both to meet Toby."

"Let's go then," Dad said excitedly.

We walked to the elevator, and as we got on, I heard Matthew ask, "Why are you following me?"

"Because it's a free country," Emery replied.

"Please go away."

"You go away."

"I'm trying to," Matthew muttered under his voice as they disappeared, and I suppressed a smile. I could sense a future friendship there.

"I'm a little nervous," Mom admitted as we went to the second floor, and Dad took her hand in his own.

"Don't be," I told her. "He's easy to love."

"I'm sure he is," she said with a timid smile.

We paused outside the room that had been housing Toby and Mateo's sleeping bodies and I said, "How about I go in first? Let them know you're coming in."

"Okay," Dad agreed, so I opened the door then closed it behind me.

"Robin!" Toby exclaimed, and a grin filled my face as I went and gave him a hug.

"I'm so glad you two are awake!" I said as I walked over to Mateo's bed to embrace him too.

"I can't believe everything we missed!" Mateo replied with a shake of his head. "What you and Alexander and your friend did to stop the fighting sounds so awesome. I wish I could've seen it."

"Yeah, well, you were a little preoccupied," I pointed out jokingly.

"Uh, yeah. I almost *died*. I mean, can you believe that? I was knocking on death's door." His voice was playful and light, but his face revealed the fear the thought gave him. "Oh, speaking of which, how's your boyfriend?"

"He's going to be okay," I answered, another round of bliss entering me as I said it. "Thanks for asking. But he's not my boyfriend anymore."

"Is that why you stopped wearing your ring?" Kodi asked, and I glanced down at my naked hand. "I noticed you haven't had it on since the battle, but I didn't want to pry."

"Then why ask now?" Mateo questioned with a roll of his eyes.

"Shut up, Mateo," she told him.

"You shut up," he shot back.

"Why don't you make me?"

"Don't think I won't!"

"Guys," Andre said, his voice firm, and they both stopped talking. "I swear you act like children."

I stifled a giggle, his words all too true. Toby was more mature than they were most of the time even though he was the youngest.

"So, are you going to answer?" Toby asked me curiously.

"Yeah. I actually lost it," I admitted sadly. "I took it off and put it on my dresser like I always did before going to sleep. So now it's probably buried deep in the rubble of the castle somewhere since I never had a chance to grab it the morning of the battle."

"I'm sorry," Toby said.

"Thanks. But this isn't the time for a pity party! I brought some people to meet you," I told Toby. I looked over to Mateo and said, "You too, but it's not as special for you."

"I understand," Mateo said with a genuine smile. "It's your parents, right?"

I nodded and Toby's eyes widened. "Really?"

"Really. They've been anxiously waiting outside."

"Bring them in then!" Mateo commanded, and Kodi punched his arm.

"Would you be quiet? Don't ruin their moment," she instructed, and Mateo actually ducked his head and listened for once.

With my own unexplainable nerves jittering inside, I opened the door and beckoned my parents in. Dad nodded in greeting to Andre and Kodi as Mom's eyes jumped between Mateo and Toby.

"Mom, Dad, this is Mateo," I pointed to him, and he raised his hand but didn't say anything, "and this is Toby."

Toby's dark green eyes were hopefully cautious as he looked them over. Mom walked closer to him and cocked her head to the side slightly as she watched him.

"Hello, Toby," she said, her voice gentle.

He offered her a small smile, his face still withdrawn, so Mom carefully sat at the edge of his bed and took one of his hands in her own. Dad came up behind her and put a hand on her shoulder as he beamed down at Toby.

"Welcome to the family, son," he said, and Toby's eyes swelled with tears.

He began to cry, and Mom wrapped him in her arms as I came and stood by Dad. He slung his arm around my shoulders and we both placed a hand on Toby, creating our new little family unit. The moment was heart-rending and somehow, I knew we'd all remember it forever.

Toby wiped his nose across his arm and, between sobs, said, "It's nice to meet you."

"Mom and Dad," Mom finished for him, and his lips quivered.

"Mom and Dad," he repeated, testing it out. His face lit up and he exclaimed, "I have a mom and dad!"

"And a sister," I pointed out. "But you can still call me Robin."

"Very funny," he told me, making a face, and I stuck my tongue out playfully.

"Let the squabbling begin," Dad said, followed by a hearty laugh.

"We have your room all set up," Mom said, and I could hear in her voice how excited she was. "We haven't decorated it yet because we didn't know what you liked, so sometime soon we'll go shopping for you. How's that sound?"

"It sounds great! I've never had a room to myself!" he replied.

"Technically, you still don't," I said. "Andre and Mateo are staying in there with you for the time being."

"Sorry to crush your dreams," Mateo commented insincerely.

"That's okay. I'll have it to myself when you two are gone, so I'm glad we get more time together before then," Toby responded.

"Speaking of which," Kodi spoke up. "When were you going to speak to the council?"

"Well, now that Ben is here and safe, we can prioritize your situation and approach them about it tomorrow in our session," Mom answered. "But, please, don't get your hopes up. If they think it'll bring any danger to Garridan, they won't allow it."

"It's a part of our history though," I said, puzzled by the idea that they'd be against us finding their infamous tree. "How could it be dangerous?"

"The unknown can always be dangerous," Dad answered with a shrug.

"But why is it unknown?" Andre asked. "I would imagine something as significant as that would be common knowledge."

"I'm sure at one point, the man and the tree *were* common knowledge. However, sometimes things are covered up for certain reasons, then that history has a way of disappearing over time." Mom shot him a warning glare I didn't understand, and Dad cleared his throat before continuing. "But that's not what happened here, I'm sure. This is just silly folklore to our people. If I remember the story correctly, the last time there was any sort of proof of his existence was well over four hundred years ago, so you can see why we'd be hesitant to believe it."

"Even if everyone on the council did believe in it, hunting it down means leaving the walls of Garridan, which in turn means the possibility of being revealed if someone were to see you using your powers," Mom added. "That's what they'll focus on."

"What if we promise not to use our powers?" Kodi asked.

"That's not something you can do. Our powers are second nature to us. It would be like promising not to swallow. You could try, but you'd end up doing it eventually," she answered.

"So, how would we convince them to let us do it?" I questioned.

"I'm honestly not sure," Mom said.

"Well, that's not very helpful," Mateo muttered with a sigh. When he caught us all looking at him, he grinned sheepishly and said, "Sorry. I wasn't trying to be rude."

Dad chuckled before saying, "It's alright. We understand the predicament you're in." He furrowed his brows, then his eyes lit up. "That's how we do it. That's how we get the council to let them hunt down the tree." Mom pressed her lips together, and I noticed her eyes tighten slightly. Dad noticed too so he added in, "If it's real."

What's that all about?

"How?" Kodi asked as I tried to figure out my parents' odd exchange.

"We appeal to their emotional side. Almost all of them had children who were sent away when the war started. All we have to do is point out that it could've been *their* kids in this situation and, if it was, they'd want them to remember their heritage even if they weren't staying in Garridan."

"That's not a bad idea," Mom replied, nodding her head slightly. "It might just work if we play it right."

Something was nagging me about how she said it. It was like there was a hidden meaning behind her words, and I couldn't shake the feeling that they were hiding something.

"Which we will because we're kind of awesome like that." Dad winked at us, and I groaned.

"This is what you're stuck with for a father," I said to Toby. "Are you sure you want him?"

Toby nodded seriously, and we all laughed. He'd want them as parents even if they were aliens. I couldn't say I blamed him though. He'd missed out on a family for sixteen years; this was his opportunity to have one.

"So, you'll update us tomorrow about how the meeting went?" Kodi pressed.

"Of course. Mateo and Toby should be discharged today or tomorrow morning, so we'll all be together to discuss it at dinner," Mom answered.

"Thank you," Kodi said as she and Mateo looked at one another hopefully.

I knew she wasn't trying to be pushy. She was just ready to be home with her family. If I were in her shoes, I'd be the same way.

CHAPTER FOUR

I sat next to Ben's hospital bed for the second time in less than two days. Only this time, he wasn't hooked up to any tubes or machines, so it was easier to believe he was going to be okay. A healer stopped by at one point to work on him, and when I asked what she was doing, she explained that twice a day they needed to basically trick his body into thinking it was being hydrated and given nutrition. It allowed his organs to keep functioning healthily but also eliminated the need for bathroom interventions. They had to do it with all patients who were in a deep sedative like state while their bodies healed after an extensive trauma.

I sat dumbfounded, realizing I'd never questioned any of those things when I'd woken up from my own week long slumber. It made sense, but I was surprised it never crossed my mind back then or even this past week when Mateo and Toby were in the same position. The healers did more for their patients than I realized.

As I pondered that information, I absentmindedly played with Ben's hair as Matthew slept in a chair on the back wall. He had to be as tired as I was since he'd been staying awake with me while my demons played out in my head. I didn't know why he was so good to me, but I was endlessly grateful for his friendship. I truly believed he was the only reason I was making it through the somnokinesis withd-rawal, but I wished he didn't feel like he *had* to help.

I looked back to Ben's peaceful face, and a yawn escaped me. I peered out the window, realizing how late it must be. I didn't want to leave him, though, and I didn't want to wake Matthew when he was finally getting some rest. I yawned again, waiting for the voices to start their attacks. I stood and bit my lower lip as I watched Ben's chest move as he breathed. Then, hesitantly, I climbed into the bed next to him.

I carefully positioned myself then pushed my hair to the side before lying my head next to his on the pillow. With my forehead touching his cheek and my arm wrapped around his stomach, I closed my eyes and fell asleep.

* * *

A loud bang sounded, echoing through the silent room like a gunshot. I bolted upright with a gasp as my heart threatened to stop beating, and wildly looked around for the threat.

"Sorry!" Matthew hissed in a whisper as my eyes landed on him. He was carrying a tray with food and walking towards me. "The door slipped out of my hands. I didn't mean to wake you."

I took a deep breath, begging my body to calm down before I had a heart attack. "What time is it?" I asked as I tried to run my fingers through my tangles.

"Twelve."

"Only twelve?" I asked with a groan. It was going to be a long night.

"Twelve as in noon, not midnight," Matthew clarified with a grin.

"Noon?" I repeated, my brows furrowing, and Matthew nodded. "But that means—"

"You slept all night," he finished as he sat the food in front of me.

"I slept all night." As the words sunk in, a smile slowly crept onto my face. "I slept all night!"

"Who would have thought that'd be something someone would get so excited about?" Matthew shook his head as he chuckled.

"So the somnokinesis effects are over? The voices? They're . . . Gone?"

"They're gone."

Hallelujah!

I cheerfully took a bite of toast. No more voices keeping me awake at night meant I wouldn't be dead on my feet anymore. It meant I wouldn't be ready to snap at any moment if someone said or did the wrong thing. It meant I could get back to being *me*.

I looked down at Ben and smiled softly. What were the odds that the same night I slept next to him, the voices disappeared? He always could drive my demons away, so maybe he had again.

"This is great!" I exclaimed, my body unable to stop dancing around.

"It is," Matthew agreed in amusement as he watched me shove more food into my mouth. "Good to see your manners came out unscathed."

I childishly opened my mouth for him to see my chewed up food, and he let out a belly laugh that I couldn't help but join in with.

"It's nice to see you so happy again," he said.

"And now you can start worrying about something other than me," I replied. He opened his mouth, but I cut him off before he could deny the request. "Maybe start with your ongoing Felicity obsession."

"I am *not* obsessed," he muttered, his eyes turning to slits.

"The picture in your wallet would say otherwise."

"I told you I just forgot it was in there."

"Uh huh. Sure, sure." I smirked at him playfully as he huffed.

"I think I liked it better when you didn't harass me. Think we can get those voices back?"

"Aren't you just *so* funny," I said dryly.

"I like to think so," he replied with a smirk, and I rolled my eyes. "Anyway," he said pointedly. "What's on the agenda today?"

I shrugged. "My parents want us all to have dinner together so we can talk about whatever happens in their meeting today." Matthew didn't meet my gaze as I talked, instantly making me narrow my eyes in suspicion. "Why?"

"No reason."

"Liar."

"Maybe."

"So, what's up then?"

He cleared his throat before admitting, "I went to see Alexander. A couple times actually."

My stomach did a flip, and my eyes widened slightly. "You did? How-how is he?"

"Bored."

I arched a single brow. "He's locked up in an underground prison, and he's just bored?"

"Garridan treats their prisoners with humanity. He's well fed and has clean living quarters. It's not like the Cyfrin compound. He isn't being tortured or anything like that so, yes, he's simply bored."

"I mean, that's good though. It's good he's okay." I slowly chewed on a piece of food before asking, "What made you go see him?"

"We had some unfinished business."

"What—"

"You should go see him too," he cut me off. "I think it'd be good for him."

"Since when do you care about that?" I questioned.

"Okay, fine. I think it'd be good for you."

"Why?"

He looked away from me with troubled eyes. "You talk about him a lot."

"No, I don't!" I exclaimed.

"In your sleep you do. Even if you only got thirty minutes of it before the somnokinesis effects hit you, you'd say his name. A lot. It was never Ben or Felicity or anyone else. Only him."

I stared, open-mouthed, as I sat there baffled by that information. It didn't make any sense. "I don't remember dreaming about him."

"Maybe he was one of the things haunting you," Matthew suggested with a shrug.

"But I never heard his voice when I'd wake up. He was never one of the voices attacking me." My curiosity piqued at that realization. "It was everyone I've ever cared about except him. Why do you suppose that is?"

"Maybe because you don't actually care about him," Matthew snipped.

I rolled my eyes and replied, "Sorry to disappoint you, but that's not it."

"Makes the most sense to me."

I ignored him as I tried to think of reasons why Alexander wouldn't have been one of my demons.

"The voices always blamed me for things: their unhappiness, their deaths, their losses," I said. "I was the villain in their stories because it was my fault things happened." I chewed on the inside of my lower lip as my jumbled thoughts tried to turn into something that made sense.

"But it wasn't real. It was just your head messing with you because, on some level, you really think you're to blame for everything they accused you of," Matthew replied, a disapproving frown forming on his face.

"I guess that makes sense," I murmured, mulling it over. "Does that mean I don't think I'm to blame for anything that's happened to Alexander?"

"Maybe so," he said with a shrug, "and maybe you were only dreaming about him for . . . *Other* reasons."

He arched his brow and I blushed at his insinuation. "I don't remember any of my dreams, so I couldn't tell you."

"Convenient."

"Shut up," I muttered, embarrassed, and he snorted.

"Nevertheless, I know you'll be worried about him a lot more now that you can think straight, and I think seeing him would put your mind at ease some."

"Maybe I'll go see him today then."

I glanced at Ben's still body and guilt gripped me like a vice. I felt like I was cheating on him, like I'd given up on our relationship. But then I remembered he had a new girlfriend. He'd given up on us first.

"I'll stay with him," Matthew offered. "I know it'll make you feel better."

"It would," I agreed. "Thank you."

He threw a banana at me and said, "Now finish eating. We just fixed one problem with you. We don't need another."

"Yes, master," I answered, the sarcasm dripping heavily.

"Shut up," he replied, and I grinned.

Surprisingly enough, even just one night of sleep had me feeling like my old self.

* * *

I ran home to find it empty and took the opportunity to take a long, hot shower. After putting on fresh clothes and weaving my hair into a loose braid, I looked in the mirror. The bags under my eyes were still there but not nearly as detrimental looking as they seemed just yesterday. Color flushed upon my cheeks, and I was happy to be leaning closer to the side of the living than to the dead.

I made the trek downtown and walked up to what I had thought was the prison, but when I looked around, I wasn't so sure. The building was small and run down, with no signs on the outside. I decided to go in anyway and heard the jingle of a bell when I pushed open the door. The inside was just as minuscule as the outside, with only two desks on either side of the room and a kitchenette against the back wall. Two bored looking men stood around aimlessly and barely gave me a glance as I entered.

"Uhm, hi," I offered up uncertainly. "Is this the prison?"

"The top half of it," one of the men answered.

I frowned as I looked around again. "Are you sure?" I couldn't help but ask.

The man chuckled. "Pretty sure, young lady. I'm Officer Sanchez. Who might you be?"

"Robin Hayes," I replied, shaking his outstretched hand.

"Hayes . . . I'm afraid I don't recognize the name," he said as he scratched the back of his head.

"That's probably because it's my adopted name. My birth name is Caldwell."

"Oh! You're Elijah and Adriana's kid, right?"

"Yes, sir."

"Well, it's a pleasure to meet you. This here is my co-worker, Officer Zetto." The other officer nodded. "And if you're looking for the prison, you've come to the right place."

"It sure doesn't seem like it."

"That's because all the real activity is underground. This here is just the place we do paperwork or check in visitors.

So, yeah, it kinda looks more like an office space than a prison," he agreed. "Who are you here to see?"

"Alexander . . ." I trailed off as I realized I didn't know his last name. "The Cyfrin's earth element."

"Ah, yes. Quite the popular one, isn't he?"

"What do you mean?" I asked as he wrote on a clipboard at his desk.

"Just that he's had a number of visitors since coming. Mostly from our Keepers of Balance. They've had lots of questions for him."

"I'm not surprised," I said, thinking of all the answers and explanations he could be carrying around. "It's okay if I see him, right?"

"Of course. I already got you checked in, so just follow me."

He walked to the door next to the kitchenette—the door I'd assumed led back outside—and when he opened it, I was surprised to see it led to an elevator. He motioned me forward, and I cautiously stepped in with him following behind me. He pressed a button, and the elevator began lowering us into the ground.

"Do, uh," I paused and swallowed. My palms were slick, and I wiped them on my pants as we descended further past the safety of the wide-open space of the outdoors. "Do the rest of the Cyfrin prisoners get visitors?"

"Most everyone has had at least one. An old friend, family member, the parents of a child who grew up there. It's been pretty somber. And dramatic," Officer Sanchez said. "Lots of anger, lots of tears."

"There's a lot of that going around," I murmured, thinking back to the trainees. The elevator came to a jarring halt, and stomach churning anxiety continued to grip me. When the doors opened, my jaw dropped to the floor. "Wow."

"Not what you were expecting?" he questioned with a grin.

"No. Not at all."

The room in front of us was modern and large, with high ceilings and lots of light fixtures. The contrast of them against the almost all white interior made it seem like we were in a normal building, not hundreds of feet underground, and it eased my claustrophobia just a tad. Garridan guards stood positioned every couple feet, while many other people were bustling around. Each wall held two hallways leading out of the room, and I tried to peer down them curiously.

"Hey Sanchez," a woman greeted us. "Another visitor?"

"Yep. She's here to see the earth element."

"Well, you know the way." The woman glanced over her shoulder and said, "Penbrooke, Chader, escort them to cell 531 in the west block."

"Follow me," Officer Sanchez instructed, walking down one of the halls to our right as the two guards trailed behind us silently.

Both sides of the hall were lined with doors spaced about eight feet apart. The doors were made of metal, and I could tell the intricate locks weren't opened with any kind of key I'd ever seen.

"Are these—"

"The jail cells," he said. "This whole place is a maze of them."

"How do the people not escape? I'm sure some of their powers could help get them out."

"These doors degenerate powers. They reflect into the rooms and make the prisoner's powers mundane," he explained. "They can still use their powers, but it's an extremely weak variation of them."

"How? How is that possible?" I asked in disbelief.

"These were made way back when the barrier around Garridan was," he answered, as if that were explanation enough.

"And?" I pressed.

He glanced over at me. "Sorry, I forgot you haven't been here long. Our ancestors were very powerful in ways we can't even comprehend. They made these cells. I don't know how we lost that kind of power, but at least we still have their inventions."

"Oh," I said, my brows furrowing as I pondered his statement. It made me wonder what else I didn't know of my own history.

We walked past another hall before stopping at a back wall. More rooms were spaced amongst it, but these ones had see through fronts instead of normal walls.

"Is that glass?" I asked.

"A stronger form of it. These cells were made with extra layers of protection for the more powerful individuals. One of which being the earth element from the Cyfrin we're going to see."

"Why is it on these ones and not the others?"

"They're bigger threats, so we just want to make sure no one's up to any funny business. We have constant patrols checking in as they walk by."

I glanced into the rooms as we passed. They were all identical in their setup: a bed on the left, a small television and bookshelf on the right, and a toilet and sink in the corner. The rooms were small, but not as small as the one I'd been locked in when I was in the Cyfrin compound the first time. Also unlike the Cyfrin, Garridan's prisoners were at least given a couple different forms of entertainment.

Officer Sanchez stopped in front of a door. "Here we are. Pembroke, Chader, and I will wait out here."

"You're not coming in?"

"Don't worry, we'll be watching the entire time from the outside," he assured me, as if he thought I was scared to go in alone.

After unlocking the door, he opened it for me, and I slowly stepped in. An immediate pulling sensation filled my chest, and I could feel the room affecting my powers. It was as if a wet washcloth had been thrown over them—I still had access to where they resided, but they were sluggish to respond to my call. The door shut behind me with a heavy thud as I stared at Alexander, who was lying on the bed with his arm thrown over his face.

"More questions?" he asked, a hint of annoyance in his voice.

"Actually, yes," I said softly, and he immediately bolted into a seated position, his tired brown eyes lighting up. "I do have a few."

"Robin," he said as he stood.

He was wearing an ugly, yellow jumpsuit that would've been unflattering on anyone else. But, on him, it worked by highlighting his complexion. His jaw was covered in stubble, giving him a rugged, manly look, and his usually well-groomed hair was amuck. I bit the inside of my lower lip just enough to cause some pain, so my thoughts didn't run wild.

"I'm . . . You . . . Uh, thank you . . . For coming," he managed to say. It was strange to see him stumble over his words. Usually, he talked with unwavering confidence.

"Of course," I replied, and he visibly relaxed, his nerves gone. "Sorry it wasn't sooner. Things have been . . . Rough."

"Matthew informed me. How are the somnokinesis effects?"

"Well, I had my first full night of sleep last night, so I think it's finally gone," I said, relief filling me once again at that.

"Good. You look like you could use some rest," he commented as he observed my face.

"You're one to talk," I shot back as I crossed my arms, knowing I looked better than I had yesterday. "I don't think I've ever seen you so disheveled."

"Well, I *am* in prison with a possible death sentence over my head, so excuse me for not being well groomed for you."

He stared me down, matching my stance, and after a moment, smiles crept onto both our faces. I let out a laugh then walked over to him and let him wrap me in a tight hug.

"I'm glad you're okay," I said as my head rested on his shoulder.

He ran his hand up and down my back as he said, "And I you."

"And, for the record, you're not getting a death sentence," I told him as I pulled back. "I won't let that happen."

"You're overly optimistic," he retorted as he pulled me next to him on the edge of the bed.

"No, I just have leverage with the council."

"I can't imagine you have *that* much leverage."

"I got them to let Ben be brought here. Why couldn't I convince them to give you a second chance?"

"Wait, you did *what?*" Disbelief swarmed over his face.

"Ben was hurt in a ski accident. He was . . . Dying." I swallowed loudly, still emotional with how close he brushed death's hand. "Yesterday, we went to the hospital in Milton and brought him here."

"The Keepers of Balance allowed an outsider into Garridan?"

"With some convincing, yes. So, who's to say they won't give you some lenience, too, if I ask?"

Alexander's brows furrowed, and his lips were turned down. A moment of silence encased us before he asked, "Is Ben okay?"

"Yeah, he is. Thanks for asking." He nodded his head slightly, so I grabbed his hand and squeezed. "And you will be too."

"We'll see."

"Is something wrong?" I asked softly, seeing the troublesome look in his eyes.

"You mean aside from being locked in an underground prison with death looming near?" he responded sarcas-ti-cally.

"Yeah, aside from those very minor things," I replied, equaling his sarcasm.

He smirked for the briefest second then shrugged. "Nope."

I pressed my lips together and cocked my head to the side as I scrutinized him. "You're lying."

"It's nothing important."

"If it's bothering you, it's important."

"To you maybe."

"Which is why I'm asking about it. Talk to me, Alexander. I know I've been wrapped up in my own stuff the last couple weeks, but I'm here now, and I want to help any way I can."

"This isn't anything you can help with."

"You never know."

"Trust me, I know. It's a pretty permanent problem."

"Sometimes just talking about a problem can be helpful," I said, knowing I was going to hit my limit with the pushiness. He was about to either snap at me to let it go or sigh and fess up.

To my delight, it was the latter. He let out a huff and rubbed his fingers over his eyes before turning his head towards me.

"When I got here, I asked about my parents."

"Oh!" I exclaimed, surprised by that revelation. I couldn't recall him ever mentioning any interest in who his parents were. In fact, I remember him telling me he had no interest in them.

"They're dead," he stated flatly, and my heart sank.

"Oh. I'm so sorry."

He shrugged one shoulder. "It's no big dent in my life. Not like I knew them or anything."

"That doesn't matter." He sat rigidly, so I placed my hand on his back. "It's okay to be upset about it."

"Yeah."

A man of many words.

"Well, I'm always here if you want to talk about it," I said.

"I know." He gave me the side eye then said, "Thank you."

"You're welcome."

"Who knows? Maybe I'll get to meet them sooner rather than later anyway."

"That's not going to happen," I insisted firmly. "I promise."

"You shouldn't make promises you can't keep," he advised, his voice calm but stern.

I sighed. "I really shouldn't. I'm going to end up disappointing someone."

"I think not saving me from a death sentence would be a large step up from just disappointing."

I looked up at his smirk and realized he was joking, so I rolled my eyes. "Glad you still have your dry sense of humor intact."

"Always."

"Well, that's not what I was referring to anyway."

"Then what?"

"Kodi and Mateo. I promised them we'd get them home with their memories intact."

"And how do you plan on fulfilling that promise when the only power remover in Garridan is Joey?"

"I kind of told them we'd find this ancient, magical tree that may or may not even exist."

Alexander snorted. "Oh, it exists alright."

My eyes widened. "How do you know that?"

"All the Keepers of Balance know that."

"All the Cyfrin's Keepers of Balance?"

"No, *all* the Keepers of Balance. The Cyfrin's and Garridan's alike."

My forehead scrunched as I remembered my parents' odd exchange yesterday and their hesitancy the couple times we'd discussed it before.

Is this the reason? Did they lie to me?

I shook my head fiercely, answering my own question. "I don't think so. Both times it's been brought up, my parents said it's just a legend, and they don't even know if it was true or not."

"They lied."

"They wouldn't lie to me!" I told him hotly, instantly on the defensive, but my anger was just a front for the hurt that began to swell. He was confirming what I'd just questioned.

"Apparently they would," he said, and I shot off the bed.

I set my jaw as my eyes narrowed. "Just because *you* deceive the people you claim to love doesn't mean everyone does. My parents are good people, and you have no idea what you're talking about."

I turned on my heel and shoved the door to his cell open as he called out to me, but I ignored him. He couldn't be right.

"I'm ready to go," I told Officer Sanchez, and he nodded accommodatingly.

As we walked away, I glanced over my shoulder and saw Alexander staring after me. I averted my gaze and listened to the echo of our footsteps as I thought of what he said. He must be misinformed. If my parents said the council didn't know anything about the tree, it had to be true. They had no reason to hide things from me.

Right?

There was no reason to doubt them but, for some reason, I was.

As we ascended in the elevator, I knew I'd be back. I felt bad for leaving so abruptly just because I was upset, but I had to talk to Matthew. I needed some answers.

CHAPTER FIVE

"How's he doing?" I asked as I entered Ben's room. I instinctively went to his side and grabbed his hand.

"He's fine, Robin. Really. That's not going to change," Matthew replied, putting down the book he was reading.

"I know. I just can't help but ask."

"I know. How was your visit? You weren't there very long."

"I kind of got angry and left," I admitted as I plopped down next to him on the couch under the window.

"Shocker." I rolled my eyes at his sarcasm, and he asked, "Angry about what?"

I tapped my thumbs together and, instead of answering, asked, "How did you know about the earth element? The one who turned into a tree?"

"I heard talks about it over the years at the Cyfrin compound."

"Like rumors?"

"Basically."

"So, how do you know if it's true?"

"I suppose I don't know for certain," he answered with thoughtful eyes. "But I don't see how there could be a record of people gaining powers if there wasn't truth to it."

"And there *are* records of that happening. My mom said so the first time we asked her about it. So why would she and my dad know that but not know how it happened? It doesn't make any sense. Unless . . ." I closed my eyes as the truth screamed out at me. "They *do* know, and they're hiding it."

"What's going on, Robin?" Matthew questioned, his voice full of concern.

"Alexander said the tree isn't a legend. He said all of the Keepers of Balance know about it and that my parents have been lying to me." I opened my eyes to see his forehead creased. When he didn't comment, I said, "You're supposed to tell me he's wrong."

"I would if I could but what if he's not? I've been wondering the same thing for a while. I just didn't want to bring it up." He turned his body towards me as I groaned unhappily. "Think about it. It's a well-known legend, but how did it originate? Who would've come up with such a story? It makes more sense to me that there's truth in it rather than it's made up. Also, look at how your parents' demeanors have changed every time it's been brought up. It's like they're afraid of saying too much."

"You noticed that too?" I asked, unsurprised at his observations, and he nodded.

"Plus, it doesn't make sense that they wouldn't know if there's any information on it or not when the council is in possession of all the original history books—old diaries, journals, maps. It's all kept in a locked room, and every member of the council knows everything that's in there."

"How do you know that?"

"From some of the defected Keepers of Balance like Toshiro. When I was still part of their inner circle, they'd discuss things like that sometimes."

I chewed on my bottom lip then stood and started pacing. "So, let's just say they do know it's true, and they're keeping it a secret. Why would my mom tell us about it in the first place? She's the one who explained it that day we left Milton."

Matthew rubbed the back of his neck. "Well, she didn't know what I knew about it, so maybe she thought a broad overview of a 'legend' would be better told than whatever I could've said. And when I didn't offer up any alternate information, maybe she thought their secret was still safe."

"Maybe," I agreed, not finding a flaw in his explanation. Matthew scoffed, and lightly shook his head. "What?"

"I never thought anything of it before, but after your parents and I got on the plane that day—when you were still talking to Ben—they asked me if I knew anything else about the tree. Which I didn't. Then they asked if I knew if it was true or not, and I said I'd only heard rumors of it, so I didn't know." The corner of his mouth turned up in a humorless smile. "They were trying to see if their secret was still safe."

My hands fell limply at my sides, and my shoulders slumped forward. "So, you think they're lying?"

He hesitated before saying, "Yes."

"I think so too," I murmured, casting my eyes downward. "But why would they lie to me?"

"I don't know, Robin," he answered just as quiet. "That's something you'll have to ask them."

* * *

Later that evening, my parents and I were sitting around our dining room table with all the trainees in attendance for the first time. Toby was still excitedly gabbing about his new house and how he couldn't wait to pick out his room decorations. Mom and Dad listened intently, not letting a single word go unheard, as the rest of the trainees talked amongst themselves.

"Is something wrong, Robin?" Mom asked, finally noticing my silence.

I pushed the food on my plate around. Without a second thought, I asked, "What did the council say about finding the tree?"

"Maybe we should wait until after dinner to discuss it," she replied as everyone instantly quieted down.

"Why? Isn't that why we were having dinner together in the first place?"

"No. It was to welcome Mateo and Toby into our home." She smiled over at Toby. "And to welcome Toby into our family."

Toby's grin reached both ears as he said, "I feel very welcomed."

"That's all we wanted," Mom responded, patting his hand affectionately.

"But I don't mind talking about the tree or whatever it is," he added. "I know it's important to everyone else."

Mom pulled her hand away, frowning unhappily. She met Dad's eyes, and he shrugged, so she wiped her face with her napkin before setting it down.

"Okay then," she said. She cleared her throat and shifted in her seat then folded her hands on top of the table and looked around the room. "Unfortunately, not many of them believe in that old legend. They don't have any deeper information than we do; just the rumors that go around."

I ground my teeth together and balled my hands into fists on my lap. "Are you sure about that?"

"Yes, honey, we're sure," she replied, and I stared into her sympathetic eyes. She was lying straight to my face. And she was good at it.

"So Mateo and I are going to lose our memories?" Kodi asked quietly, tears springing into her eyes.

"I'm afraid it's the only way you'll get to go home," Mom said, and Mateo stared down at his plate.

Andre put his hand on Kodi's shoulder as she began to cry, and a sudden rage burned at my core.

"You're lying." My cold voice sliced through the air, and my mom recoiled like I'd slapped her.

"What?"

"You're lying!" I nearly yelled, slamming my hand against the table.

"Robin," Dad said, his eyes wide.

"You're both lying," I repeated quieter. "I just don't know why."

I pushed my chair back and rushed out of the room. I didn't even stop to get a jacket before running out the door. Luckily, the air wasn't frigidly cold like it'd been last week. Spring was finally coming.

I briskly walked to the police station, and when I opened the door, Officer Sanchez was pulling on a coat.

"I need to see Alexander again if that's okay," I said.

"Two visits in one day. How did he get so lucky?" He chuckled, but when he realized I wasn't in a joking mood, he cleared his throat awkwardly. "I was just heading out, but Briggs can take you down."

"Okay, thank you."

"Have a good night."

"You too, Officer Sanchez," I replied as Officer Briggs opened the door to the elevator.

Within moments, I was back underground and headed towards Alexander's cell. When we reached it, one of the guards opened the door and I stepped in. Alexander was in the middle of doing a push up but peeked towards the door when he heard it unlatch.

"Robin," he said, immediately standing up and wiping the sweat from his face on his shirt. Without a word, I walked past him and sat on his bed, scooting back so I could lean against the wall. He sat next to me, peering into my face with concern. "What's wrong?"

I fiddled with my fingers in my lap. "You were right," I said quietly. "My parents were lying."

"I'm sorry."

"No, *I'm* sorry," I told him. "For what I said to you earlier. It's no excuse, but I didn't want to believe they would do that. I don't know why, but I had this picture in my head that they were flawless—like they weren't capable of doing anything bad. I know it's ridiculous but . . ."

"You wanted to believe someone was incapable of hurting you," he finished. "It's not ridiculous. It's a defense mechanism."

"Didn't realize I needed one," I muttered, and he smiled wryly.

"Does this mean you're going on a man hunt?"

"You mean tree hunt?" I retorted, and he chuckled.

"I suppose so."

"I don't know. I still don't even know anything about it. After my parents said the council didn't know anything on the subject, I called them liars and came here."

"Finding comfort in my presence?" he asked, only half joking.

"I was actually hoping you'd fill in the blanks for me. I only know what the legend says, and I want—no, I *need*—to know the truth. It's the only way I can help Mateo and Kodi."

"I can do that. On one condition."

"What condition?" I asked, completely blanking at what he could want.

"When you start your journey to find him, take me with you," he requested.

My mouth opened then shut again as he stared at me intently. "I-I don't know if I can do that."

"It's not going to be an easy quest, and I'll be damned if I point you to danger without being there to make sure you're safe," he replied, his low voice more serious than I'd ever heard it before.

My eyes grew soft. He only wanted to protect me and, though I didn't need it, I was grateful. I knew I wouldn't win this argument, and I needed the information he had, so I slowly nodded my head and told him what he wanted to hear. "Okay. I'll find a way."

"Okay," he repeated, his eyes searching mine. He must have been satisfied by whatever he found because he crossed his ankles and began speaking again. "Once upon a time, in a land not so far away—"

"Alexander," I said with a roll of my eyes. "This is serious."

"That it is," he agreed gravely. "So, here's how history tells it: Many, many years ago, our ancestors lived in peace with everyone and everything around them. They were good people trying to live up to the blessings bestowed upon them by nature—also known as our powers. They succeeded for a long time, but no one is perfect. People got greedy as they always do. Future generations started to create powerful weapons without thinking of the consequences."

"Weapons?" I interrupted. "What kind of weapons? Why?"

"The barrier around Garridan, the doors to these cells." He gestured towards it. "They were for protection if ever a day came when they'd need it. But, like I said, they didn't think of the consequences of making such powerful things."

"What kind of consequences?"

"The worst kind imaginable—they were draining nature. Water sources disappeared, crops died off, erratic weather began to occur." His lips turned even further downward. "Our people were responsible for thousands of deaths because of it."

"But how? How were they draining nature?"

"Our powers are rooted in nature. You could say it's our source. Whenever we use them, we take some of nature's energy to do so. Done in moderation, it's not a problem because the earth's core is constantly re-energizing. However, the amount of power our ancestors used to fuse their creations was detrimental, and they paid the price."

"What do you mean?" I questioned, hanging on to his every word. I was fascinated by learning more of our origins.

"That's what started the feud between our kind and the Norms."

My brow furrowed and I said, "I thought a Welsh man started the feud between us."

"Technically, he did. But his movement started with the allegations that our ancestors were to blame for the misbalance in nature . . . And it was true."

"So, it's *our* fault we were ousted . . . Why people were scared of us," I murmured, and Alexander nodded.

"That's correct. You won't hear about it in any classroom history book though." He shook his head in disgust.

"What happened next?" I asked.

"Nature needed to be rebalanced. The only way to make that happen was to give back some of what we took." He had a faraway look in his eyes, as if seeing it play out in his mind. "So, our people sacrificed four Keepers of Balance—the strongest person from each element."

"Sacrificed?" I repeated. "You mean *killed?*"

"Hardly," Alexander commented. "Three of them relinquished their powers and were banished to live out their days far away from Garridan. However, all three were lucky enough to not be alone. Their spouses and children gave up their powers and joined them."

"That's sweet. But also kinda sad. What happened to the fourth Keeper of Balance?"

"He absorbed the others' powers and became one with nature, vowing to never let our people take advantage of it again. His energy helps feed the earth as we continue to take from it."

"So, he became the tree from the legend?" I asked, and Alexander nodded. "Wow. That's . . . Quite the story."

"That it is."

"So, he has the powers of each element?"

"Correct."

"Then how does he grant and take away powers?"

"There's many speculations, but what most assume is that he earned so much favor with nature that they gifted him that ability and possibly more. In his last days as a human, he was very adamant that he'd keep nature safe and balance our usage of it, so it would make sense for him to be able to choose such a thing for people."

"Do you know his name? I feel weird calling him 'the tree' and also a little stupid," I admitted, and he grinned.

"Silas. Records say he didn't have a wife or children, which is why he volunteered to take on the role that he did. The only person who lost him was his twin brother."

"That must've been so hard."

"Probably. Especially when you consider the fact that his twin brother, Lyle, was one of the four Keepers of Balance that was sacrificed." Alexander's face was devious, and I could tell he enjoyed the pure shock that fell over my face.

"What?"

"Mhmm." He drew out the sound, adding to the dramatics he was trying to convey. "Silas was an earth element like their father, and Lyle was an air element like their mother.

Their parents passed away at a young age, so they were just that much more inseparable. Must've been hard for them to part ways, but at least Lyle had his wife and kids."

"As someone who's lost a sibling," Alexander averted his gaze as I said it, "believe me when I say having family by your side doesn't make it any easier."

"Of course not," he said quietly. "I'm sorry."

We sat in silence, and I pondered the possibility that I may never forgive him for the death of my mom and sister. No matter how much I tried, would I always hold some resentment towards him for it? I glanced over at the guards who were still standing at attention, their eyes focused solely on Alexander as if he could hurt me at any moment. Little did they know, he wouldn't hurt me any worse than he already had in the past.

"So, uhm, do you know how to find Silas?" I asked after the silence became too much to bear.

"Not specifically, but I know how to locate what you need to find him."

"Which would be?"

"A map, of course," he replied slyly.

"A map? Seriously?" I couldn't help but stare at him in disbelief.

"Think of how long ago this happened," he pointed out. "What else would you have expected?"

"I guess that's true. Where is it now?"

"Silas made sure he could be found if ever the need presented itself, but he also made sure it wouldn't be an easy task. He created three separate parts to the map and gave one to each of the other Keepers of Balance before they were exiled."

My brows furrowed and I said, "Wait. They're not even in Garridan?"

"That's correct."

"How are we supposed to find them then?"

"Trace the Keepers of Balances' lineages. Find their current living descendants and hope they still have it in their possession."

I groaned loudly. "What if they don't?"

"Then I guess you won't be going on a tree hunt."

I rested my head on his shoulder in defeat. I hadn't even started but was already overwhelmed by the possible 'what ifs' and dead ends I might encounter. This wasn't going to be an easy task.

CHAPTER SIX

All five of the trainees were sitting in the living room with Matthew and Claire, watching TV and playing board games. When I entered, they all stopped and stared at me.

"Where are my parents?" I asked.

"They called the council in for an emergency meeting," Claire answered.

"The trainees filled us in on what happened at dinner," Matthew added.

"When are you going to stop referring to us as 'the trainees?'" Emery asked with a roll of her eyes.

"Probably never," Matthew replied as he continued to stare at me. "What did he say?" He already knew where I'd been.

"What did who say?" Andre questioned.

"Alexander," I said, falling into an empty bean bag chair. "He had answers I wanted, so I went to get them."

"So your parents really did lie?" Kodi asked, and I nodded. "Why?"

"I honestly don't know. But I'm going to find out," I said with determination.

"Until then, what did Alexander say?" Matthew asked again.

I relayed the history I'd just learned, making sure not to leave out any details. When I finished, Matthew and Claire looked as intrigued as I'd felt, while the others stared on in disbelief.

"You know how insane that sounds, right?" Emery asked.

"About as insane as being able to control electricity," Claire remarked. "Everything around here is insane to an outside eye. Get used to it if you want to be a part of it."

Emery opened her mouth to, no doubt, say something snarky, but Kodi cut her off. "We're doing it, right? We're finding the map pieces then finding Silas?"

"Yes," I told her.

"There's only one problem with that," Matthew said.

"What's that?"

"We don't know the names of the original Keepers of Balance who gave up their powers."

"Let's figure it out then," Mateo spoke up.

"Weren't you listening?" Claire chided. "Alexander said the council are the only ones with access to all the old journals and documents referring to that history. If they don't want you to know about any of this, they definitely won't let you look through them."

"And that's the only way we can start trying to find the pieces of the map," I clarified more for myself than anyone else. I tapped my fingers against my leg as Kodi's face withdrew again.

"If we find out where they're kept, maybe Mateo can get in somehow," Emery suggested.

"Last time I snuck around for you people I almost died. So, uh, no. Pass," Mateo replied as he folded his arms over his chest.

"Baby," Emery muttered.

"*Excuse* me?" he asked with narrowed eyes before going off on her in Spanish.

"I don't understand what you're saying, so your threats are meaningless," Emery told him, sitting back in her chair with a smirk.

"You may not understand, but that doesn't mean the threat isn't real," he replied through gritted teeth.

"Enough," Matthew instructed. "You *all* need to grow up."

"Honestly," Claire agreed with a shake of her head. "I think you might be worse than me, and that's saying something."

"No one is worse than you," Matthew muttered.

"Who needs to grow up now?" Claire asked, placing her hands on her hips.

I rolled my eyes as everyone but Andre and I jumped into the disagreement. Just as I was about to silence them, a loud ringing echoed in my ear.

Please come to the courthouse. The council has requested your presence.

I flinched as the voice resonated within me, loud and authoritative. My eyes flickered around the room, looking for the source, then I realized someone must've been communicating with me telepathically.

Now.

A shiver ran up my spine, and I felt oddly violated as I stood up. "I have to go."

"What? Where?" Toby asked.

"I've been summoned by the council."

"When?" he questioned with confusion.

"Just now."

"How?"

"Telepathically."

"Why?"

"I'm not sure. I'm assuming it has to do with finding Silas," I answered with a shrug.

"She's now answered who, what, when, where, why, and how," Emery told him. "Quit being such a pest."

"I'm not a pest!" Toby denied.

"Yeah, you kinda are," she shot back.

"What crawled up your butt and died today?" Kodi asked in annoyance. "You're being an ass."

As Emery snapped back with another remark, Matthew stood and said, "I'll come with you."

I nodded in agreement, then when we were outside said, "You just couldn't stand being around them anymore, could you?"

"Not for another second," he agreed with a shake of his head, and I laughed.

They weren't an easy bunch to interact with if you weren't used to that kind of behavior. Luckily, I was all too familiar with it because of Dawn and her friends, so I didn't mind.

"Do you think I'm in trouble?" I asked.

"In trouble for what?"

"Calling my parents—and by default the council—out on their lies?"

"I doubt it," he replied without missing a beat. "I think your parents called the emergency meeting to inform the rest of the council that you already know the truth and to tell them they should let us go find Silas. I'm assuming they denied our request the first time because they thought they could pass a magic tree off as just a silly story."

"That's true," I agreed. "Do you think they changed their minds then?"

"If your parents told them that the trainees and I know the truth, too, then I think it's likely. We're problematic to them now."

"Why's that?"

"Think about it. An entire group of outsiders knows about a piece of history they've been hiding for centuries. They know we could cause them trouble if we wanted to, and they won't want that."

"Which means they'll let us do what we want," I said.

"Within reason, yes. I believe so."

I bit the inside of my cheek as I thought over that possibility and decided I had no reservations about using our knowledge to get us what we needed. "Let's go find out if that's the case then. If it's not, it's about to be."

Matthew's eyebrows shot up. "If that's not why they summoned you, you're going to blackmail them with my logic?"

"Blackmail is such a strong word," I responded. "I prefer the term . . . *Influence.*"

He shook his head in mock disgust. "And here I thought you were just a goody two-shoes."

I pushed him away from me playfully, and he grinned as we continued to walk. A short time later, we were heading up the stairs of the courthouse and waiting in the hall outside of the council's chambers. Malachi stepped out of the door and gave us both a look.

"I can't tell if that's a disapproving look or not, Dad," Matthew said.

"You two sure know how to cause trouble," Malachi responded with a shake of his head, and a small smile played at his lips, "but no, it's not a disapproving look."

"Technically, I didn't do anything. This one is all on Robin," Matthew told him, and I scoffed.

"Thanks a lot," I muttered as Malachi chuckled.

"The council is ready to see you," he said, holding the door open for us to enter.

"We asked for Ms. Hayes. Not Ms. Hayes *and* the youngest Mr. Alastair," Peter griped as he watched us walk in.

"Matthew is as much involved in this as any of us," Dad said. "He or William are going to take Malachi's place as head of the guard one day, which means he'd learn the history anyway. So, why not teach it to him now when we all know he's going to be joining our mission?"

Murmurs of agreement spread out across the room, so Chang asked, "All in favor of Matthew staying?"

All but two Keepers of Balance raised their hands, and Mom said, "The vote stands. Matthew can stay. Let's begin."

Darby leaned onto the desk she sat behind, her arms crossed over one another as she observed us. "Silas—or the magic tree as most people call him—has been seen as a legend amongst our people for hundreds of years. Very few have ever questioned the legitimacy of the story so, tell me, why do you?"

"Because I've been told it's true," I replied, making my voice ring out strongly, "and I believe the source it came from."

"That source being a man in a prison cell?" Luna questioned, and my brows furrowed.

"How do you know that?" I asked.

"We have eyes and ears everywhere," she answered.

"We also keep tabs on all the Cyfrin prisoners' visitors," Chang added.

"Okay, well, yes. The information did come from Alexander," I said. "That doesn't make it less reputable though. In fact, it makes me more inclined to believe it. He has no reason to lie to me."

"He's a Cyfrin. That's all the reason he needs," Peter stated with malice.

I glanced at him from the side of my eye before turning to face him fully. "Are you always such an angry, pompous jackass or is it just for my benefit?"

"Robin!" Mom exclaimed, her eyes narrowing. "That kind of disrespectful behavior will *not* be tolerated. Not here and not at home."

"I mean, she has a point," I barely heard Dad murmur, and Mom shot him a glare as other Keepers of Balance suppressed grins.

I wasn't done yet, though. I crossed my arms over my chest and held my mom's gaze intently. "You want to talk about disrespect? How about lying blatantly to my face? To Mateo and Kodi's faces when all they want is to go home and remember us. You don't get to talk to me about disrespect until you own up to your own misgivings."

Mom's eyes fell away from mine guiltily, and everyone began fiddling with things around them. They didn't know where to look, so they kept their eyes cast down as if that would make the situation less awkward. I looked towards Dad and saw him watching me sadly. I didn't want to hurt their feelings. I never wanted to hurt anyone's feelings, but I'd been learning it was an unavoidable and necessary evil sometimes.

Chang cleared his throat as he scratched at his patchy skin, and everyone eagerly looked his way as he said, "Robin, we called you here because we felt like you deserved to know the truth about our history."

"You mean you called me here because you realized I already knew the truth, and you were afraid I'd cause you trouble."

"She's a spitfire, isn't she?" the woman sitting next to my dad commented with a grin.

"She didn't use to be, Carmella," he answered, and I couldn't tell if he meant it in a bad way or not. "It seems the comrades she kept in the Cyfrin compound rubbed off on her. This no-nonsense attitude is definitely new . . . But efficient."

He smiled before shooting a wink my way, and I let out a silent breath of relief. He wasn't upset.

"Which means we should just cut the crap," Carmella said, her curly, black hair bouncing around her shoulders as she leaned forward and stared at me. "Right, Robin?"

"It'd make things easier," I agreed with a shrug.

"Alright then," she commented, her light brown eyes gleaming. "We called you here to confirm what your friend told you."

"Friend?" Peter asked with narrowed eyes, but Carmella ignored him.

"The legend of the tree is true, and we believe he can preserve your friends' memories if they want to give up their powers," she told me. "Mind you, we don't know that for certain, but we suspect it to be possible."

A jubilant feeling stirred in my core as the possibility of helping Mateo and Kodi became more realistic.

"We've spoken in length about the lot of you trying to find him and are basically split right down the middle," Luna said.

"But?" Matthew urged.

"*But*," she repeated, "we're aware that you won't stop at our say so. You're a very persistent individual, especially when it comes to people you care about. So, for that reason, we're going to allow you to try."

Matthew and I exchanged a glance, and a smile crept onto my face. "Really?" I asked. That was easier than I thought it'd be.

"Really," Luna confirmed.

"Thank you! Thank you so much. You won't regret it," I told them as I clasped my hands together. "We'll take our friends and go and come back before you know it."

"Hold on just a moment," Chang commented, his bushy brows rising high on his head. "We're going to allow you to go, but you'll have to follow certain rules. One of them being that we'll hand select the group going with you."

"Group?" Matthew asked.

"Yes. Not a very big one though."

"Why can't we go alone?"

"Because this isn't a completely selfless decision," Chang replied. "All of our records on Silas are extremely old. We don't even know if they're accurate anymore since our people have never had a need to use the information. So, we're hoping to gain some knowledge on this journey. We want to make sure our records are up to date but also enlarged."

"Enlarged?" I questioned, arching one brow.

"We know next to nothing about Silas' abilities," Darby explained. "We don't know how powerful he really is or what he does on a daily basis for us. We'd like to be better informed so we can continue to protect him but also be prepared if things ever started going south."

"What do you mean exactly?" Matthew asked, his stance rigid as he held his hands behind his back.

"After Silas transformed," Chang began, "his sacrifice was buried behind council walls because our ancestors thought it was best to hide the fact that someone so powerful was out there. They didn't want anyone with ill intentions to be able to locate him and destroy the pact he made with nature. Everything that happened in recent years with the Cyfrin just proves they made the right decision, but it's also made us worry. If the Cyfrin had gotten their hands on Silas' whereabouts, who knows what they could've done.

"We want to make sure he isn't controllable," Darby jumped in. "We also want to know what would happen if nature ever chose to outcast us. Don't get me wrong, we aren't planning on forging powerful weapons like our ancestors. We learned our lesson with that. However, would nature cut us off for the actions of the Cyfrin had they advanced in their plans? My guess would be yes, so we just want to be informed on how it would happen and what to expect. Does that make sense?"

"I mean . . . Yes," I replied hesitantly. "I think it does. You want to be able to have a plan in place in case that ever happened."

"Yes, exactly!" Chang exclaimed, seeming to appreciate my summarized version.

"Why didn't the people who've been granted powers by Silas in the past have any information to give?" Matthew asked.

"As far as we know, only five people have ever been granted a power by him, and they all came here directly after it happened," Peter answered. "However, those five people never discussed how they stumbled upon him or what happened when they saw him. It's as if they were bound to secrecy. When asked questions, they provided vague answers like 'I don't recall,' 'I don't remember,' or 'I couldn't say.'"

"Did you ever stop to consider that maybe those answers were true?" I asked.

"Meaning?"

"What if Silas wiped away any of their memories that pertained to him?" I suggested. "If he's trying to stay hidden and protected, he wouldn't want people walking around with knowledge about him."

"That's absurd," Peter stated.

"Actually," Dad spoke up, "it makes sense. Robin could be right."

"If that's the case, what's to say he won't do the exact same thing to everyone we send in to find him?" Carmella pointed out as she drummed her fingers on the table.

"It's a possibility," Luna said with a shrug as she pulled her long, blonde hair into a ponytail, "but we still have to try."

"I agree," Chang told her.

"How many people are you sending with us?" Matthew asked.

"We haven't planned out all the details yet, but we're thinking two Keepers of Balance and a handful of guards," Darby answered. "Then, of course, there's you and Robin and the two children who want to go home."

"It's actually three possibly," Matthew told them as I began to rub my lips together nervously. "One is still undecided."

Chang nodded, and I shifted my weight from foot to foot as he said, "Understandable. In that case it's you two as well as the three others."

"Actually," I stopped and cleared my throat, trying to work up the courage to say what I needed to say in front of Matthew. "It's us two, the three trainees . . ." My voice dropped before finishing. "And Alexander."

"*What?*" Matthew snapped as the council members broke out in varying degrees of denial.

"Robin, *why?*" I barely heard Dad ask over the hoard of rising voices.

I opened my mouth, then shut it just as quickly. I didn't have a reason other than he'd asked to come and I wanted him to, but the council would never let him see the light of day for that. As the volume in the room reached an uproar, my mind ran wild with reasons they'd allow him to go.

Mom slammed a book on her desk and yelled, "Everyone calm down!" One by one, they slowly stopped talking but continued eyeing me with contempt. "Robin. Why on earth would you want Alexander to go?"

"The Cyfrin knew a secret necessary to finding Silas," I spewed, my eyes wide as the lie flowed from mouth.

"What secret?" Dad asked.

"I don't know," I said. "He won't tell me. He said the last step to finding Silas relies on it though."

"Isn't that convenient?" Peter muttered as he shot daggers my way.

"Matthew?" Mom shifted her attention to him. "Do you know the secret?"

I glanced his way, silently begging him to play along. His glare was menacing as he stared at me, and he clenched his jaw as his hands balled into fists at his side.

"No," he finally answered, his gaze leaving mine. "Only the Keepers of Balance knew. I wasn't high enough on the food chain for information like that."

I let out the breath I'd been holding as relief flooded through me. Matthew shot another angry look towards me, and the relief vanished as my blood ran cold. He was going to kill me for this.

"The council needs time to talk through this," Chang said over the murmurs being exchanged, "but it's already getting late. Why don't we all sleep on it and plan to meet first thing tomorrow morning?"

"We can finish discussing the journey with Robin and Matthew tomorrow as well," Dad added, giving me his own disapproving look.

"All in favor?" Carmella asked, and every hand in the room lifted. "Meeting adjourned."

Matthew turned on his heel and stomped out of the room, slamming the door into the wall as he pushed it open. I ran after him, my feet slapping the ground loudly.

"Matthew!" I called out as he raced down the stairs. "Matthew, wait." I caught up to him on the first floor and pulled at his arm. "Matthew, please listen to me!"

He yanked his arm free of my grasp then backed me into the wall with his finger against my chest. His eyes blazed with anger as they bore into mine. "I swear if you don't back the hell away from me, I'll petrify you. I'll feel bad about it later, but I'll do it."

"I believe you," I replied, my voice barely an octave over a whisper. "But uhm . . . You have me pinned against the wall. I can't get any further away from you."

His lips turned white as he pressed them together, and he lifted his hand away from me. It hovered near my face shakily, and I could see him struggling to maintain his composure.

I cleared my throat and said, "You can hit me if it'll make you feel better."

"Why would *hitting* you make me feel better?" he cried out in exasperation.

I shrugged. "Because you like hitting things."

"Not *girls*."

"You've hit me plenty of times before," I pointed out.

"In *training*. Not out of anger! Is that really how you think of me?"

"No, of course not. I didn't mean it like that." I reached towards him again, but he held up his hand to stop me.

"I'm leaving now. Don't try to stop me." Before turning away from me completely he said, "Oh, by the way, how do you think the trainees are going to feel about this?" His question stopped me in my tracks. I hadn't thought about that. "I'm pretty sure I'm not the only one who's going to be pissed, so I hope it's worth it."

I watched as he walked away from me again, but this time, I didn't follow. I leaned against the wall dejectedly and moaned into my hands. I'd just created a very sticky situation.

CHAPTER SEVEN

As I walked home alone, I desperately tried to figure out how to tell Mateo, Kodi, and Andre that Alexander might be joining us on our journey to find Silas. Each conver-sation I played out in my head ended in chaos. As calm and forgiving as he was, Andre would be fine with it. Mateo could go either way depending on how I presented it. However, Kodi was a time bomb waiting to explode. She would be as angry as Matthew.

When I opened our front door, I immediately noticed how quiet it was. Quiet was never good. I slowly walked past the kitchen and saw my parents sitting at the dining room table. Mom had her hands folded neatly in front of her, and Dad was toying with a napkin.

"Robin," Mom said when she saw me. "Please take a seat."

"Where's everyone else?" I asked as I pulled out a chair.

"We asked them to go upstairs so we could speak with you alone."

"Oh," I murmured before sitting down.

"Why did you lie to the council?" she questioned.

"Why did you lie to me?" I asked in reply.

She pursed her lips, her eyes narrowing just a hair. "We didn't have a choice."

"There's *always* a choice. You did what you thought was best, and so did I. Don't harp on me for doing the same exact things you do."

"There's a *very* big difference," she stated, and I couldn't help but roll my eyes. "Don't you dare start with that attitude again young lady. We've been very lenient with you because of the somnokinesis withdrawals, but that ends now. I will not tolerate the disrespect."

"You deserve it though!" I exclaimed.

"*We* are the parents, and *you* are the child. You don't get to decide that!"

"Okay, why don't we all just calm down," Dad finally interjected, holding his hands up in front of us. "Robin, you may not like it, but we are still your parents, and we won't let you be disrespectful while you live in this house." I opened my mouth to argue, but he shushed me. "However, your mother and I do owe you an apology. Being on the council binds us in ways because we can't go against what's been decided. Our votes are unquestionable and must be followed. If they weren't, the system wouldn't work.

"We couldn't tell you the truth about Silas because that's the way the vote swung. It was never a problem for us before because . . . Well, because you weren't here. Now that you are, we're still trying to learn how to balance work with family, and we may not have gone about it in the best way this time around. I'm not trying to make excuses, but can you see the predicament we were put in?"

I glanced from him to my mom, whose expression had softened, before looking down at my hands. The annoyance I felt towards them dissipated immediately and shame took over. Of course they hadn't *wanted* to lie to me, but they were instructed to, and they couldn't disobey.

I was sure the repercussions for going against the council were substantial. Had they told me the truth, they would've been in serious trouble. What Dad said rang through my mind. They were doing the best they could.

"I'm sorry," I murmured, looking back and forth between them as I continued. "I should've realized . . . But I didn't, and I'm sorry. I didn't mean to overreact, and I would never want you to do something that would get you in trouble.”

“Thank you, honey,” Mom said, grasping my hand tightly in her own. “We’re sorry too. Like your father said, we’re trying to find that balance still, and it isn’t easy.”

“It’s okay,” I assured her. “Really.”

“See, that wasn’t so hard, was it?” Dad questioned with a wry smile.

“No, it wasn’t,” Mom said with a placating tone.

“You two can both be so hotheaded sometimes,” he commented with a shake of his head before looking at me. “It almost makes me happy I didn’t have to see you through puberty.”

“Ha. Ha,” I said dryly, and he chuckled.

“I’m serious. You and your mom going head-to-head every day.” He shook his head again. “Nope. I’m glad I missed it.”

“Enough, Elijah,” Mom instructed, swatting his hand. “We still have something else to discuss.”

They both watched me expectantly, and I ducked my head and asked, “What?”

“You know what,” Dad answered.

“Why on earth did you lie to the council?” Mom questioned.

“Because I need them to let Alexander come when we go find Silas.”

“But why?” Dad asked. “He’ll just complicate things.”

“Well, for one, he asked to go,” I told them honestly, “and I want him to. I think it’ll be good for him.”

“How so?”

I took a deep breath, gathering my thoughts. “I know he’s done a lot of bad things, but he’s not a bad person,” I finally started. “We *all* know that. We’ve seen it. He doesn’t deserve to be executed, and I don’t think he should be exiled with no memories either. If we let him make his own choices, he'll make the right ones. I know he will. He just needs to be given a chance."

My parents exchanged a look, their eyes having a silent conversation I wasn't part of. Mom looked at me gently and asked, "Honey, is it possible you have feelings for this boy?"

"This isn't about that!" I grumbled, averting my eyes. "It's just . . . He deserves a chance. He deserves a chance to be able to figure out who he is and what he wants. It's not his fault he was raised in the Cyfrin compound—just like it wasn't Matthew's—so what's the difference between them? They were both forced into that life. If Matthew was allowed a second chance, all the children of Garridan who were captured and raised by the Cyfrin should get a second chance. Don't you think?"

They looked at each other once more before Dad said, "Yes. They do. And we're going to make sure we advocate for them in that way."

"Even Alexander?"

"Even Alexander," he confirmed.

"You're not mad I lied to the council then?" I asked hesitantly.

"If Alexander stays here, I'm afraid the council won't be very forgiving in his case. He would most likely be sentenced to death because of the position of power he held." I tried to swallow away the unease that rose in my throat as he continued. "However, him helping find Silas could be a good way for him to prove himself while also buying us time to sway the council's decision. So, no, we aren't mad. We're proud of you for caring so much."

I smiled softly as Mom said, "Now we just have to convince them to let him go. Although, it might not be too hard with the lie you chose to tell. They want information about

Silas, and I don't think they'll want anything to derail them from getting it. Even if it means letting that boy tag along."

"I'll keep my fingers crossed," I commented. A thud sounded on the ceiling above us, and I remembered I still had more people to deal with. A grimace crossed my face and Dad let out one humorless laugh.

"Good luck," he said as Mom stood up.

"Kodi is going to be so angry," I told them, hiding my face in my hands.

"You reap what you sow," Mom replied, no hint of sympathy in her voice.

I groaned quietly as I pushed my chair back then slowly stalked up the stairs. I paused outside the boys' room, took a deep breath, then knocked.

"Come in!" Toby called out.

I twisted the handle and pushed the door open. "Why's the door shut if you're all in here?" I asked when I saw Kodi and Emery. The room was a decent size but having five people in it with a closed door piqued my claustrophobia.

"We wanted to give you and your parents some privacy," Andre replied.

"Some of us wanted to listen in but *somebody*," Kodi looked pointedly to Andre, "wouldn't let us."

I gave him a grateful smile and said, "Well, I appreciate it."

"Are you and Mom and Dad fighting?" Toby asked, and my smile widened at his effortless use of the terms.

I sat next to him on his bed and wrapped my arm around his shoulders. "No, we aren't fighting. We just disagreed about something, but it's fine now."

"Are you sure?"

"Yes," I assured him, "but . . . There's something I need to tell you guys. The council agreed to let us find Silas—"

"Really?" Kodi exclaimed, her eyes widening so much I thought they'd pop out of her head.

"Really," I said as she and Mateo shared a hug. "I should learn more tomorrow, but I know they're sending other people along with us."

"'Us' being?" Emery asked.

"Me, Matthew, Kodi, Mateo, and Andre," I replied. Emery scowled and my brows furrowed. "What's wrong?"

"Who said Andre was going?" she asked as she narrowed her eyes at him.

He looked down and didn't seem like he intended to answer, so I said, "Well, he's still not sure if he wants to go home or not, so he needs to come in case he decides he needs Silas' help too."

Emery continued to glare at Andre, but he wouldn't meet her gaze. After a moment of awkward silence she said, "Fine. I'm going too then."

I opened my mouth to object, but Toby spoke up first. "If you're all going, I'm going too!" he declared.

"Guys, I don't know if the council will let us bring anyone else," I told them. "Especially because . . . I kind of told them Alexander needed to go, and they're really not happy about it."

"You *what?*" Kodi asked, immediately standing up and placing her hands on her hips.

"Why?" Mateo questioned, his face hardening.

"I told them he knows a secret that we need to find Silas."

"That makes sense then," Toby spoke up, eagerly trying to avoid a fight.

"It was a lie," I admitted quietly. "I just had this conversation with my parents, and they understand, so I hope you will too."

"Oh, by all means, enlighten us," Kodi said sarcastically, crossing her arms.

"Do you realize that any of you could've ended up like Alexander? *Any* of you. Had you come into your powers sooner, the Cyfrin would've kidnapped you and raised you like they did him. Then *you* would've done awful things and hurt people. *You* would've been seen as a monster." I looked around the room as I spoke, trying to get my point across. "If you had, wouldn't you want to be given a second chance once you were finally free of the people who ruined you?"

They all exchanged looks, my words hitting them in the exact way I meant for them to. I watched as they processed what I said then added in, "This is the only way he'll get a second chance. If he stays here, they'll probably execute him. If he goes, he can prove he deserves to be rehabilitated instead."

"He tried to kill us, Robin," Kodi said with a shake of her head. "How can we trust he won't do it again?"

"Technically, he never tried to *kill* any of you. If he wanted you dead, you would be," I pointed out.

Kodi scowled. "That's not a selling point."

I sighed. "Look, I'm not trying to justify anything that happened while we were in the Cyfrin compound. Alexander did plenty of horrible things, and I'm not asking you to forgive him or even be nice to him. I'm just trying to make sure he has a fighting chance."

"Adding another lost cause to the list," Kodi muttered, but I ignored her.

"If the council decides to let him go, I'm going to make sure he earns his place in Garridan. I don't expect your help, and I don't expect you to be happy about it. All I'm asking is that you don't do anything to cause problems with him during the trip. You have every right to be angry at me, and

I won't try to change that, but I hope you remember if the roles were reversed, I'd be doing the same for any of you too."

"I can't say I'm pleased by the idea," Andre said, "but I'm not angry at you. I see where you're coming from."

"Seriously?" Emery scoffed. "If you chose to stay here, would you really want him around?"

"If he was to change his outlook on things, I don't see why it'd be a problem," he replied. "He didn't choose that life. If he's given a chance and he chooses the right path, who are we to hold a grudge against him? Robin's right. It could've easily been any of us, and, if it was, I'd want someone to give me the benefit of the doubt."

"I think he's mean and scary," Toby said, and my heart sank as he stared at his new sneakers. "But . . . He did save you."

"Yes, he did," I agreed quietly.

"He ended the war too . . . Which means he's not all bad. So . . . I'd give him a chance," he murmured.

"You will?" I asked.

"I trust you," he replied, finally looking up at me. The truth of that statement showed in his expression and warmed my heart.

"Thank you," I whispered as I squeezed his arm.

"You're all delusional," Emery commented with a roll of her eyes.

"No, we just possess some level of compassion," Mateo said in a low voice.

"You too?" Kodi asked accusingly, and Mateo shrugged.

"If he was to do something to us now, Robin wouldn't stand by him. I trust her judgement," he said.

My heart swelled at his comment. At least I had some of them on my side. I watched Emery and Kodi as they simmered in their anger and said, "I know how much I'm asking of you, and I'm sorry. I won't be upset if you can't get past this."

"I feel like you're betraying us," Kodi replied, her voice breaking.

"I'm not," I insisted. "I swear. Mateo's right. If Alex-ander was to do anything to any of you now, I wouldn't advocate for him. You are still my number one priority. I promise."

Kodi swallowed loudly and blinked away tears. "Fine. I won't cause problems if the council lets him come. But I don't promise to not be in a bad mood about it."

"I'll take it," I responded quickly, breathing a little easier. I glanced to Emery, and she scowled.

"If he even looks at me wrong, I won't hesitate to fry him from the inside out," she declared.

"I believe it," I muttered, then smiled. "Okay then. I'm glad we had this talk. Thank you for kind of understanding."

I received varying degrees of replies and nodded my head as their somber mood wafted through the room.

"Well, I'm going back to the hospital to sit with Ben," I said, standing up and walking to the door. "I'll see you guys later?"

Toby nodded and offered me a small smile. No one else acknowledged me, so I gave them a halfhearted wave and left them to stew freely.

CHAPTER EIGHT

The next day, Matthew and I stood in front of the council again. He hadn't spoken to me and wouldn't meet my gaze, so I knew he was still upset. I inwardly sighed and tried to keep the irritation off my face. Why was I the only one willing to help Alexander?

"We aren't happy about it," Chang was saying, so I turned my attention back to him, "but we need that information on Silas. Therefore, we've decided to allow Alexander to go." I fought to keep a wide smile off my face as my insides burst with joy. "However, he will be under constant supervision, and if he steps out of line even once, the guards will not hesitate to bring him back."

"Or eliminate the problem, if necessary," Peter added.

I bit my tongue, knowing this wasn't the time to get lippy with him again. I didn't want to give them any reason to change their minds.

"We're assuming you'll go tell him the good news," Luna said to me, and I nodded. "We'll want to debrief him and lay out our expectations as well, so kindly inform him that he'll be brought to us sometime in the next couple days."

"Yes ma'am," I responded.

"Until then, let's get down to business," Mom said. "Before anyone can go anywhere, we need to track down the pieces of the map."

"As I'm sure you're aware," Dad spoke up, "the three Keepers of Balance who gave up their powers and went to live among the normal people were each given a piece of that map. Silas wanted someone to be able to find him if the need ever arose. Unfortunately, with how long it's been since it happened, we don't know if they even still exist."

"If they don't, there's no way to find him," Luna added.

"Our best bet is to trace their family lineages and see if their current living descendants have them," Carmella said.

"That should be pretty easy to do," I said.

"Aside from the fact that Garridan's computers don't work the same as the ones you're used to," Matthew muttered.

"Unfortunately, he's correct," Mom agreed. "We'll have to go outside the barrier to track down the information."

"Then let's go," I said enthusiastically.

"It's not that easy," Luna replied. "Unfortunately, no one here would be very efficient working a computer in the normal world. Not to mention, there's not many of us who are comfortable with going outside the barrier."

"Then send Matthew and me," I responded with a shrug. "I don't see why everything has to be so complicated with you people . . . Respectfully."

"It's not that we try to be complicated," Mom answered. "We just want to be vigilant about keeping our presence a secret, and every time we leave the barrier, it's a chance of being found out and ruining everything we've worked so hard to protect."

"I understand that. I just don't think it's as risky as you all think it is. As long as no one uses their powers on the outside, anyone who goes out there will be fine."

"It's not just about the possibility of using our powers by accident," Chang inserted. "We're well aware that our demeanors are different than others. Not to mention, our lack of knowledge on basic things would raise suspicion."

I smiled wryly. "That's true but trust me when I say absolutely no one would jump to the conclusion that you're from a secret society full of superpowered people. If anything, they might think you're from a cult or Amish or something." Confused faces looked back at me, so I shook my head. "Never mind. Just let Matthew and me go. We'll be fine. There's no risk, I swear."

"We do need that information," Chang said as he glanced around the room.

"If they're offering, let them go," Carmella replied with a shrug. "Then none of us have to. They're probably more capable than us anyway."

"We can send Malachi with them as well," Mom added.

"Fine by me," Darby said.

"Me too," Peter agreed. "All in favor?" His eyes scanned the room then he said, "Alright. Send the kids then."

"In that case, let's show them the journals," Dad said as he stood from behind his desk. Mom, Chang, and a petite fire element I always forgot the name of followed suit—one person from each element. "Follow us."

Matthew stalked in front of me, and I followed close behind as we were led out a side door. I'd never been through this area, but it looked no different than the rest of the courthouse. The four Keepers of Balance stepped up to a thick double door that had intricate designs running along it. As I looked closer, I saw each element displayed in a row, and I realized they were all standing in front of their respective ones. They each held up one hand and a series of clicks sounded from within the door. My eyes widened as it opened.

"How did you do that?" I asked.

"Another one of our ancestors' creations," Chang answered, looking it over with adoration. "It requires one of each element to open."

"That's so cool!" I said as a smile crept onto my face.

"Yeah it is," Matthew agreed, the first acknowledgement he'd given of my existence since yesterday.

The room we entered was small, with shelves lining each wall. A collection of books and journals filled the space, and a table with four chairs sat in the middle of a tattered rug. Mom stepped up to one of the shelves and scanned over it before pulling out a yellowed journal that was completely falling apart. She carefully placed it on the table and motioned us to sit.

"This is one of the oldest pieces of history we have," she said. "The pages are very fragile, so please be careful." She flipped through the journal slowly before turning it around for Matthew and me to see. "These are the names of the four Keepers of Balance we lost to preserve our powers."

"Silas Tovert, earth; Lyle Tovert, air; Mitzi Robaday, water; Elin Windsor, fire," I read off.

"So we need to track the lineage of Lyle, Mitzi, and Elin," Matthew said.

"Correct," Mom answered.

"When can we go?" I asked.

"How's tomorrow morning?" Chang suggested. "That way you'll have the whole day."

"Where are we even going?" Matthew questioned.

"There's plenty of ancestry websites online that'll make it easy to do," I responded. "All we need is access to a computer, which means we could do it anywhere."

Matthew peeked over at me, and I immediately knew what he was thinking. Simultaneously, we said, "Milton," and it was decided as easy as that.

We left the courthouse not much later, and I walked a few steps behind Matthew as he headed down the street. The sun beat down pleasantly, so I unzipped my jacket to enjoy the warmth. It was a nice day, and all I wanted to do was stay outside and enjoy it.

"So, what boyfriend are you going to go see first?" Matthew asked with snark.

I stopped in my tracks and my brows furrowed. As he walked further away, a scowl climbed onto my face and my eyes narrowed.

That's the last straw.

I yanked a wall of water up directly in front of him and heard him sigh as I stomped his way.

"I'm tired of your crap!" I said loudly, and he turned to face me with his arms folded over his chest. "You have absolutely no reason to be angry at me so just stop!"

"No reason?" he repeated, his own eyes flashing daggers. "You're bringing Alexander with us to find Silas!"

"*So?*"

"I don't want to spend any more time with him than I have to!"

"Then don't go!" I yelled, and he pulled back as if I'd slapped him. "We'll be perfectly fine without you, so just stay here where you'll be far, far away from him."

"You'd choose him over me?" he asked, his eyebrows drawn together tightly.

I let out a wild noise of frustration as I tangled my hands in my hair to keep myself from punching him.

"I'm trying to *save his life!* If he stays here, he'll get executed. If he comes with us, he has a chance of being rehabilitated instead. What's so wrong about that? I'll tell you what—absolutely nothing! I'm trying to help him which is what *you* should be doing!"

I pointed a finger into his chest roughly. "But are you? No! You'd rather hold onto the hate you *pretend* he deserves so you can feel better about yourself! Well, guess what? You could've easily been the villain in *my* story, but you aren't because I *forgave* you. So grow up because you're no better than Alexander, and I'm tired of watching you pretend you are!"

I turned around and stomped away as the anger in me grew with every step. Why was everyone acting like I was the bad guy for helping Alexander? How could they not see the truth of the situation that sat right in front of them? I wasn't in the wrong for showing him compassion, and I was about at my breaking point in patience with everyone who said I was.

I stalked into Ben's hospital room and sat in the chair by his bed with a huff. I grabbed his hand in both of mine and brought my forehead down against it as tears threatened to fill my eyes. I was tired of fighting everyone.

"You'd understand, wouldn't you, Ben?" I asked softly. I took a deep breath then released it slowly. "I sure could use some of your sage advice right about now. You always know what to do." I smiled as I watched him sleep so peacefully. "I miss you so much, Benjamin."

Emotion overcame me, and I slowly leaned in. I hesitated for a moment then closed the rest of the distance between us, letting my lips meet his lightly. Butterflies rose in my stomach and warmth filled my cheeks. When I pulled back, I bit my bottom lip as a smile crept onto my face. Even asleep and drifting away from me, he made me swoon.

After another hour of small talk and letting myself calm down, I headed to the jail to see Alexander. When he saw me walk through the door, his face lit up, and I couldn't help but smile back.

"Knock knock," I said.

"Come in," he replied. "Anyone and everyone else sure does."

"Man, it must be so hard not having privacy," I remarked pointedly.

"Hey, I gave you privacy when you asked."

"Kind of," I said with a roll of my eyes. "But, anyway, guess who's coming on our hunt for Silas?"

"Me?" he asked with raised brows, and I nodded as I sat on the edge of his bed. He let out a huff as he shook his head. "I won't lie, I didn't expect you to actually convince them to let me go."

He sat beside me as I shrugged. "What can I say? I'm very persuasive."

"Apparently. So when do we leave?"

"Matthew and I are supposed to go to Milton tomorrow to track down the names of the ancestors who would have the map pieces. After that, we'll have to actually find them and hopefully bring them back here. So, sometime after that I would imagine."

"And I really get to go?" he asked, and I nodded again.

"The council is going to summon you sometime in the next couple days to lay down the ground rules."

"Thank you, Robin."

"Of course."

"I'm sure Matthew had words to say about it."

I shrugged. "A couple."

"A couple?"

"Maybe a few," I amended, and he arched one brow. "Okay, he's pissed, but that's his problem. If he doesn't want to be around you, he can just stay here, and I told him that."

"You did?" he asked, a note of surprise in his tone.

"Yep. And I'll tell it to anyone else who has a problem with it too."

He hesitated before asking, "Why?"

"Because you deserve a second chance and I'll do whatever it takes to make sure you get it." I caught his eye and stared at him intently. "I've been standing up for you and causing fights with everyone I care about so, please, don't make me regret it. Prove to them that what I see in you is real. Show them you're not the monster they think you are."

"I will," he replied as serious as a heart attack. "I won't let you down. I promise."

CHAPTER NINE

I sat on my bed, letting upbeat music fill the empty space. Kodi and Emery were in the boys' room when I got here—probably to avoid seeing me since they were still upset about Alexander—so I was trying to drown out the somber mood with the happy tunes of an early 2000s boy band. It wasn't helping much, so I laid on my floor, staring at the ceiling as I thought back to my argument with Matthew.

Guilt flooded my body as my harsh words resounded in my head. I knew everything I said was justified, even if it was done out of anger, but I could've been nicer about it. He didn't deserve to be blown up on.

A knock sounded at the door before Dad poked his head in.

"You okay, kiddo?" he asked when he saw me.

"Peachy," I replied.

"Okay," he said slowly. "Well, you have a visitor."

"Who?"

"Why don't you go downstairs and find out?"

I let out a dramatic sigh, not in the mood for socializing with anyone, but followed him out of my room anyway. I stepped off the last stair then stopped when I saw Matthew waiting in the foyer.

"What do you want, Matthew?" I asked wearily as I crossed my arms and looked away.

"Did you mean what you said earlier?" he questioned quietly.

I swallowed, anger and guilt battling for first place. "Yes, but I'm not going to argue with you anymore. It's done, so why don't you just leave."

I walked past him to open the front door, but he grabbed my upper arm and stopped me in my tracks.

"I'm sorry," he said before meeting my eyes. "I'm really sorry. I messed up."

"Yeah," I said as I pulled my arm out of his grip. "You did."

"Robin, I don't know how you ever forgave me for deceiving you when I first came to Milton, but I'm grateful you did. That second chance meant everything to me."

"Then imagine how much a second chance would mean to Alexander."

He leaned against the wall and looked down at his feet. "Did you know I still blame myself for what happened to your mom and sister?"

"What? No. You shouldn't." I instinctively reached out to comfort him, but before my hand landed on him, I stopped.

"I'll never not." His face was sad, and my stomach flip flopped as I tried to squander the grief that began to fill me. "However, my point is that even though I blame myself, somehow you don't. Somehow, you never did. I could never live up to the kind of person you are . . . But I think it's time I tried. If you can forgive me . . . I can forgive Alexander."

"Really?" I asked, and he nodded as a half-smile covered my face. I pulled him off the wall and wrapped my arms around him tightly. "Thank you."

"No, thank you," he said as he rested his head against mine. "For always being my voice of reason and trying to make me a better person."

"It sure isn't easy," I joked, and he pushed me away.

"I was being serious," he grumbled with narrowed eyes, and I laughed as I pulled him into a hug again.

"I know. I'm sorry. It's just too easy sometimes."

"Yeah, yeah, yeah."

"Thank you for apologizing."

"You're welcome." He gave the top of my head a quick peck.

"And, hey, I'm sorry too," I said, rubbing my arm. "I meant what I said, but I could've gone about it in a better way. And I *want* you to come. I'd probably go crazy if you didn't."

"I appreciate the apology," he replied, "but we both know I'm too stubborn to listen to rationale. I needed a harsh slap of reality, so don't even worry about it."

"Okay," I murmured.

"I'll see you tomorrow, okay?"

"You can't stay?" I asked as he placed his hand on the doorknob.

"Afraid not. My mom suckered me into helping with this home renovation thing. I just needed to apologize before I chickened out."

"You? A chicken? Never," I said with a grin. "Have fun with your mom."

"I make no promises," he replied before closing the door behind him.

I walked back up the stairs, then my smile quickly disappeared when I saw the trainees hustling back into the boys' room. I rolled my eyes—knowing they'd been listening—then plopped onto my bed with my headphones in my ears.

I thought back on Matthew's words, and warmth traveled through me. He held me on such a high pedestal, and I never wanted to disappoint him. We may have our fights, but we always found a way past them, and each time we did, I always felt closer to him. We had our differences, but our friendship worked anyway. I couldn't imagine him not being in my life.

Toby glanced around the corner of the door, and I took out my headphones. "Hey," I greeted him.

"Hi . . . Can we come in?" he asked.

"Sure." I sat up and placed my hands in my lap as Kodi, Emery, Mateo, and Andre came in behind him. "What's up?"

They all looked to Andre, and he shook his head as his lips pressed together in disapproval.

"Apparently I'm going to start this conversation. As usual," he said as he continued to stare at the others accusingly. I suppressed a grin. They always hid behind him, literally and figuratively. "Anyway, Robin, we came to tell you we overheard your conversation with Matthew earlier."

"Haven't you guys learned your lesson in eavesdropping?" I asked with an arched brow.

"It would appear not," Andre answered as the others shook their heads. "Although, I did try to tell them not to."

"Is that why you were listening right alongside of them?"

He smiled sheepishly. "I fell into peer pressure."

"Uh huh."

"Well, we wanted to apologize like Matthew did," he said.

"What?" I asked in surprise.

"We like Matthew. We think he's a good guy," Emery jumped in. "But we only know him as that because you forgave him for whatever happened in your hometown."

"If we'd known him when he was a Cyfrin member, we would've easily seen him as a bad person like we do with Alexander," Mateo said. "But we've only known him after, so we haven't judged him based off his past."

"So why is it fair to do that to Alexander when he helped us in the end?" Kodi added with downcast eyes.

"So you're saying . . .?" I trailed off expectantly.

"We're ready to give him a chance," she answered, although she still looked grim.

"Come here," I told her, holding out my hands. She crept over to me, and I gave her a quick hug. "Thank you. I know that's not easy for you."

"It's fine. Not like I'll ever have to see him again once I leave here anyway," she pointed out.

"Way to look at the bright side," Mateo said sarcastically, giving her two thumbs up. She reached over and punched him in the arm.

"I'm trying," she muttered.

"I know you are, and I really appreciate it," I told her before looking around at all of them. "I appreciate all of you. This trip will be fun. You'll see."

* * *

"This trip is a disaster," Matthew grumbled as he leaned back in his chair and rubbed his hand along his face.

"Not yet it's not," I muttered back, clicking through another page on the computer.

"I come bearing fuel," Felicity announced, setting doughnuts and coffee down in front of us before sitting down in her chair.

"Thank goodness," Matthew said. "My eyes need a break."

"Come on, Robin, you too," Felicity instructed.

"I can't. We've been here for hours and only found Elin Windsor's descendant. We need the other two," I said.

"You'll have more energy and focus when you get some caffeine in your system."

I picked up a cup and took a sip then gave her a sneer before looking back to the computer.

"Leave her be," Matthew said. "We both know she's too stubborn to listen."

"I am not," I denied.

"Then prove us wrong. Take a break."

I eyed them both for a long minute before shaking my head. "No."

"That's what I thought," Matthew said, and I made a face at the computer screen. "How's the college hunt going?"

"Amazing!" Felicity exclaimed. "I got an early acceptance letter to a school in New York and LA. I just have to decide what coast I want to live on."

"Do you want to spend your free days on the beach or at Broadway shows?" I asked as I crossed another possible lead off my list.

"Definitely both."

"Then go to New York so you can have both those options."

"That's true . . . But winter. It'd be so nice to get away from it," she said with a sigh.

"That's true," I agreed, opening a new tab and typing another name in, "but at least in New York you wouldn't have to worry about driving to places during the winter. You could just take the subway."

"True again." She was quiet for a moment, and I knew she had her thinking face on. "Oh well. I have time to figure it out," she finally said.

"You'll do great no matter where you go," Matthew told her, and her smile widened.

"I know."

"Hey," I said, squinting my eyes at the screen. I rubbed my fists over my eyes then stared at the name in front of me harder. "Hey!" I jumped up and threw my arms above my head in triumph. "I found it. I found it!"

"Found what?" Felicity asked around a mouthful of dou-ghnut.

"Mitzi Robaday's descendant!"

"Really?" Matthew asked excitedly, peering over my shoulder as I sat back down and began reading.

"Her name is Genevieve Robaday, and she lives in an assisted living center in California. She's ninety-two with no other living relatives. No kids, no siblings, nothing."

"So, she's Mitzi's *last* descendant," Matthew said.

"Looks that way."

"Good thing we didn't need to find her in ten years," he muttered. "She'd probably be dead, and we'd be screwed."

"Matthew!" Felicity chastised.

"What? It's true," he said with a shrug.

"He's not wrong," I agreed. "We probably need to go to her first just to be safe."

"Maybe Dad will take us today."

"What about that last descendant y'all need?" Felicity asked.

"Y'all?" I questioned with raised brows.

"I'm in a western play next week," she replied, as if that explained it all.

"Okay then. Well, I can't find anything on Lyle Tovert at all. It's like he never existed in the normal world," I said, leaning back in my chair.

"Maybe he didn't," Matthew replied.

"What do you mean?"

"What if he never planted roots in the outside world? What if he lived off the grid until he died?"

"I mean . . . Maybe. But he had a wife and kids. If the kids grew up and had their own children, surely there'd be a record of them eventually."

"Maybe he changed his name," Felicity suggested. Matthew and I turned to stare at her, and her eyes flickered between us as her brows lifted. "What?"

I looked at Matthew, suddenly feeling extremely defeated. "She's right. It's the only thing that makes sense."

"But if that's true, we'll never find the third map piece," he said.

"And if we never find the third map piece, we'll never find Silas, which means Kodi and Mateo can't keep their memories." I banged my head against the table as a loud groan escaped my mouth.

"Hey, you tried," Felicity said, reaching behind me and giving my shoulder a squeeze. "They'll understand."

"They're going to be devastated."

"Probably," Matthew agreed. "But Felicity is right. You tried, and they'll know you did everything you could."

I slowly raised my head as his words echoed in my ears. It would be easy to call it quits now, but I wasn't ready to. We hadn't done everything we could yet, and I wasn't going to quit at the first obstacle. Our friends deserved more than that.

"Not yet we haven't," I finally said. "We're still going to get those two map pieces. Maybe, somehow, they'll help us find the third."

"I don't think that's how they work," Matthew said.

"You never know," I replied with a shrug. "Besides, the council probably wants them whether we go find Silas or not."

"That's true."

"Does that mean you're leaving now?" Felicity asked quietly.

Matthew and I exchanged a look, and he winked at me before saying, "I mean, we probably *should*."

"Yeah, we do have a lot to do," I agreed, suppressing a smile as Felicity's face turned sad.

"I guess that settles it. Time to go."

"It was good seeing you guys again," Felicity said, trying to force a smile onto her face.

"You too," Matthew told her, "but duty calls."

We all stood, and she came to give me a hug, but I stepped back as I put my finger to my chin.

"Then again," I said slowly, "how often are we going to have a chance to hang out with you?"

"That's a fair point," Matthew agreed with a nod of his head.

Felicity furrowed her brows then put her hands on her hips. "Are you guys screwing with me?"

Matthew grinned as I let out a laugh. "Yes, we are," I answered. "The council doesn't expect us back until tonight, so we have the whole afternoon."

Felicity's eyes turned to slits as she crossed her arms and stuck out her lower lip. "You guys are mean."

"Yeah, Matthew's a bad influence like that," I said as she huffed.

"Well, in that case, dinner is on you," she told him before linking her arm in mine and pulling me away from the computers.

CHAPTER TEN

When we arrived back in Garridan, Matthew and I quickly met with the council. Despite not finding a living descendant for Lyle Tovert, they still wanted the other two map pieces—just as we thought they would. Malachi scheduled us to fly to California the next day to talk with Mitzi's de-scendant first, then to Tennessee where Elin Windsor's de-scendants lived.

It wasn't too late, so I stopped by the hospital to check on Ben. Akio said he should wake up any day now, and I was both excited and nervous about it. I was enjoying these last moments of him recovering so I could hold his hand and run my fingers through his hair. After he woke up, I'd already decided to be distant until we took him home. It was the best thing for us both.

As I walked home, my direction unintentionally veered until I was heading straight to the jail. Officer Sanchez glanced up from some papers on his desk when I entered then smiled.

"Good to see you again," he told me.

"You too," I replied. "Is it too late to see Alexander?"

"Nah, we don't have visiting hours here." He stood and walked to the elevator door. "Come on, I'll take you down."

The ride to the lower level still left me squirming. I never realized I was afraid of being underground. When was the last time I even had been?

Wait.

The last time I'd been underground was when Alexander locked me in the torture room at the Cyfrin compound.

Great. He traumatized me.

Officer Sanchez guided me through the maze of halls I was slowly getting used to. When we came into view of his cell, Alexander was doing pushups and sweat poured down his face.

When I walked into the room he said, "I don't care who you are, I'm not stopping."

"That's okay. I don't mind the view," I replied with a smirk. He looked up at the sound of my voice and smiled back as he stood. "So much for not stopping."

"You're the one exception," he said as he grabbed a wet towel and wiped his face and neck.

"Well, don't I feel special." I leaned against the glass wall, ignoring the guards that were posted outside.

"As you always should."

My eyes fell to my feet as he changed into a clean shirt then I said, "We found two of the three descendants."

"Only two?"

I nodded. "The third is a ghost trail. We couldn't find a single connection for Lyle Tovert. My friend, Felicity, said maybe he changed his name after leaving Garridan."

"That would make sense. How are you going to find his map piece though?"

I shrugged. "At this point, we can't. We're going to get the other two tomorrow though. Hopefully." He eyed me dubiously. "What?"

"No map piece means no Silas. No Silas means no rehabilitation chance for me. Guess I should prepare for execution after all."

"That's not true!" I exclaimed as I pushed myself off the wall. "You know I'll do everything I can to make sure you don't get a death sentence. As long as I'm here, you still have a chance."

"You can only prolong the inevitable for so long," he said, walking to the edge of his bed and sitting.

"Luckily for you, I'm an optimist."

"Lucky me indeed," he replied semi-sarcastically. "How's Ben doing?"

His question caught me off guard. "Oh, uhm, he's good. Akio said he should wake up any day now . . . Why?"

"I know how happy you must be that you'll get to see him."

"Not really, actually," I admitted.

"Oh?" He furrowed his brows. "Why's that?"

I sat next to him and shrugged. "It's complicated."

"People say that a lot, but usually it isn't very complicated at all. They just don't want to explain."

"When did you get so perceptive about people?" I asked, arching one brow.

"Time served will do that to a person," he replied. "So, why aren't you going to be happy to see him awake?"

I tapped my thumbs together as I looked down at them. "Because I know I'll have to ignore him. Or at least be really distant until he goes back home."

"Why?"

"Because it's what's best for us both. Just because we brought him here to heal doesn't mean our situation has changed. We still can't be together, and I still want him to move on and be happy with his new girlfriend. So, I can't make this another heartbreaking goodbye. It just has to be . . . Goodbye."

"You're very selfless," Alexander said quietly.

"Am I? Because I feel like it's pretty selfish. I'm doing it to save myself."

"No, I don't think you are. You're doing it to save him, and I admire that." He grabbed my hand and lightly traced the back of my palm with his thumb. "I have something for you. I meant to give it to you sooner, but the timing never seemed right."

"What is it?"

He let go of my hand and bent over, feeling underneath the springs of the bed. When he straightened up, he held out a familiar ring I thought had been lost forever. A small gasp left my lips, and I reached for it, taking in every inch of the intricately welded family heirloom Ben had given me.

"I thought it was gone," I murmured, one side of my lips turning up in a sad smile.

"I went to your room the day of the battle—after I locked you up. I saw it sitting on the table by the bed and took it so it wouldn't get lost. I knew how sentimental it was to you and that the castle might take a couple hits, so I didn't want it to be harmed."

"That was really thoughtful. Thank you." I carefully put the ring in the pocket of my jacket as Alexander watched with confusion dancing in his eyes.

"You're not going to put it on?" he asked, and I shook my head.

"Distance, remember?"

"I don't think there's any harm in treasuring it while you have it."

I peered up at him, trying to figure out how his mind worked. "Why are you being so understanding? Why are you asking about Ben at all? Why do you even care?"

"Because I love you, and I want you to be happy."

My heart skipped a beat then thumped faster than it was supposed to. My mouth was dry, and I tried to swallow but couldn't. He'd said that to me once before, but I didn't have time to really process it. We were in a war after all. But now, sitting here next to him, those words were center stage, and I wasn't sure how to respond.

I took a deep breath then said, "You shouldn't."

He smiled in amusement. "And why not?"

"Because I don't love you back," I murmured, struggling to not jump up and run far away from him and this conversation.

"That's my problem then, isn't it? Besides . . . I don't believe for a second that you couldn't love me after Ben is out of your life."

I shifted uncomfortably as he seemed to stare through my very soul. "That isn't fair to you," I said. "Do you really want to be someone's second choice?"

"I don't mind being your consolation prize when I know your feelings for me are real. They're there, and you mean them. They're just hidden under the ones you have for Ben right now." He lifted one shoulder, his kind eyes never leaving mine. "But I'm patient. I can wait."

"Alexander—"

"Don't say it isn't fair to me," he cut me off. "It's my choice just like it's your choice to distance yourself from Ben. I love you, and I know you could love me too. Waiting until you can get over losing your first love is the least I could do for you if I mean what I say . . . And I do."

I stayed silent; he was right. I couldn't tell him what to do or how to feel. Somewhere deep inside, a strange heat radiated in my core. I pressed my lips together to keep the smile that was forming under control. Knowing he'd be there waiting brought me an odd sense of joy. It relieved some of the burden I felt about sending Ben away—especially with what would be a less than decent memory of our last interaction. In that moment, I knew Alexander could fill the void of Ben's absence. We could be happy together.

"Now I'm *really* going to make sure you get your second chance," I said quietly, leaning into him.

He wrapped his arm around me and kissed the top of my head. It was wrong of me to use him as a fallback . . . But I didn't really care. If he was fine with it, why shouldn't I be?

* * *

"Do you think you'll get the two map pieces tomorrow?" Kodi asked as we laid in the dark.

"I hope so," I replied, turning onto my side to peer at her and Emery on the air mattress beside me. Emery snorted. "What's that for?"

"It's been what? *Hundreds* of years since those things were made?" she asked. "Do you really think people would keep something like that around for a couple dozen generations? They probably got thrown away or ruined at some point over the years."

She sounded so skeptical, voicing the concern I had myself, but I couldn't think like that. I couldn't see it as a lost cause until I knew otherwise.

"You never know," I said with a shrug that was lost on them in the blackness that surrounded us. "Some families really value heirlooms." I placed my hand over the ring I was keeping in the pockets of my sweats. "Some families value their history."

"Yeah, but what are the odds that both those families did?" Emery questioned.

"What are the odds of me getting you to stop being so pessimistic?" I shot back.

"Very unlikely."

"Can't you just try to be supportive for once?"

"I'd rather be realistic."

"And I'd rather be asleep," Kodi interjected. "Can you both just please be quiet now and stop talking about it?"

Her voice was thick, and as she rustled the sheets around her head, I could hear her sniffle. She tried to put on a brave front, but we could all see how much hurt she was going through—her and Mateo both. They were depending on Matthew and me to succeed so they could go home whole and unbroken.

The thought of them losing their memories kept me determined to do just that. They couldn't forget us. They couldn't forget the part of them that made them unique and special. They just couldn't.

CHAPTER ELEVEN

"Good morning," I greeted the tired looking receptionist. "We're here to see Genevieve Robaday."

The woman peered at me over the top of her glasses. "Are you family?"

"No, ma'am. Just old friends," I replied. "Ms. Robaday doesn't have any living family. Only us."

"Yes, that's right," the receptionist said around a yawn. "Well, it'll be nice for her to have some visitors. Let me just give her a quick call to make sure she's awake."

She grabbed her phone while I looked back to where Matthew stood. I crossed my fingers, hoping this would be an easy ordeal.

"Alright, she's all yours. She's in room 112," the receptionist announced as she hung up the phone.

"Thank you so much," I told her before heading down the hall she pointed towards.

"Easy peasy," Matthew said as we walked.

"Let's hope the rest of the trip goes like that."

Large windows took place of the walls, letting in lots of natural light. The warmth of the sun made me smile as I took everything in. It was all well-kept and inviting. I noticed the hall was lined with an assortment of vibrant flowers and instantly thought of Alexander. He'd love the atmosphere around here.

We'll have to build him a garden somewhere in Garridan so he can have a place to escape and relax. I'm sure he'll need it.

"This place is nice," I commented.

"It is. A good place to wait to die."

My head whipped towards Matthew as my lips turned back down. "What?"

"What?" he asked, tilting his head quizzically. "Isn't that what this place is? For old people to live in until they die?"

I pressed my lips together and found myself trying to contain an amused smile. "I guess it is," I agreed. "Just never heard it explained like that."

"A new perspective for you then."

"That it is," I agreed with a snort. "Oh, here's her room. You ready?"

"Let's do it," he said, knocking on the door rapidly.

A moment passed then a short, petite woman with white hair and small glasses opened the door with a smile plastered on her wrinkled face.

"Hello there," she greeted us.

"Hi, Ms. Robaday," I replied gently. "My name is Robin, and this is Matthew. We were hoping we could visit with you for a moment."

"Of course. And it's Genevieve. Please, come in." We sauntered past her as she opened the door wider, and she motioned for us to sit around a table near the bed. "Care for some tea?"

"No, thank you. We won't take up much of your time," I told her as I sat.

Matthew stayed standing behind me as Genevieve poured herself a cup of steaming liquid. As she sat across from me, she glanced from Matthew's rigid demeanor back to me, her tight-lipped smile never wavering.

"Seems you have a protector," she said to me.

"That's just his natural demeanor," I replied lightly.

"She doesn't need protecting anyway," Matthew said. "She's the fiercest person I know."

"That's so sweet," Genevieve responded, then she sighed. "How I miss the days of young love."

"What?" I asked, heat rushing to my cheeks. "Oh, no, no, no. We aren't together. We're just friends."

Her eyes skittered between the two of us again, her already wrinkled forehead scrunching even more. "He's not your boyfriend?"

"No, ma'am," Matthew answered, a hint of amusement in his tone. "She has enough of those already."

My eyes narrowed into slits as I whirled around to look at him. A smirk lingered on his lips, and I couldn't help but shoot a narrow water beam at his leg. It sliced through the material on his pants, barely grazing his skin, and he scowled as he refrained himself from petrifying me in front of a Norm.

I turned back around and cleared my throat as I tried to recollect my thoughts.

"He's just joking," I assured Genevieve, and she let out a soft chuckle, oblivious to what just happened.

"So, to what do I owe the pleasure?" she asked. "Donna said you were old friends, but I'm afraid either she or you are mistaken. I may be old, but my memory is still fully intact, and I don't remember ever meeting the two of you before."

"That's because you haven't," I admitted. "We're actually doing a history project and stumbled upon a very interesting old legend we wanted to look into more, but we hit a roadblock."

"Well, if there's one thing I know, it's history. How can I help?"

"This particular legend has a map that needs to be followed. We were hoping to find it to show our class, but it looks like it was divided into three pieces and passed down within three different families. We traced the lineages and one of them was yours." I rubbed my hand against my arm and laughed nervously. "I know it sounds silly, but we were hoping maybe you really had it."

"It doesn't sound silly at all! Why, maps were the way of the world once upon a time. Now it's all digital and compli-cated."

"That it is," Matthew agreed.

"Would you happen to have it then?" I asked hopefully.

"I'm afraid not," she replied. My face fell as I slumped down in the chair some. "But I can tell you where to find it."

"You can?" I questioned excitedly as she slowly stood and waddled to an old filing cabinet.

"That map was in my family for as long as I can remember," she said as she opened a drawer and looked through it. "We always thought it was just some silly heirloom. We never knew the history behind it, although we did have fun making up stories. When I moved in here, I had to part with many of my belongings—the map incl-uded. I didn't want to just throw it away, but I had no one to pass it on to."

She came back with a piece of paper in her hands and handed it to me. I quickly scanned it and realized it was a notice of forfeiture. The name on the top read 'Museum of Ancient History.'

"You gave it to a museum?" I questioned, and she nod-ded.

"I thought someone there could find a place for it. I even hoped someone might contact me with information if they ever looked into it," she told us, her voice growing soft. "But who knows if that'll happen before I pass."

"It will!" I told her, my heart growing heavy at her sad expression. "Matthew and I will let you know what we learn after we find the map pieces." Matthew flicked my back in warning, but I ignored him. "When our project is over, we'll come back and share what we found."

I could feel Matthew's eyes boring into me as Genevieve clasped her hands together. A wide smile danced on her face, and I couldn't help but smile back as the happiness radiated from her.

"That would be just lovely!" she exclaimed.

"It's our pleasure. Especially since you gave us exactly what we needed."

"Not quite," Matthew muttered, but Genevieve didn't seem to hear him.

"Oh, thank you!" she said, grasping my hand tightly in her clammy one.

"Of course. Well, I guess we're headed to the museum!" I announced as I stood. "Thank you again for your time."

"Anytime, dear. Please, come back and visit. It was so nice to have some company."

"We will," I promised, my stomach twisting unhappily at the lie. She was so sweet and lonely that I wished it were the truth. Maybe we could find a way to get her more visitors later on.

* * *

"This is it," I said as we stopped in front of a large building.

"Do you think they have it on display?" Matthew asked.

"I doubt it. They'd have to know the history before displaying it so they could explain what it was. I mean, unless they made something up."

Matthew glanced at me unhappily, but I plastered a smile on my face, linked my arm in his, and pulled him forward to the doors.

"Hello!" a young man greeted us enthusiastically as we walked to the front desk. "Two adults?"

"Actually, we have a question about an item that was forfeited to the museum," I replied as I looked at the man's nametag. Evan.

"Oh, something different to spice up my day," Evan said with a quirky half smile. Matthew stared at him with disdain, and I could tell he didn't like the guy's overly chipper attitude. I nudged his foot with my own. This wasn't the time to scare the poor worker. "So, what's the item?"

"It's an old map. Or maybe only part of an old map." I pulled out the paper Genevieve had given me and handed it to him. "This is the information."

Evan looked it over then tapped his finger on his chin. "Hmm . . . Can't say I've ever seen this before."

"Which means it's not on display, right?"

"Definitely. I know every single item in here, and this sure isn't one of them."

"Is there any way to figure out where it is?"

"Well, sure! I'll just check my handy dandy computer here, and we'll see what it says."

"That's so helpful! Thank you," I told him as Matthew rolled his eyes. I elbowed him in the side and whispered, "Be nice."

"He's annoying," he muttered back.

"Why? Because he's happy?"

"No, because he's fake happy. Big difference."

"Well, suck it up, buttercup," I replied with my own overly fake happiness, and he rolled his eyes again.

"Looks like it's in one of the storage rooms," Evan said as he read over his screen.

"Are there any plans for it?" I asked.

"Not that I can see. I think it's actually scheduled to be destroyed."

"*Destroyed?*" Matthew asked harshly, and Evan peered up at him.

"Yeah. Every so often, pieces that have no value or purpose get destroyed to make room for other artifacts," he explained.

"You can't destroy that!" Matthew nearly yelled, and I placed my hand on his shoulder before turning to Evan again.

"Sorry about him," I said, putting a sweet smile on my face. "He just found out that map is actually a really sentimental family heirloom. His great grandmother was supposed to pass it down, but she had one of her senior moments and gave it away instead. His whole family is pretty upset about it."

I looked back up at Matthew with sorrow in my eyes, and he arched one brow at my lie. Before he could say anything, though, Evan let out a heavy sigh.

"Man, that's rough. I'm so sorry," he said to Matthew, and Matthew nodded slightly. He wasn't a very good actor. "I bet I can get it back for you."

"Really? That would be so amazing!" I exclaimed.

"Let me make a call to my boss real quick," he said, and I nodded earnestly before walking to a bench near the door.

Matthew slowly sauntered over, his arms crossed as his eyes appraised me. I squirmed under his scrutiny as he continued to stare silently.

"What?" I finally asked.

He pursed his lips and shrugged slightly. "This trip has shown me a new side to you."

"What do you mean?"

"Oh, nothing. I just didn't realize you were such a good liar."

I made a face at him. "It's called acting," I commented with a wave of my hand. "Felicity taught me."

"I bet she did," he agreed with a snort.

"Hey, at least one of us is likeable enough to get answers."

He put his hand over his chest and gasped. "I'm hurt."

The action was so unnatural on him that I busted up laughing. "Looks like you picked up on some dramatics too."

"Just a few," he replied with a grin.

"Alright, guys," Evan said, coming up behind us. "My boss has no problem giving the map back to you. He's calling the guard with the keys to the room it's in, and he'll bring it out in just a few minutes."

"That's great!" I responded, my excitement real this time. "Thank you!"

"My pleasure," he replied with a smile before walking back to the desk.

"One down," Matthew commented as he sat next to me.

"I'm excited to see it," I said. "What do you think it looks like?"

"Old and tattered."

"That's not what I meant, and you know it."

I watched people come and go as we sat and waited. Everyone looked like they were having a great time, and it made me want to go explore the museum too. Just when I was about to say that to Matthew, a man walked up to us.

"I hear this belongs to you," he said as he held out a round tube.

"Yes, thank you!" I replied, and he nodded before walking away.

Matthew quickly unscrewed the top cap and shook a rolled up piece of parchment out. Shock filled me as he unrolled it. The paper was crisp and clean, with seemingly no wear and tear anywhere. The perfectly shaped rectangle wasn't harmed in any way.

"So much for old and tattered," I said as I stared at the drawing.

"I thought it would be torn down the side," Matthew admitted.

"Me too."

We stood there staring at it quietly as people continued to pass us by. I assumed it was the middle of the map based off the incomplete sidings. The center was an almost perfect circle of what appeared to be a dense collection of trees. Near the top and bottom, thick, black lines ran jaggedly from one side to the next, and more trees stood between them and the end of the paper.

The longer I looked, the more disappointed I became. There were no coordinates, no words, and no directional markers of any kind.

"This isn't what I expected," I admitted quietly.

Matthew rubbed the back of his neck and said, "Me neither. But maybe it'll make more sense when all three pieces are put together."

"If we can even get all three."

"Hey, what happened to positive Robin? I like her a whole lot better," he joked as he rolled the map back up.

"She was just destroyed by realistic Robin."

"Well, tell realistic Robin to shut up because we just got a piece of the map. That's huge."

"I guess," I replied dejectedly.

I knew finding one was already a triumph in itself, but I couldn't help but think of Kodi, Mateo, and Alexander. Without all three pieces, we couldn't help them. Matthew seemed to sense my distress because he threw his arm around my shoulders and squeezed.

"Come on," he instructed. "Let me buy you some ridiculously sugary snack before we head back to the plane."

The side of my lips turned up at how well he knew me. Sugar was definitely a good way to defeat my sorrows.

"Fine," I relented. "But then straight to Tennessee. Elin Windsor's descendants await."

CHAPTER TWELVE

"Here we are," Malachi announced as the car rolled to a stop in front of a quaint farmhouse.

"Cows!" I exclaimed, pointing to the few that were wandering close by.

Malachi and Matthew both stared at me with matching perplexed expressions, and Matthew said, "So?"

My smile slowly faded, and I leaned back in my seat, embarrassed. "Never mind," I muttered.

"Shall we go then, or are you going to go pet the cows?" Matthew asked. I made a face, then opened the car door and stepped out with him close at my heels.

Before we could go any further, a woman stepped out from the side of the wrap around porch with two small children in her arms. When she saw us, she stopped.

"Hello," she greeted us. "Is there something I can do for y'all?"

"Hi," I replied. "We're looking for Randy and Summer Windsor."

"I'm Summer, but it's Davitt now. Randy and I are separated," she said as she put the kids down.

"I'm sorry to hear that."

She let out a loud bark of a laugh. "Don't be. That man ain't nothin' but crazy in the head." She saw the look Matthew and I shared, so she crossed her arms defensively. "What were y'all needing?"

"We're doing a history project for school and needed some information about an old map that may have been passed down in your ex's family," I quickly explained.

Summer rolled her eyes and threw her hands in the air. "For the love of all things good, I can't get away from that stupid thing, can I?"

"What do you mean?" Matthew asked, and she sighed heavily.

"That stupid map."

"You've seen it?" I questioned.

"Only every day for the last decade or so. He was obsessed with that thing. Called it his birthright. The last few years it escalated though. He started talking about superpowers and some magical land he belonged to." Summer snorted as my eyes widened. How did Randy know about that? "Anywho, he became so obsessed he lost his darn mind. Never made no sense. When he lost his job over it, I put my foot down and made him move out. That was over a year ago."

"Does he still have the map?" I asked.

"As far as I know, he'll be buried with the stupid thing."

"Do you have his new address by chance?"

"Yes. But I'm tellin' y'all, you don't want to get involved with that."

"It's for a school project," I repeated, shrugging lightly. "Fifty percent of our grade. We're going to have to go talk to him."

"Suit yourselves," Summer said before walking inside. When she came back out, she held up a piece of paper. "Here ya go. Good luck."

"Thank you," I said as I took it. "Sorry for taking up your time."

She turned her attention back to her kids, so Matthew and I quickly jogged back to where Malachi waited. As soon as the doors were shut, Matthew asked, "How does he know about his history?"

"That's a good question," I replied, just as dumbfounded.

"Who?" Malachi questioned. "Where's the map piece?"

"They're separated. Randy has it," Matthew answered, "and apparently, he's obsessed with it. His ex said he's been talking a bunch of nonsense about superpowers and a secret world."

Malachi raised both brows high into his hair line. "Doesn't sound like nonsense to me. Sounds like he knows about Garridan."

"But how?" I asked. "Everything about Garridan is secret."

"Even the best kept secrets have slip ups" Malachi replied. "If Elin Windsor told her descendants about their heritage, it could've lived on in the form of ancient family history or folklore . . . If that's the case, Randy must see the truth in it."

"Whatever the reason, it sounds like he won't give up the map piece easily, so what do we do?" I asked.

"We could steal it," Matthew suggested.

"That seems cruel," I replied.

"So?"

"No. If it really means that much to him, it disappearing could drive him to real insanity or suicide or who knows what else."

"That sounds dramatic."

"No, it's just a sad reality to our world."

"Not mine."

"Really?" I challenged, crossing my arms as my eyes narrowed. "Because I could easily give examples of real insanity I've witnessed in *your* world."

Matthew opened his mouth to respond but Malachi quickly intervened. "Alright, you two. That's enough," he said, holding out one hand towards each of us. "I agree that stealing the map is a bad idea. Besides, as members of the Garridan guard, it's our job to protect our home from any threats, and that certainly includes outside ones. We need to talk to this man and figure out what he knows about our world. See if he poses any danger."

"That's a good point," Matthew agreed.

"I say we go speak with him and decide from there what to do about the map piece if he won't let us have it," Malachi said.

"That's really all we *can* do," I replied, leaning into my seat and buckling.

Matthew followed suit as I read Randy's address to Malachi. He plugged it into the car's GPS, then we were on our way. As we drove, I couldn't help but wonder what Randy knew and how he had come to believe it so fiercely. When Matthew first told me about my heritage, I had a hard time believing it even with proof. How did Randy believe it with none?

Maybe he's had proof too.

"Hey . . ." I said slowly. "Do you think somehow Randy could have some sort of powers?"

"What do you mean?" Matthew asked.

"It's technically in his DNA, right? What if somehow it surfaced, and he came into some powers?"

"Hmmm." Malachi's forehead creased as he thought it over. "I don't see how that could've happened. Elin Windsor's powers were stripped from her completely when she relinquished them. I think that includes DNA."

"Didn't her husband leave with her?" I asked, and Matthew nodded. "Could it have still been in his DNA?"

"As far as I'm aware, giving up your powers means giving up all rights to them, and that includes passing it onto your future lineage," Malachi answered.

"Oh." I looked out the window somewhat dejectedly.

"Why do you ask?"

I shrugged. "I guess I just don't understand how he'd hear a story like that and believe it. Even if it is a family story. Not like they have any proof."

"Maybe he's just crazy," Matthew said, and I rolled my eyes.

"How can you call him crazy for believing in the very thing we know to be real?"

"All I'm saying is, right now you don't know what else he believes. What if he also believes in unicorns and dragons?"

"We're trying to find map pieces to lead us to an enchanted tree," I said dryly. "Don't tell me unicorns and dragons are any less believable than that."

Malachi chuckled. "I swear you two bicker like an old married couple."

"At least if we were old, I wouldn't have to deal with her shenanigans much longer," Matthew said.

"You'd miss them when they were gone," I shot back. "Or have you already forgotten how miserable you were when I was in the Cyfrin compound?" He shot me a look with narrowed eyes, and a smirk rose on my face. "Oh, yeah. Claire told me."

"I'm gonna kill her," he muttered.

I grinned as Malachi let out a bellow of a laugh. He patted Matthew on the shoulder then turned down a busy road packed with rundown apartment buildings. After pass-ing by the first one, he pulled over and turned the car off.

"Let's go talk to Mr. Windsor, shall we?" he asked before stepping out of the car.

He didn't usually interact with people when we were out-side of Garridan, so I knew how important this was to him. He'd spent his whole life protecting his home, and that would never change.

"Summer said it's apartment 2B," I said as we walked up a rickety flight of stairs. When we got to his door, I turned to Malachi. "Did you want to take the lead on this?"

"No, that's perfectly alright," he said. "You're more likely to get him to open up than Matthew or me. You're more inviting than we are."

I gave him a small smile at the compliment then knocked on the door. When no one came, I knocked again but still received no answer.

"I guess he isn't home," I said.

"Well, let's go get some food then. We can come back after," Malachi replied.

"Can I help y'all?" a low voice asked from behind us.

Matthew looked him over suspiciously and said, "We were just leaving."

"Did you need something from the man that lives here?"

He was wearing a nice business suit and had an aura of authority about him. He was nearly a head taller than Malachi and looked just as strong as Matthew, but his dark blue eyes looked sad on his otherwise cheerful face.

"Yes," I finally answered, "but he isn't home, so we were just going to come back later."

He shuffled past us and jingled some keys around in the lock. He turned the doorknob and stepped into apartment 2B. "Looks like he's home now," he said as he threw the keys into a bowl by the door.

"You're Randy Windsor?" I asked.

"In the flesh," he responded. "What can I help you folks with?"

"Actually," I started, glancing between Malachi and Matthew. I said a quick silent prayer they wouldn't kill me then continued. "We came to help you."

Randy's brows furrowed, and he crossed his arms as he leaned into the doorframe. "Is that right? With what?"

"Your map."

Randy's eyes widened as he pushed himself straight up again. I could feel the two sets of eyes behind me staring intently, and I knew without looking that Matthew's were narrowed and Malachi's were full of concern.

"How do you know about my map?" Randy asked harshly.

I took a deep breath, fighting with myself on what I was about to do, then slowly drew a line of water bubbles in front of me, letting them dance in the space between us.

"Robin!" Matthew hissed as Randy's eyes widened even more.

"It's okay," I told him without looking away from Randy. "Right, Randy?"

He opened his mouth then shut it just as quick before licking his lips and nodding fervently. "Yes. Yes! Please, come in."

He stepped aside so we could enter, and I smiled gratefully as I passed him. His apartment was old and in need of some obvious repairs but looked clean. The biggest mess I could see was some scattered magazines on a coffee table. With how Summer described him, I'd expected to find a disheveled man in a dark, dirty home. To my surprise, I was very wrong.

Randy sat down on his couch and motioned for us to join. I took the seat opposite him while the other two continued to stand. He nervously began twisting his hands together as he stared at me.

"Can we see the map?" I asked, and he immediately jumped back up.

"Of course. Let me go get it right quick," he said.

When he was out of earshot, Matthew snapped, "What were you thinking?"

"It was the only way to approach the situation," I whispered. "He's been ridiculed and called crazy for who knows how long. He needed to know we weren't going to do the same. Otherwise, he would've just slammed his door in our faces."

"Because you're such an expert on reading people," he said sarcastically.

"I took AP psychology in high school, thank you very much. I'm *excellent* at reading people," I shot back. For good measure I added, "And, look, it's working."

His narrowed eyes finally loosened just the smallest bit, and he shook his head as his teeth ground together. "I know you mean well, but if this ends poorly, Dad is going to be paying the heaviest price. Not you. Your actions have consequences for others when it comes to Garridan's safety."

I glanced to Malachi, who placed his hand on Matthew's shoulder. "It's okay, son. It wouldn't be the first time I've been in trouble, and I know how to take care of myself."

"I'm-I'm sorry," I stuttered, the sudden guilt all consuming. "I didn't think . . . I didn't realize . . ."

I felt stupid. Of course Malachi would suffer the consequences if our trip here went sideways. He was in charge of us but, more than that, he was the head of the guard. He was held to an extremely high standard.

"It's okay, Robin," Malachi assured me, but I shook my head.

"No, it isn't. I should've known better," I replied, my mouth set firmly. "I didn't even think about you having to answer to the council . . . But nothing will go wrong. I'll play this right, I swear."

"Here we are," Randy announced, breaking up our serious conversation as he gently placed the map piece on the coffee table.

It was just as well kept as the first. The black line continued on the top and bottom of this one but ended where a vast mountain range began. The mountains took up the whole right half of the paper, but the land on the left was open and clear. Trees lined the small space between the black lines and edges of the paper, just as they had in the middle section.

"This must be the right side of the map," I commented, tracing the top line with my finger. "The middle piece probably connects perfectly with these two lines. I wonder what they are."

"Maybe a barrier of some sort," Malachi said.

"There's more pieces to this?" Randy asked, his face lit up at the thought.

I peered up at him and nodded. "There's three total, and we need them all for a very important trip."

"What kind of trip? What's the map lead to?"

I sat up straighter and clasped my hands together. "Randy, I'm going to be completely honest with you. I made a mistake showing you what I did outside. I wanted you to trust us and believe that we didn't think you were crazy but, by doing that, I put us in jeopardy. You see these two behind me?" Randy glanced at them and nodded. "They're part of our world's military. They keep us out of harm's way and make sure there's no threats to our people—both inside threats and outside ones."

Randy's eyes skipped over the three of us before he raised his hand to his chest. "Outside threats as in *me?*"

"Yes," I replied. "So, if you don't mind, we'd like to ask you some questions, and we need honest answers."

"I understand. . . But only if you'll answer mine in return."

"That's fair. The ones I can, yes, I'll answer," I assured him.

"Okay, then ask away!" he exclaimed.

"What do you know about this map?" Matthew asked.

"Just what's been passed down through my family. My memaw and pawpaw used to switch up the story when all us grandkids came to visit, but the history was always the same." Randy leaned forward, his eyes sparkling. "Our family wasn't originally from here. They came from a secret world. One that was hidden directly under our noses. One where magic was real."

"When you're a child, you hear plenty of make-believe stories," Malachi spoke up. "What made you believe this one was real?"

"I didn't always," Randy admitted. "I used to think it really was just a story and that the map was an old relic from some voyage or something. At most, I thought maybe it was a pirate's map, but certainly not magic."

"What changed your mind?" I asked.

"I saw it," he almost whispered, the smile on his face wide.

"Saw what?"

"*Magic.*"

"How?" I asked.

At the same time Matthew asked "when" and Malachi asked "where."

"Summer and I used to be foster parents," he explained. "We always had youngins coming and going, but there was this one little girl . . . She started acting real strange, so I began payin' her extra mind. One day I followed her to our old barn and, I kid you not, this one-hundred-pound girl was lifting our tractor with one hand! That's when I started second guessing everything.

"A few years later, something similar happened with another one of our placements. But this one . . . He was on a different level. He was manipulating the light somehow. It was the most amazing thing I'd ever seen."

I glanced back at Matthew. What were the odds that two different kids from Garridan were placed in his home?

"What happened to those children?" Malachi asked.

"The boy's real parents were able to take him back home, but the girl . . ." he hung his head. "She was kidnapped. She was walking home from school with her foster siblings, and they said she was yanked into a van. The police never got any leads."

The boy was found and taken back to Garridan, and the girl was kidnapped by the Cyfrin. How different their stories ended.

"What was her name?" I asked curiously, only remembering one person with super strength in the Cyfrin compound.

"Anna."

I looked at my feet as her image flashed in my mind. She was the same one who'd almost killed Toby during the battle, but I suddenly felt a new sense of sympathy for her. Her life could've been so different, but the Cyfrin turned her into a killing machine. She was currently sitting in a jail cell awaiting sentencing from the council. Her lack of remorse was pushing them towards choosing execution, just like with the rest of the Cyfrin's inner circle.

Maybe I needed to advocate for her like I was with Alexander since she was also a child of Garridan who'd been kidnapped. If she was willing to change, she deserved a second chance too. The only problem was she didn't want anything to do with Garridan and continuously chanted her hatred for us. The council wouldn't keep her around if she was going to cause problems, so maybe I could convince them to banish her with no memories like the majority of the Cyfrin members instead.

Randy cleared his throat, breaking me out of my train of thought. "But, uh, anyway, after that I started trying to research my family history more. I did get pretty obsessive over it, but I never learned more than I already knew, which was next to nothing."

"So, you really don't know anything more?" Matthew pressed, and he shook his head.

"I'm afraid not. I was so upset I fell into a deep depression. Lost my family, my job . . . Everyone called me crazy—said I needed to be institutionalized. I started thinking maybe they were right." He glanced up and moisture filled his eyes. "But I wasn't crazy after all . . . It really is all true, isn't it?"

"Yes," I told him quietly. "It's true."

Tears ran down his cheeks, and he sobbed a couple times. "A couple months ago I gave up on it all," he said. "I decided to throw the map out and start working to get my family back instead. I got a new job and started saving my money. I was gonna wait till I was a solid man before going back to talk to Summer and see my kids. Show her I was responsible again . . . I was gonna do that next week . . . And now here y'all are making me second guess it all."

He took a deep breath as he wiped his sleeve over his face. He stared down at the map for a while, the silence stretching on. Finally, he picked it up and handed it to me.

"I never could throw it out, but now I don't have to. Take it," he told me.

"Are you sure?" I asked in surprise, not expecting the conversation to turn this way.

"Yes. Now I can truly tell Summer I'm over it and that I got rid of the map she hates so much—the map she blames for our marital problems."

"I don't understand," Malachi said. "I thought you had questions. I thought you'd try to get us to take you to our home."

"I'd be lying if I said the thought didn't cross my mind," Randy admitted. "But . . . This last year has shown me what's truly important and that's my family. I've been working to get them back, and that's what I intend to do. Knowing my family history is true . . . It's unimaginable to finally get that confirmation, and I'll keep it near and dear to my heart as long as I live. Knowing magic is out there gives me hope for this world . . . But the only magic I want anything to do with is my kiddos' imaginations. I've seen life without them, and I don't want it. I'd rather sacrifice knowing your world than never seeing mine again."

"That's very noble," Malachi told him. "I commend you for that, but I still have to ask: Are you going to share this encounter with anyone?"

"No," he answered sadly. "This is my secret to keep now."

"I'd like to believe that," Malachi said. "However, we'll be checking in frequently for a while. I still consider you a threat, but as long as you keep your word, we'll leave you in peace."

"Understood."

"Robin, Matthew, let's go home."

Randy walked us to the door, and Matthew and Malachi immediately left. Before I could follow, Randy said, "Wait! I almost forgot. Whenever my pawpaw would tell us stories, he always said there was a secret hidden in the map."

"A secret?" I asked.

"That's right. He said you had to have a certain light to see it though." He scoffed and shook his head. "I tried every light known to man with no luck, but maybe you'll have a better chance."

"A secret that can only be seen with a certain light," I repeated. Wasn't the strangest thing I'd heard. "Okay, thanks for the tip."

"You're welcome."

"It was nice meeting you," I told him, grasping his hand in my own. "Good luck getting your family back."

"Thank you," he replied. He held onto my hand a moment too long as he hesitated. "Could I see it one more time? The magic?"

I smiled at the hopeful look in his eyes then pulled the water from around me into a big ball. I stretched it out, looping it around him as he watched in awe. I slowly backed out of his home, controlling the water as long as I could while I walked to the car.

Two map pieces down. But was there any way to find the third?

CHAPTER THIRTEEN

As the plane soared through the sky, we stared at the map pieces that sat on the table in front of us. The one from Randy was indeed the right side, and the longer I looked at it, the more I felt like I recognized the terrain. I couldn't quite put my finger on why though.

"If we could just figure out where this is, we could go," Matthew said.

"What about the left side?" I asked.

"I don't see why we'd need it if we all agree Silas is in that middle section of trees."

"Then, technically, we didn't need the right side either."

"Maybe not, but it definitely helps. The more visual we have, the better chance of figuring out the location."

"I feel like I've seen it before," I murmured. "I really do. I just can't place it."

"Try harder," Matthew said, and I arched a brow at him. "And I mean that in the most loving way, of course."

"Oh, of course," I muttered, knocking him with my shoulder. As I looked down at the map again, a little bit of hope sparked. "Do you think we could really still find him without the last piece?"

"I don't see why not," Matthew answered.

"I wouldn't be so sure about that," Malachi spoke up, and I peeked up at him in disappointment.

"Why?" Matthew asked.

"Silas created three map pieces for a reason. Even if you knew exactly where that grove of trees was, I'm fairly certain you still couldn't get to it without the map fully intact."

"What does the map being intact have to do with it?"

"That map was forged with the powers of nature. Do you really think its only purpose is to point us in the right direction?"

"No, I suppose not," Matthew admitted.

"Well, there goes that idea," I said with a heavy sigh.

"Don't look so discouraged," Malachi told me as he handed me a drink. "Let's wait and see what the council thinks."

* * *

I pulled my hair back into a ponytail then stretched my arms high above my head. All this flying had made me tired, and I was beyond ready to go to sleep, despite the early hour. When we stepped off the plane, a full welcoming committee stood near the parking lot. Matthew's family, my mom, and all five of the trainees waved eagerly as we walked up, and I could see excitement on most their faces.

"Did you get them?" Kodi asked.

"Can we see them?" Claire questioned.

"Tell us all about your trip!" Mom exclaimed.

"Yes, yes, and that'll be better told over a hot meal," Malachi replied after giving Susan a kiss. He pulled both map pieces out of his bag and carefully unfurled them on the hood of a car, placing them in alignment. "We have a lot to discuss with the council."

"I'm sure," Mom said as she placed her arm around me and observed what we'd brought home. "But I'm also sure you're all exhausted from your trip, so that can wait until tomorrow. We'll bring them to our house for now, and you can tell us how everything went over dinner."

"Sounds good to me," I said. "I'm ready to crash."

"Robin!"

Dad's voice caught my attention, and I saw him jogging towards us. His face was slightly red but plastered with a huge smile.

"Honey, what is it?" Mom asked when he got closer.

He grabbed my upper arms and, around his panting, exclaimed, "It's Ben. He's awake!"

Everyone started talking excitedly, but I couldn't hear their words around the ringing in my ears. He was awake. The moment I'd been dreading since knowing he was okay was finally here, and the weight crushing down on me was immense. It was time to say goodbye.

Again.

Dad finally noticed my expression, and his brows knitted together in concern. "Are you okay?" he asked, but I didn't answer.

I shook my head slowly then pulled away from him. "I-I have to go," I murmured.

I walked away from their stunned and confused faces, not bothering with an explanation. I couldn't be around them right now. I had to go see Ben.

But I couldn't. Not yet.

"Robin," someone called from behind me, but I didn't turn around. "Robin, hold on!"

Toby ran up next to me and grabbed my hand as he kept up with my pace. He didn't say anything, just walked with me as I stewed in my own sorrow. The sun began to set as we came into town, but we didn't go to the hospital. Instead, we somehow stopped in front of the jail. I looked up at the old building, torn about going in.

I should go see Ben but seeing him would be heartbreak. Seeing Alexander would be comfort. I bit my lower lip as double guilt washed over me—guilt for avoiding Ben, but even more guilt for using Alexander.

Toby squeezed my hand, then released it. "Go see him. I'll walk you to the hospital after."

I stared, unblinking, as my brain tried to process his remark. "What?"

"I know why you want to see him, and I don't blame you," he replied.

I finally glanced at him. "You don't?"

"No. You're hurting. You're losing the type of love he's ready to give you, so it makes sense you want to see him. It won't make Ben leaving any easier, but it might help get you through it."

"When in the world did you grow up and get so wise?" I questioned in disbelief.

He grinned. "Andre said it first. I just thought you needed to hear it."

A light laugh escaped my mouth. That sounded more accurate. "Wait," I said as realization dawned. "You guys have talked about it? About me . . . And Alexander?"

He looked away sheepishly, messing with a rock on the sidewalk. "A little."

"Well, that's awkward," I muttered, the familiar flow of blood touching my cheeks.

"It really wasn't bad. I swear. Kodi and Emery were complaining about him—as usual—so Andre put them in their place. He reminded them what you risked to keep them safe and that, in the end, Alexander chose the right side. He told them you both deserved a chance to be happy, even if it's with each other, and it's not our place to say otherwise."

It never failed; Andre was always the voice of reason to them. I didn't know how he stayed so accepting, but knowing he defended me when I wasn't around was comforting.

"Does that mean you'd be okay with having Alexander around?" I asked hesitantly. "If that's the way things were to work out?"

He ran his fingers through his oily hair, and I made a mental note to help him choose a better shampoo.

"In the end, yeah," he replied. "It might be a little hard at first, but I just want you to be happy. So I'd be willing to get to know him."

I pulled him into a hug and whispered, "Thanks, kid. I'll be right back, okay?"

"Okay."

I ventured into the building and waved at Officer Sanchez. "Are you ever not working?" I asked as he stood to meet me at the elevator door.

"Sure seems like I'm not, but I get my days off like everybody else," he replied with a grin.

I held my breath as we descended. There wasn't any type of pressure change, but my chest suddenly felt very heavy, and I struggled to breathe normally. My eyes watered, and I knew I was about to have a breakdown. Each step became a race against time as my emotions threatened to take over.

Alexander sat on his bed, leafing through a book. He took one look at me after walking in and immediately tossed the book to the side. Before he could get up, I crawled onto the bed and leaned against him.

"What's wrong?" he asked as I buried my face in his chest, but I couldn't speak. Instead, I cried. "Hey, it's okay."

He held me tighter as the tears freely flowed. Matthew would've done the same. So would my parents or Toby or even the other trainees. So why did I come to him for comfort instead? Was Andre right? Was it to fill the void of what I was about to lose? If it was, would Alexander feel used? If the situation was reversed, I would.

After another agonizing minute, I slowly stopped crying and took some deep breaths to calm down. I sat up and wiped the moisture off my face as Alexander carefully watched my every move. I glanced over at the guards standing at attention along the wall.

"They probably think I'm crazy," I commented with a sniffle.

"Who cares what they think?" Alexander replied, holding my hand as he waited for me to explain my emotional trauma.

"We found the two map pieces we went for," I told him.

"I don't care about that right now," he said, his eyes intently staring into mine. "What's wrong? Why are you crying?"

I looked away, but he gently grabbed my chin in his fingers and directed my gaze back to him.

"Robin, what's wrong?" he asked again.

I swallowed around the lump in my throat and finally said, "Ben's awake."

"Ah," he said as understanding dawned. He rubbed his lips together, carefully considering his next words. "Saying 'I'm sorry' sounds like the wrong sentiment."

"Just a little," I agreed, the corner of my lip twitching.

"How did it go?"

"How did what go?"

"Seeing him."

"I haven't yet."

Alexander's brows furrowed. "Why not?"

I shrugged. "I came here instead."

His eyes appraised me tenderly. "I think you need to go see him."

"Why?" I asked more harshly than I intended. "You don't want me here with you?"

He chuckled and said, "I always want that. But what I want is meaningless compared to what you *need*."

"And what do I need exactly?" I asked sarcastically, folding my arms over my chest.

"To see the man who holds your heart," he answered softly.

My lips pressed together as I scrutinized him. There was no malice in his tone nor animosity in his eyes. He meant it.

"I don't understand you," I told him. "How are you so okay with this? How do you not feel . . . Used?"

"After what I did to you, I have a lot to make up for."

"So, you're loving me out of pity?" I accused with a grimace.

I could see him wrestling to keep a smile off his face as he grabbed my hands. "I love you because you're everything I wish I was raised to be—kind, caring, thoughtful. I have no pity for you whatsoever. I love you because you're the embodiment of what the world should strive to be."

"I'm not though," I choked out, his words resonating in me. "I have plenty of flaws."

"That you do," he agreed, no longer hiding his smirk. "You're extremely self-critical, stubborn to a fault, and overly protective. But you make up for it with your beauty and charm."

"Wow, thanks so much," I muttered.

"Sarcasm. Another flaw I'd say," he teased, and I shoved his arm. He laughed then became serious again just as quick. "Robin, I already told you I'd be here whenever you're ready to move on. I don't care if it takes weeks, months, or years even. Until then, I'm perfectly okay helping you through it any way I can. I don't feel used. I feel . . . Needed. So, please, don't harbor guilt for allowing me that."

"Are you ever going to not surprise me?" I asked quietly.

"Robin."

"Yes?"

"Go see Ben."

* * *

I paced outside Ben's hospital room door, wiping my palms on my jeans every couple seconds. As Toby eyed me, he started mimicking my nervous tick, my own anxiety rubbing off on him. I stopped in front of a picture frame and stared at my reflection then pulled my hair down and ran my fingers through it. When I was done, I turned back towards Toby.

"How do I look?" I asked.

"Pretty. You always look pretty," he responded.

I went and gave him a hug. "Thank you."

I stepped in front of Ben's door again and peeked in the small, glass window. He was sitting on the edge of the bed, combing through his hair. Someone had brought him clothes to change into, and they fit like a glove. The red and black plaid shirt was out of character, something he never would've chosen for himself, but the style suited him.

My eyes took in every detail of his face as I stared, searing it to memory. I took a deep breath before letting it out slowly.

"Alright. Wish me luck," I said more to myself than Toby.

"Good luck," he responded anyway, his voice wavering.

I knocked quietly then let myself in, shutting the door behind me as I leaned into it. Ben stood when he saw me, his whole face lighting up as his smile reached both ears. His eyes skimmed over me head to toe, taking in everything he could just as I'd done to him. He took a step towards me, but I held up my hands.

"Wait," I said, stopping him cold.

"What's wrong?" he asked, his thick brows knitting together.

"Nothing," I replied, intertwining my hands in front of
me.

"I know that's not true. Am I contagious or something?"

"No, no. Of course not," I said with a forced laugh.
"You're healthier now than you've ever been in your entire
life. Did anyone explain what happened to you?"

"Yeah, your dad did actually," he responded as he
rubbed the back of his head. He let out a short, forceful
exhale. "I can't believe I almost died."

"I can't either." I bit my lower lip, the image of him lying
on that hospital bed knocking at death's door instantly
bringing tears to my eyes.

"Hey, it's okay. I'm fine," he assured me, taking another
step closer. "From what I hear, I have you to thank for
that."

"I couldn't let you die," I whispered, remembering the
agony of thinking I'd lost him. "I couldn't live in a world
where you didn't exist."

His expression mirrored my pain, and he reached towards me. All I wanted was for him to wrap his arms around
me so I could be enveloped in him—to be held in his strong
arms as my head rested against his chest, listening to his
strong heartbeat while his musky scent filled my nose.

But I couldn't.

I side stepped his advance and held my hands out again.
"Stop."

"Why won't you let me touch you?" he asked, a mixture
of confusion and hurt dancing in his voice.

"I'm just . . . Trying to keep my distance."

"Why?"

"Because you're going home soon."

"So?"

"What do you mean 'so?'" I threw my arms up. "You're going home, Benjamin, and I'm staying here. That means another painful goodbye neither of us needs." I sighed and lowered my voice, trying to smile. "We're both moving on and that's great! No need to go backwards, right?"

His eyes tightened and his lips turned down. "You've moved on?" he asked accusingly.

"What?"

"You said 'we're both moving on,'" he repeated.

"No! I mean . . . Sort of . . . But still no." I fumbled around the words. I couldn't tell him about Alexander. Not like we were *actually* together anyway. "You did too, though, so why does it matter?"

"What? I haven't moved on at all."

"I mean you must've a little if you have a girlfriend." I rolled my eyes.

"What girlfriend?" he exclaimed in bewilderment.

"*Your* girlfriend!"

"I don't *have* a girlfriend!" He studied me for a quick second before adding, "Other than you, I thought."

"You don't?" I asked, my voice wavering with sudden uncertainty, and he shook his head.

We stared at one another as tension filled the air between us. I opened my mouth then closed it again. I was going to kill Claire.

"So, uhm," Ben averted his gaze as he shifted his weight from one foot to the other. "Do you have another boyfriend?"

"No," I answered too quickly, and his amber eyes met mine again with heavy accusation.

"But there's somebody?" he pressed. I couldn't answer, and that's the only confirmation he needed. "Who is it?"

"No one you know," I replied quietly. He moved his jaw side to side as he stared at the ceiling. The light glistened off his eyes, and I tried to fight back my own tears as he blinked his away. "I should go."

"That's it? You come in here with unfounded allegations then leave as soon as you find out they aren't true? You have nothing else to say to me?"

"I have a lot to say. I just don't think I should." My head dropped to the floor. "A quick and simple goodbye is better."

"Really? Because I think this is the worst goodbye we've had yet," he said, his voice thick.

"I'm sorry," I replied, my voice breaking. I walked towards the door, but before I reached it, I remembered what was in my pocket. I grabbed the ring and looked at it with sad adoration before holding it out to him. "Here."

He glanced at it. "Are you serious?" he snapped, finally angry. "You meet someone else, so you're going to throw away everything related to me?"

"No! It's not like that!" I exclaimed.

"Then what's it like?" he asked sarcastically. "Because from my point of view, it seems like you're burning every bridge possible."

"I just don't think we should keep hurting each other! We've had enough goodbyes."

"You think having to say goodbye to you hurts worse than being cast aside for another man? I'd rather have a million goodbyes than know you're in love with someone else!" His eyes blazed with such uncharacteristic anger it was unsettling. He took a couple deep breaths as he stalked around the room then said, "I know how selfish that is, but it's the truth."

"We can't keep doing this to each other. You and I were over the first time I left for Garridan, and we both know it." My voice wavered. All I wanted to do was cry, but I couldn't. Not yet. "I don't want you to spend the rest of your life alone. I want you to love and be loved like you deserve . . . And it can't be by me. Not anymore. So, please," I held the ring up again. "Take the ring, Benjamin."

"You remember what that ring signifies don't you?"

"Of course I do."

"And you still want to give it back?"

I nodded, unable to answer out loud. Of course I didn't want to, but I had to. My heart shattered as he swiped at his cheeks. He watched me for a moment and shook his head lightly. But, finally, he held out his hand and I dropped the ring in it.

"I'll always love you, Robin," he said as I ran out the door.

CHAPTER FOURTEEN

I sat on the floor against my bed, wallowing in my own self-pity as everyone else visited downstairs. No one stopped me when I came in, and no one had bothered me since. They must've known I was in a bad mood.

My stomach rumbled, and I sighed. Dinner was being made, and its sweet aroma met my nose invitingly. I guess it was time to face the music. Before I could make the decision to go down, a soft knock sounded at my door, then Ben walked in.

I jumped up with wide eyes as my heart hammered in my chest. "Ben! W-what are you doing here?"

"Your dad invited me earlier," he replied, sticking his hands in his jean pockets and avoiding my gaze. "I wasn't going to come after what happened, but Matthew convinced me to."

"Oh . . . Good. That's good."

"Is it?"

"Of course. You deserve a good meal, and my dad's a really good cook." I nodded my head trying to convince myself as much as I was him. "Plus, you can meet all my new friends."

"What's the point?" he asked. "Not like we're together anymore."

I rubbed my hand against my arm, his harsh demeanor hard to swallow. It didn't fit him and made being around him that much harder.

"I'm sorry," I whispered, and he sighed.

"No, I'm sorry," he replied, rubbing his hand over his face. "I came up here to try to clear the air so it wouldn't be tense downstairs around everyone. I didn't mean to make a jab at you."

"You have every right to though."

He walked to the wall that held all my pictures, and a sad smile played on his lips as he grabbed one of the two of us. "I guess you aren't burning *every* bridge," he commented quietly.

"You know I never wanted things to end this way, right?" I asked.

"I know."

"And I hope you'll believe me when I say I didn't end things with us because of someone else. It would've happened eventually no matter what."

"I know," he repeated, his voice cracking slightly. "It doesn't make me any less jealous though."

"I know." I looked down at my hands, fidgeting with my fingers.

"Matthew told me who he is."

"Matthew *what?*" I asked, my mouth falling open.

He's a dead man.

Ben turned around and leaned against the wall with his arms crossed. "He told me about Alexander."

I swallowed loudly, imagining the awful things Ben must think of him. "You can't trust everything Matthew says about him. They don't have the easiest history."

"He told me."

"He did?"

Ben nodded. "Yeah. He definitely had negative things to say, but he also told me how good he is to you. How he helped you survive in the Cyfrin compound. How he's the one who ended your guys' war."

"Matthew told you about *all* of that?" My voice was hoarse. I never wanted Ben to know about my time with the Cyfrin.

"Yes. He told me everything." His eyes tightened as he watched me. "You've been through hell and back, and I wasn't there."

"It's not your fault."

"I know that. What I'm trying to say is . . ." he trailed off and looked at the ceiling as if gathering his thoughts. "I wasn't there. I wasn't *here*. There's a lot in your life I can never help with or understand anymore. Everything Matthew told me made me realize that and . . . You deserve to be loved by someone who can actually be here with you. Someone who can help you through the crazy power drama and understand every part of your life . . . And that's not me. The rational part of me knows that."

"Ben," I murmured, but he held up his hand.

"Let me finish." He took another deep breath, and his eyes narrowed slightly. "The rational part of me knows that, but I'm only human. I don't care about the rational stuff right now because it's crap, and I'm not ready to accept that I'm losing the love of my life."

I could see him trying to compose himself as he dug his fingers into his palms. It was taking everything in him to stay calm and everything in me not to throw my arms around him and tell him everything was going to be okay.

"You've always wanted the best for me, and I know that's all you're trying to give me now." He shrugged and shook his head as a humorless laugh left his mouth. "Maybe that means you love me more than I love you, though, because all I want is to keep loving you forever. I'd rather pick the option that keeps us together, not the one that's better for you. And I know trying to hold onto you . . . It's selfish. But I don't care. It's what I want, but you've taken the choice away from me, and it pisses me off. It pisses me off that I have no say in it."

He ran his fingers through his hair and let out a sharp breath as my blood boiled. I set my jaw and glared as I fumed.

"Like hell I took the choice away from you!" I snapped.

He recoiled from the venom in my voice. "What?"

"I asked you to come to Garridan with me, and *you* chose not to."

"Because of my family! You're mad at me for staying with them when they needed me?"

"No! I've never been mad about that, and I'm not even saying it was the wrong choice. All I'm saying is that it *was* a choice and *you* made it. Not me. So don't you dare try to make me the only bad guy in all this because we both played a part."

"You're saying it's my fault then?" he asked defensively.

"*No*," I emphasized. "But what did you expect to happen after I left? That we'd maintain a long-distance relationship forever?"

"No," he said quietly, looking at his shoes. "I honestly thought you'd end up coming back eventually."

"You thought I'd give up everything here to be with you?" I asked. He nodded and I pressed my lips together. "Even though you wouldn't even consider doing it for me?"

"That's not the same thing."

"How is it not?"

"We didn't even know if I *could* come with you! Your parents said that old tree was a legend."

"Well, they lied! He's real, and we're going to find him. We already have two of the three map pieces we need, so we'll be seeing him and all his magical glory soon enough." He blinked rapidly at that news, so I crossed my arms and said, "What about now, huh? It's a possibility, so would you stay here with me if you could?"

He opened his mouth then shut it again as his eyes looked everywhere but at me. I shook my head as I fought back tears. He didn't need to say anything for me to know his answer.

"We should get downstairs," I said.

"Yeah. Yeah, we should," he agreed. He stepped towards the door then hesitated, glancing back at me. "Hey, the whole reason I came up here was to say I don't want our last interaction to be hateful. That didn't really work out, but can we try to be civil until I go home tomorrow?"

I swallowed around the lump in my throat, trying to diminish the anger I still felt. "Of course."

He nodded, his eyebrows pulled together tightly, then left the room without another word. I stared after him as I tried to compose myself. He was right—this was our worst goodbye yet.

I followed him down the stairs a minute later and plastered a smile on my face. The adults were gathered in the kitchen while everyone else lounged in the living room. I plopped down next to Toby on the ground, purposely sitting as far away from Ben as I could.

Matthew was next to him on the couch, and when I caught his eye, I scowled. He cocked one brow, and I glared harder so he'd know he was in trouble. He was going to get an earful later about what he told Ben.

"So, what do you think about Garridan?" Claire asked Ben.

"It's not what I expected," he admitted.

"Why do all you outsiders keep saying that?" she asked with a pointed look in my direction.

"I'll let the outsider comment pass," I told her with a sweet smile. When I glanced at Ben, he looked confused, so

I explained, "I said the same thing when I came here. I told them I thought it would be more grandeur."

"That's what I thought too," Ben said.

"But *why?*" Claire prodded.

"I guess we've seen too many movies," I replied with a grin that Ben matched. When we caught each other's gaze, both our smiles faltered, and we quickly looked away from one another.

"So, uh, how are you all connected?" Ben asked.

"Claire's my sister," Matthew answered. "The others are the trainees from the Cyfrin compound I told you about."

"We have names, you know," Emery muttered.

"That's Emery," I told Ben. "Then we have Andre, Kodi, Mateo, and *this* is Toby." I wrapped my arm around his shoulders. "My parents are adopting him."

"Oh, that's awesome," Ben said, and Toby nodded vigorously.

"It's all Robin's doing," he said proudly.

"I don't doubt it," Ben replied. "She's always been that caring."

"Hey, that means you would've had a brother-in-law had Robin not broken up with you," Emery popped off with. All eyes flashed to her with mixed amounts of disbelief. "How's that going anyway?"

"You don't have to answer that," Andre told Ben as he shook his head disapprovingly at Emery. "Sometimes she just doesn't know when to stay quiet."

"We're all thinking it," Emery said with a roll of her eyes. "Why not address the elephant in the room?"

"What elephant?" Claire asked, oblivious to the meaning of the phrase.

"Because it isn't any of our business," Mateo said. "Do you want to talk about the problems you and Andre are having?"

Emery glared at him. "What problems?" she asked curtly.

"You really want me to announce them to the whole room?" Mateo questioned.

Emery eyed him suspiciously then gasped. "You were spying again?"

"Yep," he replied, unashamed. "So, do you really want to bring up personal problems?"

Emery's hands began to crackle as small sparks leapt from her fingers. The reflection of them danced in her eyes, but Mateo didn't back down. The tension between them radiated through the whole house as we watched on expectantly.

"I think you both need to calm down," I said carefully, trying not to add fuel to the fire.

Emery scoffed. "You're not in charge of us anymore, Robin."

"No, but it is my house, and I don't think my parents would approve of you ruining it over some hurt feelings."

"Hurt feelings?" she hissed as she turned on me. "You really think this reaction is over some hurt feelings?"

"Hey," Andre said, standing up next to her. "I'm the person you're mad at, so stop trying to take it out on them."

"Stop telling me what to do!"

She flicked her wrist towards him, letting her electricity travel out her hand and into his shoulder. He grunted as his body absorbed it, his face contorted in pain.

"That's enough!" I snapped, dousing her in water from head to toe.

Her eyes blazed, and she pulled more electricity into her palms. Only this time, she cried out in pain and fell to the floor.

"Are you okay?" Kodi asked as she knelt beside her.

"No!" she yelled. "I electrocuted myself!"

"How?"

"How do you think?"

Everyone looked towards me, and realization dawned. "Ooh, that makes sense," I said, followed by an awkward laugh. "Water, electricity . . . Not a good combo."

No one knew what to say as she continued to scowl at me. I averted my eyes and pursed my lips as Toby spoke up.

"On the plus side, having that big of a weakness makes her less scary," he commented.

I tried to suppress a grin but failed and began giggling. Toby joined in then Mateo and Kodi. Soon everyone but Emery, Ben, and Matthew were laughing.

"Is this normal?" Ben asked Matthew.

Matthew grimaced. "Since they got here? Yeah. Pretty much."

"Sorry," I managed to say. "There's definitely never a dull moment."

"I can see that," Ben replied, his eyes thoughtful as he watched us.

"Did you know you couldn't use your powers if you were wet?" Mateo asked.

"Duh," Emery replied.

"Then why did you try right now if you were *soaking* wet?" Kodi asked.

"I was angry."

"And you paid for it," Matthew commented.

"Why didn't you tell us that before?" I questioned.

"Because of exactly what Toby said," she replied. "It's a weakness."

"Kids, dinner!" Mom called out.

We filed into the dining room—where a second table had been added—and Dad dried Emery off as the rest of us took our seats. Somehow, Ben ended up sitting directly across from me, and I became very interested in my food so I wouldn't have to look up. Questions about our trip began to fly, and we took turns explaining different parts. Matthew and Ben whispered back and forth as Matthew filled him in on the things he wasn't understanding.

"When can we see the map pieces again?" Kodi asked, practically bouncing in her seat with excitement.

"How about right now," Dad suggested.

"They'll get dirty around all the food," Mom said.

"I'll put them on the shelf on the wall," he replied, motioning towards it.

"I don't think they'd get dirty anyway," I spoke up. "They're in perfect condition. There's no way there's not some sort of protection spell or something on them."

"Oh, alright," Mom relented. "Go get them, Elijah."

Dad quickly complied then placed them against the wall on the shelf so they were in alignment. Everyone broke out in excited chatter as they stared at them, questioning the same things we had and pointing out their flawless appearance.

Ben's chair scraped the floor as he stood, and I watched as he walked towards them with a perplexed expression on his face. He traced the dark lines with his fingers as everyone quieted down.

"Is there something wrong, Ben?" Mom asked.

"I don't think so," he replied. "It's just . . ."

"Just what, son?" Dad questioned.

"I think . . . Actually, I'm positive I've seen the other part to this map."

Questions flew his way left and right as I slowly stood. He caught my eye and I asked, "Are you sure?"

"Yeah. The lines on here are so unique and strange. I've only ever seen them on one other map, and they were in the exact same position."

"Do you remember where?"

"Of course. At my house."

My jaw dropped open. "W-what?"

"It's my dad's map," he explained. "He used to use it as a bedtime story prop all the time when Mahka and I were little. Then again with Dakota."

"When's the last time you saw it?" Malachi asked.

"It's been a while. I think the last time was when Dakota was eight or so, which would've been four or five years ago."

"Do you know why your dad has it?" Mom questioned.

"He used to say it was a family heirloom. We have a lot of those though." Everyone stared at him, slack jawed and wide-eyed. He glanced around the room, not understanding our stunned silence, then looked at me. "What? What is it?"

I opened my mouth, but no words came out. Matthew stood and shook his head in bewilderment before answering.

"You're a descendant of Lyle Tovert."

CHAPTER FIFTEEN

"Tovert...Toves...Tovert...Toves," Ben kept repeating to himself.

We were on our way to Milton, not only to drop him off, but also to retrieve the last piece of the map we thought we'd never find. Ben seemed in a trance. We tried to answer his questions as best as we could after the big revelation, but it was a lot to take in. Matthew said he went to sleep as soon as they got home then stayed quiet all morning.

"Do you think he's okay?" I asked Matthew as I glanced at Ben from the corner of my eye.

"He's fine," he replied. "Just processing."

"For someone who was so accepting of us having powers, I'm surprised it's hitting him so hard. Not like it affects him directly at this point."

"No, but it's a part of his history. His life may not be any different, but I'm sure he's connecting some dots," Malachi said as he sat next to us.

"What do you mean?" I questioned.

"When your bloodline contains an elemental power, it doesn't just go away," he explained. "Yes, the power itself is gone, but the connection isn't. No matter how many generations have passed, you'd still have a bond with the element."

"So, had we asked Randy or Genevieve what their favorite element was, they would've answered fire and water?" I asked.

Malachi's brows furrowed. "I'm not sure why you'd ask them that, but yes."

"It's actually a really common question in the normal world," I said with a grin.

"Strange," he responded, scratching his chin. "But, anyway, Ben's bloodline contains two elemental powers—earth and air. You've known him most of your life. How does he speak of those two things?"

"Huh," I said as the dots began connecting in my own head as well. "He's really in touch with them both. His whole tribe is though."

"If Lyle Tovert founded their tribe, it's very likely he brought them up on the same principles he always lived by when it comes to nature. By now, it's engraved deep in all of them, so they have a respect for it that most don't. But only Ben's bloodline has a real connection."

"Huh," I repeated as I peered over at Ben. Now I understand why he was acting this way. He may not have any powers, but his whole life had still been shaped around it. I stood up and slowly walked over to him. "Can I sit?"

He glanced at me and nodded before looking back down at the ground. "I don't know why this is getting to me so bad," he said.

"Because your whole life has been shaped by something monumental that you didn't even know about," I replied.

"That's a pretty spot-on deduction."

"Yeah, well, Malachi came up with it," I admitted, and one side of his lips turned up slightly. "I don't know if this is the right time to ask, but what are you going to tell your family?"

"What do you mean?"

"We need that map piece to find Silas. How we go about getting it, though, is entirely up to you." I instinctively reached out to grab his arm, but immediately stopped and shoved my hands in between my legs. "I lied to Genevieve about it but told Randy the truth because those were the right decisions for those situations. But I'm not sure what the right one is here."

"I'm not sure either," Ben said.

"Well, whatever you decide, we'll go with it. And I'll help answer any questions I can if you want to tell them the truth."

"I appreciate it." He pressed his hands together tightly as he let out a slow breath. "But I don't think the truth is best right now. Maybe sometime in the future but not now. They'll already be too overwhelmed with me coming home."

"Okay. If that's what you want." I offered him a timid smile then stood to go back to my seat.

"Hey, Robin."

"Yeah?" I asked as I looked at him over my shoulder.

"Thanks."

"You're welcome."

* * *

"You ready?" I asked Ben as we pulled up to his house. He took a deep breath and nodded. "They're going to be so happy to see you."

"Last time they saw me I was nearly dead," he commented. "I can't imagine how that feels."

"It's absolutely horrific," I said quietly. His eyes turned sorrowful as he realized the meaning behind my words, but I continued before he could say anything. "It's been more than a week since I promised them I'd bring you back alive, so don't keep them waiting any longer. I'm sure they're still a mess of worry."

"Yeah, you're right. Let's go."

Matthew and I followed him out of the car as he slowly sauntered up the steps of his front porch. His shoulders rose, as if taking a deep breath, then he opened the door.

"Honey, I'm home!" he called out as a wide smile appeared on his face.

The house was silent for only a second, then the pounding of feet met my ears from both upstairs and down. Kiona reached us first. When she saw Ben, both hands flew to her chest, and she leaned against the wall for support as quiet sobs shook her entire body. Ben leaped forward, wrapping her in his arms before she collapsed and supporting her weight as she clung to him.

"Oh, Ben," she whispered.

"Ben," Jeremiah said when he reached them. He placed his hand firmly on Ben's shoulder, looking him up and down, then joined in on the hug. "You're alive."

"Ben!" Mahka and Dakota yelled as they stampeded down the stairs. Ben laughed as they crashed into him, the family hug complete.

I leaned into Matthew as my chin quivered. Everything that happened between Ben and I in Garridan was worth it in this moment. I would go through it again and again if it meant keeping him alive another day. Matthew placed his arm over my shoulders, and we stood there and watched as the Toves family was reunited.

Jeremiah caught my eye and smiled through his tears. "Thank you," his gruff voice managed to say, and I nodded in acknowledgement.

Ben caught Mahka in a headlock, and Mahka playfully punched him. Kiona swatted Mahka's hands away, and he laughed as he ran up to me.

"Badass," he said so only Matthew and I could hear, and I grinned. "I gotta see that kind of magic in action one day."

"I already told you we don't call it magic," I replied, nudging him with my shoulder.

"Well, whatever you call it, I still want to see it. Think you can take me there one day?"

"I doubt it," I said, and he began to pout. "The council barely agreed to your brother coming, and he was nearly dead."

"But you convinced them to."

"With some help."

"So what's to say you won't convince them again?"

"Don't get your hopes up, kid," I said with a wry smile.

"Oh, they're already up. Way up." He grinned at me and started backing away. "I'll get to go there."

"Mahka."

"One day," he said before turning his back to me and rejoining his family.

"He's going to be awfully disappointed," Matthew said with a shake of his head.

"Maybe," I agreed before rubbing my lips together as my mind raced. "Maybe not."

Matthew's eyebrows shot up. "Getting some more unrealistic ideas?"

"Maybe," I repeated with a shrug. "Maybe not."

He shook his head again, and I leaned back into the wall. As I watched the Toves family cling to one another, I thought of all the possibilities that could open up to Garridan if they would stop hiding behind the barrier. If they could have a little bit of trust, they wouldn't have to stay cut off from the rest of the world. I didn't know if it was something I could ever bring up to the council, but the idea of it left my mind spinning.

A while later, we were all sitting in the backyard drinking lemonade and enjoying the warmth of the sun. Matthew and I had been dodging questions all afternoon as we tried to scrape up lies about the medicine in Garridan and why it wasn't available to the general public. After a certain point, I think they realized we were hiding something but stopped asking questions. They were just happy to have their son alive and well.

I noticed the pitcher was nearly empty, so I offered to refill it.

"Can you bring out more cookies too?" Dakota asked.

"Of course," I replied before heading into the house.

As I stood in the kitchen restocking the cookie tray, Ben came up behind me.

"Hey, we'll need to ask your dad about that map piece soon," I told him without looking up. "It's starting to get late, and Malachi probably doesn't want us here after dark."

"Of course," he said. "I'll ask him as soon as we go back outside."

I could feel his eyes on me, so I looked up and asked, "Is something wrong?"

"No. It's just . . ."

"Just?" I pried.

"I never actually said 'thank you' to you," he said, an unusual timidness on his face, as if he didn't know how to interact with me. "For saving my life."

"I didn't do anything really," I replied, kicking my foot against the floor. "It's Akio and the other healers you should be thanking."

"Oh, I did."

"Of course you did." He wouldn't be him if he hadn't.

"But you're the reason they were able to heal me. Without you," he paused and swallowed, "my family would be in shambles right now."

"They wouldn't be the only ones."

"Meaning you?"

"Yes, but also Felicity and basically the whole senior class. She told me they've held so many tributes and fundraisers for you. The whole school loves you, you know."

He shrugged halfheartedly as color flushed his cheeks. "I know you suck at accepting praise, but are you going to let me say thank you or not?"

"If you must," I replied playfully.

His eyes bore into mine, intent and serious. "Thank you."

I smiled softly. "You're welcome."

Before I knew what was happening, he took a step forward and I was wrapped firmly in his embrace. I tensed up as he placed his chin on my head but, after a moment, I relaxed into him. I placed my arms around his waist and inhaled his scent as his warmth radiated through me. He held onto me tightly then gently kissed my forehead.

This is where I belong.

Tears pricked my eyes, and I blinked them away before they could fall.

But I have to find somewhere else to belong now.

All too soon, he let me go. His face was filled with as much emotion as mine, but he didn't say anything. Instead, he walked away, and I followed like nothing had happened.

"Hey, Dad," he said when he landed on the patio. "Do you remember that old map you used to tell us stories with? The one you said was a family heirloom?"

"Of course," Jeremiah replied.

"Do you think we could see it?"

"Sure." He stood and stretched before going inside. Ben, Matthew, and I followed him to his study, and he began going through his desk drawers. "What's the interest anyway?"

"Robin and Matthew have been tracking down old maps for a school project. I thought they might be able to borrow ours," Ben told him.

Matthew glanced at him at the word 'borrowed.' There was no way the Keepers of Balance would let us give it back once we had it.

"I don't see why not," Jeremiah said. He rummaged around for another moment then sat back with a triumphant smile. "Here it is. Still in perfect condition."

We gathered around it excitedly. Sure enough, the black lines on it mirrored the others. These ones curved in the middle of the paper, though, connection the two into one. On the upper left-hand side, a stream of water was drawn, ending where the black line began. Trees littered the bottom right-hand side but there was open space around the water source.

"I knew I recognized it!" I exclaimed.

"What?" Jeremiah asked.

"Oh, sorry, it's just uh—" I faltered, unsure what to say.

"We found a map that had similar markings," Matthew spoke up quickly. "It must lead somewhere in the same region as this one."

"Oh, I see," Jeremiah said. "I was never under the impression that this one actually led anywhere."

"What do you mean?" Ben asked.

"It doesn't have coordinates or anything like that, so I just assumed it was a fake."

"But you said it was a family heirloom."

"Oh, it is," Jeremiah replied as his long braid fell over his shoulder. "But that doesn't mean it's a legitimate piece of work. When it was passed onto me, my father made me memorize a poem and said I had to pass that down as well when the time came. That's another reason I've always thought it was just a joke of some sort."

"What was the poem?" Matthew asked.

"'One with powers and one without must come to show you're ready. Peace between our lands is needed; the alternative is deadly,'" he quoted, then he chuckled again. "Silly, isn't it?"

We all forced out our own laughs. "Sure is," Ben agreed.

"Well, you two are more than welcome to borrow it," Jeremiah told Matthew and me.

"Thank you," I replied. "We appreciate it."

"Of course."

"Jeremiah!" Kiona called out.

"Coming!" Jeremiah answered. "I'll be right back."

As soon as he was out of ear shot, Matthew pounced on me. "You know where this is?" he demanded.

"Yes, but we'll get back to that," I said. "Did you hear what he said? 'One with powers and one without must come to show you're ready.'"

"What's it mean?" Ben asked.

"It's honestly pretty straightforward," Matthew replied. "Someone without powers has to go find Silas with us."

"But why?" I asked.

"Silas and the others were cast out because they used too much of nature's energy. He vowed to never let that happen again. Maybe in his mind, that's the only way to balance it out—keeping us and normal people equal."

"That would make the second line make sense," I agreed. "Without peace between us, one of our worlds is doomed."

"The council isn't going to like this."

"Not at all." I glanced over at Ben, who had gone quiet. His eyes were squinted, the lines on his forehead protruding, and I could tell he was in deep thought. "What's wrong, Ben?"

He didn't speak and, after a long moment of silence, I didn't think he was going to answer at all. Finally, he looked at me then Matthew.

"Take me with you," he said.

"*What?*" I asked as my jaw unhinged, but he ignored me.

"You need someone without powers and who better than someone you know and trust?" He kept speaking directly to Matthew. "Someone who already knows about Garridan."

"No," I said, shaking my head vigorously. "No, no, no, no, no."

"It would be the easiest solution," Matthew said. "Are you sure you want to volunteer for this though? I'm not sure what all it'll entail."

"Yes, I'm sure."

I stuck my hand on my forehead as my heart raced. We were supposed to go our separate ways, not prolong our sudden awkwardly tense encounters.

"Let me call my dad to get in touch with the council. It'll be their decision after all," Matthew said. He gave me the side eye then left the room, pulling his cell phone out as he went.

"You can't do this," I told Ben.

"Yes, actually, I can," he replied, crossing his arms.

"Okay, fine, but why would you want to? This isn't your problem and—" I bit the inside of my lower lip.

"And what?"

"And Alexander is coming too."

"I know. Matthew told me."

"Then why do you want to go? You're already angry just thinking about him. Do you really want to see him in person? See him around me?"

His eyes narrowed slightly then relaxed just as quick. He shrugged, trying to seem nonchalant. "I think it'd be good to see that actually. Maybe it'll help me accept it."

"It's not really my problem if you accept it or not" I said hotly.

"And it's not my problem if you don't want me to go."

"Why are you doing this to me?" I groaned.

"I'm not doing anything *to* you," he denied, sticking his hands in his pockets. "I'm doing it *for* you."

"What?"

"You were right when you said I made a choice before. I chose to stay and, in the moment, it was the right thing. But things are different now, and I'm choosing to go. I'm choosing more time with you, no matter how good or bad it is. I'm choosing to give us a chance to work things out."

"It's too late for that," I whispered, my heart dropping into my stomach.

"I don't mean a relationship. You've already made it clear we're over, and I would never push myself on you. I just mean a friendship.

"Ben."

"Just let me do this, Robin, please." His voice was barely audible as his sad eyes held my gaze hypnotically. "I couldn't live with myself if we had such a bad breakup we couldn't even stay friends, and I don't think you could either. If we can't mend our relationship, at least this will give us time to figure out how to not hate each other."

"I don't hate you."

"But you don't like me."

I looked at my shoes. "No, I guess I don't right now."

"And I don't particularly like you either. So, I think this could do us both some good," he insisted earnestly. "We both have a lot of healing to do. Maybe if we have more time to talk it'll help."

I contemplated it. Maybe he was right, and this would be a way to salvage a friendship. Or maybe he wasn't, and this would turn into an even longer, more difficult trip. Either way, I didn't want him to have to live with any regrets.

"Fine," I said quietly. "If you're allowed to go, I'll play nice as long as you do."

"That's all I'm asking," he replied.

"We're good to go," Matthew announced as he came back into the room. He glanced from Ben to me, his eyes wary. "Is everything good here?"

"As good as can be expected," I replied. "That was a quick call."

"Your mom and dad made an executive decision to say yes," he explained. "They're getting the council together now to tell them, but they didn't want us to have to sit and wait while they bickered it out."

"Thank you, Mom and Dad," I commented, knowing how long it could've taken the council to reach a decision.

"Now to talk to mine," Ben said, pressing his lips together. "They aren't going to be happy about this."

"Maybe you should stay then," I said.

"Not happening," he replied. "Do you guys mind waiting here?"

"Of course," Matthew responded, sitting in Jeremiah' chair. After Ben left, he asked, "Are you okay?"

"I'm frustrated."

"He's not coming to cause any problems. He just wants time to make amends."

"How do you know that?" I asked with my hands on my hips. "Were you spying on us?"

"Please. That's Mateo's specialty," he replied with a wave of his hand. "Ben talked to me about it last night."

"I thought you said he was quiet all night."

"A minor lie."

"Well, what did he say?" I asked.

"He said he wished he had the time to make amends. If there was any way for him to stay in Garridan for a while longer, he'd do it so he could make sure neither of you regretted how things ended."

"That's basically what he just told me," I said quietly.

"Did you think he was lying?"

"Ben's not a liar."

"Then?"

I shrugged. "I don't know. I guess I just didn't expect him to get over being so angry this quickly."

He snorted and leaned back in the chair. "He might be a saint, but he's definitely still angry. And jealous. Going on this trip with us, with Alexander, it's going to be torture for him."

"Then why did he even offer to go?" I asked in frustration.

"Wake up, Robin," he shot back, just as frustrated. "Why do you think? He's not the type of person to let his emotions get in the way of helping somebody else. Esp-ecially somebody he loves. Don't make any mistakes, he jumped on this chance for *you*. Not for himself. He doesn't want *you* to regret how things ended. He could care less about himself, and you know it."

I looked at the aging carpet under my feet. Of course that was the real reason. He could say it was for us both until he was blue in the face, but it wasn't the truth. It was for me. He was doing this for me. That realization made me want to curl into a ball and jump over a mountain ledge. I never deserved him.

Matthew and I stayed quiet until Ben poked his head around the doorframe and said, "Let me pack a bag really quick then we can go."

"How'd your parents take it?" Matthew asked.

"Okay, I think. Mom started crying and Dad's concerned about me finishing school. But they trust me and know I wouldn't be running off without a good reason."

"You know you won't be able to talk to them for a while, right?"

"It'll be okay. I'll be okay." He glanced at me and said, "We're *all* going to be okay."

CHAPTER SIXTEEN

"Welcome, Mr. Toves," Luna greeted Ben as Matthew and I stood on either side of him.

"It's an honor to be here, ma'am," he responded with a smile. "And, please, call me Ben."

"Isn't he a charmer?" Luna commented as she returned his smile, and he blushed slightly. "It was very brave of you to volunteer your help to our quest. We aren't keen on outsiders, but you'll be treated with nothing but respect while you're with us."

"I appreciate it."

"Now, the Alastair family has already offered to accommodate you while you're here. You'll stay with them in their home until we start our journey, and they'll see to your needs as they may arise. After we leave to find Silas, they'll provide you with protection. Do you have any ques-tions?"

"No, ma'am. I understand, and I'm ready to help in any way I can."

Luna's eyes sparkled as she watched him, clearly smitten by his charm. My lips pressed together in annoyance. She was too old for him.

"Know that any less than satisfactory behavior will not be tolerated," Peter said, his cold gaze unhappy. I'm sure he didn't want Ben, or any other person without powers, here. "We'll be keeping a close eye on you."

"I understand, sir. You need to keep your land safe," Ben said, and Peter glared harder.

"Now that that's out of the way," Mom spoke up, "let's look at these map pieces, shall we?"

She carefully placed them in a row on the table in the middle of the room. As soon as they were all touching, a light glow began to radiate. I squinted as it brightened, then it was gone as suddenly as it had appeared. When I looked back at the map, it was no longer three separate pieces but one continuous map.

"Well, that'll make it easier to transport," Carmella commented as we stared at it with intrigue.

"It's definitely a magic map, that's for sure," Juan said.

"How do we go about finding the location?" Dad asked.

"Oh," I said, a little embarrassed I'd forgotten to tell them. "I actually know exactly where it is."

"That would've been useful to know before," Peter muttered.

"I only figured it out when we saw the last piece."

"That might make this whole endeavor a lot easier," Chang said. "If we know the location, we can just have a teleporter pop on over."

"William, would you please have Charles come here immediately," Mom commanded.

William nodded in acknowledgement then walked out of the room.

"I also think we need to call in a photokinesis user," Matthew said. "We were told there's a hidden message on the map that can only be seen with a special light. No nor-mal light worked, so I'm assuming it has to be something only our people could see."

"Very astute, Mr. Alastair," Chang said before turning to another guard stationed in the room. "Can you call Kenji in here please?"

"Right away," the guard replied.

"Anything else worth mentioning?" Peter asked as he drummed his fingers loudly on the desk.

"No, that was it," I replied.

"Good," he said.

The Keepers of Balance began talking amongst themselves, so Ben murmured, "They're an intimidating bunch, aren't they?"

I couldn't help but smile. "You get used to it."

"Then you're *so* used to it you begin to argue and defy them," Matthew said with a pointed look my way.

"Hey, it's always been for good causes," I defended myself.

"I can't picture that from you," Ben told me. "I don't think I've ever seen you be disrespectful to a grown-up before."

"I wouldn't call it disrespect—" I started.

"It's definitely disrespect," Matthew cut me off with a smirk.

"It's not for no reason though!" I exclaimed.

"Even so, I just can't imagine it," Ben said.

"I've probably done a lot of things you couldn't imagine," I replied, ruining the lightness of the mood.

"Being here has changed you," Ben noted.

I shrugged. "All life experiences shape you in one way or another."

"Some for the worse."

"So you think I'm a bad person now?" I questioned accusingly.

"That's not what I said."

"Yes, it is."

"No, it isn't."

"Sorry, man," Matthew inserted, "but it kind of is."

"Thanks for the help," Ben muttered. "I'm sorry. I didn't mean it like that."

Before I could ask how else he could've meant it, the doors opened, and Charles walked in with William.

"Hello, Charles," Mom greeted him.

"Adriana," he replied with a nod of his head. "What can I do for you?"

"We have somewhere we need you to go. Get the lay of the land and let us know if you can take us there."

"Okay. Where is it?"

"Robin?" Mom beckoned me closer.

"You know where the Amazon Rainforest is, right? In Brazil?" I asked Charles.

"Of course," he replied.

I placed my hand on the map. "This is in the eastern part of it. It's not on many maps in the normal world because it's tucked into the forest so well. But lucky for us, I did a school project on the Amazon Rainforest a few years back and found a newly updated map with this on there."

"Are you sure it's the same spot?" Mom asked.

I nodded. "Definitely. I remember because it's so unique. These black lines are actually a deep canyon. The river flows into it and escapes through underwater caverns in the mountain range."

"I've seen this before as well," Charles said.

"Really?" I questioned in surprise.

"Oh, yes. I study maps vigorously. All teleporters do. We'd be pretty useless without them since we're stuck within Garridan's barriers. It's the only way for us to know enough to transport ourselves to certain locations when asked. And this," he pointed to the map, "is as you said, very unique."

"Can you go there then?" Dad asked.

"Of course. I'll be back in a jiffy," he replied before closing his eyes and disappearing.

"Whoa," I heard Ben whisper.

Dad chuckled and said, "Be prepared to say that a lot, son."

"And I thought Robin's powers were cool," Ben said, his voice full of awe.

"Uhm, excuse me, my powers are way cooler than that," I told him with raised brows.

"Everyone is entitled to their own opinion," Matthew said. "Even if it's wrong."

I scoffed. "Like petrifying things is just so awesome."

"It's obviously the best," he replied, and I rolled my eyes. "Okay."

Charles reappeared suddenly, making me jump, but his brows were furrowed deeply together.

"What's wrong?" Mom asked.

"I couldn't find anything," he answered.

"Well, I'm sure Silas wouldn't be right out in the open."

"No. I mean there was literally nothing there," he clarified. "I was stuck in this black world where nothing existed."

"I don't understand," Chang said, all the Keepers of Balance now listening. "You couldn't make it there?"

"No, I made it. But it was . . . Nonexistent. There was no sky, no ground, no trees, no anything."

Everyone exchanged confused glances.

"Are you sure?" Darby asked.

"Yes, ma'am. I'm positive," Charles replied.

"I suppose it makes sense," Matthew said.

"What do you mean?" Peter questioned.

"Ben's dad said someone without powers had to go too. Maybe Silas won't appear without both present."

"That's true," Mom said. "Charles?"

"I'm on it," Charles replied before walking to Ben and making them both disappear. We waited around anxiously, and when they finally reappeared, Charles shook his head.

Ben stumbled over to Matthew, his legs barely holding him up. I suppressed a grin as the grown-ups started speaking again.

"Does that mean we can't go?" Darby asked.

"It's on the map, it can't just be non-existent," Juan commented.

"People have stumbled upon it before," Chang pointed out. "So it has to be there."

"Normal people. None of our kind," Luna replied. "What if our people can't go?"

"That makes no sense," Dad said.

"Screwed again," Peter muttered.

As they continued speaking over one another, I thought back on everything I'd learned thus far about Silas and the history that led him into becoming the infamous magical tree. That's when it hit me.

"I think I know why Charles can't see him," I said loudly to be heard over all the voices.

"Why's that?" Juan asked.

"Think about it. Silas' sole purpose for existing is to keep the balance between us and nature. He could've just told someone where he was going, but he didn't. He made an elaborate map and separated the pieces." I looked around at all the faces staring at me. "He didn't want anyone to be able to find him easily because we might abuse the power he has. We could be a threat to everything he's worked to protect."

"So we need to prove we're worthy before he'll let us find him," Matthew stated, catching on to what I was getting at.

"Exactly."

"How would we do that though?" Darby asked.

"I think we've already started by bringing Ben here," I replied. "'One with powers and one without must come to show you're ready.' Silas wants peace between our lands, but our ancestors screwed up and caused a huge war that led us to go into hiding. Bringing Ben doesn't undo that mistake, but it shows we've advanced enough to have civil relations with the people who once thought we were their enemy."

"Where do you get off speaking about our ancestors like that?" Peter asked angrily.

"You know it's true," I shot back, suppressing the urge to roll my eyes. "You all do." I looked at my mom accusingly. "You told me only half the truth when you explained why Garridan went into hiding. I learned the rest from Alexander. And if he knows it, he learned it from the Cyfrin's Keepers of Balance, which means it's common knowledge to the council. Right?"

Mom looked away, rubbing her lips together as I radiated my annoyance towards her. How many other lies had she told me?

"I knew that boy was going to be trouble," Peter said.

"That's completely beside the point," I told him. "It's true, right?"

"Yes," Dad finally answered. "It's true."

"So, not only do we have to prove we won't bring harm to nature, but we also have to prove we won't bring harm to Ben's people," I said. "Which is why he's here."

"How do we prove the rest?" Juan asked, and they all looked at me expectantly.

I blinked rapidly and said, "I have no idea. But I just gave you half your answers. Can't you figure the rest out yourselves?"

"Robin," Mom chastised.

Half the room looked bemused while the rest looked annoyed. I didn't care though.

"What?" I asked. "I've only been a part of this world for a year yet, somehow, I still understand more about it than any of you. Why is that?"

"Robin," Mom said again.

"Because we hide our transgressions behind our good deeds," Chang said, and everyone turned to look at him. "After this trip, I think it'd be wise of us to start teaching the true history of Garridan. We aren't perfect, and we certainly aren't above people with no powers. Everything that happened with the Cyfrin over the last decade should've taught us how dangerous that mindset is."

"Maybe that's what finding Silas is all about," Matthew said. "Showing us our downfalls and coming to terms with them."

"And also learning how to do better," Dad added.

The doors creaked open, and a younger man with small glasses and a bowl cut hairstyle walked in.

"A conversation for a later time," Luna said before speaking louder. "Hello, Kenji. Thank you for joining us."

"My pleasure," Kenji answered, his pitch an octave too high. "How can I help?"

"We need you to shine some light on this map," she replied. "Literally."

"Okay," he said, his brows furrowed at the strange request.

He sauntered over slowly then held up both hands. They began to glow, first dully then more intensely. His palms became translucent as the glaring light radiated in straight lines. It was like looking at a flashlight. He placed them a good distance away from the paper, illuminating it. At first, nothing happened, but after a moment, shimmering letters slowly appeared.

My eyes widened as I watched the kind of thing I'd only seen in movies. There were three places where groups of words came into view—below the stream on the left, across the grove of trees in the middle, and next to the mountain range on the right. One on each part of the map that'd been fused together.

"What does it say?" someone asked from the back of the room.

I slowly read the script on the left. "*Only the pure will be allowed inside my sacred ground. If your heart is wise and true, the way across is found.*" My forehead scrunched up. "What does that mean?"

"I don't know, but the other two are just as cryptic," Dad said. "*Take the risk, make the jump. Come see what lies beyond. Put your trust in me to see the tree beyond the translucent pond.*"

"And the third?" Chang asked.

"*We've all lost loved ones through the years. It's shaped us to who we are. Through all the pain, suffering, and tears, you must learn to accept your scars. If you can't, you won't advance. You'll seal your fate forever. Stuck in the past, locked in the fog, life will reach you never,*" Matthew read.

"What are these?" Mom asked.

"They seem like riddles giving hints to find Silas," Ben murmured, unsure if he should be speaking or not.

"That last one sounds like a warning too," Matthew said.

"How do we figure out what they mean though?" Luna asked.

"Well, the first one is easy enough," Ben answered. "Only a pure hearted person can enter the land Silas is on."

"But what about 'the way across is found' part?" I questioned.

"My guess is it means we'll be shown the way as long as our intentions are good," he replied with a shrug. "I could be wrong, but that's what it sounds like to me."

"I have the feeling we won't understand them completely until we're on the journey," Chang said.

"You're probably right," Mom agreed. "Silas hasn't made any of this easy thus far, so I can't imagine the trek through the woods is going to be any better."

Kenji lowered his hands, and his light disappeared. Half the room gasped when the writing dissipated as well.

"Guess we'll need to write those down," Peter grumbled.

"Now that we actually have everything in place with the map, we should discuss the logistics," Darby said as the Keepers of Balance took their seats again. "Who to send, when to go, supplies, etc."

"Agreed," Luna replied. She gave Ben a once over. "I can't imagine you'd like to stand there through all this. Go home with Matthew. Malachi can fill you two in later."

"Same to you, Robin," Mom said to me. "We'll discuss it at dinner."

"Okay," I agreed. "See you guys at home."

"Bye, kiddo," Dad replied before I headed out of the room with Ben and Matthew.

"You guys are more than welcome to go to my house," I told them. "I'm sure Claire is already there with the trainees."

"Are you not going?" Ben asked.

"I have an errand I need to run first," I replied.

"She's going to go fill Alexander in on everything," Matthew informed him, and I scowled.

Ben pressed his lips into a hard line before a forced smile took its place. "I'm sure he'll appreciate that," he said through gritted teeth.

He walked ahead of us, and I punched Matthew in the arm. "You're walking on thin ice," I whispered angrily.

"I'm just trying to help him prepare. If he can't handle knowing you're going to talk to Alexander, do you really think he's going to be able to handle seeing you with him?" Matthew asked.

I rubbed my lips together. "I didn't think about that. I suppose I should say thank you . . . But I'm not going to."

"You'll thank me later."

"We'll see," I retorted before strutting away.

CHAPTER SEVENTEEN

"I thought you'd come back sooner," Alexander remarked as I sat on his bed.

"Things got a little crazy," I replied with a sigh.

"Ben?"

"Sort of."

"How did seeing him go?"

"Pretty terrible," I admitted, leaning my head back against the wall. "He ended up coming to my house for dinner that same night, and we had another less than pleasant conversation."

"I'm sure he was just hurting," he said. "He's back home now, so both of you will have a chance to come to terms with things."

"Actually, that's where things got a little crazy. Ben isn't back home."

"Ben isn't back home?"

"Not anymore."

"Care to elaborate?" he asked, his disheveled face seeming too tired to understand anything other than a direct explanation.

"We found the third map piece and were told someone without powers had to be present in order for us to find Silas," I explained. "When Ben heard that, he volunteered."

"And the council agreed because he already knows of our existence." He smiled wryly, his eyes dancing mischievously. "Smart boy."

"What?"

"Ben. Joining us on our journey." He chuckled humorously. "It's a grand gesture to win back your favor."

"That's not why he's doing it," I denied.

"Isn't it?"

"I mean, in a way, yes. But not in the way you're thinking. He wants us to be friends. He's concerned I won't be okay if things between us end badly and we hate each other."

"And you believe that?"

"Yes," I answered with confidence. "Ben isn't a liar."

Alexander watched me, observing every detail of my expression as I looked back at him. He cocked his head to the side slightly and said, "Whatever you need to believe."

I could tell he wanted to say more, but he kept himself in line, and when I didn't reply he asked, "How did you find the last map piece anyway?"

"We found Lyle Tovert's descendants."

"Really?"

I nodded, then said, "It's Ben."

"Ben?" Alexander repeated, the shock resonating off his usually well composed face.

"Ben," I confirmed. "He's a descendant of Lyle Tovert."

"Huh. Can't say I saw that coming."

"Can't say I did either."

We sat in silence for a while, both wrapped up in our own thoughts. Whenever I'd glance over at him, his face was distant and cold like how it used to be around Toshiro. I couldn't figure out why he seemed so distressed by the news though.

"When are we leaving?" he asked.

"The council's discussing all that now. I'm sure someone will relay the information to you after it's figured out."

"The sooner the better," he mumbled, and I once again noted the exhaustion that radiated from him.

"Are you okay?" I asked, gently placing my hand against his cheek.

He leaned into it and sighed. "Just tired and ready to get out of this hell hole. Being drained of my powers for so long seems to be having a negative impact on my overall state."

"It's hurting you?"

"In an odd sense, yes."

"I'm sorry, Alexander," I murmured, wishing there was something I could do. "Just hang in there a little longer."

"Don't have much other choice, now do I?" He sighed again then carefully pushed my arm away. "Go home, Robin."

"You don't want me to stay?"

"And see me like this? No. I'd much rather be miserable without witnesses."

"It's going to be okay," I told him as I stood.

"So you keep saying."

I walked to the cell door, glancing back to see his eyes already closed. Once he was out of here, I would never let him come back.

* * *

Laughter met my ears as I walked into my house. A smile formed on my face at the sound, and I peeked around the corner to see everyone chilling in the living room. Even Matthew was grinning widely.

"What's so funny?" I asked as I stepped into the room. All eyes hit the ground, their smiles disappearing immediately—all except Matthew's. "Am I really that much of a party pooper?"

"No, of course not," Claire assured me, but she wouldn't meet my gaze.

Suspicion crept up my spine as I looked harder at everyone. Their smiles weren't completely gone, they were just trying to suppress them.

"What's so funny then?" I asked again, crossing my arms.

"Ben was just telling us a story. That's all," Mateo answered, the corners of his lips wobbling.

I gasped and pointed at Ben. "Are you telling them stories about *me*?"

That did them in. They began laughing again as I pursed my lips and peered up at the ceiling.

"I'm sorry," Ben said around a chuckle. "They wanted to know what you were like before you knew about Garridan."

"And you chose to tell them what story exactly?"

"All the embarrassing ones," he admitted, his sly smile showing no shame.

"Ugh, thanks a lot," I groaned as I plopped onto the floor next to Kodi and Emery.

"You were really a clumsy kid, huh?" Toby asked.

"*No*," I replied. "My mom just sucked at buying the right size shoe."

"And that's why you fell into the cutest eighth grade boy and pulled his pants down?" Emery questioned with a smirk.

"Benjamin!" I yelled as heat rose to my cheeks. Everyone started laughing again as my heart thumped faster in my chest. "His pants were way too baggy and already falling down anyway!"

"Uh huh, sure," Emery said.

"It's not that funny," I muttered, picking at the carpet as they all slowly got their bearings and stopped laughing.

"Sorry, Robin, but it *was* funny," Andre said.

"No more embarrassing stories," I demanded as I glared at Ben.

He held his hands up and nodded. "No more."

"How's Alexander?" Matthew asked, shutting down the rest of the small smiles that lingered on faces. He was going to cause trouble if he wasn't careful.

"Tired," I replied.

Emery snorted. "I'm sure sitting in a cell all day can be *very* taxing."

"It isn't the cell. It's the door," I shot back, and her brows furrowed.

"What?" she asked.

"The door to his cell was forged by our ancestors as a weapon. It degenerates a person's powers," I explained. "I don't think they ever learned the long-term effects of it, though, because it seems like it's starting to drain the life right out of him."

"Poor thing," she muttered sarcastically.

I shot her a warning look but noticed Matthew's concerned expression next to her. At least someone else cared.

"I take it you don't care for Alexander?" Ben asked.

"Considering one of the first times we interacted he almost killed me, no. Not particularly," Emery replied.

Ben frowned at that revelation, looking to me then to the rest of the trainees. "What about you guys? What do you think of him?" he asked.

"Can we not do this now?" I questioned.

"He's going to be around the guy," Emery said. "Doesn't he deserve to know how dangerous he is?"

"He isn't dangerous," I snapped.

"None of us are his biggest fan," Andre said.

"You too?" I asked, feeling betrayed.

"None of us are his biggest fan," he repeated, "*but* we also all agreed to give him a chance. In the end, he helped stop the war. He saved Robin from Toshiro, and he willingly turned himself in to be arrested even though he knew it meant he might be executed."

"Yeah," Toby agreed softly. "We realized we could've had the same experience with Matthew if he'd still been in the Cyfrin compound when we were. But since we only knew him here, we like him even though he's done lots of bad things too."

"Some of us," Mateo said, looking from Emery to Kodi, "are just having a harder time accepting that than the rest of us."

"I'm sure Ben hates the guy as much as we do, and he doesn't even know him," Emery commented.

"No, actually, I don't," Ben said, and I looked up at him in surprise. "I'm a pretty levelheaded guy, and I try not to judge people based on other's opinions. I've heard both good and bad things about him, but all I really care about is what he does from this point forward now that he's in Robin's life." He glanced over at me, his eyes soft. "I'd be lying if I said I wasn't concerned, but that's just because I love her and want what's best for her."

I chewed on my bottom lip as a weight landed on my chest. My throat began to close as I tried hard to keep in a sob. My eyes sank to the floor as Matthew cleared his throat to take the attention off me.

"I'd say we could all learn a thing or two from Ben," he said.

"You included," Claire replied softly.

"Me included," he agreed.

The front door opened, and my dad called out their arrival.

"We brought Chinese!" he hollered before he and Mom came into the living room with four large bags. They placed them on the coffee table, and Andre and Mateo moved from their spot on the couch to the floor.

"Well, thank you, boys," Mom told them as she and Dad took their place.

"We have lots to tell you, so dig in," Dad commanded. After we sorted out all the food, he said, "We're leaving in two days."

"Who's included in the 'we?'" I asked.

"Because we're currently three Keepers of Balance short, we decided it was best if only two of us go so the rest can stay focused on our duties here," he replied. "Since neither an air nor earth element were lost, that'll be me and Luna."

"Why Luna?" I heard myself say.

"Why not Luna?" Dad asked in return, raising his brows. "I didn't realize you had an issue with her."

"I don't!" I exclaimed quickly. "I was just curious is all."

I could tell he didn't believe me, but Mom answered, "She and Chang are both very powerful, but he has a slight edge on her, so it'll be best to keep him here to help us stay balanced. However, we figured sending her is still more than enough to counteract anything Alexander might do if he were to present a problem."

"Makes sense," I agreed before stuffing my face with some food.

Both my parents and Matthew eyed me suspiciously, but Mom continued anyway. "Since only two are going, we're only sending five guards."

"Which ones?" Matthew asked.

"You, your brother and father, Vivi, and Demetri," Dad replied.

Matthew nodded appreciatively. "Solid group. Vivi is a teleporter and Demetri is a camouflager," he informed the rest of us.

"We're also sending Akio. You can't go on a trip like this without a healer."

"And you trust him to be that person?" Claire questioned.

"Of course," Mom responded. "He may have lived in the Cyfrin compound, but he was never loyal to them."

"Plus, he helped us so much during the battle," I told her. "He's the only reason half of us are alive."

"Okay," she said with a shrug. "No arguments here. I was just wondering."

"Aside from that, it'll just be you kids and Alexander," Dad said.

"*All* of us?" Emery asked. "Toby and I included?"

"Yes, the council approved the two of you going as well," Mom answered. She looked over at Toby. "Although, I'd personally much prefer if you stayed here with me."

"I can't let them go without me," Toby replied as he messed with his fingers.

"Actually," I said softly, knowing his feelings were about to be hurt, "I think you *should* stay here."

His lower lip stuck out. "You don't want me to come?"

"Of course I do, but we don't know what's going to happen out there, and I think we'd all feel better knowing you were safe at home if things don't go as planned."

"I get it. You think I'm a burden."

"No!" I exclaimed, glancing around the room for some help. "No, no. Of course not."

"My power could keep me safe," he said earnestly.

"I don't think a jungle is going to have any forms of metal for you to protect yourself with," Kodi pointed out gently.

"What about Ben?" Toby asked. "He has no powers, and you're letting him go."

"You already know why he's going," Mateo said. "We need him to find Silas."

"And you don't need me," he said dejectedly.

"We *do* need you," I assured him. "But what we need from you right now is to stay here and look after Mom.

She's going to be a basket case with all of us gone, and you can help her through it."

"I can?" he asked, his face perking up.

"I'd be forever grateful if you did," Dad told him, squeezing his shoulder. "I'll feel much better knowing she isn't alone."

"Plus, it'll give us a chance to spend some one-on-one time together," Mom said, her eyes sparkling with excitement. "Wouldn't you like that?"

"Well, yes," he answered hesitantly. He looked back at Dad and whispered, "You really think she needs me?"

Dad suppressed a smile and whispered back, "Definitely."

Toby nodded firmly then said, "Okay, then. I'll stay."

"I appreciate you thinking of me, Toby," Mom said.

"And just like that, the baby of the family has learned his place," Emery said teasingly.

"I'm not a baby," he said with a scowl, and I giggled at how offended he sounded.

Mom slowly looked around the room affectionately. "It'll be strange having the house so quiet again. You haven't been here long, but I've grown fond of each and every one of you. So, please, all of you look out for one another." Her eyes landed on Mateo and Kodi. "And you two, never forget where you come from as you find happiness in your own world."

"We won't," Kodi replied as she grabbed Mateo's hand and tried to smile. It came out more like a grimace, though, and Mateo nodded.

"We definitely won't," he told my mom.

"Well," Mom said, plastering a smile on her face as she tried to lift the gloomy feeling that fell over the room. "Let's enjoy the time we have left together."

"Hear, hear," Mateo said, lifting his drink to the air then chugging it before transforming into some sort of tiny bird.

He flew up, and I pulled some water from the atmosphere, turning it into a maze around him. Emery flung her electricity into it, adding a sense of danger as he weaved in and out of the labyrinth I'd created.

He chirped loudly and Kodi said, "He said give him a real challenge," so I decreased the extra wiggle room between him and the humming water. Dad added a small amount of wind to the mix, satisfying Mateo's yearn for danger.

The rest of the evening passed in a similar fashion as we all showed off our talents for Ben. By the time we went our separate ways, we were all exhausted from overusing our powers and hurting from laughing so much. As I curled up in bed, all I could think of was how perfect our time together had been. It was a nice memory to have, especially knowing how much everything was about to change.

CHAPTER EIGHTEEN

The day was warm with just enough wind to be enjoyable. Everyone lounged around outside while we waited for the plane to be fueled and loaded with supplies. Aside from Toby, the boys all wore cargo pants with crew cut T-shirts and light jackets thrown over their shoulders or tied around their waists. Kodi, Emery, and I had opted for jeans but matched their pick in tops. Andre and Matthew chose combat boots that matched the rest of the guards, but everyone else was in sturdy tennis shoes.

Courtesy of my mom, we each had individual backpacks full of imperishable snacks, extra clothes, and other items she considered necessary for survival in the woods. I questioned some of the things she'd packed—including the snacks since Alexander or Luna could make berries and nuts on demand—but decided not to point that out since making the bags was her way of feeling useful.

As Mateo got Toby in a headlock, a car drove up, stopping just outside of where we stood. Two guards got out, both surveying the land as if danger lurked nearby. One of them opened the door to the back seat and Alexander stepped out, his own eyes inspecting the surroundings. When they landed on me, the side of his lips twisted up slightly, and I smiled in return.

His hair was trimmed and his face shaved, his bare skin making him appear younger. Someone had graciously given him proper attire, so he was as ready as any of us to brave whatever came our way in the wilderness. As he walked towards us, he and Ben checked one another out, the judgement obvious on their faces.

"Hello," Alexander greeted us all collectively.

"Hi," I replied.

"Alexander," Matthew acknowledged.

A few of the others muttered their own welcome, then Ben stepped forward. My breath caught in my throat as my heart skipped a beat.

Please don't let there be any drama. Please don't let there be any drama. Please don't let there be any drama.

"Hi, I'm Ben." He stuck his hand out, but Alexander just stared at it.

You could hear a pin drop as we waited to see what would happen. After another tense moment, Alexander grasped Ben's hand in his own.

"Alexander," he said.

"Nice to meet you," Ben replied as the two stared each other down. They tightened their grips on one another, both their eyes narrowing slightly.

"Likewise," Alexander said.

My eyes darted between them, and I let out an awkward laugh and said, "Oh, would you look at that. I think it's time to board."

As luck would have it, my parents, William, and Malachi walked up to us as Akio and the two other guards entered the plane. Relief flooded through me, immediately followed by concern when I noticed their expressions.

"What's wrong?" Matthew asked.

"We aren't entirely sure," Mom replied as she held onto Dad's arm. She was going to miss him.

"I've already been checking up on Randy Windsor. I figure if he was going to tell anyone what he learned, it'd be within the first couple weeks," Malachi explained.

"Oh, no," I said. "Did he tell?"

"Not that we've picked up. He did exactly as he said and went to Summer. In the last couple days, he's been spending time with his kids and even took her out on a date."

"That's great!" I exclaimed. "What's the problem then?"

Malachi glanced at my parents then said, "I was just informed that he's dead."

"Dead?" Matthew repeated as my mouth dropped open. "How?"

"It looks like foul play."

"That's awful," I said.

"That's not all. William convinced us to check on Genevieve Robaday after learning about Randy. It appears she's also deceased."

"W-what?" I stuttered.

"Well, she *was* old," Matthew responded.

"Her death wasn't natural, son," Malachi told him, and the air rushed out of me as if I'd been punched. "She was killed."

"That can't be a coincidence," Matthew said.

"We go find the descendants of the Keepers of Balance who were ousted and get their map pieces and they both wind up dead days later? Of course that's not a coincidence!" I cried out.

"Wait, what about my family?" Ben asked in a panic, his eyes wide. "What about my dad?"

"We've already sent guards to stand watch," Malachi assured him. "Whoever did this won't be able to touch him."

"Yeah, but who could've done it?" Matthew asked.

"Who do you think?" Alexander asked quietly. We all turned our attention to him as he said, "Mallory."

Just the mention of her name made my blood boil. With all the craziness going on, I'd forgotten about her and the others that hadn't been brought in.

"Why would she do that?" Andre spoke up.

"She doesn't need a reason," Alexander replied. "Since she was born, she's been taught people without powers are beneath her. She would have no remorse killing each and every one of them just because she can."

"That's horrible," Ben said, his face ashen.

"It was the way of the Cyfrin," Alexander responded with a slight shrug. "She never had a chance to learn anything different."

"Unfortunately, he's right," Matthew said. "She knows no compassion." He looked at his dad. "So, what do we do? We can't let her keep roaming free."

"No, we most certainly cannot," Mom agreed. "We'll be setting up extra teams to track her down. They've been evading our current forces, but I'm confident we can find her with enough manpower."

"I hope so," I murmured.

"Me too," Ben said distractedly.

He wouldn't stop worrying about his family until she was caught. Mom must've noticed this as well because she stepped up to him and put her hand on his shoulder.

"We'll protect your family as if they were our own. I promise," she told him, and he nodded as a grateful smile pulled at his lips. She met each of our gazes then said, "Don't let this distract you. You *all* need to stay focused on your own mission. You don't know what's going to happen while trying to find Silas, so, please, be smart and don't let this cloud your judgement."

"Of course," Matthew agreed as the rest of us nodded.

"We're ready to go, sir," a guard called out, and Malachi nodded.

Mom and Toby took turns giving each of us—except Alexander—a big hug. Toby's red rimmed eyes swam with tears as he held on extra long to Kodi and Mateo.

"I'll miss you guys so much," he told them around loud sniffles.

Mateo mussed up his hair and said, "We'll miss you too."

"Try not to forget me."

"We're going to do our best," Kodi responded with a sad smile.

Toby weakly waved as they turned towards the plane, then he buried his face into Mom as she wrapped her arm around him.

"Keep your head up," I told him, and he nodded earnestly, but the tears kept flowing. As I walked away from them, Mom called out to Andre, and I paused to hear what she said.

"Whatever you decide to do, make sure it's what will make *you* happy. Don't do something you'll regret later on, even if it's for someone you love," she advised.

He gave her another long hug and said, "Thank you," before following the rest of us onto the plane.

It was a larger vessel with plenty of room, and I said a quiet thanks for that since no one aside from me wanted to be anywhere near Alexander. He sat at the back of the plane, and the two guards who'd already been in the plane plopped down on either side of him.

"Guys, this is Vivi and Demetri," Matthew introduced, and we greeted them with an assortment of gestures.

Vivi was a tall, lanky woman in her early twenties with bright green eyes and brown hair pulled into a tight bun. She waved at us, her plump lips raising into a smile. Demetri nodded once, his stoic face never changing. His dark, buzzed hair and sharp features fed into the serious persona he radiated as his blue eyes stared straight ahead.

"My own personal 'guards,'" Alexander muttered, crossing his arms and leaning his head back as he closed his eyes. "Joy."

Malachi entered the cockpit with William at his heels. Dad, Luna, and Akio chose the seats closest to them so they could converse. The rest of us scattered around the remaining seats in the middle, sitting quietly and fastening our seatbelts.

The overall mood was somber as we began to ascend. I thought of Randy, who'd gotten his life back together just to have it stolen away. His kids were young, so they may not understand that he was gone for good. Maybe that was for the best.

Genevieve certainly lived a full life, but she still didn't deserve to be killed. I cringed as I wondered how they died. I wanted to believe it was quick and painless but knowing what I did about Mallory, I couldn't imagine it was.

I glanced around the plane. Andre and Emery were holding hands, the closest they ever came to PDA.

I hope they work out whatever they're going through before Andre needs to decide if he's leaving Garridan or not.

Mateo was chatting with Ben, neither looking happy as they kept shooting looks in my direction.

I wonder what they're talking about.

Kodi's eyes were closed, and her hands gripped the edges of her seat so tightly that her knuckles were pure white.

She must be scared of flying.

Alexander and Matthew were watching one another intently but, to my surprise, it wasn't with animosity.

They'll be okay eventually. I just know it.

"Who wants to play a game?" I asked suddenly, needing a distraction from my jumbled thoughts.

"A game?" Alexander questioned, raising both brows. "Seriously?"

"What's so wrong with that?"

"Just seems a bit childish is all."

I made a face at him, expecting nothing less. He probably never played a game in the last ten years, if ever.

"Robin loves playing games," Ben said with a bite in his tone. "Don't belittle her for that."

"Au contraire, I was doing nothing of the sort, my friend," Alexander responded bitterly.

"Really? Sure seems like it from over here, and I won't stand for it."

"You won't stand for it," Alexander repeated with a sneer. "And what, pray tell, are *you* going to do about it?"

"Whatever it takes to protect Robin," Ben replied firmly, his mouth set in a tight line.

"There's nothing to protect Robin from when it comes to me. I'd never harm her." He gave Ben the side eye, his smirk lingering on his face. "But there are many other things out there, you know. Things that *will* hurt her. Things I'm sure we'll see on this trip. And what are you, a *Norm*, going to do about it when you won't even be able to protect your-self?"

"Is that a threat?" Ben asked, daggers shooting from his eyes.

Alexander waved his hand dismissively. "Simply an observation. You can't very well do anything to save Robin if you're already dead yourself."

"Enough!" I yelled with a glare. "*I* am not a damsel in distress. I'm a powerful water wielder with deadly abilities, or don't you remember?" I glanced to Alexander. "I don't need saving, and I certainly don't need your guys' toxic masculinity and egos fighting on my behalf when I'm sitting right here!"

"Amen, sister," Emery murmured, and I scowled at the grin on her face before pointing to Ben.

"You said you weren't going to cause any problems and you," I turned my finger to Alexander, "said you'd help me through this. If you can't shove your male chauvinism far, far away then neither of you better say another word to me or about me the rest of the trip. Otherwise, it'll be the two of you who need rescuing from *me*."

I folded my arms over my chest with a huff and sat down, staring out the window as I tried to calm down.

"Way to go guys," Mateo commented, and Emery snorted.

Someone sat beside me and sighed dramatically.

"What?" I asked without looking at him.

"They both mean well," Matthew replied. "Don't be too angry with them."

"Since when do you defend Alexander?" I questioned, turning on him with a frown.

"I told you I was going to forgive him, and I meant it," he replied. "I've even gone to see him a couple more times."

"You didn't tell me that."

"I didn't want to disappoint you if I couldn't keep my word," he admitted. "But the visits went . . . Fine. Not great, but definitely not bad. He harbors no ill feelings towards me like I do him, so he's more than happy to accommodate my attempts at reconciliation."

"Well, I'm proud of you."

"Don't be too proud. I've still got a lot to work though."

"But you're trying. That's all that matters to me."

"And that loving and forgiving attitude is exactly the reason you won't hold a grudge over those two hot heads."

"A compliment wrapped in a demand. Smart," I commented with a wry smile.

"It's their first interaction with one another. Surely you didn't expect it to go smoothly."

"I had hoped."

"Then you're naive."

"Don't let Ben hear you say that," I remarked sarcas-ti-cally. "He'll have your head."

"I highly doubt Ben has any problem with anything I may say to you, negative or not," he replied with a smirk. "He'll save that—what did you call it—*male chauvinism* for anything Alexander may offend him with."

"Ha. Ha," I said dryly.

"It'll be okay." He patted my shoulder. "Just give it time."

"Hopefully we aren't around one another long enough for that."

"You're going to miss him when he's gone."

"You think I don't know that?" I snapped.

"Maybe you should think about enjoying the time you have with him instead of spending it being angry."

"You know I can't do that."

"No, you just think you can't. There's a difference." He stood and glanced down at me. "I'm not saying be all lovey dovey with him. Just be a friend. That's all he's asking for and, honestly, I think it's what you need if you're going to survive this trip."

I frowned unhappily then peeked over at Ben as Matthew walked back to his seat. Our eyes met, and he smiled apologetically, but all I could do was look away. Everything would've been so much easier if he'd just stayed in Milton like he was supposed to. But since he hadn't, maybe Matthew was right.

All Ben wanted was for us to find a way to not hate one another. There was nothing wrong with that, and I definitely didn't want us to part ways on bad terms. If he played nice like he'd promised, so would I.

* * *

A couple hours had passed but I still sat by myself staring out the window. Everyone had taken their turns trying to talk to me, but I brushed them aside. My dad plopped down next to me and poked my arm repeatedly. I rolled my eyes and turned towards him.

"Yes, father?" I asked.

"Oh, *father*, is it?" he questioned, his eyes swimming with amusement. "Well, *daughter*, I just came to tell you life sucks so get over it."

"Seriously?" My eyebrows shot up at his unusual callousness, and he chuckled.

"Of course not," he replied. "I mean, it's true, but I have a much more sensitive and understanding way I was going to present it."

"Thanks for the life lesson."

"Come on, Robin. This isn't like you. I know you're hurting, but do you really want to become that person who takes their own problems and inflicts them on others?"

I sighed heavily. "No. Of course not."

"Look around, kiddo. Ben is miserable, Alexander is . . . Well, I believe he's upset. It's hard to tell since he's always so angry."

"Dad."

"Yes, right. Anyway, they're both upset, and all your friends are down in the dumps because they're concerned about you. It's a pretty somber mood in here and, as much as I hate to say it, it's because of you." I looked down at my hands as he continued. "I'm not saying you have to pretend to be happy for their benefit, but maybe you should try to find the light in this dark tunnel for yourself. That way, you can enjoy the time you have with the ones who are leaving before they're gone."

"You're right," I murmured. "I'm sorry."

"You never have to apologize for how you feel, kiddo," he replied as I leaned into his hug. "I just wanted to give you an outside perspective."

"I needed it. Thank you."

"That's what I'm here for. Now, go. Make peace before we land."

"Make peace?" I repeated, arching one brow.

"That's what I said. Now shoo!"

I stood up and let him usher me away as I made the quick decision to go to Alexander first. That was the least complicated of the two. I could feel everyone's eyes on me as I sat beside him.

"Should I hold your hand to really rile them up?" he asked with a devious smile.

"*No.* You should not," I replied.

"Just thought I'd ask."

"You're not funny."

"No, not usually," he agreed, and I rolled my eyes as he grew serious. "I apologize for my behavior before. I wasn't trying to cause any problems. Being cruel to someone beneath me is just my natural instinct, I'm afraid."

"That'll change over time," I replied. "No one expects you to disregard what's been branded into you overnight. But he isn't beneath you. He may not have powers, but he's braver than all of us combined. You want to know why?"

"Do enlighten me."

"Because he'd risk his life for me or any of the others despite knowing he's completely powerless. He's the weakest of us all, and he knows it, but he'd still jump in front of us if danger came our way."

Alexander didn't reply as I looked towards Ben. He routinely glanced our way but immediately averted his eyes every time he realized I was still watching him.

"I see why you love him," Alexander said softly. "He's the opposite of me in every way."

"I love him for different reasons than why I'm attracted to you," I told him. "And that's a good thing."

"How so?"

"Because it proves you aren't a replacement of him."

"What do you mean?"

I pressed my lips together as I tried to figure out how to explain what I meant. "If I was to fall for someone exactly like him . . . It wouldn't be because I loved them. It'd be because they gave me back part of who I really did love. At least I can say for certain, that's not what's happening with you. I like you for you. Not for what you can give me of Ben."

"I suppose that makes sense."

"In a twisted kind of way, right?" I said with a small smile.

"Indeed." He returned my smile, but it didn't meet his eyes. "Although, seeing you with him is actually quite harder than I thought it'd be."

"Imagine how he feels," I replied. "We both need to give him some grace."

"Not my strong suit."

"Please?" I asked. "For me?"

He exhaled sharply. "I'll do my best."

"Thank you." I patted his hand then stood to hit my next mark. I stopped in front of Mateo and asked, "Mind if I sit here for a minute?"

"It's all yours," Mateo replied, happily obliging.

As soon as I sat, Ben spewed out an endless slew of words. "I'm so sorry about all that. I don't know what got into me. I really did mean it when I said I wasn't here to cause any problems. I would never try to insinuate you're a damsel in distress. It's just, well, I get overprotective, and I know that's not my place anymore but—"

"Ben," I cut him off. "Breathe." He did as I said, taking a deep breath. "I'm not mad anymore, okay? I know you meant well. You always mean well."

"Sometimes it gets the best of me," he admitted with a wry smile.

"It does," I agreed. "But you wouldn't be Ben if you weren't always trying to do what you thought was right."

"Does that mean you forgive me?"

"If you don't interfere with conversations between me and Alexander again, yes."

"Of course! Not my place. I'll keep the jealous rage to myself."

"I'd appreciate it," I replied.

He said it as a joke, but the seriousness layered in his tone told me there was truth in it. He was raging on the inside. I rubbed my lips together as I realized just how hard this was for him.

"So, are we good then?" he asked hopefully.

"Of course."

A half smile lit up his face and he said, "How about that game now?"

CHAPTER NINETEEN

"Look!" Mateo called out, pointing to the window next to him.

I looked through the one closest to me and let out a gasp as my eyes widened.

There was nothing but green almost as far as the eye could see. The thick canopy of trees was vast with a never-ending variety of hues that radiated under the setting sun. Different water channels weaved in and out of the forest, some murky and some a beautiful shade of blue. It was a sight like no other.

"It's beautiful," Andre said from beside me.

"Imagine what the forest floor looks like with all the different flowers and animals," Emery replied.

"Kodi, you have to see this!" Mateo exclaimed.

"Nope, I'm fine right here," Kodi responded, her eyes planted firmly on the plane floor.

"Have you ever seen anything so extraordinary?" Ben asked as he stared out in awe.

"I sure have," Alexander murmured, and when I looked over at him, he was watching me. My cheeks flooded with heat, and I suppressed a smile as his simple words made my heart flutter.

As we all continued to leer outside, a familiar territory took shape. The river we followed flowed right into a massive opening in the earth. The valley made an almost perfect oval but was cut short by a mass of mountains that sat out of place in the terrain. The middle of the oval held the tallest group of trees, which seemed thick and unwelcoming. It was the map's location.

"Alright, kiddos," Dad said from the front of the plane. "Time to buckle up."

We all took our seats again, and Mateo tried to comfort Kodi as we began to descend. Her already pale face had reached a sickly ghost-like hue, and I tried not to laugh. If anything happened to the plane, there was more than one way we'd all remain safe because of the powers we had on board. Being afraid seemed silly.

"Where did we land?" Matthew asked.

"On what would be the west side of the map," Malachi replied. "Good thing there's such a wide-open space on this side, otherwise we would've had to parachute down."

"P-parachute?" Kodi choked out.

"Dude, we're already on the ground," Emery told her. "Calm down."

"We're going to canvas the area then camouflage the plane. We'll camp out in here tonight then head out first thing tomorrow morning," Malachi said. "Let's go, troops."

William, Matthew, Demetri, and Vivi followed him out of the plane as Luna took a seat next to Alexander. He appraised her with a less than ecstatic expression, and she stared back, unfazed. I watched through the window as the guards spread out in different directions, zoning the area for possible threats. Ten minutes later, they were all back by the plane talking, and Malachi gave us a thumbs up.

"Anyone ready to stretch their legs?" Dad asked as he and Akio stood.

"Yes! Yes, yes, yes," Kodi replied excitedly, running ahead of the rest of us.

When I stepped outside, my senses went on overdrive. The field we stood in was bare of everything other than luscious green grass that rose around my calves. But beyond the tree line there was a leafy paradise. The squawking of birds echoed through the umber-brown forest in the distance, and the churning water rushing into the valley roared. The smell of the water hit me like a ton of bricks, and I breathed in deeply as my feet gravitated towards it.

The river was a comforting deep blue that begged me to jump in and go for a swim. Jagged rocks cut through the top in places, dividing the liquid before it swirled back together. I stepped closer to the edge where the waterfall began and peered over cautiously. The drop was a good hundred feet down, and the waves looked unforgiving. I gulped as I backed away. Falling in there was a death sentence.

"Someone's going to fall down there," Andre said.

I turned to see all the trainees and Ben looking at the hole in the ground as cautiously as I'd been.

"Who?" Emery asked.

"That brown haired guard," he replied.

"Vivi? How?" I questioned, and he shrugged.

"I can't see that. Just her falling."

My stomach churned at the thought.

"Well, let's just go tell her to stay away from it then. Problem solved, right?" Ben asked.

"Yeah," Mateo agreed. "Easy peasy."

"I don't think it'll change even if we do that," Andre replied slowly.

"Why not?" Emery questioned.

"Sometimes my visions are crystal clear—sharp in color and contrast. Other times they're dull or murky," he explained. "I've slowly come to realize that the clear ones have always happened no matter what. The dull ones, though, don't always."

"So some visions are solidified, and others are . . . What?" Kodi asked. "Dependent on a different variable?"

"Yes, exactly," Andre replied. "And this one . . . It's set."

"Shouldn't we still warn her though?" I asked. "What if you're wrong and something *can* still change it?"

"I'm not wrong," he said.

"He isn't," Alexander said as he stepped up behind us. "I'm surprised you figured that out on your own, Andre, but you're right. Clear images are what *will* happen, while dull ones are what *could* happen. Many people have tried to change the outcome of a vision they saw coming, but that only makes it worse. You're better off keeping things like that to yourself."

"You *would* think that," Kodi muttered.

"I don't say it with malicious intent," Alexander told her. "I say it as a caution. Trying to change the outcome of a vision set in stone is dangerous to anyone involved. You'll likely end up dead with her."

"You can change your destiny but not your fate," Ben said softly.

"What?" I asked.

"It's the old destiny versus fate argument," he replied. "People believe you can change your destiny but not your fate. It's the exact same concept as what Andre is seeing."

"I suppose it is," Andre said, his brows drawn together. "Dull is destiny and clear is fate. Huh. I never thought of it like that."

"In layman's terms, yes. That's exactly right," Alexander said with a slight nod of approval.

"Then I can't tell her," Andre concluded, his eyes tight. "And I shouldn't have told any of you. Now it's everyone's burden to bear. I'm sorry."

"You don't have to go through that alone," Emery told him, placing her hand on his arm.

"But he should," Alexander stated.

"Another unexpected sentiment," Kodi said sarcastically.

"The less people who know, the less chance of someone trying to stop it from happening. Which means less people getting hurt," Alexander retorted. "But if you want to risk your life pointlessly, by all means, go ahead. I won't lose any sleep over it."

He turned on his heel and walked away as we stared after him.

"I see why he has trouble making friends," Ben remarkeded. I shot him a look, and he held up his hands defensively. "On the flip side, I see his point. It comes off crass, but everything he said makes sense."

"Unfortunately it does," I agreed. "Guess that means we all need to keep quiet about what Andre saw."

I received different levels of agreement, then we walked back to the plane as the sun started to disappear entirely.

"Everything is safe and secured," Malachi told us. "The guards and I will take turns keeping watch tonight, so you can all sleep soundly."

"Elijah and I are also going to be taking turns sleeping," Luna added before peeking over at Ben. "We'll make sure there's nothing to fear."

I bit my tongue to keep myself from shooting her a nasty look.

If she keeps this up, we'll have one less Keeper of Balance returning home.

I quickly kicked the back of my heel, shocked at my own thought. She was barely flirting, let alone doing anything worth getting violent over. Even if she did make a move on Ben, it wasn't my place to get possessive.

I suddenly felt a new wave of respect for Ben. If I felt like this over harmless flirting, I couldn't imagine the genuine rage he was fighting back at seeing me with Alexander—someone who loved me and whom I was falling for.

"Tonight, we feast!" Dad exclaimed playfully. "Enjoy it while you can because every other meal will be whatever fruits and veggies Luna can conjure up."

"Unless we can find an animal to cook," Matthew pointed out, and Kodi's face turned pale.

"What's wrong?" Mateo asked as they walked to the plane. "You're not a vegetarian."

"No, but I don't want to hear some poor animal's distress," she replied.

"Oh, yeah, that would suck," Mateo said.

"Just make sure to cover your ears then," Emery said, and Kodi scowled.

Not wanting to leave the fresh air yet, I plopped onto the ground and was joined by Andre, Matthew, Alexander, and Ben. We soaked in the last of the sun rays as Akio joined Malachi in pacing around the field. Meanwhile, Dad and Luna stacked twigs and branches in a pile. Luna pulled out a match, but Ben was on his feet and pulling it out of her hand before she had a chance to light it.

"Have you two every made a fire before?" he asked hesitantly.

"No," they both replied.

"Okay, well, lesson one: clear out the brush," he said as he pocketed the matches. "If you start a fire here, all this grass is going to catch on fire too."

"Oh, how smart!" Luna exclaimed, and I scoffed as my eyes rolled to the back of my head.

"Your jealousy is showing," Matthew said under his breath. "And I'm not the only one who sees."

He nodded towards Alexander, who was watching me too. I looked down and picked at the grass as embarrassment crept through me. Ben continued to make the fire—with my dad and Luna watching with interest—but I kept my focus on Andre and Matthew as they talked about what was to come.

Soon enough, food was made and ate, then everyone began to turn in for the night. As the sounds of heavy breathing and snores sounded around me, I tossed in my recliner chair uncomfortably. I looked out the window wh-ere Luna sat with one of the guards. William paced not too far away from them, his eyes peeled on the forest. I peered up, and my breath caught in my throat at the number of stars that lit up the dark sky.

I quietly snuck around the sleeping bodies in the plane and shivered slightly at the cool breeze that touched my skin when I stepped outside. William gave me a nod of acknowledgement as I walked to the center of the field. I stared up then fell onto my back, letting the grass envelope me like a blanket as I breathed in its earthy scent. The twinkling stars were brighter than I'd ever seen them, and I couldn't help but smile at the joy their beauty brought me.

Grass rustled under heavy footsteps, and I thought one of the people on watch was coming over. When I glanced up, though, I was surprised to see Alexander instead.

"May I join you?" he asked.

"Of course," I replied, and he lowered himself next to me.

"What are you doing?"

"Just enjoying the stars."

"One of my favorite pastimes as well," he noted, and I gave him a look. "Yes, I know. Gardening and star gazing? How very un-villainesque."

"You read my mind," I joked.

"You're an open book."

"I am not!" I denied. He raised his brows, staring me down until I caved. "Okay, fine. Maybe I am."

"You should be careful about that. It may not serve you well sometimes."

"What do you mean?"

"Earlier when you were watching Ben with Luna," he said, his voice low, and I rubbed my lips together, knowing exactly what he was referring to. "You were jealous."

"Yes," I admitted softly. "I'm sorry."

"Why are you apologizing?" he asked with his lips turned down.

"Aren't you mad?"

"Why on earth would I be mad? I may be a bit jealous myself about it, and I'd be lying if I said it didn't hurt some, but I have no claim on you. You've barely ended things with the man. I'd expect nothing less than for you to act that way."

"Then why are you bringing it up?"

"I wanted to point out that if *I* can see that emotion so clearly on you, I'd imagine Ben could as well," he replied. "If you two are trying to find a way to remain friends, I don't think either of you will benefit from knowing the other still desires you."

"But we both know that whether we hide our jealousy or not," I said quietly, letting my eyes travel over the stars as I searched for answers that weren't there.

"Robin." Alexander hesitated, so I looked over at him. "Can you be happy? Without Ben in your life, I mean. Can you thrive? Or will you always just be merely content?"

I took a deep breath and looked away, his question catching me off guard. "Don't you think it's way too early to be asking me that?" I questioned with an edge in my voice. "Like you said, we've barely broken up. Of course my answer is going to be 'no' right now."

"I know."

I sat up as emotion bubbled through me. "Why are you asking me that then? You're the one who said you'd wait for me to get over him. You're the one who said you thought I could love you one day too. You're the one—"

"I know what I said, and I meant it." He sat up beside me and grabbed my hand. "But after seeing you interact with him—seeing the way you both look at one another—it just makes me concerned."

"Concerned about what?" I asked in exasperation.

"That you won't ever love anyone the way you love him," he replied gently, "and, to me, that's a tragedy. Yes, I think you could love again. Yes, I think you could love *me*. But to what avail? How true will your happiness be?"

My chin began to tremble, the annoyance disappearing as crushing heartbreak took its place. My breath was shaky as I exhaled, Alexander's words breaking the wall I tried to put up. Without permission from me, I started spewing word vomit.

"I'll always love him. I know we're young, and people don't think high school sweethearts are forever but . . . I know without a doubt that he's the love of my life." I sniffled and pulled my legs to my chest as if that would hold me together.

"Sure, I'll move on eventually. I'll fall in love again and be happy but . . . He'll always be in the back of my mind, ya know? I'll always wonder how he's doing and if he's happy and what our life together would've been like. He'll always be the one that got away." The corner of my mouth turned up slightly. "He'll be that person that I reconnect with after my husband dies, and it'll be like no time has passed at all."

"What?" Alexander questioned.

"Like in all those romance movies," I explained. He still looked troubled, so I said, "Never mind," then sighed. "I'm just afraid he'll always be my biggest regret. Could I have fought harder for us? Was there something I could've done to convince him to stay with me in Garridan? I mean, why wasn't I worth changing his life for? Why am I not enough? Why won't he just stay with me?"

A broken sob escaped my mouth. Alexander wrapped his arm around my shoulders, and I buried my face in his chest. I thought I heard soft footsteps walking away from us but didn't give it much thought. A guard must've seen my breakdown and retreated.

After a while, the tears stopped, and I sat back up, wiping my cheeks. "I'm so sorry," I told Alexander, embarrassed by the lack of control over my emotions.

"Don't be. You're grieving a loss," he replied.

"How can you still be willing to wait for me when you know I'd choose him over you if the chance came?" I asked quietly. "You deserve better than that."

"Do I though?" he asked with a humorless smile. "After every horrible thing I've done, this seems like karma's take on justice. Loving a girl who can be happy with me but never truly love me with all her heart. Seems fair. Not like anyone else could ever love me anyway."

"That's not true!"

"Isn't it? I may live in Garridan, but it'll never be my home. I'll never be accepted. I'll never make friends. I'll never know what it's like to not be hated."

"Have you . . . Have you ever considered doing what Kodi and Mateo are doing?" I asked hesitantly.

"No."

"Why not?"

He looked at me with a mixture of emotions swimming in his eyes. "Because you're here." He looked up at the sky then gave my hand a light squeeze. "Come on. We need at least a little bit of rest before the sun rises."

I let him help me off the ground, then we walked back to the plane. As I got settled back in my seat, I glanced over at Ben then quickly did a double take. I squinted through the dark, swearing I'd seen his eyes open and watching me. But when I looked again, they were closed, and his chest was rising and falling rhythmically.

Must've just been my imagination.

CHAPTER TWENTY

"Hey," Ben greeted me as he walked up with his hands in his pockets.

"Hi," I replied with a smile as I continued cleaning some of the mess from breakfast.

"How did you sleep?"

"Not great. Those seats are pretty uncomfortable."

He chuckled. "That they are. I tossed half the night myself."

I wasn't sure how to respond, so I asked, "Did you need something?"

"No, no," he replied quickly. "Just wanted to say hi. Need any help?"

"Sure. You can dry." I tossed him a towel and went back to twirling the dirty dishes in the river water.

"You'd think it would've been easier to have brought paper plates and plastic utensils."

"You know, believe it or not, I don't think I've ever seen those in Garridan."

"Really?"

"Yeah." I sat there dumbfounded. "Huh. Strange."

"But very environmentally friendly," Ben pointed out with a grin.

"True. Maybe that's why actually."

"What else can you tell me about Garridan?" he asked nonchalantly.

"A lot. What do you want to know?"

"Anything."

"Why the sudden interest?"

"I've always been interested, but I never really had time to ask. The one time you came to Milton, I didn't want to waste it with silly questions."

"It's not silly," I assured him softly. "It makes me happy you're asking. I'd like to share that part of me with you. I've always wanted to."

"And I want you to too," he replied, his own voice just as soft as we watched one another. "So, any other *strange* things about Garridan?"

"Where to begin?" I laughed lightly. "So, there's no pets. There's birds and ducks and turtles and all that kind of stuff outside but no dogs and no cats."

"None?" he asked, flabbergasted.

I shook my head. "None. I keep telling my parents they need to introduce them into their world because everyone would *love* it but, so far, no luck."

"That's crazy!"

"I know!" Both our smiles reached our eyes, and my heart stirred. We could have genuine conversations like before after all. "Also, there's no college. There's smaller schools for specific powers that need to be better refined—like healers—but that's it."

"What if someone needs a lawyer?"

"That's what the Keepers of Balance are for."

"Vet?"

"Why would we need one if there's no animals?"

"Touché."

I laughed, the lighthearted feeling taking a weight off my shoulders. Maybe we could do this after all. We could still be friends. We could talk without there being any bad blood. He really knew what he was doing when he volunteered to come with us. One day, I might just have to tell him that.

We continued to discuss Garridan and all the different powers it held within its walls as we finished the dishes and walked back to the plane. As we got closer, I noticed Kodi talking to Vivi. Both their expressions were bleak, and I knew exactly what she was doing.

"Oh, no," I murmured.

"What?" Ben asked.

"I think Kodi told Vivi about Andre's vision," I replied. I handed him the dishes I was carrying. "I'll be right back."

Vivi was already walking away as I came up. I crossed my arms as I stared at Kodi, but she wouldn't meet my gaze.

"What did you do?" I asked.

"Nothing," she replied, her voice an octave too high.

"Kodi."

"Yes?"

"Did you tell her what Andre saw?"

"Of course not."

"Kodi."

"Yes?"

"You're lying."

"Maybe."

"Kodi!" I exclaimed.

"Stop saying my name like that!" she insisted, looking at her feet. "She deserved to know."

"If Alexander is right, which we have no reason to doubt that he is, then you just put your life at risk too."

"Yeah, because Alexander is always so trustworthy," she muttered, and I sighed.

"He has no reason to lie, and he knows a lot more about people's powers than we do. You can hate him all you like, but you can't disregard his knowledge."

"Whatever," she said before shuffling past me.

I let out a frustrated growl then rubbed my hands over my face. She was about to surpass Emery in the attitude department.

"Alright, everybody, gather around please," Dad hollered. When we were all in hearing distance he said, "We're going to have a quick debriefing session. Please listen while Malachi and William go over the plans."

"Okay, guys," Malachi said. "All the backpacks are packed, and the plane has been secured, which means we're ready to head out."

"As you know," William spoke up, "our mission is to find the tree known as Silas. We believe he's in this center portion of trees, so once we get across the valley, it should be a straight shot to him."

"I don't think it'll be as simple as that," Alexander said.

"And who asked you?" William asked in annoyance.

"Nobody, but it's still true."

"What makes you say that, Alexander?" Luna asked, stepping up next to him as if he were going to cause an issue.

"There are three incantations on the map, one of which is on the complete opposite end of where we are currently. Silas wasn't so daft as to create it for fun. There's a reason it's there, which means we'll somehow need to get to that side as well."

"Or maybe it was simply for whoever started on that side," Luna suggested.

"Perhaps, but I doubt it."

"We don't even know what those words mean. They could just be the works of a crazy man," William said.

"Silas was anything but crazy," Alexander replied.

"You have no way of knowing that."

"Don't I?"

"Do you?" William asked with narrowed eyes.

"Well," Malachi interjected, seeing his son's growing agitation. "I suppose we'll get our answers soon enough. Getting over that valley is a simple enough task, but we perceive this trek will be anything but easy. So, please, everyone keep your eyes sharp and expect the unexpected."

"Almost everyone here is more than capable of protecting themselves if something happens," Luna added, "but let's try to watch each other's backs regardless."

"And let's all keep a special eye on Ben," Dad said, his face apologetic as Ben scowled unhappily. "We want to take him back home in one piece."

"I got you, man," Mateo told him, slapping him on the back.

Emery snorted. "If he had to choose, I don't think you'd be at the top of his list of protectors."

"Like you would be?" he shot back.

"Electricity is pretty deadly."

"I could turn into a lion and eat you."

"Not if I fry you from the inside out and eat you first."

"Let's get going," Malachi inserted, ending their strange rebuttals.

As we marched closer to the edge of the canyon, I grew more and more uncomfortable. The place where my powers resided slowly emptied, becoming a distant feeling. With every step, they were yanked further from their home, and I suddenly felt empty like I had when Isaac stole them away.

"What's happening?" Matthew asked, and I realized everyone's faces had the same look of confused agony.

"What's wrong?" Ben questioned as his gaze jumped from person to person.

"Our powers are gone," I answered quietly.

"What? How?"

"I don't know."

"It's the land," Luna said. Her eyes closed as she carefully continued to walk, and she held her hands up by her waist as if sensing the earth beneath her. "It's absorbing them like how a power canceler would."

"I can feel it too," Alexander agreed. "The ground is pulsating under us."

"Does that mean we can't use our powers the entire trip?" Akio asked, his frown deepening his wrinkles.

"I wish I knew," Luna replied, her thin brows furrowed.

"So much for getting across the valley being easy," Emery said. "What are we supposed to do now? Build a bridge?"

"Repel down the side?" Mateo suggested.

"Jump?" Dad proposed, and most of us rolled our eyes.

I stepped closer to the edge, staring down at the bubbling water below as it churned unforgivingly. Suddenly, the ground began to tremor, and my knees almost gave out beneath me. Ben grabbed my arm and pulled me back before I lost my balance into the drop off. A piercing ringing sounded in my ears, and I covered them as my eyes closed tightly.

"Welcome to Zohara, my eternal resting grounds," a deep-toned voice radiated through my head. When I opened my eyes, I could tell by everyone's expressions that they were hearing the same thing I was. "Your trials begin now. Be prepared because I will push each and every one of you to examine who you really are. Are you worthy of seeking me out? Only time will tell." The voice paused, and a chill crept up my spine. "To get across the gorge, you must sacrifice your own. For each individual you eliminate, four others will be transported to the other side. I suggest you choose wisely."

The ringing in my ears disappeared, and I rubbed my arms to try to get the lingering cold out of my body.

"He can't be serious," Dad said.

"There's no way," Luna agreed.

"That goes against everything we stand for," Akio added.

"Some sort of sick joke," William said.

I thought back to Andre's vision then glanced to Vivi, who looked pale. Was this why Andre saw her falling?

"We can find another way across," Matthew said.

"How?" Demetri asked. "Our powers are gone."

"Maybe we can just walk until the canyon ends," Dad suggested.

"The map showed no end until the mountain range," Luna reminded him as she twisted a lock of hair around her finger. "Which means we'd have to find a way to climb that, and we don't even know if it's possible without seeing it."

"Plus, who knows how long it would take to walk that far," William added.

"The answer seems obvious to me," Demetri said.

"What would that be?" Malachi questioned.

"Do as Silas instructed," he replied, and it was instantly met by harsh disagreement. "If that's what was directed of us, it's only smart to listen."

"How can you possibly think sacrificing a life is okay?" I asked in disgust.

"I'm not saying it's right, but if it's what we need to do to find Silas, I don't think we have a choice but to do as he wants," he replied.

A small argument broke out, no one listening to anyone else as our voices rose. I shook my head and pressed my lips together tightly.

This shouldn't even be a conversation.

"Demetri, no!" Kodi yelled.

My head snapped towards her just in time to see her jumping forward as Demetri pushed Vivi over the cliff. Vivi screamed wildly and frantically raked her arms around, knocking Kodi over the edge with her.

"Kodi!" Mateo cried out.

Alexander sprung forward, grabbing Kodi's hand as she fell. He landed on his stomach with a thud, the weight of her dragging him halfway into the canyon, but he held on tightly. Ben and Matthew dived in to help, grasping Kodi under her arms and pulling her to safety. She fell into Alexander, shaking uncontrollably, and he awkwardly pat-ted her back as she clung to his shirt.

Vivi's bloodcurdling screams echoed around us as she plummeted to the bottom. I faintly heard the splash of her body hitting the water and fell to my knees as William punched Demetri in the face.

"What the hell were you thinking?" he yelled.

"I solved a problem like we've always been taught to do," Demetri answered, staring straight ahead as he moved his jaw around.

"We don't solve problems like this!" Malachi inserted angrily. "What right do you have to choose to end someone else's life? You *murdered* her, Demetri."

Before Demetri could reply, his body began to ripple. In the blink of an eye, he disappeared from in front of me and reappeared on the other side of the valley. Andre, Matthew, and Luna followed immediately after.

"It-it worked," Ben said, dumbfounded.

"What kind of monster makes you kill your own?" Mateo asked in horror as he knelt next to Kodi.

"I don't know, son," Dad answered, his eyes wet.

"One like Toshiro," Akio responded, his voice barely over a whisper.

"How do we decide who's next?" Emery asked shakily as she stared at the canyon with wide eyes.

"We don't," I replied harshly.

"But you just saw—"

"No," I cut her off, full of hostility. "We will *not* kill another person. We shouldn't have killed even one! Our own interests in finding Silas doesn't give us the right to compromise our integrity." I looked at Mateo and Kodi, who had inched far away from Alexander. "Is going back home with your memories intact worth killing someone?"

"No," Kodi managed to squeak.

"Absolutely not!" Mateo exclaimed.

I looked at Dad and Malachi. "How about the council? Is learning about Silas worth sacrificing your own citizens?"

"Not in the slightest," Dad answered, his lips in a hard line.

"Vivi was a wonderful person," Malachi said, his brows knitted tightly together. "Nothing is worth what just happened to her."

"Then let's figure out how to get those four back over here and go home," I said, my voice unwavering in my command. "Our hunt for Silas is over."

The ground started to shake again, and I leaned forward to steady myself as it intensified. The rumbles of the earth overtook all my senses as it got louder, and my whole body vibrated. The grass brushed against my ankles in an unruly pattern as the trees in the distance swayed angrily. I watched with wide eyes as large chunks of rocky dirt jutted out from both sides of the canyon. They connected in the middle with a deafening boom then everything became still, and all was quiet. We had a way across.

Ben offered me his hand, and I took it gratefully as I stood on shaky legs. We all stared at the path before us with open jaws.

"What just happened?" Mateo asked.

"I'm-I'm not sure," Dad replied, just as stunned as the rest of us.

"Look, something happened to Demetri," William said, pointing.

I looked over and saw his body convulsing on the ground. Luna held him on his side, but he began to screech and thrashed away from her. Malachi carefully stepped onto the walkway. When he confirmed it was safe, he darted across with Akio right at his heels.

They tried to calm Demetri down, but he clawed his face, leaving bright red marks behind. He stood frantically then fell to the ground again as bubbly froth dripped from his mouth. He took a loud breath in, then another, then went limp.

"Help him!" Luna commanded Akio.

"I can't," he said, falling to his butt as his head sagged. "He's already dead."

The rest of us slowly sauntered across the passage one at a time, eyeing it with distrust as Dad asked Luna what happened.

"I don't know. He was fine before the bridge popped up, then he just fell to the ground after," she explained as her hands got knotted in her hair.

"I don't understand what's happening," Ben murmured, grabbing the back of his neck as he stared at Demetri's body.

"You're not alone," I assured him quietly. "We're as lost as you are."

"Actually," Alexander said, rubbing his chin thoughtfully, "I think I've got it figured out."

"Do you really?" I asked as everyone eyed him.

"Silas said he was going to test each and every one of us to see if we were worthy of seeking him out. He also said our *trials* begin now."

"Right. And?" Emery asked.

"Do you remember what the riddle was on this side of the map?"

"Uhm . . . *Only the pure will be allowed inside my sacred ground,*" I started.

"*If your heart is wise and true, the way across is found,*" Matthew finished.

"Exactly," Alexander stated. We stared at him, not understanding, and he sighed. "Only those that Silas deems worthy can find him. To weed out the ones who aren't worthy, he's going to give us trials we have to pass. My guess is three since there's three incantations on the map. This first one was a test of a pure heart basically."

"Okay, I get it," Andre said. "He told us to kill to find him, but what he really wanted was for us to refuse and decide finding him wasn't worth murdering our comrades."

"Precisely," Alexander said. "Once that decision was made, the bridge across appeared because he found us 'pure of heart.'"

"That makes sense," Dad said, and Malachi nodded. "Good work, Alexander. At least one of us could make some sense of all this."

"But what happened to Demetri?" Akio asked.

"He killed Vivi. It was his punishment from Silas," Matthew responded quietly.

We stared at his body, and I swallowed around the lump in my throat. We knew this wasn't going to be easy, but I didn't expect to lose two team members in the first five minutes.

"We should transport his body back," Luna said.

"Why?" Kodi asked angrily. "Vivi's body won't be brought back. And if it wasn't for Alexander, neither would mine."

"I understand your anger," Dad told her. "But, right or wrong, we can't in good conscience leave him here to rot."

"Since we don't have a teleporter anymore, I'll place a petrification on him, and we can load him into the plane," Matthew said. "That way his body will be preserved and not start to smell."

I felt around inside and realized my powers were back. I leaned into them, breathing deeply as they swam through my body. It wasn't much, but it made the day seem less gloomy.

As Demetri's body was taken care of, I joined the trainees.

"Are you okay?" I asked Kodi.

"I'm fine," she replied. "A little shaken still but fine." She glanced towards Alexander. "Why did he save me? He used to *want* us dead."

"No, he didn't," I said. "He was just doing what he'd been trained to do by the Cyfrin."

"Now that he's not under their rule, I think we'll get to see the real Alexander," Andre said.

"Just like you've been trying to tell us," Mateo said to me.

Kodi looked at the ground. "I feel like I should say thank you but . . ."

"You don't have to," I said.

"You don't," Emery agreed, and Kodi nodded, but she continued to glance over at him uncertainly.

Maybe this was the start of them seeing Alexander as less of a villain.

CHAPTER TWENTY-ONE

As we began our walk to the tree grove, the mood was still somber from the events at the gorge. The further we got away from it, though, the lighter the mood became. Aside from Malachi, William, and Matthew, everyone was chatting or laughing.

"Thank you for what you did for Kodi," I told Alexander as I caught up with him.

"There was no reason for two to die," he replied.

"She's grateful, you know. She just isn't ready to tell you that yet."

"And she may never be. None of them may ever be after what I put them through, and I can't say I blame them."

"They'll come around. So will the people in Garridan." I placed my hand on his arm and smiled reassuringly. "You won't be hated forever."

"Your optimism is refreshing but highly unlikely."

"You don't really believe that, do you?"

"I do, actually," he replied with a shrug.

My lips turned down. "Well, I'll never stop giving them reasons to like you."

The corner of his mouth twitched. "I believe that too." He looked at me with soft eyes. "My own personal advocate."

"As long as you need," I replied.

Emery's raised voice caught my attention as she yelled at Andre. He walked past her, annoyance written all over his face, and she violently kicked at the ground.

I bet she's picturing his face beneath her foot.

"I'll be right back," I said to Alexander absently as I went over to her. Her eyes were narrowed, and she scowled harder than I'd ever seen. "Is everything okay?"

"Absolutely peachy," she replied sarcastically.

I stopped and touched her shoulder, and she looked at me with a little less hate. "What's going on with you two?"

She glanced at the ground as her shoulders raised in a shrug. "A lot."

"Want to talk about it?"

"Not really," she replied unconvincingly as she walked away from me.

I followed after her, staying by her side as I observed her expression. "I don't think that's true."

"Because you're just all knowing?" She bit her lip as her nose grew red, and I realized she was trying not to cry.

"Hey, talk to me," I insisted as my brows furrowed. "Why are you crying?"

"Because I'm frustrated."

"At Andre?"

"Yes." She glanced over to where he stood talking to Ben and Akio. "And no." She took a deep breath and after a moment said, "We both went and met our birth families a couple weeks ago."

"You did?" I asked in surprise, and she nodded. "Why didn't you tell me?"

"You were a little preoccupied with the somnokinesis withdrawals. Oh, and being a total nightmare to be around."

I frowned at the reminder. "I'm sorry."

"You couldn't help it."

"I'm still sorry though. I hate knowing how awful I was. Especially if it made me miss out on some important things you guys were going through. I never wanted you to go through it alone. I wanted to help you transition here."

"Well, we don't always get what we want," Emery commented.

"Yeah, I know." After an awkward pause, I asked, "So, how did meeting your families go?"

"Depends on who you ask."

"Okay, well, I'm asking you so?"

She smiled wryly and softly said, "It was great."

A smile lit up my face. Her reply was so simple yet so impactful.

"My parents were so nice and inviting," she continued. "They gave me the biggest hug when I introduced myself."

"I'm surprised you let them," I said with raised brows, and she grinned.

"I was pretty tense at first. Almost hit them, actually." Her eyes danced at the memory, and I tried to suppress a laugh at the image. "But then it just kind of felt right somehow, and I hugged them back. I can't explain it."

"You don't have to. I understand."

"They were just so happy to see me. I've never felt that loved or wanted." She glanced at me, her cheeks reddening slightly. "It was nice."

"I'm glad. You have a sister, right?"

She nodded. "Her name is Ember, and she looks so much like me it's scary. She's married and has a kid of her own. He's three. Cute as a button."

"That's awesome."

"Yeah. Kid loved me for some reason."

I snorted. "And here they say kids are a good judge of character." She socked me in the arm, and I let out a trill of a laugh. "Kidding. I'm happy you clicked with them so well."

"I really did. Especially my dad. He has the same powers as me and showed me some things he and his team are working on for Garridan. It's really neat and gave me a lot of ideas."

"Like what?"

"It's hard to explain to someone who doesn't understand electricity. But basically, ways to hone Garridan's electrical use into more substantial areas that will actually lessen the usage overall. That way, the extra electricity can be put towards newer technology that won't drain nature like our ancestor's accidentally did."

"Oh, wow. That seems like a big undertaking."

"It definitely is, but my dad loved the ideas and said I could work with him and his team to actually make it happen. It'll take some time—well, a lot of time—but I'm really excited about it. If it works, I can help Garridan so much."

"I'm excited for you," I told her. "It sounds like you finally found where you belong."

"I think I did," she agreed. "I'm happy . . . I'd just be happier if Andre was happy too."

"What happened when he met his family?" I asked.

"It's just his dad and it was a disaster."

"Why?"

"His dad was so sad. He could barely look him in the eye because he looks so much like his mom."

"Because his mom is gone," I commented quietly.

"Yeah. She passed away not long after they had to give up Andre. I guess she got really depressed and she ended up committing suicide."

A gasp escaped me. "That's awful!"

"I know," Emery agreed as she stared over at Andre with sad eyes. "His dad seemed like a really nice guy, but he just couldn't handle being around Andre. I hate to say it, but I think he might blame Andre for his mom dying."

"That's not Andre's fault at all!"

"I know that but . . . Well, you know better than anyone what grief can do to a person. Andre's dad didn't say he blamed him or anything, it's just the vibe I got."

"Does Andre know you think that?"

She nodded. "He thought the same thing. He was hoping to have a relationship with the guy, but now he feels like his presence will only make things harder for him."

"Is that why he's still considering leaving?"

"Yeah."

"That's a really tough situation," I murmured.

"He has every reason to go, and no reason to stay."

"No reason except you."

"I don't think that's enough," she whispered.

I rubbed my lips together before saying, "I understand."

"How could you possibly understand?" she snapped. My eyes traveled towards Ben, whose face was lit up with a wide smile as he jostled Mateo away from him. Emery noticed my stare and said, "Oh. Maybe you do understand."

"It isn't an easy feeling."

"No, it definitely isn't."

"Just remember everything else you have waiting for you in Garridan," I said quietly. "A family who loves you, friends you'll never lose, important plans for your future . . . You have so much going for you. Don't let a guy—even such a special one—ruin how happy you are about all that."

"Are you saying that for me or for you?" she asked with a raised brow.

The corner of my lip turned up. "Both."

"At least you have another option waiting for you when Ben is gone."

"It's not the same."

"Yeah, I figure, but at least you have a backup plan."

My forehead creased. "That's not what Alexander is."

"Isn't he?"

"What am I now?" Alexander asked, and I realized Emery and I had fallen to the back of the group where he strolled, escorted by Luna.

"Nosy," Emery responded.

"On the contrary," he replied. "It's only natural to be attuned to your name."

"Doesn't mean you have to—"

"Everybody down!" Malachi yelled, cutting her off.

Alexander pulled me to the ground, bracing his body over mine as a wave of heat hit my skin. A bright green light blinded me for a moment then pierced the outer layer of trees we were venturing towards. It was hard to see since they were still quite a ways away, but their bark seemed to snap off, leaving deep indents in the trunk. At second glance, I realized they were slightly charred as well.

I peered ahead, my eyes searching madly for Ben. When I saw him on the ground unscathed, I let out a sigh of relief. He was looking at me as well, his expression matching my own.

"You can get up," William said, a flickering ball of protection already surrounding us. "Nothing is getting through my force field."

"What was that?" Emery asked.

Alexander helped me off the ground as we glanced around for the source of the threat.

"It looked like some sort of laser," Matthew answered.

"But it was so hot," Malachi said. "I've never known a laser to transmit that kind of heat."

"Whatever it was, it burned the trees," I said.

Malachi squinted towards them. "It did indeed. Lasers don't burn like that. Fire does."

"I didn't see any fire," Matthew replied.

"It had to be there in some form. I'm sure of it," Malachi stated.

"Was it sent by Silas?" Luna asked.

"I know I'm a stranger to all this, but I would say no," Ben said.

"Why's that?" Matthew asked.

"He considers this his sacred ground—his final resting place," Ben replied. "I don't think he'd do anything to destroy it. Not even char a few trees."

"If we go by that logic, we have to assume it was an outside threat then," William said.

"You mean there could be someone else here?" Kodi asked nervously as her eyes skirted over the terrain.

"If there is, they have to be good people," I said. "Otherwise, they couldn't have gotten across the valley."

"Unless they killed their own to do it," Alexander pointed out. "When Andre, Luna, and Matthew were transported across with Demetri, nothing happened to them."

"If Silas doesn't want bad people on his land, why would he allow them to stay?" Dad asked.

"I mean . . . Maybe they'd be tested at the next trial," I suggested. "Matthew, Luna, and Andre didn't have a choice in coming over, so they couldn't prove themselves, but Silas wouldn't punish them for that. He'd just make them prove themselves next time. Maybe the other people here are the same way."

"Or maybe they're hiding in the tree line on the other side of the gorge," Malachi said.

"Or maybe they followed us over the bridge afterward," William countered. "It was still there after all."

"Who could possibly be here at the same time we are? No one from Garridan," Luna said.

I glanced over at Matthew then Alexander. Both their faces looked as grim as I felt.

"It's Mallory," Alexander said, his lips pressing together as he shook his head.

"That would explain the heat," Malachi said. "They must also have someone with a laser ability with them and they forged their two powers together when they targeted us."

"Great," Emery muttered. "Not only do we have to worry about these 'trials' killing us, but also madman Mallory and her maniac pals."

"How did they find us though?" Mateo asked.

"Arthur can locate power sources, remember?" I said. "They've probably been tracking us every time we leave Garridan." My brows furrowed as my heart sank. "Which means we led them right to Randy and Genevieve."

"This is why you shouldn't use your powers outside of Garridan," Dad said sternly. "This is why the council is so strict."

"You're not really trying to say it's her fault, are you?" Ben asked defensively.

"Of course not, son," Dad replied. "But there's a lesson to be learned for her here, and she knows what it is." He looked at me with a no-nonsense expression and I averted my eyes, ashamed. "We'll discuss that later though. For now, we need to figure out what to do about Mallory and Arthur and the others."

"We're sitting ducks out in the open," Matthew said.

"Yes, and as long as they're hiding, we'd lose valuable time trying to search them out," Malachi said. "I propose we keep moving forward with William's protection. Matthew and I will take the rear and watch our backs as we go. At least in the trees we'll have better coverage."

Luna and Dad discussed that possibility for a moment before nodding their heads. "We trust your judgement," Luna told Malachi. "Let's get to the trees and decide from there what to do."

I kept my eyes down as we scurried forward. Mateo rubbed my shoulder as he and Kodi passed me by, but all I could feel was shame. I trailed behind everyone except Mal-achi and Matthew as I got lost in my own thoughts. Ben slowed his pace until I was by his side, and he nudged me with his arm so I'd look up at him.

"Randy and Genevieve dying wasn't your fault," he told me.

"If I hadn't used my powers when we were around them, Arthur never could've tracked us," I said. "Mallory and her lackies wouldn't know about them or the map or Silas or anything. Randy wouldn't be dead. Genevieve wouldn't be dead. Your family wouldn't be in danger, and they wouldn't be here trying to hurt us now. It *is* my fault."

"You didn't pull the trigger that killed them, Robin."

"Actually, knowing Mallory, they were probably burned to death." Ben stared at me, horrified, and I lifted one shoulder as I shook my head. "My world . . . It can be a dangerous one. That's why the council has such strict rules. My dad's right. I needed to learn that. I'm always pushing the council to ignore them or just bypass them because I think they're silly but . . . They're not. Our worlds . . . They just don't go together. Silas' generation proved it before, and Mallory definitely proved it now."

Ben was quiet for a minute. "I don't think that's neces-sarily true. Even in the normal world, people and countries are fighting for power. We live with violence every day."

"You're forgetting one big difference though," I said, sorrow weighing heavy on me. "Someone from my world could wipe out an entire city in one sitting."

"So could a nuke."

"Ben!" I exclaimed. "This is serious."

"I know that, and I *am* being serious. There are monsters in every world. I don't think that should stop you from do-ing what you're doing."

"What am I doing?"

"Trying to muddle the line between Garridan and the rest of the world," he answered. "It may not be intentional, but every time you've gotten them to let you leave or when you convinced them to bring me there, it's what you've done. You've been showing them Garridan doesn't have to be completely cut off. You may even be showing them they can lower their guard."

My eyebrows scrunched at his interpretation of my actions. That hadn't been my intention at all.

Is that what I was doing?

"Garridan is too afraid of the outside world. They don't want to risk destroying everything they've worked for," I said with a shake of my head. "They'd never let their guard down, especially after all this with Mallory. Honestly, because of her, the council will be harder than ever about enforcing the rules." I looked up at him with a wry smile. "So, even if you and I do manage to come out of this as friends, it's almost pointless. We'll never see each other again anyway."

"I wouldn't be so sure about that," he replied softly. "There's other ways our story can end."

"What do you mean?"

"Just . . . Have a little faith in the unknown. I have the feeling our days of seeing each other won't be over after we find Silas."

He said it with such certainty, his eyes filled with nothing but love as he stared at me. I opened my mouth to ask what he meant again, but he strutted away without another word.

"What was that about?" Matthew asked as he crept up behind me.

"Eavesdropping?" I accused.

"Unintentionally. So, what was that about?" he asked again.

"I honestly have no idea." I watched Ben's hair bounce as he walked next to Andre and Emery.

"Does he know something we don't?"

"It sure seems that way, doesn't it? Or maybe he's just being his overly positive self," I added with a small smile.

"I'm not so sure about that," Matthew said, his forehead scrunched as he thought on it more. "I'm going to find out what he knows."

"You do that," I replied with a shake of my head as he jogged to catch up to Ben.

"So much for watching your backs," Malachi commented as he watched his son leave his post.

I grinned. "I'll take his spot."

"At least I can count on one of you kids."

"I'm just better like that," I joked, and he laughed before taking another scan of our surroundings.

After walking another two hours, we were finally coming up on the tree line. I sighed in relief, my throbbing feet begging me for respiration.

"Finally," Kodi groaned.

"I don't think I could walk another step," Emery grumbled.

"Just a little bit longer," Dad assured them. "We'll stop once we get some coverage from the trees."

"Thank goodness," Mateo said, followed by a dramatic sigh, and Andre nodded in agreement.

"You all need to buck up," William said.

"They aren't soldiers, son," Dad reminded him. "Don't expect them to have the same stamina that you do."

"Yes, sir," William replied as Malachi shook his head in mock disappointment.

"Look, there's something up ahead," Luna said, and everyone's focus turned to that.

"I don't see anything," Dad replied, squinting as he looked.

"I see it," Malachi murmured. "It looks like a translucent force field."

"Does that mean we can't go any further?" Akio asked.

"I guess we'll find out," Matthew replied, walking forward.

"Be careful," William told him as he created a space for him to exit the force field around us.

Matthew cautiously advanced, his eyes darting to and fro as he took in the nearly invisible barrier in front of us. When he got close enough, he slowly raised his arm, reaching out to touch it. He hesitated right before his fingers landed on it then brushed his hand the rest of the way forward. The second his skin made contact, he evaporated.

"Matthew!" William and I yelled simultaneously.

My fingers and toes began to tingle. A strange pulling sensation traveled through my body just as everyone in front of me disappeared one by one. I took a step back and lifted my hands, as if that would somehow help, but the rest of my anatomy stretched forward—almost painfully—and the world around me went black.

A marble effect of colors spiraled around as my body became nothing but dust caught in a windstorm. I didn't have time to panic or think before I was suddenly on the ground in one piece again. I looked around wildly as I ran my hands over my body to check for injuries. Our group was scattered about, slowly sitting or standing and looking as confused as I felt.

Monstrous mountains towered above me and in the distance was a grove of trees. On either side of the mou-ntains, deep holes maimed the ground and ran forward as far as the eye could see.

"What happened?" Ben asked, his face pale.

"We teleported," Matthew answered, offering him a hand.

"That didn't feel like the time Charles teleported us," I muttered, feeling queasy myself.

"All teleporters are unique with the traveling process," Malachi said. "Some have good side effects and others don't. This one, though, that was a doozy."

"Are you saying there was a teleporter around and we didn't see them?" Alexander asked.

"No. This was definitely different," Malachi answered. "It's as if a station, if you will, had been set up. The teleportation powers were there alone."

"Is that even possible?" William asked.

"We just saw that it is," Malachi said. "It must be Silas' doing."

"But why?" Kodi asked.

"And where are we?" Mateo added.

"We're on the opposite end of where we started from," I said as I stood. "This is the right side of the map."

"So, you're saying that grove of trees," Emery pointed towards them, "is the exact one we *just* reached?"

"Yep."

"Which means we have to walk all the way over there *again?*"

"Yep," I repeated grimly, about to throw myself back on the ground. Half the group groaned, and I sighed heavily.

"Why would Silas send us all the way to the other side?" Andre asked.

"To pass the second trial," Alexander answered.

"It makes sense why we needed all three map pieces," Matthew said. "He knew we'd be traveling to each spot."

"So, what's the second trial?" Akio asked.

"Your guess is as good as any of ours," Matthew responded as he pulled out a pad of paper. "The words on this side of the map said: *We've all lost loved ones through the years. It's shaped us to who we are. Through all the pain, suffering, and tears, you must learn to accept your scars. If you can't, you won't advance. You'll seal your fate forever. Stuck in the past, locked in the fog, life will reach you never.*"

"Does that mean anything to anyone?" Luna asked.

"Well, the first half is simple enough," Ben said. "Accept the pain of the past or you won't move on."

"Literally or metaphorically?" I questioned.

"It's hard to say," Alexander said. "It mentions 'the fog' though. Not *a* fog but *the* fog. So maybe it's literal, and we'll be captured in an endless fog if we can't move on from whatever ails us."

"I don't see any fog," William said.

"Doesn't mean it won't creep up on us," Matthew replied.

"Or maybe its metaphorical, and we just need to sit and reflect for a while," Dad suggested.

"You want us to sit and . . . Reflect?" Kodi asked, her nose scrunching.

"What could it hurt?" Dad replied.

"Our timeline," Luna said.

"Our mental health," Emery added.

"Would you rather continue on and risk failing the trial and seeing what the consequences of that entails?" Alexander asked them.

Everyone exchanged looks then, one by one, sat down. I leaned against a rock sticking out from the ground then pulled my water bottle from my bag. I met Matthew's eyes then Ben's, Mateo's, Kodi's, and Emery's. The awkward silence started to become amusing, causing pursed lips and suppressed smiles to form. I pressed my own lips together to keep from grinning.

"This is only going to work if we all stop looking at each other," I said loudly before closing my eyes and leaning my head back. I breathed in deeply, trying to concentrate.

What am I supposed to reflect on?

Silas' words talked about the loved ones we've lost. Did that mean my mom and Dawn? A lump formed in my throat.

Nope. Not going there.

Instead of thinking about anything, I focused on my breathing. Reflecting was for the birds. I started to relax my body as my mind fluttered around uselessly. The sun shone down, and the birds cawed as they flew overhead. If we weren't in danger, I'd enjoy this.

"Mind if I sit?" Alexander asked.

I peeked out of one eye and saw him standing above Kodi. She hesitated and looked at Mateo, who only shrugged, then nodded. He cleared his throat as he settled next to her.

"I thought we were supposed to be reflecting," she said.

"That's what I'm doing," he replied, staring straight a-head. They sat in silence for a while before Alexander spoke again. "A lot of what I have to reflect on is far in the past, and there's nothing I can do to relieve the weight of my misgivings."

"Sounds like a personal problem."

Alexander's lip twitched. "That it is. However, there's a few people who are heavy on my mind that are very close by. Perhaps something can be done to ease that."

"Doubtful."

"I'd still like to try."

Kodi pressed her lips together, and Mateo nudged her gently. "He did save your life," he reminded her.

"I didn't save her life to gain forgiveness," Alexander stated. "If you don't want to listen to an apology, that's your choice. Maybe you can do me a favor instead."

"Seriously?" Kodi asked incredulously.

"I just . . ." he glanced my way, and I quickly closed my eyes again hoping he'd think I was asleep or too busy reflecting to pay attention. "I have questions."

"About?" Mateo asked.

"Your world," he answered.

Kodi and Mateo side eyed one another before their curiosity got the best of them. "What do you want to know?" Kodi asked.

"I'm not entirely sure," he said, his brow furrowed. "Why do you two want to go back? What's so appealing that you'd give up your powers to return?"

"Well, for me, it's my family more than anything," Mateo answered. "My little siblings still need me, and I just can't picture any type of life without them in it."

"But they aren't your real family," Alexander said.

"They may not be my biological family, but they most definitely *are* my real family," Mateo replied firmly. "Genetics don't determine family. It's just like with you and Matthew. You aren't blood related but you still consider each other brothers."

"I see," Alexander said. "What about you, Kodi?"

"My parents play a part for sure but also . . . I just like my world better," she said. "Don't get me wrong, it has its flaws and there's days I'd rather be anywhere else, but it's still home. I can go anywhere and do anything without being defined by some stupid power level. In my world, everyone is considered equal, and that's the way it should be. Plus, there's a ton of different cultures. I could travel my whole life and still not know all the different people in the world."

"That does sound intriguing," Alexander said.

"It is," Kodi agreed. "When I get home, I'm going to travel as much as I can. I could never be happy confined to one place like the people of Garridan are."

"You'll just have to save up money first," Mateo commented with a grin.

"How does one do that?" Alexander asked.

"Seriously?" Mateo questioned.

"I'm familiar with the use of money, and I remember it being important when I was younger and in your world. But we didn't have it in the Cyfrin compound. Everything we needed was just . . . There."

Mateo and Kodi exchanged another glance. "You get a job," Kodi said.

"What sort of job?"

"Any job that's hiring. Most people start out in fast food or retail," Kodi explained. "But you can go to school to train for a specific job that interests you."

"Like what?"

"Well, the big ones that need a college education in our world are doctors, lawyers, vets, that sort of thing. But you can go to trade schools for jobs like plumbing, electrician, welder, etc.," Mateo answered. He must've noticed Alexander's perplexed expression because he said, "You don't know what any of that is, do you?"

Alexander lifted one shoulder, his face hardening slightly. He didn't like not knowing things.

"I suppose your world is too complicated for me to understand," he said grimly.

"Nah," Mateo said with a wave of his hand. "It would just take time to learn. No different than us trying to learn about Garridan while we were there."

"If you were thrown into our world like we were yours, you'd adapt," Kodi told him.

"I suppose I'd have to," Alexander said quietly.

"Is there any reason why you're asking?" Kodi questioned, her eyebrows furrowing slightly.

"No," he replied almost harshly, and she narrowed her eyes.

Before she could say anything, her eyes fluttered shut, and she slumped over. I opened my mouth to call out to her, but a familiar feeling filled my body—a feeling I would never forget. My head whipped around, searching for the person responsible as the groggy sleepiness crept through me. My eyes began to close just as I saw a handful of blurry figures appearing out of nowhere.

CHAPTER TWENTY-TWO

"Wake up, Robin," a distant voice said, and I could barely feel my shoulder being shaken. "Wake up."

"Is she okay?" another voice said.

"She's fine." The voice became clearer, and I recognized it as Matthew's. "They all are. They're just sleeping. They'll wake up when they're ready."

"Why are you waking her up then?" the second voice, Ben's voice, asked.

"The Cyfrin used somnokinesis on her for a long time, so she had horrible withdrawal symptoms for weeks," Matthew explained as he shook my shoulder again. "When you've gone through that, it's best to not be touched by that kind of power again. The longer she's asleep, the longer the somnokinesis is in her, and that's not ideal for someone who could easily slip into those side effects again."

"I see," Ben said, and I could hear all the anger he was feeling in those two simple words.

I let out a small moan, trying to fight the strength of Darnell's powers, but my eyes refused to swim through the haze around me.

"My dad and Akio are waking up," Matthew said. "Stay with her. I'll be right back."

As he walked away, Ben gently pulled me onto his lap with my head resting on his arm. He pushed my hair out of my face then rested his hand against my cheek.

"You're the strongest person I know," he said quietly as his thumb stroked near my ear. "I can't even imagine everything you've gone through lately, but here you are still fighting—still trying to help others. No matter how many times the world wrongs you, you're still the selfless and caring person I love."

He swallowed loudly then inhaled deeply as I began to succumb to the sleep that pulled at me again. When he spoke again, his voice was full of emotion.

"You're more than enough, Robin. You're worth changing my life for, and I'll never forgive myself for letting you think otherwise."

Wait, what, I thought before I was overcome by darkness again.

* * *

"Robin. Robin!"

I whined loudly, just wanting to be left alone.

"I swear if you don't open your eyes, I'll petrify you into next year." I struggled to open one eye, peering out from the blurry space to see Matthew with his arms crossed. "That's better. Sit up."

He pulled my unwilling body into a sitting position, and I slouched into him as I tried to wake up completely. "What do you want?" I snapped.

"Someone's cranky," he noted with amusement.

"I'm not ready to wake up."

"I know, but you have to. We need to get the somnokinesis out of you."

I blinked once, then again, then sat up quickly as I looked around. "Darnell really was here?"

"Yes," Matthew answered grimly. "They all were. They ransacked our supplies while we were sleeping, and I'm assuming took off to hide again. They left us with nothing."

"Well, water has an easy solution," I said as I lifted the palm of my hand with some liquid sprouting from it. "We can live without clothes and toiletries, even if it is gross, and Alexander and Luna can both make food."

"They're both passed out."

"That's unfortunate," I commented as my eyes found their sleeping bodies.

"We'll just have to see what we can find here. Berries, mushrooms, animals, anything."

"Kodi's going to love that," I said as I continued to look around.

It was already getting dark. Only half our team was awake, and I suspected the rest would sleep through the night. Ben sat next to Andre, who was holding Emery's hair back as she leaned over the backside of a rock.

Wasn't Ben over here earlier, or did I just imagine it?

"Is Emery okay?" I asked.

"Darnell's powers didn't work on her fully," Matthew replied. "She's just nauseous from it."

"There are worse things."

"You would know."

Malachi and Akio walked to where Ben, Emery, and Andre sat. Malachi motioned us over, and we quickly obliged. I plopped onto the ground as I yawned, not ready to stay standing.

"Half our group is still asleep," Malachi stated, "and now we know for sure that a threat is out there possibly hunting us. They didn't kill us when they had the chance, which makes me think they want to toy with us a little longer. Maybe pick us off one by one."

"Who is it exactly?" Ben asked. "What are their powers and . . . Danger levels, I guess I'll call it?"

"Mallory is a fire element," I said. "She's younger than us, but she's crazy. Killing is second nature to her, but she's extremely limited. She has to have a source to gain fire from. She can't just pull it out of thin air like I can with water."

"She usually keeps a handful of lighters on her to get it from," Matthew added.

"But with Robin here, she has to know she's vulnerable," Andre said. "Robin drenched her one time at the Cyfrin compound, and her lighter got wet, so she couldn't fight back with her power."

"Compared to others with her element, she's very weak," Malachi said. "But still dangerous, nonetheless. There's also Darnell, who has somnokinesis powers. He's the one who put us all to sleep in one clean sweep, so I'd say he's a threat. We can't do much to protect ourselves if we can't even stay awake."

"He can't penetrate forcefields though. So if William can keep a constant one around us, we should be safe enough from him," Akio said.

"True, but maintaining that for too long isn't ideal," Malachi replied. "A few hours max is all we can expect, and he's asleep right now so, unfortunately, we don't have him to rely on."

"Arthur is with them as well," Matthew said. "He can locate power sources, but he's not any kind of threat. He's definitely not a fighter, physically or power wise."

"After talking with Alexander, we also know a camou-flager named Jenson is with them," Malachi cont-inued. "That's probably how they're hiding actually. He's a decent fighter from what we were told. Aside from that, Alexander wasn't too informative if anyone else was unaccounted for. He knew the big names in the compound, not all the 'little people' as he put it."

"We didn't exactly associate with the members who lived in town," Matthew admitted. "Only during the yearly gala."

"Which means there may be more people with them that we don't know about," Malachi said.

"We know there's one for sure," I pointed out. "Whoever has that laser power."

"True," Malachi replied. "So, really, we're a little blind on what we could be up against."

"That's not very reassuring," Ben said with a sigh.

"Don't worry, Ben," Malachi told him. "We won't let any harm come your way."

"It's not just me I'm concerned about," he replied, glancing from me to Matthew.

"We can take care of ourselves," Matthew assured him, and I nodded in agreement.

"Doesn't make me worry any less," Ben said with a frown.

"Nonetheless, we will *all* be okay," Malachi said, looking from one face to the next. "I don't like it, but we need to send people out to look for food."

"Too bad Alexander's asleep," Emery muttered. "The one time he could be helpful."

"What do you mean?" Ben asked.

"He could make some berries or nuts or something," Matthew replied. "Luna too. Once they're awake, food and water won't be an issue between them and Robin. But, for tonight, it's up to us to gather something ourselves if we want to eat."

"Our people here need to be protected as well," Malachi said. "They can't do anything to ensure their own safety right now, so whoever stays needs to be on high alert."

"Whoever goes needs to be as well though," Akio said. "We don't know how far Mallory and the others went, or if they'll try to attack again."

"Sounds like a picnic either way," Emery commented.

"Matthew and I will stay," Malachi said, ignoring her. "We're much better suited to the task of protecting than hunting down food."

"I'll stay as well," Akio told him. "Just in case anything happens while the others are sleeping and they need a healer's attention."

"Sounds good," Malachi agreed. "Robin, Andre, Emery, are you good with finding food? It's not going to be safe out there in the open."

"We've been through worse," I replied with a wry smile. "Besides, Emery and I will probably make a deadly team if we combine our powers."

"That's what I like to hear," Malachi said with a chuckle. "Just be safe, okay? I could never face your father if I let something happen to you."

"We'll be fine. I promise."

"I want to go too," Ben said.

"I don't think that's wise, son," Malachi replied. "We can better protect you here."

"I trust Robin to keep me safe."

"Or you'll distract her just enough to where she can't keep herself safe," Matthew said.

"Just for that, let him come," I said as I made a face at Matthew. "He's as safe with us as he is with you guys."

I could tell Malachi was hesitant to agree, but Emery stood and crackled some lightning in her palm. "Wanna fight for him?" she asked playfully.

Matthew rolled his eyes as Malachi half smiled. "No, I suppose I don't," he said. "If you want to go, Ben, it's your choice."

"Thank you," Ben replied before looking at me with a grin. "Let's go foraging."

"We'll see you guys in a little bit," I said, giving Matthew a reassuring look as he scowled.

"Let's create a perimeter around the others," Malachi said as Ben, Emery, Andre, and I walked away.

"We better find something good," Emery said. "I'm starving."

"You were just throwing up," Andre replied. "How can you even be thinking of food?"

"Because I'm hungry," she stated with a look that dared him to argue.

"I wish they hadn't taken our flashlights," I said as I squinted through the ever-growing darkness.

"At least the stars and moon are bright enough to light a way," Ben responded.

"Do you really think we'll find anything out here?" Emery asked.

"Surely there's something edible," Andre replied. "This is the most luscious place on the planet."

"Should we break off into two teams to cover more ground?" Emery asked.

"We're already split off from the others," I said, "so it's probably better to stay together."

"I think so too," Andre agreed.

"Only because you're scared of the dark," Emery said, and he rolled his eyes.

"Why are you so mean to him?" Ben asked suddenly. I raised my brows and looked away, knowing the attitude he was about to get.

"Excuse me?" Emery snapped.

"Why are you so mean to him?" Ben repeated as Andre and I exchanged a glance. "I don't know how long you two have been together, but you don't act like you love him."

"*Excuse me?*" she repeated, her voice filled with venom as she stopped walking and placed her hands on her hips.

"I'm just an impartial outside eye but, to me, it seems like he does nothing but treat you well, but all you do in return is give him grief," Ben told her.

"What are you—a psychologist?" she hissed, her hands sparking with the light blue hue of electricity. "Sure, I'm not the nicest person, but he knew that when he asked me out."

"Maybe he thought you'd be nicer when you got out of the Cyfrin compound. Now he knows you're always a jerk, and that's why he wants to go home instead of staying with you."

"That's not true!" she yelled as Andre and I looked on, not knowing what to do. *What is Ben doing?* "He knows I'm an ass, and he loves me anyway!"

"How do you know?"

"Because he told me!"

"Too bad you don't love him back."

"I do too love him!" she cried out before placing both hands over her mouth as her eyes jumped to Andre.

"You do?" Andre asked, his face lighting up.

She slowly lowered her hands and nodded. "Of course I do. How could I not? You're . . . Amazing."

"You never said it back," Andre murmured as he walked up to her. "All these weeks I've been waiting to see if you'd say it back, and you never did. I thought you didn't feel the same way."

"I do, Andre," she said as he grabbed her hand. "I just . . . I'm no good at this. I suck at emotions. I didn't know how to let myself say it back in case you changed your mind."

"You know you don't have to put up that hard exterior with me," he said. "And I'll *never* change my mind."

Ben nudged me with his arm and tilted his head to the side. I nodded and followed him away from Andre and Emery so they could have some privacy. We didn't wander too far, just enough to where we couldn't hear them.

"You did that on purpose, didn't you?" I asked him.

"Yeah," he admitted sheepishly.

"I gotta say, I'm a little relieved. I thought you'd gone crazy there for a minute. Everything you were saying was so unlike you."

"I know, and I didn't mean any of it. It's just the push she needed."

"How did you know that?" I asked. "How did you even know what was going on between them?"

"Mateo told me. I didn't ask, I swear," he insisted as he threw his hands up defensively.

"I believe you," I said with a laugh. "He's a big eavesdropper and, turns out, a huge gossip. Not a great combo."

"I haven't been around them very long, but they're all pretty easy to pinpoint. It wasn't hard to guess what would rile Emery up enough to admit her feelings. No sane, meaningful conversation would've done the trick."

"You're not wrong," I said as I shook my head. "Why did you do it though? You're not usually one to butt into other's lives."

He stuck his hands in his pant pockets and looked at the ground. "I guess I just didn't want them to have any regrets. I know what that's like, and I'd do anything to go back and change it if I could."

He looked up, his wide eyes meeting mine as I pressed my lips together sadly. We stared at each other for a long moment, then he reached out and stepped towards me as he opened his mouth to say something.

"Hey, let's hurry and get some food," Emery demanded as she and Andre walked up behind us. The look she threw Ben was somewhere between deep hate and sincere gratitude, but she didn't acknowledge him.

I cleared my throat as Ben stepped back again. "Yeah," I agreed. "Let's go."

CHAPTER TWENTY-THREE

"I'd say we did pretty good," Andre said as we were walking back to the campground.

I could see the faint flicker of light and smoke billowing up. At least one of them knew how to build a fire.

"It'll be enough to last until tomorrow for sure," Ben agreed, surveying our packs full of grapes and edible ferns. "Not very filling, but at least we won't be starving."

A sudden heat hit me from behind and I started to sweat as the air around me thinned. "What is that?" I asked as I fanned my face.

"What's what?" Emery questioned.

None of them seemed to have any idea what I was talking about.

"You don't feel that heat?" I asked before clearing my throat.

"No," Emery replied as Ben and Andre shook their heads. "Are you okay?"

My eyebrows scrunched then my eyes widened as realization dawned. "Mallory!" I yelled as I threw a fountain of water around the four of us.

"Where?" Emery asked, wildly trying to peer around the water.

"I don't know," I muttered.

We stood there encased by the only thing that would keep Mallory's fire away, but without being able to see anything, we were helpless.

"You have to lower the water, Robin," Emery said.

"If I do, we could all get burnt to a crisp," I replied.

"If you don't, we're sitting ducks to the other's powers," she shot back.

I looked from her to Andre to Ben. Andre nodded in agreement, and I bit my lip as I contemplated it. She wasn't wrong, but was it worth it?

"Okay," I finally said. "I'll lower it just long enough to see what's out there. Then we need to run towards camp."

"Okay," Andre agreed, and Emery nodded once.

"Okay," I repeated. "Get ready."

I took a deep breath then let the liquid barrier around us fall. My eyes searched our empty surroundings, desperately trying to locate the danger.

"I don't see anything," Ben said.

"I don't either," Andre responded.

"Me neither," I said, "but she's out there. I know she is."

"Let's just back away while we can," Emery said.

"You can run, but you can't hide," Mallory's snippy voice called out. My head whipped from one side to the other, but I still didn't see her. "You *ruined* my life when you took the Cyfrin away from me. I thought it'd be fitting to do the same in return—take everything from *you*, that is."

"Where is she?" Andre grumbled as we tightened our stance beside from another.

Mallory cackled. "I considered killing you all at once but picking you off one by one seemed more fun."

A miniscule line of fire scorched Emery's upper arm, and she yelped in surprise. I threw water in the direction it came from, hoping to drown Mallory's powers.

"Missed me," she said, and I could picture her sneer as another fiery shot enflamed Andre's shirt.

I immediately put it out, but Mallory was fast to lash out again. I raised the water from the ground, letting it drench us to the bone.

"It won't do much, but at least our clothes and hair won't catch fire so easily," I muttered as I glared at the empty space ahead of me. "You guys need to run. Let me hold her off."

All three of my comrades were quick to object, and I ground my teeth together.

"Aw, isn't that sweet," Mallory said, before letting out a snort. "Makes me sick. You know, Robin, if I just take you out now, I can make the others suffer." She paused then said, "I think I like that plan. Are you ready to join your fake mommy and sister in the afterlife?"

I saw red as she laughed. Her body appeared directly in front of me with her hands lifted, and a blinding orange radiated from them. Before I could do anything to react, Ben yelled 'no' and pushed me out of the way. I landed on the ground, and looked up as he cried out in agony. Mallory's burning inferno encased him with a vengeance, and I let out my own scream as he fell onto the grass beside me.

I submerged his body in the cool liquid that could ease his pain then sent a jet stream flying towards Mallory. It struck her in the side, and she screeched as it pierced through her skin.

"Emery!" I called out, and she flung a surge of electricity into the water.

Mallory's body quivered, and her eyes rolled to the back of her head as she fell forward.

"Grab her!" someone yelled, and she disappeared again. Heavy footsteps thudded away from us then everything went silent.

"Are they gone?" Emery asked breathlessly.

"I don't know," I said through gritted teeth as I watched our surroundings.

"We need to get him back to Akio," Andre said, tearing through my tunnel vision, and I looked down. He knelt next to Ben, who was clenching his fists and jaw. Burns covered the better half of his body, and I could tell he was trying to contain his agony.

"What the hell were you thinking?" I yelled at him as I fell to my knees.

"I didn't . . . want you . . . to get hurt," he managed to say between deep breaths, and it took everything in me not to smack him.

"You idiot! I wouldn't have gotten hurt!" I cried out. "You can't just jump between me and danger. You're going to get yourself killed!"

"I just . . . wanted to . . . protect you."

I sighed heavily, then swallowed around the lump in my throat. "You idiot," I repeated quieter. "You can't protect me here. I have to protect you so, please, don't do that again. Okay? You've taken care of me most of our lives. Let me take care of you this time."

He nodded, flinching at the motion. I bit my lip, trying to ignore the urge to puke as I stared at his split, disfigured skin. The blackened wounds flaked as he moved, and the smell of burnt flesh wasn't helping.

"Can you walk?" Andre asked him, and he nodded again with less motion. "Let's *carefully* help him up. Try not to grab the places where his skin is burned."

Ben let out a pained groan as Andre and I helped him off the ground. We put his arms over our shoulders to help ease some of the weight on his legs as we walked. Emery slowly followed, backing up as she kept her eyes peeled for another attack.

"Are you okay, Em?" Andre asked without looking back.

"A little toasty but nothing as severe as Mallory got," she replied.

I glanced over my shoulder. The ends of her hair were charred, and her fingertips were dotted with black. She'd electrocuted herself to attack Mallory.

"I'm sorry," I told her. "I didn't think about you being wet."

"No biggie," she said. "Could've been a lot worse. Let's just get back to camp before someone else decides to show up."

I nodded, focusing on the space ahead of us. The trek was pure torture as I watched Ben's face twist in misery. He huffed out breaths between low moans, having to stop every couple feet as his legs became too wobbly.

"We're almost there," I murmured as he stopped again. "Just a little bit further."

"How are we looking Emery?" Andre asked as he glanced back.

"Still not a sound," Emery replied, her eyes never leaving the space behind our backs.

As we came closer to the campground, I saw the outlines of the three men standing on duty. Ben slumped over, and I struggled to hold him up.

"Matthew!" I yelled, my voice breaking slightly. "Malachi!"

"They're back!" Malachi called out as he, Matthew, and Akio jogged our way.

When they saw Ben's limp form between us, they picked up their speed. Malachi and Matthew took mine and Andre's places, taking on his full weight with ease as we rushed to where the others were still lying, completely ignorant to our events.

"What happened?" Malachi asked as they gently placed Ben on his back, and Akio knelt beside him.

"Mr. Macho Man thought he could take on fire," Emery explained as she plopped to the ground.

"He jumped in between me and Mallory," I clarified as I sat on the opposite side of Akio.

"Of course he did," Matthew said with a shake of his head.

"Always the protector," I murmured as I stared at his marred face.

"Will he be okay?" Malachi asked Akio.

"Of course," he replied, his hands already traveling over Ben's body. "Give me an hour, and he'll be good as new."

"Wonderful," Malachi responded before peering at me. "Sounds like we need to talk."

I nodded, gave Ben one more glance, then stood and joined the others.

"We got enough food to last everyone tonight and to-morrow for breakfast," Andre was telling Malachi and Mat-thew.

"That's great," Malachi replied. "Thank you for going out to find it."

"We didn't mind," Emery said.

"Nevertheless, it sounds like you had quite an encoun-ter," he said. "What exactly happened?"

"They have a camouflager with them," I said with a shake of my head. "We couldn't see where they were, and Mallory started taunting us."

"Yeah, first with her whiny voice then with her power," Emery added with disgust.

"She said we ruined her life when we took the Cyfrin away from her, and she was going to make us pay," Andre said. "She's not going to stop attacking."

"We have to stop them while we're still here," Matthew said, his arms crossed tightly across his chest. "If they fol-low us back, they're going to cause chaos. They'll probably reveal themselves to the normal world and go on a giant killing spree just to draw us out."

Malachi rubbed his hand over his face then said, "Unfortunately, I think you're right. They need to be caught before they can do any true damage to Garridan."

"Tell us what to do, and we'll do it," I said. "She's hurt enough people already."

"Not until tomorrow," he replied firmly. "We aren't doing anything without a full force behind us. Especially when we don't know if they have any more surprise companions."

"When everyone wakes up, we'll fill them in and devise a plan," Matthew agreed.

"Until then," Malachi said, "let's all keep our eyes peeled. We can't let our guard down for a second."

He directed us to designated spots that created a half circle around our sleeping comrades. Since we were directly in front of the mountains, we didn't have to worry about both sides, which gave us a fighting chance. We just had to maintain safety on the front, and that was easily done with the number of us that were awake and able.

Emery sat close on my left side, and I scooted closer to her.

"Are you and Andre . . .?" I trailed off, raising my brows insinuatingly.

She smiled softly—a look that was odd on her usually downcast face. "We're good," she said. "We're more than good."

"Is he planning on staying now?"

"I'm not sure," she answered with a shrug. "He kept telling me he wasn't basing his decision solely on me, and I guess he really meant it."

"Did you think telling him how you felt about him would sway his decision?"

"Yeah." She fiddled with a leaf and realization dawned on me.

"Is that why you didn't tell him sooner?" I asked.

"Partly," she admitted. "I didn't want to be the reason he stayed and ended up miserable."

"Do you think he'd really be miserable though?"

She shrugged again. "I'm not the most delightful person to be around."

"It's endearing once you get used to it," I said with a grin.

"Oh, thanks," she muttered sarcastically.

"Andre is a really sensible person." I placed a hand on her shoulder. "Your feelings for him may play a part in his decision but, in the end, he'll choose what's right for him. If he decides to stay, don't let yourself feel guilty. Just . . . Be happy. Okay?"

She nodded and glanced at me, her eyes less guarded than usual. "Thanks."

"You're welcome."

I scooted back to my spot, letting my gaze travel over the trees in the distance. Were Mallory and the others camped out in there or were they somewhere closer just waiting to strike? All I knew was I'd be on edge the rest of this trip unless they were caught.

* * *

A twig snapped behind me and I whirled around, immediately on the defensive. My adrenaline faded, repl-aced by relief when I saw Ben walking up with his hands in the pockets of a pair of sweats. He'd also changed his charred shirt out for a tight-fitting sweater.

"I think you need a bigger shirt," I commented with a smirk.

He pulled at it uncomfortably. "Mallory's gang didn't leave many options behind from our extra clothes, so I'm afraid this is what I'm stuck with."

"On the plus side, it really brings out your athletic build," I said, my grin widening as his face flushed a deeper shade of red. "If it was any smaller, we might be able to call it a crop top."

"Okay, I get it," he mumbled, running his hand through his hair. I let out a laugh but didn't say anything else. "I really screwed up, didn't I?"

He sat beside me, and I shrugged. "It definitely wasn't the smartest move," I answered.

"I didn't even think before I jumped in front of you."

"It's just in your nature—being protective, I mean. But I hope you learned your lesson."

"Definitely. Around here, *I'm* the damsel in distress," he replied lightheartedly, and I smiled.

"That about sums it up," I confirmed. "How are you feeling?"

"As good as new. But, sadly, I can't say the same for my hair though."

I reached out and ran a piece through my fingers. "You're lucky I got you wet when I did, otherwise it would've been a lot worse. It definitely needs a good trim though."

"I'll do it as soon as we get home."

"You mean when *you* get home," I said.

He blinked a couple times and furrowed his brows as he quickly said, "Yeah. Yeah. That's what I meant."

"I'm sure you're ready to go back to your life, huh?" I asked softly. "Your normal, uncomplicated life."

"You sound jealous."

"I guess I am a little bit. Sometimes I wish I could go back to the way things were. It was so easy compared to all this. It was simple."

"And a lot less life threatening."

"That too."

"You know . . . Technically, you're going to have a chance to give this all up," Ben said slowly. "When we find Silas. You could leave this all behind too."

I inhaled deeply and looked ahead. Without hesitation, I said, "No. I can't. I'd be lying if I said I never thought about it but . . . Garridan's my home now. For better or worse, I belong there. Even if it is the more complicated choice."

"I get it," Ben replied as he looked down at his hands. "It's good to know where you belong. It's worth all the craziness that comes with it."

"Exactly," I said, looking towards him as a sudden sadness ran through me.

If only he thought where he belongs was with me.

CHAPTER TWENTY-FOUR

I was helping Matthew and Ben divide our scarce food supply when the others started to stir. One by one, they slowly sat up, rubbing their eyes or grumbling as they looked around.

"What happened?" Alexander asked as he stood and stretched.

"Darnell put everyone to sleep," Malachi answered, "then they stole all our supplies."

"We had to go foraging for food last night," Emery added. "Nearly died for it too."

"Don't be dramatic," I muttered with a roll of my eyes.

"Okay, fine. *Ben* almost died for it," she corrected.

"Yeah, but it was his own fault," Matthew said, shooting him another disapproving look.

Dad walked up, throwing his arm around me as he squinted at the sun. "You're going to have to explain that in much more detail," he instructed.

"Just as soon as everyone can listen," Malachi agreed. "Don't really feel like explaining it ten times."

"Sounds good to me," Dad replied as a groggy Luna dragged her feet towards us.

Everyone else slowly joined us around the campfire we still had going. We handed them small portions of food, which they gratefully took as they listened to our encounter of the night.

"Can't believe we slept through all that," Mateo said as he popped his neck.

"Don't worry, you'll get your chance to make up for it," Emery said. "You can be the bait."

"I'm sorry, bait?" he asked, and she nodded wickedly.

"We have a plan to catch the remaining Cyfrin members," Malachi explained.

"It better be a foolproof plan," Alexander said. "They won't go down easily."

"They never have," Matthew replied.

"What's the plan then?" Alexander asked.

"And what's this about being bait?" Mateo questioned.

"We want to send out who they perceive as weak so they'll attack," Matthew answered.

"Excuse me?" Mateo asked. "One, I'm not weak. And two, that's messed up."

"You wouldn't be alone," Malachi said. "We'd all be there but hidden under a form of camouflage—we want to use their own strategy against them essentially."

"We don't have a camouflager with us," Luna pointed out.

"No, but we have William," Malachi replied, gesturing towards him with a proud smile upon his face.

"I'm afraid I don't understand," Luna said as she scratched at her matted hair.

"Go ahead, son," Malachi told William, so he cleared his throat and stood.

"I accidentally dipped into a new ability," he explained, standing rigidly as we stared at him. "Long story short, I found a way to make a mirror of sorts with my force fields. If standing on the outside of them, you can't see in. You see the reflection of the surroundings."

"That's so cool!" Mateo exclaimed.

"Didn't seem particularly useful until now," William replied with a shrug.

"It's definitely something to be proud of," Dad said to him. "Honing in on a new ability is always exciting!"

"I agree," Malachi said.

"There's a flaw in that plan though," Luna said. "If it's a reflection, and not truly camouflage, the Cyfrin members might see there's something there that shouldn't be. Especially if we're reflecting the backs of whoever we're walking behind."

"We'll walk far enough back and to the side so that hopefully won't be a problem," Malachi replied. "It's a risk, but it's the only plan of attack we have."

"But they really do have a camouflager. If you can't see them, you're not going to get very far in an attack," Alexander pointed out.

"We already thought of that," I told him. "We mixed up some sticky powder last night. When they start attacking, Dad's going to fly it through the air so it attaches to them. Even if just a little bit sticks, we'll know where they are."

"After we catch them, Matthew will petrify them until we can bring them back to Garridan," Malachi finished.

"Not a foolproof plan, but I suppose it's better than nothing," Alexander replied. "I'm not the bait, so I don't really have any objection."

"And who exactly *is* the bait?" Kodi asked, crossing her arms.

"Well, you, Ben, and Akio are the first to come to mind," Malachi said apologetically. "Not that we think you're weak, but the Cyfrin members will since they base strength on power. We may add in Andre as well."

"Oh, thanks," Andre said with a shake of his head, despite already knowing that.

"Not me?" Mateo asked. Emery smirked, and he scowled at her less than funny joke from earlier.

"Fine. When do we go?" Kodi asked.

"I'd say as soon as our breakfast feast is over," Dad replied with a grin. No one returned it so he huffed playfully. "Tough crowd."

"They're just grumps. Must be the after effects of Darnell's powers," Emery said.

"I always woke up in a pretty good mood after Darnell put me to sleep," I commented with a shrug.

"No, you didn't," Matthew and Alexander said simultaneously.

They glanced at one another with slightly narrowed eyes, and I rolled my own.

"Okay, I only woke up in a mood when *you*," I pointed to Matthew, "would be yelling in my face to get me up. And *you*," I pointed to Alexander, "were a moody jerk first thing in the morning for no reason. You get what you give."

"She was never grumpy with us," Kodi said.

"Yeah, maybe if you two were more likable, people wouldn't be in such a bad mood around you," Emery said.

"You're one to talk," Matthew said.

"I am nothing short of loveable," she shot back. Snorts and mutters of sarcastic agreement rose around us, and she narrowed her eyes. "Wow. And to think I call most of you friends."

"As entertaining as you all are," Malachi said around a chuckle, "we should really get going. I'd like to reach the forest and get camp set up before dark. We'll need the extra daylight hours to survey the land and hopefully catch some dinner."

"Not to mention, we don't know where we'll run into the enemy," William said. "Or how long it'll take to get past them."

"Plus, we still have the next trial to think about," Luna added.

"You think it's still somewhere ahead of us?" Dad asked.

"No offense, but I don't think reflecting was the trial. Especially when you consider what the first one was," she replied. "It's going to be something big."

Mateo groaned, so I patted his hand and said, "It'll be okay. We'll get through it."

"And it's going to take all of us working together," Matthew agreed. "We saw how turning against one another turned out, and we don't want that to happen again."

"Yes, no more sacrifices," Akio murmured.

We sat quietly for a moment, finishing up our food and drinking the water I provided from large leaves. When we were all done, Malachi beckoned us to get up. Since we didn't have any supplies to gather, we began walking. Andre, Kodi, Ben, and Akio took the lead. The rest of us followed as far behind as we dared, relying on William's unique 'camouflage' ability to stay hidden.

"Sorry you had to face Mallory alone last night," Alexander said as he walked beside me.

"She's an easy opponent," I replied. "Besides, I wasn't alone."

"Ah, yes. Wonder boy saved the day."

I snorted. "Definitely not."

"You weren't lying when you said he'd jump in front of people regardless of being powerless."

"No, I wasn't. He's always been a protector."

"You know him well."

"Well, we did grow up together. I probably know him better than he knows himself."

"And he you."

"Yeah, probably," I agreed.

He was quiet for a moment then softly said, "I think you two should find a way to remain in each other's lives."

My brows furrowed. "I mean, that's what we're doing. We're working on being friends, and I think it's going pretty good so far."

"Just make sure it stays that way."

"What? Why?" I questioned.

"Because things have a way of evolving without our knowledge."

"What the heck does that mean?"

"It means . . . Save the relationship you want to save without worrying about any of the other stuff," he replied, and I stared at him in confusion. "Me, Garridan's barrier, the council—none of it matters if you give up trying."

"But I'm not giving up," I said with frustration. "Ben and I are working it out. I think we'll both be fine being friends by the time this journey is over."

"That's the problem."

"*What is?*" I basically growled as I ran my hands through my knotted hair.

"Friends," he muttered.

"But you just told me to keep working on being his friend!"

"No. I said save the *relationship* you want to save." He grabbed my arm and stopped walking, letting the others get ahead of us. His eyes bore into mine with a burning intensity. "If you had to choose between me and Ben, you'd choose Ben. You said so yourself. So why not choose him now while he's here?"

"B-because I . . ." I clamped my jaw shut as I blinked rapidly and tried to gather my thoughts. "Because after we find Silas—"

"Who cares about after?" he cut me off.

"I-I mean, I do," I stammered.

"We don't know how things are going to end. *You* don't know how things are going to end. Even Andre rarely sees the future concretely. So, what's to say the only reason you and Ben don't end up together is because you didn't fight hard enough?"

My mind was jumbled, none of his words making sense. The more he said, the more confused I became.

"Are you saying . . .?" I trailed off, unsure what he was saying. "What in the world *are* you saying?"

"I'm saying fight for the relationship you want to save," he repeated. "Fight to save your relationship with Ben."

I swallowed loudly, my hands sweaty as I wiped them against my jeans. "What about you?" I asked.

"We don't know how things are going to end but sometimes . . . Sometimes we do," he said softly as the back of his hand brushed my cheek. "And I know how this is going to end. You have no future with me."

I stepped back, his words like a slap in the face. "Alexander, what is happening right now?"

"I just—" he paused and took a deep breath, his face full of an unusual uncertainty. "I just want you to be happy. I need to know you're going to be happy."

"I'm going to be happy," I said. "With or without Ben, I'll be happy."

"I don't think you will be."

"So . . . What?" I asked, blinking rapidly. "You're giving up on me? You're taking back everything you said and aren't going to wait for me to get over Ben? Is that what this is about?"

"I don't want you to get over Ben. I want you to fight for him to stay in your life. Fight the council to change their rules, fight with him to stay with you, whatever you want. Just fight."

"No!" I snapped. "I'm done fighting. Ben made his choice, and, apparently, so have you."

I turned around and stalked away from him, tears welling in my eyes.

What the hell is going on?

I stomped by Matthew and Luna and spat out, "Trying to get a good listen?"

"Hardly," Matthew said as he kept pace next to me. "Just doing our jobs. Can't have anyone falling behind." I didn't say anything, so he hesitantly asked, "What was that all about?"

"I have absolutely *no* idea," I muttered as I wiped a tear off my cheek.

"He was sort of spewing nonsense."

"Glad I'm not the only one who thinks so," I replied sarcastically. He scratched the back of his neck, and I could tell something was on his mind. "What are you thinking?"

"I just don't understand his sudden demeanor change. Don't get me wrong, he's always been hot then cold but, when we talked, he was so insistent that he'd be there for you. He was adamant about it, actually. It was basically an 'I'm going to be in her life so get over it' type of conversation."

"I don't understand either. Even just yesterday, he said the same thing he's been saying," I told him as I played with a strand of my hair. "That he didn't mind waiting until I was over Ben. That he'd help me through it any way he could." I glanced back at Alexander and met his closed off eyes. "What changed in the last twenty-four hours?"

"I don't know," Matthew replied, seeming just as confused as I was. "But I can find out."

"Don't bother."

"Why? Don't you want to know?"

I watched my shoes scrape across the grass as I walked. "No. If this is what he wants, that's his decision. Nothing I say is going to change his mind and knowing why isn't going to make me feel any better. I already learned that with Ben."

Another tear slid down my cheek, and Matthew quietly asked, "Why are you crying?"

"Because I'm frustrated!" I replied loudly. I pressed my lips together, then quietly admitted, "And I'm tired of wondering why I'm not enough."

"Hey, don't say that!" Matthew exclaimed. "You're more than enough!"

"Sure doesn't feel like it. All the people who claim to love me have no problem leaving me."

"I love you, and I'm not going anywhere," he said as serious as I'd ever seen him.

"The only real man in my life," I replied jokingly, a small smile creeping onto my face, and he grinned.

"You know it." After a minute of silence he said, "Try not to let this get you down too much. Ben, I understand, but Alexander . . . You didn't love him anyway. You just liked the comfort of knowing someone would be there for you when you were ready."

I pursed my lips, his words hitting me like a freight train. He was right.

"Besides, a man doesn't define your worth," he added.

"You know, I don't think I've ever heard you talk so sentimentally," I said.

"Don't get used to it either. This is a rare moment, so just take my advice and say thank you."

I nudged him with my shoulder, and he grinned again. As we walked, I watched the clouds move overhead, letting his words sink in. Everything he said was true, and I was in no worse shape than I'd been in before. Alexander's announcement may have hurt, but it didn't affect my life in any significant way.

I'd still be without Ben and finding a way to move on. Only now, I didn't have the promise of being loved by someone after. But that was okay. Maybe it was for the best anyway. Besides, Alexander deserved to be with someone who loved him completely, and that wasn't me.

"Can we stop for a minute?" I asked Matthew and he nodded.

We waited for Alexander and Luna to catch up to us, then I walked next to Alexander as Luna and Matthew fell back to make up the rear of the group again. Luna gave me a sympathetic smile, but I averted my eyes without reacting. I didn't want her to know how humiliated I felt that she witnessed such a vulnerable moment.

"I'm sorry I reacted like that," I told Alexander.

"I apologize for being so cryptic," he replied, "and for going back on my word to you."

"You have nothing to apologize for. I understand. It's what I've been saying this whole time. You deserve to be with someone who loves you back, and that's not me. I always knew it wasn't fair to ask you to wait around while I got over Ben, and I'm actually glad you finally see that too."

He chuckled once without humor. "That's not why I'm going back on my word at all, Robin. I'd still wait for you if I could."

"What do you mean? If that's not the reason, what is?"

"I can't say exactly."

"Oh, okay. I get it. You don't owe me an explanation anyway."

"I would explain if I could. I just . . . Can't." His voice was strangled, as if he were actually bound to secrecy.

My brows furrowed. "I won't lie, I'm actually really curious what's going on with you now. Especially when yesterday you were saying the exact opposite. Is everything okay? Did something happen?"

He peered up at the sky, watching the clouds that passed us by. "All I can say is Andre had a vision. A clear vision. A *fate* vision as you all named it."

"Oh," I murmured, not expecting that answer. "Was it a vision of us? Were we not together?"

"Something like that," he said, but I could tell there was more to it.

"You're not going to tell me?"

"We already witnessed what happens when someone tries to change a vision set in stone. I'm not going to put you in a position to do that."

"Maybe I wouldn't though. I can accept that we aren't going to be together," I insisted, my curiosity running through the roof.

The side of his lips turned up in amusement. "Nevertheless, I'm not going to give you any chance to be put in that predicament."

"Fine," I grumbled. "But I'm here if you need me. You don't have to go through this or anything else alone."

"I know," he replied, his eyes soft. "Thank you."

And just like that, we were fine. Somehow, I knew there'd be no lingering awkwardness; no drawn out, longing stares; no hurt feelings or regrets. He and I could easily fall into a friendship. I smiled at that thought then looked towards Ben. We'd get there one day too.

CHAPTER TWENTY-FIVE

We were nearing the edge of the forest, and I looked up in awe at how tall the trees were. The chirping of birds was louder than ever, and I could make out the colors of different flowers inside the tree line. It was going to be beautiful in there.

"Should we take a break?" Luna asked Malachi as she finished the water I'd just given her.

"We're almost there," Malachi replied. "Just a little further, and we can set up camp."

"Okay," she said with a sigh.

Everyone was getting grumpy. Lots of complaints about sore feet and being tired were coming from the group. I slung my arm over Dad's shoulders as he started falling be-hind.

"Just a little further," I told him. "You can do it, old man."

"But I don't wanna," he moaned playfully, and I shook my head.

"Buck up," Emery said. "Like you weren't *just* complaining that your feet hurt," he commented with raised brows, and she shrugged.

Ahead of us, Andre grunted loudly and fell to one knee. His hand was pressed to his shoulder, and when he pulled it away, blood dropped down his fingers.

"This is it," Malachi whispered loudly and we all took on defensive positions.

I looked around, desperately wishing I could see the threat. A green beam appeared from seemingly nothing, tearing into Andre again. He yelled out in pain as a wave of fire fanned out in front of the four people we chose to be bait.

"Elijah, now!" Malachi hollered as he held up his hands.

A nearly translucent ripple jumped forward, passing the vulnerable group members up front and hitting the fire. The flames stopped in their tracks, unable to flow any further, and Malachi began pushing them back.

At the same time, Dad dumped the backpack full of powder onto the ground, and a rush of wind that sent my hair flying easily picked it up. As it lifted into the sky, Dad directed it above the fire then straight ahead. The powder latched onto the objects in front of it, showing us just enough of six figures that stood in a line.

"There they are!" William called out.

I lifted my arms to attack, but Matthew jumped in front of me. "Stop! You'll wash the powder off of them," he said urgently. "We got this."

He took off after his dad and brother, who were already in pursuit of the fleeing Cyfrin members.

"We aren't going to help them?" Kodi asked my dad.

"This is their job, not ours," Luna replied. "They're well trained for things like this."

"Akio, fix Andre's shoulder," Dad said. He looked towards the rock-like statue of Darnell, who had been stopped by Matthew's petrification. "We'll keep his body here until we go back to Garridan."

"If this is how a fight goes between just a couple of you, I'd hate to see what your war looked like," Ben said.

"It wasn't pretty," Mateo replied. "We all had our own near-death moments."

Ben glanced towards me, and I could see the uneasiness in his eyes. Knowing I'd had a brush with death rocked him to his core, just as his brush with death had rocked me to mine.

"We should keep going," Luna said. "No point in standing here waiting."

She and Dad continued walking while the rest of us followed uncertainly.

"It feels weird letting other people go fight when we could be helping," Emery said.

"I know," Mateo replied. "We could be kicking butt too!"

"It makes me anxious actually," I said. "What if they start losing, and no one knows? There's only three of them, and we have such powerful people here. Why shouldn't we make sure they're okay?"

"I'll admit it's a tad strange for me as well," Alexander commented. "In the Cyfrin compound, the Keepers of Balance were always first to go."

"Because they cared about everyone else?" Ben asked, and every single one of us let out a snort.

"No," Alexander replied. "Because they considered themselves the strongest and were bloodthirsty. They wouldn't sit back and let everyone else do the killing when they could do it themselves."

"Oh," Ben murmured, his mouth in a tight line.

"After Mallory and her group are captured, the Cyfrin can't hurt anyone else," I assured him. "It took twenty years, but they're not a threat anymore."

"Thanks to you guys," he said as he looked us over.

"Well, I don't want to brag," Mateo started.

"Then don't," Emery said with a roll of her eyes. "If there's anyone to thank it's Robin . . . And Alexander."

"Yeah," Kodi agreed quietly. "Who knows how things would've turned out if Alexander hadn't switched sides."

"Why did you?" Ben asked him.

"Honestly . . . Robin," Alexander admitted.

"Ah, yes," Emery said. She interlaced her fingers and batted her eyelashes. "True love conquers all."

"Doubtful," Alexander replied, not catching her sarcasm. "I meant her ability to see the good in the world. I'd always been wary of the Cyfrin's ways, but they gave me a home when I had none. They raised me and protected me. So, despite not fully agreeing with their methods, it was hard for me to question their belief system. I only knew what they told me."

Everyone listened intently as Alexander shared more than he ever had with anyone aside from me. The surprise on their faces said everything they were thinking and I, too, was shocked he was telling them what he was.

"Then along came Robin with her unwavering moral compass," he continued. "She saw through a lot of my facade and, despite my insistence, didn't believe I was as awful as I claimed to be. Seeing the world from her per-spective was refreshing. It made me realize there was something else worth fighting for instead of power."

"Which would be?" Emery probed, and I could see her itching to make fun of the answer she thought he was going to give—love.

He glanced at her then said, "A better world."

Her face fell slightly, and she muttered, "Oh."

"That's a *good* thing," Andre told her with a roll of his eyes.

"Well, I know that," she grumbled.

"That's commendable," Ben told Alexander. "Being in Garridan must be exciting then. You can help them keep balance in the world."

"Not likely. The council would never trust me to sit be-side them and help," Alexander responded. "But I've seen that perhaps I can help elsewhere."

"What do you mean?" I asked.

He shot me a wry smile and said, "That would be telling."

Somehow, I knew he was talking about Andre's vision. Maybe he'd seen Alexander doing something in Garridan that I couldn't be a part of since I'd be taking on the responsibilities of a Keeper of Balance. Maybe he'd seen him finding his place there after all. The thought made me smile, hoping it was true.

"Where did your dad and Luna go?" Ben asked.

I looked ahead and realized they were nowhere to be seen.

"Maybe they're hidden by one of these huge tree trunks," Alexander replied, his eyes appraising the nature around us as we entered the tree line.

"Dad!" I called out as I cupped my hands around my mouth. "Luna!"

As we walked further into the forest, a dense fog began to accumulate around us.

"Where did this fog come from?" Kodi asked, squinting to see in front of her.

The ghost-grey mist further enwrapped us in its embrace with each step we took. Then, in the blink of an eye, gone were my friends as they were devoured by the quick moving substance. It clung to me unforgivingly, swirling before my eyes as I swatted at it.

"Ben!" I cried out, but I was met with silence. "Ben!" I tried again but still received no reply. "Mateo, Kodi, Alexander, anybody!"

Why aren't they answering? There's no way they can't hear me. It's just fog.

"Andre, Emery, where are you?" I called loudly before murmuring, "Where is everybody?"

The fog rippled away from me, forming a large circle that I was in the center of. I whipped my head around in confusion as an eerie silence descended. Two dark figures appeared in the distance, moving through the mist slowly. I couldn't see their faces, just that one was tall and the other as small as a child. My heart hammered in my chest, and I tried to swallow, but my throat was too dry.

"Ben," I whispered as I stood paralyzed with fear. "Kodi . . . Dad?"

My breaths came in short, silent gasps as the figures loomed closer. I shut my eyes tightly, begging the figures to disappear. When I opened them again, the figures were gone. I sighed in relief then took a deep breath to try and compose myself.

"Robin."

For the second time, I stood paralyzed, but this time not with fear.

"Robin," she repeated, and I slowly forced myself to turn around.

My hand flew over my mouth as tears welled in my eyes. My knees buckled together, and it took everything in me not to fall over.

"What's wrong, little bird?" Dawn asked, her sweet voice full of concern as she grasped my adoptive mom's hand.

"This isn't real," I whispered. "This isn't real."

"What do you mean?" Dawn asked, her big blue eyes watching me intently. "What's wrong?"

"You're not here," I said around a sob. "This is just a trick from Silas."

"But we *are* here," Mom said, reaching out and grabbing my hands.

My eyes widened at her touch. Her fingers wrapped around me tightly, and I went slack jawed. I could *feel* her.

"I don't understand," I said as grief threatened to overwhelm me. "You're dead . . . You're both dead. But how can I feel you if you aren't real?"

"You're talking nonsense," Mom chastised. "We've been waiting for you here all this time. We've missed you so much!"

She pulled me into a hug as Dawn clung to my waist. Without a second thought, I melted into her, letting her hands rub my back as I sobbed into her shoulder. The feeling was so familiar. I fit perfectly in between them as they held me. It was like nothing had changed; like all this time without them was just a dream, and now I was back in reality.

When I pulled back, Mom watched me lovingly. "Let's go home," she said, and I nodded eagerly as I picked Dawn up.

She laughed gleefully as we walked towards the billowing fog. As we stepped closer, a bell of warning went off in my head. My brows furrowed, and I stopped.

"Wait," I murmured as I glanced around. "This isn't right."

"Yes, it is," Dawn replied as her contagious smile lit up her face. "You're supposed to be with me and mommy."

"We can go be a family again," Mom agreed. "It'll be like nothing ever changed."

"But things did change," I said, setting Dawn down. "Everything changed."

"You can forget all that now though," Mom insisted. "You don't ever have to think about it again."

"I-I can't do that. I don't want to forget," I said more to myself than her as the fuzziness in my head started to clear. "I can't forget. I've been through too much to go back now."

"Robin, please," Mom begged, a tear sliding down her face. "Don't leave us."

"I wish things had been different," I whispered, a lump forming in my throat. "But you were killed. You're gone.

Now I'm doing what I can to make you proud . . . And you wouldn't be proud of me if I gave up everything I've gained since losing you."

Dawn's chin quivered, and she whimpered, "You don't want to stay with me and Mommy?"

I knelt down and grabbed the top of her arms. "That's all I want, sunshine," I said softly. "But I have people here who need me still. I have to go back to them."

"I'll miss you," she said, her voice wavering as her lower lip stuck out.

"I'll miss you too," I replied as my heart shattered. I pulled her into me, and she wrapped her arms around my neck tightly as she cried. I stood with her still in my arms and handed her to my mom, fighting the urge to never let go. "Take care of her for me."

Mom nodded and sniffled as she ran her fingers through Dawn's hair. "I love you, Robin," she said. "And, for what it's worth, I'm *extremely* proud of you."

I choked back a sob as I fell into her embrace once more, then I quickly pulled myself away and turned around, running as fast as I could before I had a chance to change my mind. I ran blindly as the fog warped around me, not caring if I slammed into a tree trunk or tripped over a plant. But nothing ever got in my way. Instead, the fog lifted, and I ran straight into open air.

I stopped, breathing heavily as I looked around. Members of our group were scattered about, some standing and some sitting, but all red-faced and teary eyed.

"Robin!" Dad exclaimed when he saw me. He ran up and threw his arms around me. "I was so worried you wouldn't make it out."

My chin quivered and I sobbed as I fell into him. My legs gave out, but Dad easily caught my weight and lowered me to the ground. I leaned into his chest, gripping his shirt mercilessly as he ran his hand over my back.

"Shh," he said as he held me. "It's okay, kiddo."

Another hand grabbed my knee, and I squinted through my blurred vision to see Ben sitting in front of me. His red lined eyes mirrored every emotion I was feeling, and I let out another pitiful cry as the healing wounds of my mom and sister's deaths were reopened.

Grief. Agonizing grief. It never got easier.

After a while, my tears slowed. I let go of my dad's shirt and reached my hand out. Ben immediately took it and squeezed as our eyes met. He took in an exaggerated breath then blew it out slowly, beckoning me to do the same. I focused on him, matching his breaths and letting it calm my emotions. I rubbed my lips together and sighed before leaning away from my dad.

"Are you okay?" Dad asked.

"No," I admitted. "But I will be."

"We're here for you, kiddo," he said, squeezing my shoulder. "In any way you need."

"For as long as you need," Ben added, and I smiled sadly.

"Does that mean forever?" I asked, the joking tone I intended to have not quite coming through.

"Yes," Ben replied seriously.

I opened my mouth to ask what he meant, but Kodi came running up and frantically said, "Mateo never came out."

"What?" I asked, immediately standing up.

"He never came out of the second trial," Kodi reiterated, wringing her hands together.

"That's what that was," I murmured with a shake of my head. I replayed the words on this side of the map to myself.

We've all lost loved ones through the years. It's shaped us to who we are. Through all the pain, suffering, and tears you must learn to accept your scars. If you can't, you won't advance. You'll seal your fate forever. Stuck in the past, locked in the fog, life will reach you never.

"So everyone just had a horrible experience," I said. "Not just me."

That explains everyone's misery.

"Unfortunately," Dad replied. "The guards and remaining Cyfrin members went through first. Everyone but Mallory came out. They captured the others, and Matthew petrified them. Then you kids started popping up one by one."

"But Mateo still hasn't!" Kodi almost yelled. "He's still in there."

"What happens if he doesn't get out?" Ben asked.

"I think . . . I think he'd die," I answered, and Kodi's face turned from concerned to horrified. "Choosing to stay in there with your lost loved ones means staying with them forever. In death."

"No!" Kodi exclaimed. "We're so close. He's so close! He has to make it back to his family."

"I'm afraid there's nothing we can do," Dad told her gently.

"Says who?" I asked as my eyes skirted over the fog.

"Robin," Dad said in a warning tone, already knowing what I was thinking.

"I'll be right back," I assured him before sprinting away.

"Robin, stop!" Dad yelled, but I ignored him and everyone else who called my name. I wasn't losing anybody else today.

I ran through the fog blindly once again, turning around and around as I desperately searched for Mateo. My eyes raked the unending blanket but saw nothing. I bit the inside of my cheek as anger boiled through my blood. This was ridiculous.

"Silas!" I screamed, looking up. "Silas! If you can hear me, please stop this! I understand you're trying to protect yourself and the balance of nature, but, please, let me help Mateo! He's not a threat to you. He just needs help moving past whatever he's stuck on."

I turned in another circle as my voice wavered. "We all need a little help sometimes. We all had help moving on before, and that's the only reason we made it out of this stupid fog! So let me help him now. Please!"

The silence that followed was deafening as I stood absolutely still. When nothing happened, I hung my head.

Like that really would've worked.

I looked up again and took a step forward. To my surprise, the fog thinned, and I could make out two shapes in the distance. A smile formed on my face as Mateo's voice reached my ears. I found him.

CHAPTER TWENTY-SIX

"Mateo!" I called out as I stepped into his fogless circle.

He looked up in surprise, his face wet with tears. The girl across from him was young—maybe fourteen or fifteen—with long, curly, black hair; deep-set, light brown eyes; and an upturned nose that mirrored Mateo's. Her features were so similar to his that I wondered if they were somehow related. But he was adopted and never knew his birth family, so why would a real relative show up for him here?

"Robin, what are you doing here?" he asked as the girl smiled at me.

"I'm here to help you," I said, walking up to them.

"Help? With what?" he questioned, his brows furrowing. "Everything's fine."

"No, Mateo, it's not," I replied softly. I motioned towards the girl. "She isn't real."

"Of course she is," he said, reaching out and holding her hand. "See. I can touch her."

"I know, but it's just Silas' powers. It's his second trial."

"What do you mean?"

"The second trial was—" I stopped and took a shaky breath before continuing. "Cruel. He showed us all people we've lost so we could realize we've grown from that loss. You need to say goodbye so you can come back with me."

"But Maria said I could stay here with her. We don't ever have to be a part again," he said, a smile lighting up his face.

"All that means is you'll die too," I said as gently as I could.

His smile disappeared as his eyes hardened. "What? No. That can't be."

"I'm sorry, Mateo, but it is. If you don't go back with me, you'll die. You'll be stuck here with her forever, and you'll never see the rest of your family—or anyone else—again."

"But sh-she's my family too," he said hoarsely. "She always has been . . . I just didn't know how much."

"What are you talking about?" I asked, looking back and forth between the two of them.

"Maria and I were dropped off at the same place when we were two. There were no instructions and no note, so the agency never knew if we were actually siblings." He shrugged one shoulder. "They suspected but had no proof. Anyway. When we were adopted, it was by a set of siblings—my mom and her dad. So we grew up as primos, and we were as close as any two people could be."

He stared at her with adoration as her smile remained unwavering. I could see the love between them, and it pained me when I remembered he'd somehow lost her.

"How did she die?" I asked quietly.

He took a shaky breath. "It was two days after her quinceañera. She was on a rough side of town—I still don't even know why, we never went over there—and she walked in on a robbery at a gas station. They shot her. She uh- she died before the ambulance got there."

"Oh, Mateo. I'm so sorry," I said, even though I knew firsthand those words meant nothing.

"We were always so close. I swear we could read each other's minds sometimes. I just assumed it was because we shared a bond over the thought that we might be blood related." His Adam's apple bobbed up and down as he swallowed, and Maria wrapped her arm around his waist. "Then guess what I found out while we were in Garridan?"

"What?"

"We *were* related."

"You were siblings?" I asked, my wide eyes brimming with tears.

"We were mellizos."

"Mellizos?" I questioned.

"*Twins.*"

I opened my mouth then shut it again. He was a twin. Maria was his twin. I looked towards her and saw the resemblance between them with new eyes. He'd lost his twin sister. No wonder he was having a hard time leaving her.

"Mateo, I know nothing I say can help the grief you're feeling," I started. "Believe me when I say I understand that. I can't force you to leave Maria but . . . What about everyone else you'll be leaving behind?"

He set his jaw tightly, his gaze never leaving Maria's.

"Your family is so important to you, so I can only imagine you're just as important to them," I continued. "Are you ready for them to lose you forever? For your little siblings to feel the grief you're feeling?"

He glanced at his feet as he grasped Maria tightly.

"If you stay, I'm sure you'll be happy. But your family won't be. It'll take years for them to recover. Some may never. Are you ready to put them in that position?"

He blinked rapidly as streaks of liquid fell from his face. "No."

"Then you need to let her go."

"How?" he asked as he pulled her into a hug.

"By remembering that she's already gone," I whispered, my mom and sister's faces flashing in my mind.

"It's not that easy!" he snapped. "You don't understand!"

"But I do!" I replied earnestly. "Remember my mom and sister? The ones who were killed by the Cyfrin? That's who Silas showed me. I got to hug them, and they told me I could stay with them. They told me we could all be together again." I swallowed loudly as I fought down my own grief.

"I had to fight with myself to choose to leave them so I could get out of this ridiculously horrifying fog and go back to everyone else. And guess what? *All* of them had to choose to leave someone they'd lost before as well. It's not just you, Mateo. We all went through it. So, yes, I do understand."

Mateo stood wordlessly for a moment, then closed his eyes. "I-I don't know if I can do it," he whispered.

"What would Maria want?" I asked.

"She'd want me to choose my family," he replied without hesitation. "She was all about making life better for them."

"Then do this to honor her. Come with me so you can get back to your family. Do what she'd want you to do."

He hesitated, staring at Maria as he struggled with his decision. Then, finally, he nodded before grabbing her shoulders and looking her in the eyes.

"I love you so much, Maria," he said, his accent thickened by his emotions. "We'll be together again one day . . . Just not today."

"That's okay, Mateo," she replied, placing her hand on his cheek. "You're not done yet. I understand."

"I miss you," he murmured.

"I'm always with you. Give mi padres y hermanas a huge hug from me, okay?" He nodded and she said, "Te amo, primo."

"Te amo, *melliza*," he corrected with a small smile.

He took a step back, and I reached out my hand. He gripped it tightly, and I slowly pulled him away from Maria as she waved. He turned to look back at her one last time then leaned into me for support as we walked further and further away.

"I'm sorry, Mateo," I said. "I'm so sorry."

He nodded through his tears, and I rubbed his arm as we came through the thick of the fog into what I thought was the clearing. To my surprise, we entered another circularly shaped hell hole instead.

"Mallory?" I asked, disgust evident in my voice when I saw her standing with two adults.

She turned towards me slowly with slanted eyes and a huge scowl. "What are *you* doing here?"

"Just trying to make it back out of the fog," I replied.

"*Back* out?" she asked with a snort. "Let me guess, you came back in for that blubbering idiot."

"Yes, actually, I did," I said defensively.

"Well, you got him, so why don't you just go on your merry little way."

"With pleasure."

I turned around with the intent to leave, but a nagging feeling in the back of my mind made me stop. I couldn't just leave her here. I sighed and faced her again.

"You should come with us," I told her, and she laughed.

"Why?"

"Because if you stay here, you'll die."

"Yeah, and?"

"Well, uh." Her answer threw me off guard. "You're too young to throw your life away."

"Oh, please. Like I have anything to live for anyway."

"Sure you do! Everyone does."

"I don't."

"Mallory—"

"Would you just get the hell out of my happy place?" she yelled, and I saw the shimmer of tears in her eyes. "Just go!"

"I can't just leave you here," I told her.

"Yes, you can. I want you to. Let me stay with my parents. I *want* to stay with my parents." Her chin quivered slightly. "Please. I just want to be with them, even if it's in an afterlife."

I opened my mouth, but no words came out. She sniffled then looked up at her parents. She was the spitting image of her mom but with her dad's curly, fiery hair. When she glanced at me again, all the hate was gone. Her eyes were wide and innocent, and she didn't resemble the murderous maniac I'd come to know. She looked like a kid—a scared, little kid who just wanted her parents to comfort her.

"I'm staying with my parents," she said softly.

"Okay," I murmured. "Okay."

Her parents each grabbed one of her hands, and they walked away from Mateo and me with smiles lighting up their faces. As they hit the edge of the fog, their figures radiated light. I held up one hand to block my eyes, then they disappeared entirely.

"Well, that was unexpected," Mateo said quietly.

"Agreed," I replied. We glanced at one another, and one side of my lips pulled up in a forced smile. "Let's get back to the others."

He nodded, and we headed through the mist once again, but this time we ended up in the open field where everyone waited.

"There you are!" Andre exclaimed.

"Thank goodness," Dad said, breathing a sigh of relief.

"Mateo!" Kodi cried out, and he fell into her open arms as Emery and Andre circled around them.

I watched them surround him with a heavy heart, knowing the pain he was feeling was unfathomable. No one could ease that, but being surrounded by people who loved you was a small comfort.

"And you say *I* try to save everyone," Ben said with a shake of his head as he came up to me.

A sad grimace filled my face. "Maybe we're equal in that department," I replied.

"I'd say so." He peered at my face more intently then asked, "Are you okay? What happened in there?"

"Too much heartache for one day."

"Come here."

He held out his arms, and I leaned into them without a second thought. They circled around me tightly, and I breathed in his scent, letting it calm me as my head rested on his shoulder. I looked around the camp they'd set up and saw most everyone still looking pretty somber. Matthew and Alexander leaned against the same tree, both their expressions pained. They kept glancing my way but wouldn't meet my gaze.

"What's up with those two?" I asked, motioning towards them as I pulled away from Ben.

"They're both feeling pretty guilty."

"About?"

He hesitated. "About who you saw in there."

"Of course they are," I said with a shake of my head. "They both think it's their fault my mom and Dawn are dead."

"I mean, isn't it technically Alexander's?" he asked with furrowed brows. Then he held up his hands defensively. "Not trying to start anything, I swear."

"I know you aren't. And, no, it's not. The only person to blame for it is dead."

"Toshiro?"

I nodded. "Alexander tried to stop him. He told Toshiro not to do it and that there were other ways, but he wouldn't listen. So, no, it's not Alexander's fault just like it isn't Matthew's. But neither of them will stop blaming them-selves regardless."

"Unfortunately, I think we'd all feel the same way if we were in their shoes."

"I know. I just hate it for them though."

"I know you do." He reached out and intertwined his fingers in mine then immediately let go. "Sorry. Habit."

"It's okay," I assured him, a light blush fluttering over my face.

"I don't want to cause any problems between you and Alexander."

"You won't, I promise."

"He's just that understanding, huh?" he asked, semi-sarcastically.

"In some ways, yes, but that's not why. Alexander and I . . ." I shrugged one shoulder as I took a cleansing breath. "We're never going to be anything more than friends."

"Oh." He tried to contain it, but I could see the happiness radiating in his eyes. "Can I ask why?"

"There's a couple reasons," I admitted. "When it comes down to it, though, it's because I don't love him." I peered up at Ben and met his soft eyes. "You know what he told me earlier?"

"What's that?"

"To try to save my relationship with you."

"Huh. Maybe he's got some sense in there after all," he joked, and I shoved him away from me. He chuckled before saying, "I'm just kidding, but I will admit I like him a little better now."

"Of course you do," I muttered with a roll of my eyes.

"So . . . What did you say back to him?"

I shrugged one shoulder as I stared at the trainees, who had sat in a circle on the ground. "That I was done trying. You made your choice and I have to accept that. There's no point in fighting for us anymore."

"What if—" he stopped and bit his lip as he shoved his hands in his pant pockets. "What if there was?"

"Was what?"

"A point in fighting for us. Would you do it?"

"You know I would," I replied quietly. "But you've made it clear your family and tribe need you, and I'm trying to be understanding of that. So, please, don't play the 'what if' game and break my heart all over again."

I walked away from him, crossing over to Matthew and Alexander and stopping in front of them. I crossed my arms as they both stared up at me with guilt ridden eyes.

"Stop looking at me like that," I said sternly. "I can't ease the guilt you feel, but I don't want to see it because you both know I don't blame either of you for what happened to my family. So." I gave them both a long stare. "Stop sulking. I'm fine. Okay?"

They both nodded halfheartedly as I held out my hands. They stared at them blankly, so I motioned for them to grab them. They glanced at each other then both grabbed one hand, and I pulled them up from their pity party.

"I don't know how you do it," Alexander murmured.

"Do what?" I asked as we walked towards the others.

"Stay strong."

"I don't. Didn't you see my emotional breakdown earlier?" I smiled humorlessly.

"And, yet, you put that emotion aside to go save Mateo then came to kick our butts into gear too," Matthew said. "Alexander is right. You're the strongest person I know."

"Only because I have a supportive circle," I muttered, their words of praise embarrassing me.

"Always so humble," Alexander said.

"Yes, she is," Matthew agreed, and I made a face.

"Find something else to bond over," I told them as we reached Dad, Malachi, William, Luna, and Akio. The trainees made their way over to us as well, and when we were all in attendance I said, "Mallory is gone."

"Gone?" William asked. "Gone where?"

"Dead," I clarified, clasping my hands behind my back. "She, uh, she stayed in the fog."

"You left her behind?" Matthew asked with an arched brow.

"I tried to get her to come with us, but she wouldn't," I explained.

"Let me guess," Alexander said. "She saw her parents."

I nodded, and Matthew shook his head and said, "I'm not surprised then. She always wanted to know them."

"Well, with her gone, that means we have no more Cyfrin members to concern ourselves with," Luna said. "The others were all captured and petrified. We'll just have to transport them back to Garridan when we're done here."

"Hopefully the remainder of our trip will go smoothly then," Dad replied.

"Just remember we still have one last trial to pass," Malachi said, and Dad ran his hand over his face.

"As if the first two weren't enough," William muttered.

"Silas is doing his job well," Dad said. "At least we know he's truly doing what he vowed to do so long ago. Garridan is safe with him guarding nature."

"Nevertheless, I'll be glad when this is over and we can return home," Luna said, and many of us nodded in agreement.

"Are we going any further today?" Matthew asked.

Luna, Dad, and Malachi exchanged glances before Dad said, "No. I think we could all use a break. We'll keep going tomorrow morning."

"In that case, let's go find some dinner," Matthew said.

"You mean an animal?" Kodi asked, and he nodded. "Just kill it before you come back. I don't want to hear it's suffering."

"Will do," he replied.

"We can have a nice side of fruits too," Luna said.

"And we have all our supplies back," Emery pointed out.

"Which means I can get into some clothes that fit," Ben commented, and we laughed as he tugged at the neck of his tight fitted shirt.

"Let's get to it then," Malachi said. "I think we're all ready to just relax a little."

The Alastair family set off in search of meat while Luna, Akio, and Dad gathered wood for a fire. I sat against a tree with Ben sitting closely on one side and Emery and Andre lounging on the other. Alexander stood beside Kodi and Mateo, and I could hear him asking more questions about their lives. I wondered why he was suddenly so curious but decided it was just his way of trying to make amends.

I leaned my head back and watched the sun beams that tried to creep through the small gaps in some of the trees. The air was humid, which made the mossy floor of the forest wet with dew. I could sense the vast amount of water that hung in the air. It was invisible to the eye, but I could feel the intensity of it all around. I imagined the temperature would drop uncomfortably low when nighttime came, but at least we had our supplies back.

I closed my eyes, letting the image of my mom and sister sit center stage. A shaky breath left my mouth, and I swallowed around the lump forming in my throat. I still missed them so much and I wasn't sure if today's encounter had made that better or worse.

Ben grabbed my hand and squeezed. I clasped onto it, letting his presence comfort me as my eyes stayed shut. At least I could be grateful that he was still alive. Even if we never saw each other again after this trip, I was glad he was at least here with me now.

CHAPTER TWENTY-SEVEN

"It's so humid," Mateo grumbled as he wiped the sweat dripping from his face.

I swiped droplets of liquid from my own forehead and nodded. Boy, was I wrong thinking it'd get colder as the night progressed. Everyone had soaked through their clothes, the dampness creating an unpleasant smell. I'd give anything for a shower with lots of soap right now.

We'd put the fire out ages ago, the heat radiating from it too much to handle, but now we were plagued by utter darkness. To conserve battery life, the flashlights were only on when someone took it to go to the bathroom or rummaged through their backpack for a snack. Most of us had resorted to standing, the creepy crawlies on the ground too interested in bothering us. I shuddered as a remembered the scorpion that had found its way onto my neck.

"I'm bored," Emery grumbled, and I could barely make out her shape against the tree next to me as she shifted her legs.

"We could play a game," Alexander said, the mocking undertones in his voice evident.

"If I could see you, I'd be glaring," I told him, and he chuckled.

"I think a game is a great idea," Mateo said, and Alexander groaned.

"I wasn't being serious," he replied.

"Guess you should watch what you say then," Emery told him.

"You're all such children," he stated.

"Does that mean you aren't playing?" Matthew asked coyly.

"That's precisely what that means," he agreed.

"Your loss," Kodi told him. "What are we playing?"

"Truth or dare?" Mateo suggested.

"That's so lame," Emery muttered.

"No way!" Mateo disagreed. "It could be the most epic game of truth or dare ever. Just think—truth or dare with *powers.*"

"Ben doesn't have any powers though," Andre pointed out. "And mine would be no fun."

"I don't mind," Ben said. "It'll be fun to see what everyone else has to do."

"Truth or dare it is then," I said. "Is everyone but Alexander playing?"

"I think I'll sit this one out as well," Matthew answered.

"Have you ever even played it before?"

"Nope, but the name is pretty self-explanatory."

"Oh, come on. It's fun!"

"Pass."

"Fine," I relented. "Who wants to go first?"

"I'll go," Kodi said. "Alexander, truth or dare?"

"I said I'm not playing," Alexander replied.

"Truth or dare?" she repeated, her voice as hard as steel.

The prolonged silence got hard to handle so I said, "Ask someone else, Kodi."

"No," she said firmly.

"You're gonna ruin the game," Mateo told her.

"No, he is," she replied.

Alexander sighed heavily, and I could just imagine him rubbing his forehead in irritation. "Fine," he snapped. "Truth."

"What's your biggest fear?" Kodi asked.

He was quiet for a moment then said, "I suppose starting over."

"Oh, yeah, that's hard," Emery commented. "I did it a lot when I'd switch foster homes."

"Same," Andre agreed. "Every once in a while, there'd be some super nice person that would take you under their wing and that made it easier."

"I'm sure it did," Alexander said.

"In your case, that person is Robin, so that's gotta make it a little better," Mateo said.

"At the moment. I'm afraid that's not going to be the case for long though," Alexander replied, and my brows furrowed.

"Why?" I asked. "I'll always help in any way I can. Just because we're not . . . You know . . . Doesn't mean I'll write you off."

"That's not what I mean at all."

"Then what *do* you mean?" I questioned, not understanding.

"I believe I already answered my truth," he replied briskly. "The game isn't called 'A Thousand Questions.'"

"It's twenty questions actually," Mateo commented.

"What?" Alexander asked.

"Never mind," Mateo replied.

"Mateo, truth or dare?" Emery asked.

"Dare," he answered.

"I dare you to find a scorpion and sit it on your head."

"That's stupid!"

"It's not stupid. You're just scared!" Emery shot back.

"Ugh, fine," he mumbled. He grabbed a flashlight and turned it on. "I'll be back."

"Until then," Ben said, "Andre, truth or dare?"

"Truth," Andre answered.

"Do you know what you're going to do when we find Silas?" Ben asked.

Mateo's flashlight washed over us for a second, and I saw Emery staring at Andre hopefully as she waited for his answer.

"I do, yes," Andre said.

When he didn't offer up more of an explanation, Emery impatiently snapped, "Well?"

Andre chuckled and said, "Well, little miss snippy, I'm staying in Garridan. It feels right."

"Really?" Emery prodded, her voice slightly thicker than usual.

"Really."

I looked down at my feet as I heard them share a kiss.

"Here's your stupid scorpion," Mateo muttered as he walked back up to us with the creature firmly between two fingers.

"You know what to do," Emery replied with a grin as he set the flashlight down, illuminating us as the light spread across the sky.

Mateo gulped, staring unhappily at the thrashing scorpion.

"Don't be a baby," Emery said, and I rolled my eyes at her.

Mateo flinched as the scorpion came closer and closer to his head.

"It's okay, Mateo," Kodi told him. "He isn't going to hurt you, I promise. He's just going to crawl down your back once you set him down."

"You can talk to bugs too?" Andre questioned.

"Not exactly. Scorpions are distant cousins of spiders under the category of Arachnida, which means they're technically animals," she explained. "His voice is faint—almost like a static filled radio station—but it's there."

"Okay then," Mateo said, taking a deep breath. He lowered the scorpion onto his head then squeezed his eyes shut as it immediately ran down his backside. He shivered, running his hands over his body as if there'd be more bugs, then looked at Emery. "I hate you."

"Big baby," Emery replied.

"Hey, Emery," I said, crossing my arms. "Truth or dare?"

"Dare, of course," she replied.

"I dare you to go electrocute William," I said.

"Easy," she said with a smirk.

Everyone but Matthew stared at me like I'd gone crazy. I met Matthew's gaze, and he grinned knowingly as Emery quietly snuck up closer to where William stood with the other adults. She took one more step then raised a hand.

Just as it came alive with electricity, the low hum of a force field sounded as it enwrapped William's figure. In the same instance, he whirled around and flung his arms forward. A piece of his force field broke off and slammed into Emery, knocking her to the ground roughly.

"What the hell?" she grumbled as she shakily stood back up.

"Nice try," William said before turning his back to her again as Malachi and Dad laughed.

"William has this peculiar sixth sense of knowing when people are sneaking up on him," Matthew explained as Emery wiped the leaves from her backside. "We think it might come from his powers, but we aren't entirely sure."

"And you knew that?" Emery asked me accusingly.

"Yep," I replied with a smirk.

"That *hurt!*" she exclaimed.

"Don't be such a baby," I told her, and she glared as she realized the motivation behind my dare.

She stomped back to where Andre stood trying to suppress his own smile as Mateo grinned wildly.

"Thanks, Robin," he said.

"Glad to be of service," I told him, and he laughed.

"Robin," Alexander said, and I looked up at him. "Truth or dare?"

"I thought you weren't playing," I commented.

"I've done my due diligence and answered a question. I think that entitles me to ask somebody else something."

"Okay then. Truth."

"What do you hate most about your powers?"

My brows wrinkled together. "I don't hate my powers."

"Perhaps not, but there's always *something* every single one of us dislikes about them regardless," he replied.

"Well," I rubbed my lips together as I thought about it. My powers were the best thing that ever happened to me. They completed me in a way I didn't know I needed. They'd given me so much, but at the same time, they'd taken as much as they'd given. "I guess . . . I hate how they took everyone in Milton away from me. My classmates, my family, Felicity, Ben." I glanced over at him then quickly looked away when I found him already staring at me. I cleared my throat uncomfortably then said, "Who's next?"

The next couple of hours proceeded in a similar fashion until, one by one, we all started to fall asleep. I leaned against a tree trunk, fighting to keep my eyes open as my legs threatened to collapse underneath me.

"You need to lay down and get some sleep," Ben said as he came up next to me.

I stifled a yawn then said, "I can't put my head on the ground again. I know I'm being a squirmy girl, but I just can't."

"How about you put it against me instead then," he suggested. He noticed my hesitation and said, "Come on, it's just so you can get some sleep. Don't overthink it."

"Well, if you're willing to brave the bugs, I guess it's worth a shot," I finally said.

"Good." He slid down the base of the trunk and wiggled around before finding a comfortable position. "Come on."

I bit my bottom lip before kneeling next to him. He ushered me closer, and I let him wrap an arm around me as my head fell onto his chest. It moved up and down in a soothing, rhythmic motion and my eyes fluttered shut as his heartbeat lulled me close to sleep.

"Goodnight, Benjamin," I murmured.

"Goodnight, my sweet love," he whispered, and a smile crept over my face before I fell into the awaiting darkness.

* * *

"What does the council hope to gain by finding Silas?" Ben asked Dad and Luna.

We'd been walking for a couple hours, the mood much lighter and happier than it'd been yesterday. Alexander and Luna were constantly shifting the terrain in front of us, removing the never-ending shower of vines that would've otherwise proven to be problematic.

As they cleared the way, we were able to see much more of the forest, and we were all enjoying the vast array of vegetation and birds we'd been encountering—each bea-utiful and unique in its own way. For being so dark, the rainforest floor was a lively place, but we'd been fortunate not to run into any wild animals yet. When we did, Kodi would come in very handy.

"Information mostly," Dad answered Ben.

"As well as some peace of mind," Luna added.

"We just want some concrete answers on how much power he truly wields and how our people can continue to live right in nature's eyes," Dad said. "It's a bit unnerving knowing at any moment our powers could be taken, and our world would just cease to exist."

"What would happen if something like that did occur?" Ben asked.

"Well," Dad breathed in deeply, becoming thoughtful. "We'd have to find a way to live amongst a people we know nothing about. It'd be quite the learning curve."

"I'm sure most of us would stay banded together for a while but, after time, we'd spread out and slowly lose knowledge of our existence altogether," Luna said.

"Do you think it'd be hard?" Ben asked quietly. "Learning to be someone in a new world?"

"Of course," Dad replied before nodding towards the trainees and me. "I see what they've gone through being thrust into a place they know nothing about."

"Having people to help with the transition made things easier," I spoke up. "It was still hard, don't get me wrong, but having someone there to guide me and answer questions definitely helped the culture shock to not be too much."

"Do you think . . . maybe . . . well . . ." Ben trailed off, his eyes swimming with unsaid words.

"Think what?" Luna prodded.

"I know how opposed the council is to interaction with the outside world but . . . Do you think that's a little closed minded?" Ben asked hesitantly. "Not to sound disrespectful, but what if your downfall is your own misguided rules?"

"What do you mean?" Dad questioned.

"Imagine how close the Cyfrin were to getting your world cut off from nature," Ben explained. "If that had happened, you'd have absolutely no knowledge of how the outside world works. You'd have no idea how to live or survive in it."

"Well, we would've had Robin," Dad pointed out.

"That's kind of my point, actually," Ben said. "You would've been okay but only because you had contact with someone from the outside. If you hadn't, you would've been in a lot of trouble."

"I think what he's trying to say is it would be in Garridan's best interest to consider the fact that communic-ation with people on the outside might just save our skin some-day," Matthew said as he stared straight ahead. "Keeping connections to the normal world would ensure our survival if ever a day came that we became a part of it."

"Yes, exactly!" Ben exclaimed as he pushed his hands into his pockets. "That was way more eloquent than what I was saying, but it's exactly what I was trying to get at."

"I see your point," Dad said warily, glancing to Luna and Malachi. "It's just . . . It's not that easy of a thing to decide on. There's a lot of factors we have to consider."

"Like who would be trustworthy enough to take on such a role for us," Malachi said.

"My family would be," Ben replied earnestly. "We're descendants of Lyle Tovert after all. Your history is our own, and they'd be more than happy to honor that. They'd be proud to actually."

I peered at him from the side of my eye, trying to figure out what he was up to. Could he be trying to find a way for us to stay in contact after this trip was over? Or was he sincerely interested in helping Garridan? Knowing him, it was probably the latter with the former just being a huge plus.

"I see where you're coming from, son. I really do," Dad said. "I'm just afraid the council's own fear will make them deaf to such a suggestion."

"Maybe at first," I said, "but they'd see the logic in it after their fear faded."

"It's not something I would expect to change overnight," Ben said. "I'm sure it could take months—if not years—to get everyone in agreement on something so monumental. But I do think it's something you should consider bringing to the table."

"I believe you're right," Luna agreed hesitantly as she pushed two large tree trunks to the side. "It'd be worse to be thrown into the normal world with no assistance or allies."

"What do you think, Dad?" I asked.

"I agree to a point," he replied as he scratched his head. "But there's that part of me that thinks of what Mallory did to those poor people, and I go back to believing we should stay separate from that world entirely."

"This is different than that though," Luna pointed out. "This would be limited contact with select people. It wouldn't be a free for all for our worlds to mingle."

"True," Dad agreed, but I could see he was still hesitant, and I knew that's how the rest of the council would be as well. "As head of the guard, what do you think, Malachi?"

Malachi cocked his head to the side, his eyes heavily guarded as he stared at the throng of monkeys passing us by. "It's a very abstract situation," he replied. "I can see both sides, and they both have their pros and cons."

"Look at it this way," Matthew said. "If Garridan ever came to an end, we'd be completely screwed without some outside help. We'd benefit more by having an ally. What's the absolute worst that could happen if the council chose to go that route?"

"Your ally could spill the beans to their world," Akio answered.

"And no one would believe it because that sort of thing is make believe to them," I replied.

"We could have another psychopath from our world go crazy, hunt our allies down, and kill them," William said.

"Which is really more of a 'them' problem than an 'us' problem if you think about it," Matthew said, shrugging off the incredulous looks thrown his way.

"So, really," I spoke up as I shook my head at Matthew, "I think the main point here is that we'd benefit more than we'd lose if we chose to have contacts in the normal world."

"I might have to agree with them," Malachi said slowly. "It's definitely something worth considering at least."

"So you'll talk to the council about it?" Ben asked hopefully.

Luna and Dad exchanged a long look before they both nodded. "It'll be a main priority when we return," Luna answered, then she snorted. "Peter is going to go absolutely berserk."

Dad sighed. "So will some of the others. I foresee many long nights over this one."

Ben looked over at me and smiled gleefully. I walked closer to him and asked, "What brought that on?"

"Well," he paused, and his expression turned bashful. "I actually have something I want to tell you. I—"

"Everybody stop!" Kodi cried out.

We immediately did as she said, and my eyes darted around the lush greenery for danger.

"What's wrong?" William demanded, his hands ready to throw up protection.

"We're being hunted," she answered as she scanned the murky water we'd been following.

"By?" William pried.

"Crocodiles," she replied in a low voice.

The corner of Mateo's mouth turned up in a smirk as the rest of us relaxed. "So scary," he said.

"Just tell them to leave us alone," Alexander told her, and she glared back at him. "What? Might as well use your powers while you have them. You'll miss them when they're gone."

"Who's going to miss them more—me or you?" she retorted, and my brow furrowed at the comment.

"Why would he miss your powers?" I asked, but before she could answer, loud splashing caught my attention.

The algae covered swamp swarmed with activity as four massive crocodiles broke through the surface. Their yellow tinted eyes watched us eagerly as they made landfall, and all I could do was stare at their razor-sharp teeth.

"Uh, Kodi, you're up," Mateo almost whispered as he stepped behind her.

Kodi cautiously walked past us, each step slow and deliberate as she got closer to the crocodiles. She stopped a couple feet away and cleared her throat. I couldn't make out what she was saying as the reptiles hissed loudly, but they must not have liked what they heard because one of them lunged at her aggressively.

She screamed and fell onto her butt as all four crocodiles advanced, snapping their jaws. William placed a force field between them and Kodi as Emery let loose a strike of electricity that fried the ground near where the crocodiles stood. They stopped walking but continued to bellow at us. Emery struck near them again, careful not to hit their bodies, and this time they backed away. After a moment, they slid back into the water and disappeared underneath the murky liquid.

Mateo went and helped Kodi off the ground, and I could see her visibly shaking as they walked back to the group.

"What the hell happened?" Alexander asked.

"Well, they, uh, they said it was nice to meet me and, uh," she cleared her throat as she tried to continue. "They said they hoped I could forgive them, but they didn't care that I could speak their language. They said food is food, and they'd eat me anyway."

I scratched my head as I slowly nodded, trying to process the exchange. If it wasn't so scary, it might be a little humorous. "Well, alrighty then," I finally said. "Guess we shouldn't think we're safe from the animals after all."

Alexander opened his mouth, but I shot him a look, daring him to say the flippant comment I could see coming from a mile away. He pressed his lips together and shrugged, but the amusement flashing in his eyes was obvious.

"Surely we're getting closer to the middle of this grove," Dad said.

"All we can do is keep on walking and find out," Malachi replied.

"And pray we don't run into any jaguars," Emery muttered.

Kodi flipped her the bird. Alexander opened his mouth then shut it again as he shook his head. At least he was being nice.

CHAPTER TWENTY-EIGHT

"What's up with you and Alexander?" I asked Kodi as we trudged through some mud.

"What do you mean?" she asked as she smacked a bug on her arm.

"The comments you've been making lately. It's like you know something the rest of us don't." She ducked her head, avoiding my gaze like the plague, and my eyes widened. "You do, don't you?"

"Maybe," she mumbled.

"Well, what is it?"

"I can't say," she replied, still not looking at me.

"Why not?"

"Because he asked me not to."

"Alexander?"

"Yeah."

"What would he possibly tell you that he couldn't tell me?" I asked more to myself. "You guys don't even like each other."

One corner of her mouth twitched as she finally met my eyes. "Ironic, isn't it?"

"More like frustrating. Maybe I should go ask him."

"I wouldn't. He's . . ." She shook her head as she gathered her words. "Struggling. You'll just make things worse. Trust me."

I glanced over at Alexander, my curiosity at an all new high. What could possibly be going on with him?

"He's okay though?" I asked.

"He will be, I think. It'll just take some time."

I nodded absently, trying to figure out what he could be struggling with and why he'd confide in Kodi of all people. After a minute of outlandish possibilities filling my head, I sighed and tried to shake off the questions. Instead, I focused my attention on Kodi as she stared at the wet ground in annoyance.

"What about you?" I asked.

"What about me?"

"Are you okay?"

"Yeah, why wouldn't I be?"

"Just asking," I replied with a shrug. "We're getting closer to finding Silas. I'm sure you have mixed emotions about it."

"Not really."

"Really?"

"I mean . . . I guess I kinda do but not in the way you might be thinking. I'm sad to be leaving all of you behind knowing I may never get to see you again, but other than that, I'm just really excited to be going home."

"No second guesses about leaving?"

"Nope."

"Not even about giving up your powers?"

She shook her head. "I know it seems like a big deal, and maybe to everyone else it is, but I actually can't wait to be rid of them."

"Really?" I asked, perplexed by that. I couldn't imagine my life without my powers after getting them.

"Don't get me wrong, I've loved having them, and it was awesome to be able to talk to my dogs at home, but . . ." She rubbed her nose. "I don't like this world. I don't like what it does to people, and I don't like what it did to me. I'd rather be normal."

"Normal is just a matter of perception," I pointed out.

"Maybe, but I like *my* normal. I like my boring, safe life."

"I can understand that." I bit my lip as a question tried to pass my lips. I didn't want her to think I wasn't supportive of her decision.

"What?" she asked, seeing my hesitation.

"It's just . . . Do you think you might get *bored* of your boring, safe life one day? I only ask because I'd hate for you to look back and regret this decision later on."

"I don't see that happening."

"How can you be so sure?"

"I guess I can't, but I don't plan on my life staying boring and safe. For a while, yes. I'm going to soak in the tedious, repetitive days and enjoy the things I found annoying before." She smiled at the thought before continuing. "But later on, I want to travel the world. I want to learn about other cultures and live how other people do. I want to diversify myself and not be tied down to one person or place. My life will have excitement—just not with powers or world saving problems. I'll leave that up to you."

I smiled as she elbowed my side. "I think you'll have an amazing life then," I said. "I just wish I could see it happen."

"Me too. That's the hardest part about any of this. We've gotten so close; I can't imagine not being able to talk to you or Andre or Toby or Emery anymore."

"At least you'll still have Mateo."

"Definitely. We've already agreed there's no way we'll lose touch with one another. We're 'kindred siblings' now as he put it."

"I'm glad." I sidestepped a thicker mound of mud, my shoes squishing through the ground regardless. "And who knows? If the council comes around to the idea of outside allies, maybe they'll also come around to the idea of communication with others like you and Mateo."

"That seems like a very big 'maybe,' but I'd love if it ever happened."

"Even if it's fifty years down the line and we'll all old and grouchy?" I asked playfully.

She snorted. "We're all grouchy already so what's the difference?"

I laughed as William called out to her.

"Want to try your luck at getting these animals to move?" he asked.

"Because that worked so well last time," she replied sarcastically.

"I don't think these ones can eat us," he responded, unamused. "They're just right in the middle of the walkway, and I'd rather not give them a reason to attack."

"I suppose I'll try," she said before jogging to the front of the line.

The short stall in movement allowed me to catch up to Matthew, and as we walked side by side I asked, "What do you think it'll be like to find Silas?"

"Unreal," he replied. "I keep imagining how it'll go, but they're very uncreative scenarios. I'm sure reality will be much more mind boggling."

"Do you think he'll help Kodi and Mateo?"

"I don't see why he wouldn't. Their desires are extremely pure. They're not looking to put anyone in danger or anything like that."

"Yeah," I agreed. "Do you think he'll answer my dad and Luna's questions?"

"I'm not so sure about that," he admitted. "They don't have ill intent, but you know what they say: Knowledge is power. And there's no guarantee someone else from Garridan wouldn't use the information for their own benefit."

"Silas has stayed safe and kept his word all these years by being smart," Alexander spoke up from behind us. "I don't see him giving up his secrets for the sake of the council's comfort."

"Some of them will have a fit if we come back empty handed," I said.

"Maybe it'll entice them to take up Ben's offer," Matthew replied.

I glanced back at where Ben was walking with Akio and my dad. They were absorbed in their own conversation, and I could only imagine what had them so distracted. A smile played on my face.

"It'd sure be nice to be able to talk to him after we get back," I admitted.

"I know," Matthew replied.

"I still say you should keep fighting to be with him," Alexander said.

"Then it's a good thing no one asked you, isn't it?" I popped off with as irritation filled me. He arched one brow, which infuriated me even more, and I snapped as I whirled on him. "I don't understand you! Why are you suddenly so fixated on my relationship with Ben? Just two days ago you were saying you loved me and wanted to be with me. How does Andre having a vision change that?"

"It didn't change anything," he snapped back. "We already went over this."

"Yeah, and that's all fine and dandy, but what does Andre's vision have to do with you obsessing over Ben and me?" I asked in frustration, raising my hands in the air. "I understand why you're saying we'll never be together, and I honestly don't even care about that because I'm happy to be your friend. What I don't understand is why you have the nerve to keep talking to me about something you know nothing about. It's not your place to have an opinion, and it's really not your place to continuously tell me that I should be doing more."

"Why are you being so blind?" he basically growled as a thick vine encompassed my wrists and pulled them together tightly. I glared at his irate expression as he pulled me towards him and continued. "I'm trying to help you! Someone needs to push you, and I'm more than happy to be the bad guy who does it if it means having the reassurance that you'll be supported after I'm gone."

"That doesn't even make any sense!"

At that point, everyone was staring as our conversation grew to a heated argument. Ben walked up with a disgruntled look and one hand outstretched towards Alexander.

"You need to calm down and let her go," he told him, his lips pulled down in a scowl as he motioned towards my confined grip.

"This is none of your concern, Norm," Alexander snapped.

"Just remember who you're calling a Norm," I barely heard Kodi say, but it slid from my mind as Ben stepped closer to Alexander.

"Leave her alone," he demanded.

Alexander appraised him for a moment then said, "You're right. I should be talking to you about this instead. Tell me, how stupid can you be to give up on her?"

"My relationship with her is none of your business," Ben replied sharply.

"You have a woman who loves you with every fiber of her being, but you're too spineless to man up and accept it."

"That's not—"

"You can't claim to love her if you aren't willing to sacrifice anything to be with her."

"She could—"

"*She* has made enough sacrifices in her short lifetime. What have you ever given up? What hardships have you faced in your privileged little life? Besides, why should she give up anything for someone who can't do the same in return?" Alexander scoffed and shook his head before sizing Ben up. "She speaks nothing but your praises, but I'm failing to see the appeal. You're nothing like the caring, selfless person she describes. All I see is a selfish coward and a poor excuse of a man who isn't deserving of someone like her."

"You don't know anything about me, and you sure as hell don't know anything about our relationship! Now let her go before I—"

"What?" Alexander cut him off in amusement. "What are you going to do? Fight me?"

"No."

"Why not?" Alexander took one step closer to him.

"I'm a pacifist."

"Well, guess what? I'm not, and I'm tired of your crap," Alexander spat out as he pulled his arm back.

I jumped in between them and yelled, "Stop!" but it was too late. Alexander's fist connected with my face, and I fell backwards from the force of it. The vine around my hands disappeared but not with enough time for me to catch myself before my head slammed into the ground.

Matthew and Ben were by my side in an instant, both their eyes flashing as they pulled me up.

"I am so sorry, Robin," Alexander said hoarsely.

"I should kill you right now," Matthew told Alexander fiercely as the throbbing in my cheek made my eyes water.

"Allow me," Ben spat out, standing up and taking a step forward with raging eyes.

"That's quite enough of that," Dad said harshly, his voice ringing with authority as a strong wind pushed them both back. "I consider myself a very laid-back man, but I will *not* tolerate this blatant disrespect to my daughter. I won't pretend to understand your individual relationships with her, but that's okay because it's none of my business unless she wants it to be. She is more than capable of coming to decisions regarding you both without any interference from me or anyone else. So, next time you get the urge to butt your nose into a situation that doesn't concern you, don't. Do I make myself clear?"

"Yes, sir," Ben replied quietly.

Alexander didn't answer, his narrowed eyes looking far into the forest.

"For the record, I have strong opinions about both of you, but you don't hear me voicing them. You'd be wise to learn the art of holding your tongue," Dad added before kneeling next to me. "Are you okay, kiddo?"

"I've had much worse," I replied with a wry smile, and he chuckled as Ben's face twisted unhappily. "Don't look so upset, Ben."

"He *hit* you," he replied.

"So have half the people here," I said with a shrug. "Besides, it was an accident."

Akio came beside me as I stood and ran his hand over my face. The cool, prickling sensation soothed the pain, and I gave him a thumbs up.

"Thank you," I said, and he nodded as I turned back towards Ben. "See? Good as new."

"Doesn't make it any better in my book," he muttered, and I patted his arm before looking at Alexander.

"I'm sorry," he repeated, and I grinned, trying to lighten the mood.

"It's okay. Kodi's punches hurt worse than yours anyway," I told him jokingly.

"You better believe it," Kodi said with a smirk as Alexander rolled his eyes.

"Let's keep going, shall we?" Dad suggested.

"We don't have to do that actually," William replied as he and Malachi came around a tree. "We scouted ahead while you were preoccupied."

"What did you find?" Dad asked.

"The thing we've been looking for."

"You found Silas?" Luna exclaimed.

"The entrance to him, I believe," William clarified, motioning us forward. "Come see for yourselves."

I, along with everyone else, eagerly followed. My heart thumped wildly, the anticipation eating away at me at the prospect of being so close to our goal. We wove through a dense collection of trees, and I let out an inaudible gasp at the sight in front of me.

A wall of tree trunks towered over us as high as the eye could see. There was no sign of the greenery and branches that sat somewhere above the clouds. Their colossal size was easily five times larger than a normal tree, and they were merged together, creating an impenetrable shield.

"The trees are forming a circle," William said as I gawked over the image. "I can only imagine the thing they're protecting is Silas himself."

"I'd have to agree," Akio replied quietly as his eyes tried to take in the scale of the tree trunks.

"This is extraordinary," Dad murmured.

"This isn't real life," Ben said, his jaw opened wide.

"Have you ever seen anything so massive?" Mateo asked with wide eyes.

"I can't believe you're giving this kind of life up," Emery said to Kodi.

"The trees . . . They're speaking," Alexander said in a hushed tone, and I turned to stare at him.

"What?" Matthew asked, his expression as perplexed as I felt.

"I hear it too," Luna said, closing her eyes and holding both hands up, as if feeling something the rest of us couldn't. "But I don't think they're speaking."

"They're singing," Alexander replied, and she nodded as the rest of us stared on in confusion.

"What exactly are they singing about?" Matthew asked.

"Part of it is the words from the map," Alexander answered. "Then a warning before we try to go any further."

"*Take the risk, make the jump. Come see what lies beyond. Put your trust in me to see the tree beyond the translucent pond,*" Luna whispered. "It's kind of eerie, I have to admit."

"Eerie or not, this is what we came for," William said. "We need to find a way inside."

"Mateo, can you fly up and see if there's any openings anywhere?" Malachi asked.

"Can do," Mateo replied before shifting into a vibrant toucan and whipping his wings into action.

"Is this normal for Garridan life?" Ben asked.

"Definitely not," Dad replied. "I'm as stunned as you are."

"If this is the outside of where Silas lives, imagine what the inside looks like," Matthew said with a shake of his head.

"I bet it's beautiful!" Akio exclaimed.

"Or it's nothing but a barren waste land meant to lead us to our deaths," Alexander said.

"I hate to agree with Sir Punch-A-Lots, but I agree with Sir Punch-A-Lots," Emery said, and I shot them both a disapproving look.

"Silas wouldn't bring us this far just to kill us," Dad said.

"Technically, he didn't bring us here," Emery pointed out. "We came on our own and paid the price. Two people already died. What's to say more won't?"

"Pass the trial, and you'll be fine," Matthew replied with a shrug. "Silas' goal isn't to kill everyone. It's just to weed out the bad seeds."

"Vivi wasn't a bad seed," Kodi said harshly.

"No, she wasn't," Matthew agreed with a shake of his head. "She just paid the price for one, unfortunately."

"This trial doesn't sound so bad though," I spoke up, trying to sound reassuring. "It's obviously about trusting Silas, so just stop doubting him. We'll all be fine."

"I've heard that before," Emery muttered, and I sighed.

"Fine. Be all gloom and doom," I told her. "I'll keep hoping for the best."

"And I'll expect the worst."

"You do that."

"She's a handful, isn't she?" Ben asked with a shake of his head as he came beside me.

"They all are in their own ways," I replied. "So are you."

"You aren't so easy yourself," he said, and I snorted.

"Oh, please."

"It's true."

"Uh huh."

We grinned at one another and the lightheartedness in his eyes stirred something in me. As I stared at the deep amber tones that had always drawn me in, I found myself stepping closer to him. He cocked his head to the side slightly, trying to read into my approach, then reached out towards me. I knew I needed to stop, but the pull between us was intense, and I was tired of missing him.

Squawk.

Mateo landed on his feet as his upper body twisted back into human form. I took a big step away from Ben and cleared my throat. He brushed his fingers through his hair and walked towards the barrier as I focused on Mateo.

"There's no end to these tree trunks," Mateo said. "No matter how high I flew, they still went higher, and I didn't see a single opening when I circled the outside of it."

"How are we supposed to get in then?" Matthew asked.

"Would this help?" Ben asked.

He was standing next to the barrier, pointing near the ground, and I realized the bark was slowly shifting. My eyes widened, and I clasped my hands over my ears as loud cracking echoed around us. Two tree trunks separated then broke off from the rest, intertwining around themselves as they formed an archway.

We had a way in.

"How did you do that?" Matthew demanded.

"I don't know. All I did was run my hand along it, and it started moving," Ben replied.

"I wonder . . ." Alexander murmured.

"What?" I asked.

"Ben is a descendant of Silas, who happens to be an earth element. Which means Ben could've been as well had his ancestors stayed in Garridan," he said. "So, I just wonder if maybe Silas could sense that."

"Sense that an earth element is near?" Akio asked.

"That wouldn't make sense because you and Luna are here too," Kodi pointed out.

"No, sense that he's family," Alexander corrected.

"An interesting theory," Malachi said. "Or perhaps this is the reason we needed someone from the normal world to come on the journey with us."

"To get us into Silas' hiding place," William said with a nod. "Could be."

"Are we going in or not?" Mateo asked as he shifted from one foot to the other. His hands kept balling into fists then releasing.

"Yes," I told him, walking to where he stood with Kodi. I placed one hand on each of their shoulders. "Let's get you two home."

Kodi's eyes lit up, and she grabbed Mateo's hand tightly. I looked over at Dad and Malachi, and they both nodded.

"Matthew, William," Malachi called out. "Let's go."

The guard took their cue and shuffled through the archway, fanning out like a well-oiled machine to check for possible threats. The rest of us slowly trailed behind and as I stepped through the opening, I was completely underwhelmed.

"I guess barren wasteland was right after all," Emery muttered.

"This wasn't what I was expecting," Andre said.

"I mean . . . The tree is really big," Akio said.

"But it's dead," Kodi replied in disgust.

"Surely that can't be Silas then . . . Can it?" Mateo asked.

They all looked at me, and I opened my mouth wordlessly as I lifted one shoulder. "I don't know," I admitted quietly as I looked around.

We stood at the edge of a large clearing with nothing but a big tree rooted in the very center. The land beneath our feet was as dry and brown as the Sahara, and the tree stood naked and brittle. There was no sign of life anywhere.

"What now?" Ben asked.

Dad and Luna exchanged a glance, neither of them having an answer either, as the guard members walked around the grounds, searching for any sign of a next step. The loud cracking from before started out of nowhere, and I jumped in surprise. I whirled around to see the opening shrinking as the two tree trunks fused back together.

"Great!" Emery exclaimed. "Now we're stuck here to rot."

"Don't be so dramatic," Matthew said. "This isn't a trap. We're just missing something."

"Missing? No. Not seeing? Yes." I winced as the familiar sound of Silas' voice echoed through my head.

"What the heck does that mean?" Mateo asked.

As if answering, the tree lifted slightly, sitting on its own small, circular island as a shimmery pool of liquid appeared all around it. The different hues of pink and purple res-embled a sunset reflecting on the water as it reached out as far as the eye could see. It was absolutely beautiful.

"You've all come very far the last few days," Silas said, "and you're almost to your desired destination. However, one more trial stands between you and I. You've shown your strength, but now I need your bravery. One of you must perform the ultimate sacrifice. One of you must go so the rest of you can find answers. Which one it is, is up to you. Good luck."

I shook my head as his voice became a distant sound. Everyone shared looks of concern. Silas' words were another unforgivable request.

"Did he really just tell us to sacrifice someone's life *again*?" Kodi asked.

"We already learned our lesson on sacrifice with the first trial," Andre replied. "This has to be a trick somehow. He wouldn't test us on the same thing twice."

"I agree," Luna said. "But what could he have meant then?"

"The first trial was whether we'd sacrifice someone for our own gain or not," Alexander pointed out. "This one sounds more like will one of us sacrifice ourselves for everyone else. If that's the case, it's two entirely different tests."

"So, one of us has to sacrifice ourselves for the rest to get out of here?" Mateo asked as he ran his hand over the back of his neck.

"No," Dad said firmly. "Absolutely not. We will *not* sacrifice anybody for any reason."

Everyone stood still for a moment, waiting for his words to trigger the passing of the trial like mine had done the first time, but nothing happened.

"What are we going to do?" Luna asked.

"There has to be something we're missing," Malachi said.

"Seems pretty straightforward to me," Alexander muttered.

"Go ahead then," Emery told him. "Kill yourself."

"No one is killing themselves," Dad repeated harshly.

I tuned them out—having no desire to listen to the argument I knew was coming—as I ventured near the water around the tree. I knelt down and ran my fingers through it, expecting to feel wetness, but was surprised when they brushed nothing but smoke. It looked exactly like a liquid but was actually just a dense gas. Strange.

The words on the map played in my head.

Take the risk, make the jump. Come see what lies beyond. Put your trust in me to see the tree beyond the translucent pond.

I rubbed my lips together as I repeated it again and again and watched the swirling of the fog-like substance, letting it sooth me as I thought. That's when it hit me—this was the pond referred to in the riddle! Which meant something was beyond it. If that were true, this would have to be our way out, and the poem literally said to make the jump. It must be referring to jumping into the pond.

Right?

The longer I pondered it, the more sense it made. Silas said we needed to be brave and one must go so the rest could find answers. I glanced over my shoulder where the group was still bickering. Most of them would be too afraid to jump through the pond without knowing it wasn't a death sentence. If I did it first and somehow got a message back to them, they'd come through as well and get their answers from Silas.

I bit my lip. There was no guarantee my theory was right. If I was wrong, I could be jumping to my death.

"Be brave," Silas said quietly in my head and, in that moment, I knew I had to do it.

"Stop thinking what you're thinking," Matthew said as he came up behind me.

I stood as I glanced at him. "What do you mean?"

"You're thinking about sacrificing yourself."

"No, I'm not."

"I can see it on your face." He crossed his arms. "Besides, I know you."

"No, I just . . ." I trailed off and looked back at the pond. "I think I know the answer to Silas' words and the riddle on the map."

"Does it involve you dying?" he pressed.

"I mean, I hope not."

"That's not good enough."

Ben started walking our way, and I looked from him to Matthew then back again. His brows furrowed at my expression, and he quickened his pace. I looked back at Matthew, whose face was stern.

"I'm sorry," I whispered.

"Robin, no!" Matthew yelled, reaching his arm out to grab me. But I'd already jumped back, and his hand missed me as I fell through the gassy pond.

Silas, please don't kill me.

CHAPTER TWENTY-NINE

I was sinking.

In a churning cascade of colors that exploded around me, I was sinking deeper and deeper. My hands desperately clawed at the air, like that would stop my downward tumble, but it didn't make a difference. I held my breath, unsure if I could breathe in the gas that enveloped my body, and my lungs begged for air. Finally, I stopped struggling, and that's when I realized I wasn't sinking.

I was floating.

My arms raised above my head without my consent, and my eyes followed with intrigue.

Was this death?

A bright light caught my attention, and I wondered what it belonged to. I swam towards it, the motion slow but manageable. This is what I imagined being weightless in space felt like. I made my movements wider and more forceful, the ache for a breath pushing me higher and higher. Then, as suddenly as I was in it, my head broke through the surface of the pond, and I inhaled greedily.

A coughing fit spasmed out of my mouth as I pulled myself out of the pond. I flopped onto my back and brea-thed heavily as I tried to catch my breath. My lungs ached, but at least I wasn't wet.

"You could've breathed in there you know," Silas said with a chuckle, his voice outside my head this time.

I glanced around but didn't see him as I thought I would. Instead, I was met with the same surroundings I'd just left. Only now, they were lively. The ground was lush with thick, green grass and an assortment of wildflowers and bushy plants. Gone was the lifeless tree, and in its place stood a beautifully blossomed sapling, whose limbs stretched far and wide.

That wasn't the strangest thing though. The people I'd jumped away from were all around me, but they were translucent versions of themselves. I could barely hear their muffled words as they spoke and moved around, and I stepped back to see what was happening.

Matthew and Alexander banged their fists against a force field that William had formed around the pond. Luna had her hand on Dad's shoulder as he stared wordlessly at the scene, and the trainees clung to one another with horrified shock glued to their faces. But it was Ben who drew my attention.

He'd fallen to his knees in the same spot I'd just been standing. His eyes were almost hollow as he stared into the pond, but a deep anguish lingered in them. He was an emotional person in general, but there were no tears in his eyes now. Somehow, that made his expression worse. He looked absolutely broken.

I knelt in front of him and tried to place my hand on his cheek to assure him I was okay, but it went straight through instead. I couldn't touch him.

"Your family and friends hold a lot of love for you," Silas said.

I stood, whirling around to find him, but the urgency wasn't needed. This time, there he was, standing directly in front of me with his hands clasped together.

He was tall with long, black hair and deep brown eyes. His facial shape was the same as Ben's, but his nose and lips were narrower, and his hairline sat further back on his forehead. Aside from the color, his kind eyes were a mirror image of Ben's.

"Silas?" I asked hesitantly, and he nodded.

"Welcome," he replied.

"What is this place?" I gestured around as my eyes traveled over it again.

"My home," he answered as he looked around lovingly.

"Why does everyone else look translucent? Are they really here? I don't think they can see me."

"You could say we're in a different dimension. One very close to theirs but just far enough away that I'm safe from harm. We can see what's happening on their side, but they can't see what's happening on ours," he explained.

"So, are you really here then? I thought you turned into a tree."

"I am here as much as you are. This is a place where my human body can separate from my tree body, so I can interact with the few guests I get. It also allows me to travel all throughout Zohara so I can make sure things are safe and in working order."

"Is the tree I saw before you too?"

"It is, and it's my most vulnerable state," he answered. "If any harm comes to me on that side of the veil, all this would come crumbling down." He motioned around us. "I'm useless over there though. I have no way to protect myself when in tree form, so I spend most of my time here."

"I hope you know how crazy that all sounds," I commented with a shake of my head.

"It's definitely strange, even for a child of Garridan," he replied with a smile. "I dare say I'm the most complex thing about our way of life."

"I would have to agree."

"It's best not to overthink it," he advised. "You'll go mad. Let's talk about you instead, shall we?"

"What about me?"

"I'm not surprised you were the one to take a leap of faith to find me. I was betting on you from the moment you stepped off the plane."

"You could see us?" I asked.

"I can see everything in Zohara."

"Oh."

"Your group is searching for a multitude of requests. Let me ask you this: What would you say if I couldn't help but a few of them?"

"I'd ask you to take care of Kodi and Mateo," I replied without hesitation. "They deserve to go home to their families."

"Even if it meant you losing your request in return?" Silas questioned.

My brows furrowed. "I don't have a request."

"Not yet you don't, but you will soon."

"I'm not sure what that means, but I'd still choose helping Kodi and Mateo over myself no matter what it was I wanted."

Silas observed me for a moment with one hand stroking his chin. "I can see you truly mean those words and for that, I'm going to grant your request when you ask."

"Thank you?" I replied slowly, still confused.

"It's individuals like you who will keep Garridan safe and thriving. Don't ever lose sight of who you are and the values you hold."

"I won't," I said quietly.

A muffled thud caught my attention, and I glanced over my shoulder to see Matthew in a scuffle with William. Matthew pinned him to the ground then pointed towards the force field around the pond.

"Take it down!" Matthew's dampened voice yelled.

"It's a suicide mission!" I barely heard William yell back. "She isn't dead!"

"You don't know that!"

They started rolling on the ground again but were quickly separated by two branches that sprouted from the ground. With his hands pinned to his side, William's force field disappeared.

"This isn't helping anyone," Luna chastised as she drew them further apart. She glanced towards my dad and quietly asked, "What do you want to do, Elijah?"

"I don't . . . I don't know," he murmured as he stood unmoving. "I don't know."

My heart shattered at the scene.

"They think I'm dead," I said softly as I walked in front of him. "I'm okay, Dad. I'm right here." I strode back to Ben and spoke louder. "I'm okay. I'm right here!"

"They can't hear you, Robin," Silas reminded me gently.

"I know but look at them. There has to be a way for me to tell them I'm okay. They can come over here too, right?"

"Of course. All they need to do is jump through the pond to reach us."

I brought my attention back to Ben and stared at him intently. "Understand, Ben. Please understand."

I closed my eyes and gathered the liquid around me. With as much concentration as I could muster, I shot the stream into the pond. I could feel it searching around, trying to figure out where to go. I breathed deeply and guided it through the gas, desperately trying to sense what I couldn't see. By some small miracle, it pushed through the last of the smoke, coming out on the other side of the veil.

I opened my eyes and could see the water rising from the pond. It felt different, almost out of tune with me, but I pressed it forward as it caught Ben's attention. Sweat beaded on my forehead as I twisted the water into two separate creations—a bear and a giraffe.

Ben's eyes lit up, immediately recognizing the animals from the friendship bracelet he still carried around. He glanced over his shoulder, but no one was paying any attention to him as they continued to argue. Without a second thought, he dove headfirst into the pond, disappearing as a translucent form then reappearing the same instance as solid as me.

As he pulled himself out of the hole, his eyes raked his surroundings. When they landed on me, relief filled his tension ridden body.

"Robin," he choked out as he stood, and I ran into his arms. "I thought I'd lost you."

He clutched me tightly, pressing my head into his chest as he took in shaky breaths.

"I'm okay," I assured him. "I'm fine. I'm right here."

"That was the worst five minutes of my life," he murmured into my hair.

"Imagine going through that for days," I replied, thinking of his ski accident.

He pulled back and cupped my cheeks in his hands. "Robin, there's something I need to tell you. I love you."

"I know," I said.

"No, just listen!" he insisted. "I love you and you love me. Which means nothing else matters. We can get through everything else as long as we have each other. So." He took a deep breath and the corner of his mouth lifted slightly as my heart threatened to jump out of my chest. "I want—"

"Robin!"

I glanced past Ben to see Matthew coming out of the pond followed closely by Alexander and my dad. Ben released me and stepped to the side, nodding at me to greet them when I hesitated.

What was he going to say?

Matthew gave me a quick hug before my dad wrapped me in a long one. I smiled over at Alexander, and he only nodded in reply, but I could see the relief in his eyes.

"You guys came through!" I exclaimed.

"We couldn't let you die alone," Alexander commented, and Matthew rolled his eyes.

"Akio could sense you weren't dead," Matthew said. "So these scaredy cats finally let us through."

"We weren't scared," William said as he came up beside us. "Just being cautious."

"We couldn't have everyone jumping to their death after all," Luna added as she and Malachi appeared. She glanced around and her eyes widened when she saw the trainees lined up by the pond on the other side of the veil. "This is amazing."

I peeked over to where Silas had been standing, but he was nowhere to be seen, so I pulled my focus back to the pond as the rest of our group made their way through. After many more relieved greetings and lots of awe-inspired comments of our surroundings, Alexander finally asked the question I'd been waiting for someone to bring up.

"Is this Silas?" he asked, pointing to the massive tree.

"Technically, yes," I responded. "But he was also here in human form just a minute ago." I looked at Ben and said, "He has your eyes. Well, I guess technically you have his eyes."

He smiled softly. "I didn't think there'd be many similarities seeing as how many generations have passed."

"Where is he now?" Kodi asked.

"Probably just hanging around listening," I replied as I surveyed our surroundings. "He's been watching us since we got off the plane."

"Because that's not creepy at all," Emery commented.

"He's just trying to keep his home safe," I said. "You can't fault him for that."

"No, but some would try," Silas' voice boomed around us. He stepped out from behind the tree with a smile on his face. When he spoke again, his voice was normal. "And I've been watching you for much longer than that." He chuckled as if the revelation was amusing. "Welcome. You've all worked hard to get here. I'm sorry for the troubles you faced along the way, but I hope you each learned something about yourselves over the last couple days."

No one responded as they stared at him with varying degrees of awe, so I decided to ask the question on my mind.

"I thought you said this side of the veil allowed you to travel all throughout Zohara," I started, and he nodded.

"That's correct."

"Does it allow you to travel outside of Zohara too?"

"Unfortunately not. I have to stay close to my roots," he replied as he beckoned towards the tree.

"How have you been watching us then?" I asked curiously.

"The answer to that, like everything with me, is again complex," he said. "I think the simplest way to explain is to compare it to a power seeker. They can find and monitor people by their power surges. My ability is very similar but exponentially greater. I keep tabs on each individual who possesses a power at all times, but it's not just their powers I see.

"It's also their intents and desires. I see their character and know who they are as a person. I know if they're good or bad, and I see when they're struggling with themselves morally. I don't see anyone physically, but I still know who they are better than they know themselves. I know each of *you* better than you know yourselves."

He met each of our gazes as most of us shifted uncomfortably at the information.

"Okay, now it's even *more* creepy," Emery mumbled.

"If you have all that knowledge, why didn't you ever do anything to stop the Cyfrin?" Alexander asked with narrowed eyes. "You had twenty years to intervene but never did. Why? Do you know how much death you could've stopped? How much trauma could've been avoided?"

"You are angry for yourself," Silas replied calmly. "For what you had to endure."

"Of course I am!" Alexander yelled.

"The boy has a point," Malachi said. "The Cyfrin wanted to take over the world. That must be the very definition of abusing nature's gift to us. Why sit here and do nothing?"

"History must be allowed to play itself out," Silas answered. "The tragedies that unfolded were necessary for other events to happen."

"That sounds like a load of bull crap," Kodi muttered then her eyes widened, and she said, "Respectfully, of course."

"I will never intervene unless absolutely necessary. And though it took twenty years, I wasn't needed to weed out the threat of the Cyfrin." Silas looked around at us again before focusing on Dad and Luna. "My intervention means the end of Garridan's existence entirely. If I'm ever truly needed, it'll be to preserve nature. Not my birthplace."

"In that case, we were more than happy to take care of the Cyfrin ourselves," Dad replied, his voice cracking nervously.

"You're a good man, Elijah," Silas told him. "You've done well in your position. Keeping Garridan safe isn't an easy feat, so I applaud you and the other council members for how you handled such a large threat. Just remind them all to learn from it. To grow from it."

"Yes, sir," Dad answered.

"The same goes for you, Luna," he said as he turned towards her. "You're still young and haven't been on the council very long, but you've seen so much already. I know you've lost some friends and need to find replacements for them. When you do, teach them well. Let the Cyfrin's doings be a valuable lesson to any new leader of Garridan."

"Of course," Luna answered, her eyes wide as she stared at him.

He clasped his hands together and smiled again. His demeanor reminded me a lot of Ben.

"I know you have many more questions," he said, "but I must warn you, everything you learn here won't return home with you. It'll be wiped from your memories so asking what you want to know is somewhat futile."

"We're not going to remember this?" Akio asked.

"You'll remember your journey and what you've gone through and learned about yourselves. You'll also remember me. However, the details will be foggy. You won't be able to recall the specifics of the trials you endured nor what we speak of here that involves me."

"So we can't take any information on you back to Garridan," Luna said with a shake of her head. "How pointless."

"Is it?" Silas questioned. "Is what you discovered about yourself worth nothing?"

"Oh, w-well of course not," she stuttered. "I just meant—"

"I'm fully aware of what you meant," Silas said harshly, holding up one hand. "However, I care very little about what you came here seeking. My job is to protect nature and in order to do that, I must keep certain details hidden from Garridan. If I wanted you to have records of me, you would've had them long ago."

Dad and Luna exchanged a somewhat guilty look that reminded me of children getting chastised. Silas looked at them gently and when he spoke again his voice was softer.

"It's my job to protect nature," he repeated, "but it's *your* job to protect Garridan. You must find a way to do that regardless of the unknown."

He leaned back as a tree stump sprang from the ground, easily catching him so he was sitting upon it. He crossed one leg over the other and placed his hands on his knee.

"Now," he said calmly as he appraised us, "how about we get to your last trial?"

CHAPTER THIRTY

"What do you mean 'last trial?'" Emery asked as she placed her hands on her hips. "There were only three on the map."

"You can't expect to come here and me perform favors without some proof of merit," Silas replied. "But don't worry. This is a simple assessment."

"What is it?" Alexander asked suspiciously.

"We'll get to that," Silas assured him. "First, I need to send some of you back home."

"So soon?" Dad asked.

"There is nothing for you here," Silas replied. "The ones who need to stay will, but for the rest of you, your time is done."

"Wait, who's staying?" Mateo asked. "You're gonna let us say goodbye to everyone first, right?"

"Of course, child," Silas responded. "Andre, Emery, Matthew, Robin, Kodi, Mateo, Alexander, and Ben. You'll be staying with me a while longer. As for the rest of you, say your goodbyes if you so desire."

I watched quietly as Dad, Luna, and Malachi exchanged words and hugs with Mateo, Kodi, and Ben. Akio grasped each of their hands tightly, looking surprisingly sad, and Emery was frantically grabbing onto Andre, an uncommon terror in her eyes.

"You said you were staying!" she exclaimed.

"I am," he replied, his hands enveloping hers.

"Then why aren't you being sent back to Garridan?"

"I'm not sure. Why aren't you?" he countered.

I rubbed my lips together, puzzled by that question. The people who were staying versus leaving made no sense to me. If Mateo and Kodi were the only two who wanted something from Silas, why were the rest of us not being sent away as well? There was no rhyme or reason to it.

"We'll see you soon, Robin," Dad said as he came up next to me. "Right?"

"I think so," I replied hesitantly. "I'm not planning on asking to give up my powers."

"You better not," he replied sternly, and I could see the worry in his eyes. "I don't know what I'd say to your mother and Toby."

"Just tell them I'll be home for dinner," I said, trying to give him a reassuring smile, and he squeezed my shoulder.

"It was lovely meeting all of you," Silas said to the group he was about to oust. "I hope you'll remember our interaction as a positive one and strive to keep Garridan the best version of itself it can be. With that being said, I hope I never have to see any of you again."

He raised both arms and swept them away from his body. Dad, Malachi, and everyone else simultaneously disappeared, and I tried to swallow down my nerves. Silas smiled at us widely as we stood stationary in front of him.

"Don't look so worried!" he exclaimed. "Nothing bad can happen from this challenge. Well, your request could get denied but no physical harm."

"What about mental?" Matthew asked.

"To be determined," Silas replied apologetically.

I glanced over our group, seeing that none of them looked reassured. I cleared my throat and took a step forward.

"Could you maybe tell us what exactly the trial is so we can calm down?" I asked.

"Of course, of course!" he rapidly agreed. "This one is simply about trust and selflessness. Four of you have something you want from me. The other four are the people from your search group that you were closest to. They'll help in getting you what you want."

I already knew he was referring to Mateo and Kodi but who were the other two? Had Andre or Emery changed their minds? I knew for sure it couldn't be Matthew.

"Let's start with Mateo," Silas said. "Andre will be helping you."

The two glanced at one another then stepped forward. I wrapped my arm in Emery's, trying to calm her fidgeting.

"Uhm," Mateo said, rubbing his palms on his jeans. "I was hoping you'd take my powers and send me home without losing my memories of them."

"I can do that. But I need you to earn it."

"How?"

"This is a lesson in truths—the truths you've been hiding for understandable reasons. But now is the time to tell those truths and let the only people who can help you do so." Silas watched Mateo knowingly and raised his brows. "You know what I speak of, don't you?"

"Yes, I think so," Mateo murmured. He pressed his lips together and inhaled deeply before turning towards Andre. His eyes jumped over the rest of us as he shifted from one foot to the other. "Ever since you decided to stay in Garridan, I've been . . . Struggling . . . Thinking you're being selfish."

"Selfish?" Andre repeated in surprise.

"Yeah." Mateo scratched the back of his head uncomfortably then peeked over at Silas. "This is what you meant, right?"

Silas nodded. "Continue."

"Well," he started, his voice wavering. He cleared his throat then tried again. "I know it's not fair thinking that, but I just can't help worrying about your family. I mean, I know you've only been with them for a couple years and you're an adult and all that but . . . They took you in. They loved you. Can you imagine someone you considered a son disappearing and never knowing what happened to them? Can you imagine the pain they're feeling every day wondering if you're alive or dead?"

Andre's face clouded over as he pressed his lips together in a firm line. His Adam's apple bobbed as he swallowed, and I could basically see the guilt ripping through him.

"What the hell, Mateo?" Emery snapped as she looped her arm through Andre's. "Are you trying to guilt him into leaving me?"

"No!" Mateo exclaimed. "No, of course not! I just- well, I was hoping Andre would be okay with me going and talking to them when I get back."

"You'd do that?" Andre asked.

"Of course I would!"

"What will you say?"

"I'm not entirely sure," Mateo admitted. "But I'd let them know you're okay and that you love them."

Andre gave him a mournful smile and nodded. "I'd honestly be so grateful. Thank you. That means a lot."

"Sorry I kinda judged you," Mateo replied with a nervous chuckle.

"It's water under the bridge. Besides, you're not wrong."

"A hard truth *and* an act of selflessness," Silas said to Mateo, looking pleased. "I'll be happy to grant your request."

"Really?" Mateo replied, his face lighting up with a smile.

"Yes, but first." He looked around. "Kodi, you're next."

"I don't have any hidden truths though," Kodi replied with wide eyes. "I want to go home with my memories intact too, but I don't have anything to reveal. I swear."

"In this instance, you're the receiver of the truth," Silas told her. "Your roadblock will be if you can be selfless enough to assist the one giving the truth."

"Okay," Kodi responded slowly, her eyes drifting over all of us. "So, who has something they want to get off their chests? I'm ready to get out of here."

I noticed Emery pursing her lips and shifting uncomfortably as she rubbed her arm.

"Emery?" I asked curiously.

"What?" she asked, keeping her eyes on the ground.

"Are you okay?" I questioned.

She didn't reply, and Kodi eyed her suspiciously. "Em? Is he talking about you?" she asked.

"I don't know what you're talking about," Emery replied curtly, but I noticed her eyes glistening.

"If you have something that'll help Kodi get home, you have to do it," Andre told her gently.

She peeked up at him from around a strand of hair that had fallen into her eyes then whispered, "I don't know if I can."

"Of course you can," Kodi jumped in encouragingly.

"It's not that simple," Emery replied, her face more distraught than I'd ever seen it. She looked back up at Andre.

"It can't be that bad," he said.

"You'll see me differently."

"No, I won't. I promise."

"You can't promise that."

"Sure I can," he insisted. "You're always so pessimistic, but usually things aren't as bad as you make them out to be. Whatever it is, it'll be okay."

She inhaled shakily and wrapped her arms around herself, as if they would keep her from falling apart. Without looking at any of us, she finally spoke in a hushed tone.

"Six months before the Cyfrin took me, I had a baby," she said.

My jaw fell open, but I quickly closed it in case she decided to glance my way.

"Oh, Emery," Andre murmured, his brows drawing together in concern.

"I gave him up for adoption, but the family I chose for him fell through and he wound up in foster care instead," she continued as a tear escaped her eye.

Andre put his arm around her, and she shuddered as we all watched with varying emotions.

"I'm so sorry," Kodi said quietly, reaching out and touching her arm. "I can't image how much strength that took." She glanced at Silas. "But what does it have to do with me?" Silas nodded towards Emery and Kodi turned towards her again. "Em?"

Emery licked her lips before looking at Kodi. "I didn't want my baby to have the life I did in foster care, so I reached out to the adoptive family to see why they didn't want him at the last minute," she said. Her eyes hardened slightly. "The parents said their other child didn't want a little sibling. That she convinced them they were too old to take on that kind of responsibility and that she'd never love him like a little brother because of the weird age difference."

"What was their age difference?" Andre asked as Kodi's face withdrew more and more.

"Nineteen years," Emery replied, her eyes never leaving Kodi's face.

I looked between the two a couple times then asked, "Can someone explain what's happening?"

"It was me," Kodi whispered. "I'm the other child in that story."

"You? You convinced your parents not to adopt a baby?" I asked, trying to hide my disdain. "Why?"

"I-I didn't want things to change," she replied, near tears. "And I'm not a baby person. They're loud and needy." She saw Emery's glare and rushed to backtrack. "Not your baby, though, I'm sure. I just- I just . . . I'm so sorry!"

"Me too," Emery muttered.

"How can I fix it?" Kodi asked desperately.

"You can't," she snapped. "I don't even know where he is anymore."

"I may be able to help in that department," Silas spoke up. "There's very little I can see in the normal world when it doesn't concern a person from Garridan. However, I've been able to keep somewhat spotty tabs on your son since he has the blood of Garridan flowing in his veins."

"How is he?" Emery asked, all contempt draining from her face. "Is he safe?"

"Yes, he is," Silas assured her. "He's been in a very good foster home—a foster home not far from Kodi's parents in fact."

Understanding dawned on Kodi. "You want me to talk to my parents about him again," she said. "Tell them it's okay to adopt him."

"An act of selflessness," I said quietly.

After a moment of thought, Kodi grabbed Emery's hands in her own. "Of course I will. I won't let your kid grow up in foster care, and I'll tell him how much you loved him when he's older."

"Don't say it if you don't mean it," Emery replied harshly, trying to pull her hands away, but Kodi held on tighter.

"I *do* mean it. I swear!"

Emery eyed her. "I don't want my kid to grow up unwanted."

"But he's not unwanted. My parents were so excited to have him." Kodi dropped her hands to her side as she stared at the ground near her feet. "I just ruined it for them."

"That's messed up," Alexander muttered, his arms crossed over his chest.

Kodi shot a scowl in his direction. "I know that!" She looked back at Emery. "Let me make it right."

"Do you really want to or are you just trying to get home?" Emery asked quietly.

"I'd be lying if I said it wasn't both, but I really do want to. Knowing it's *your* kid . . . I'll love him like my own birth brother."

"Really?" Emery questioned as more tears ran down her cheeks. Kodi nodded eagerly, and Emery hugged her fiercely. "Thank you."

"That's two," Silas commented with a soft smile. "Shall we move on to Alexander?"

I swiveled around to look at him, questions bubbling in me. He met my gaze, apologetic but resolved, then stepped up. He placed his hands behind his back and stood with purpose in front of Silas.

"I'd like you to take away my powers as well," he told him, his words like a punch to the gut as my jaw dropped open. "And I don't particularly care if I remember anything or not."

"You're leaving?" I asked, taking a half step towards him.

"I don't belong in Garridan," he replied without looking at me.

"Yes, you do. It's your home."

"I may have powers, but Garridan is most certainly not my home. There's nothing for me there." I cast my eyes downward as a lump formed in my throat. He must've realized how it sounded because he turned towards me and said, "I didn't mean it like that. It's just—"

"I understand," I told him, trying to smile. "I'm not enough for you to stay. That's why you said we'd never be together. It's why you suddenly switched gears about Ben."

"You're more than enough," he said, reaching out and grabbing my hand. "Anyone would be crazy to leave you if they had the choice not to."

He shot a pointed look towards Ben, but I brought his attention back to me before another argument could start.

"Why are you then?" I asked, and I could hear the sadness in my own voice. I was okay with him deciding we would only ever be friends, but it did still sting. Rejection always did.

He glanced towards Andre then said, "Remember I told you Andre had a vision?" I nodded. "This was it. Me leaving Garridan behind and starting a new life."

"And you thought that meant we couldn't be together."

"Robin, believe me when I say leaving you is the last thing I want to do, but being with you isn't in my future. Not unless you chose to leave and come with me." He let out one humorless laugh. "But if you left, it'd be for *him*. Not me. Am I right?" When I didn't answer he said, "That's what I thought."

"Where are you going to go?" I asked.

"Hell if I know."

"You can't just wander the streets without knowing anything about anything! You'll be homeless and jobless and probably wind up in a mental institution for not know-ing how simple things work. You can't do this without having some sort of plan!"

"He can come home with me," Kodi blurted out, and we all looked at her in shock.

"Seriously?" Mateo asked as his eyebrows raised far into his hairline.

"If I'm already performing one act of selflessness, why not two?" she replied with a shrug.

"That's an interesting offer, but I think I'd rather take my chances on my own," Alexander said.

Kodi placed her hands on her hips and glared. "It's rude to deny someone's hospitality."

"And when have you ever known me to be nice?" he countered.

"You know what, you little—" she started but I quickly cut her off.

"You should take her up on her offer. You don't know how that world works. As much as you hate it, you'll need help, and it'll be better coming from someone who knows why you don't understand." I grabbed his hand in both of mine. "It'll help me sleep at night knowing you're okay. Please. Go home with her. Let her help you get adjusted."

His eyes softened as he took in my pleading expression. "Okay," he said. "Just until I can stand on my own two feet."

"Thank you!" I exclaimed, throwing my arms around him. He hugged me tightly and I sank into it a little deeper, knowing this might be the last time I ever saw him.

"Don't say I never did anything for you," he said as he pulled away.

"I could never," I replied with a small smile.

He glanced towards Kodi and said, "You better have comfortable beds."

"I'm regretting this already," she muttered.

"This situation has brought me great joy," Silas said, a tender smile filling his face. "However, I'm afraid you're missing one little detail."

"And that would be?" Alexander asked.

"You haven't passed your trial."

"Kodi just performed another act of selflessness. What more do you want?"

"I need an act of selflessness from *you*."

"Okay," Alexander replied in annoyance. "Who's fessing up to a truth then because I'm ready for this to be over."

Silas' gaze traveled to Matthew, who was staring very intently at the pond. Alexander followed Silas' look, real-izing Matthew was the person who would help him get his request granted.

"I'm sure you have many truths you could spill," he said. "Choose one and spit it out."

"That's not how this works," Silas reminded him sternly. "There's a specific truth he needs to reveal so I can then see if you can be selfless. I'm sure Matthew knows exactly what I'm referring to."

"Matthew?" I questioned when he refused to speak.

"I honestly could care less what you have to say," Alexander said. "So just say it so we can be done with this."

"You think you're so strong," Matthew finally replied with a small shake of his head. "You think nothing can hurt you—that your skin is so thick nothing can penetrate it. But you're wrong. This will hurt you. This will make you hate me as much as I always claimed to hate you."

"Then I guess it's a good thing I'll likely never see you again," Alexander said, folding his arms impatiently.

Matthew set his jaw then glanced at me before looking at Alexander. He took a deep breath and stood up straighter as they stared each other down.

"Alexander."

"Matthew."

Matthew swallowed loudly. "I killed your parents."

"Matthew," I gasped, my stomach twisting as my heart skipped a beat.

"You . . . Wait you *what?*" Alexander asked in disbelief.

"I killed your parents," Matthew repeated. "They died because of me."

"No. That's not true," Alexander said crossly, shaking his head back and forth.

"It *is* true. Remember the battle we had with Garridan when I was about thirteen? The one where we lost two of our Keepers of Balance?"

"Yes," Alexander replied through gritted teeth.

"Remember the woman who spared your life in battle?" Alexander nodded so Matthew continued, his voice shaking as it lost its edge. "That was your mother. I'm not sure how she knew who you were, but she did. So Toshiro instructed me to help him while he made sure she wouldn't be a problem."

"Matthew, that's enough," I said quietly, touching his arm, but he shook me off.

"We followed her as she ran to get your father. No doubt she wanted to tell him she found you. But she never made it. She was too distracted, so she never saw us coming." Matthew's chin wobbled, but he pressed on. "Toshiro wanted her to suffer, so he only had me petrify her feet and hands so she couldn't run or use her powers. She stood there trapped as he taunted her, telling her how proud he was of you, how many of her people you'd killed."

Alexander's whole body shook as Matthew paused. I once again tried to get him to stop but he wouldn't.

"Toshiro made sure her death was slow. When it was clear she couldn't take anymore, he finally stopped, and I unpetrified her and caught her body as she fell to the ground. Her blood ran down my hands. I stood above her as she stopped breathing. Then I helped track down your dad."

"You bastard!" Alexander roared as he launched himself towards Matthew. He easily knocked him to the ground and wrapped his hand around his throat, but Matthew didn't try to fight back.

Ben took a step forward, but I held my hand up to stop him. In trying to help, he'd only make the situation worse. Alexander tightened his hold, and Matthew's face turned a bright shade of red as he lay there, doing nothing to stop the end that was inevitably coming.

"You sorry son of a—"

"Alexander!" I yelled, cutting him off.

"Stay out of this, Robin," he hissed.

"You know I can't do that," I replied firmly. "I can't let you kill him."

"He deserves it!"

"No, he doesn't."

"He killed my parents."

"No, Toshiro did."

"He *helped*."

"And how many people's parents have you killed?" I asked, slowly walking towards them.

He gritted his teeth, his eyes tightening. "It's not the same thing. He was supposed to be my brother."

"A brother you were going to kill because Toshiro told you to," I reminded him. He glanced my way as I stepped closer, and I barely recognized his lifeless eyes. "The Cyfrin controlled you both most of your lives. You both did awful things for them. Terrible, unspeakable things. But this was *their* fault. Don't let them make you do one more thing you'll regret. Because you *will* regret this. I know you will, and so do you."

Alexander's fingers tensed, causing the grip on Matthew's throat to grow worse.

"Alexander . . . Don't do this." I held his gaze as I fought back tears. "Please. If not for yourself then for me. Don't kill him . . . *Please!*"

My voice broke, and Alexander's brows rose slightly as his eyes turned sorrowful. He finally released his hold and fell onto his butt as Matthew gasped for air and coughed uncontrollably. I fell to his side as he rolled onto his hands and knees, placing my hand on his back as I tried to make sure he was okay.

"Get me out of this place *now*," Alexander spat out, standing far away from us now.

"I'm afraid your trial isn't over quite yet," Silas told him.

"Like hell it isn't!" Alexander yelled.

"What more does he need to do?" I questioned as Ben helped Mathew to his feet.

"His act of selflessness," Silas replied.

"He just showed an incredible amount of restraint and didn't kill Matthew," I said. "I'd say that was pretty selfless."

"He needs to show forgiveness."

"Forgiveness and selflessness are two entirely different things. You can't really expect him to show forgiveness when he just learned what happened to his parents." I placed my hands on my hips, the idea of it sounding ridiculous. "Not even a saint could show forgiveness that quickly!"

"I know I couldn't, and I'm a pretty forgiving person in general," Ben spoke up quietly before addressing Silas directly. "You can't honestly tell us you could either."

"Alexander deserves to leave and start over," I said with unwavering conviction. "Don't keep him here on some impossible technicality. He let Matthew live. Let that be his selfless act."

Silas watched Alexander for a long minute as Alexander actively ignored him. His eyes traveled over each of us, looking thoughtful, before landing on me.

"I can see your logic on the matter," he said. "So, just this once, I'll let you persuade me. The boy's request shall be granted with the others."

"Does that mean we can go *now?*" Alexander asked, his hands balled into fists.

"We still have one more request to take care of but yes. I suppose I can send the rest of you away," Silas agreed. "I don't need an audience. Say your goodbyes quickly then we'll get to Benjamin."

I glanced towards Ben curiously but let the wonder drain away as Mateo came up and hugged me. I held onto him tightly and tried to hold back tears as I pulled back and smiled.

"I'm gonna miss you," I told him, and he nodded, unable to speak.

I yanked him in for one more quick hug then turned towards Kodi, who was in an emotional goodbye with Emery. As soon as she was done, she wrapped her arm around me.

I leaned my head against hers and whispered in her ear, "Look after him."

She glanced towards Alexander, who was standing stiffly with no intention of speaking to anyone.

"I'll do my best," she replied.

"That's all I'm asking for," I said, knowing it wouldn't be an easy transition for either of them. "Take care of yourself, okay?"

She nodded, and I let her go before stepping back. Ben placed his arm around my shoulder, and I leaned into him, grateful for the comfort. I'd miss Mateo's jokes and lighthearted grin and Kodi's unique resilience. They would forever hold a place in my heart, no matter how much time passed.

The group we'd formed while in the Cyfrin's clutches would always feel incomplete without them, but I was thankful they were getting what they wanted. Their families would be overjoyed at seeing them again and that thought brought me enough solace to let them go without crying.

Alexander met my gaze, and I held up one hand, barely waving it. He nodded his head slightly, and I knew that was the only acknowledgement I'd get. At least I'd gotten a hug from him earlier.

"Everyone ready?" Silas asked. He pushed his arms out away from his body as he had earlier, then there were only three of us left in his domain—him, Ben, and me.

CHAPTER THIRTY-ONE

The air was still, silent. A light breeze passed over us, pushing my hair back slightly. I licked my lips as Silas watched Ben and me. He didn't speak, as if he was waiting for one of us to say something first. I glanced up at Ben and he peered down at me, then I looked back at Silas.

"I still don't have a request," I said.

"You will after you hear his," Silas replied, nodding towards Ben. "Go ahead, my boy. I already know what's in your heart. It's time to tell her."

Ben nodded then turned towards me, looking nervous as he rubbed his hands on his jeans. The sides of his lips drifted up in a smile as my forehead creased.

What was his request?

"Robin."

"Benjamin?" I questioned, my stomach twisting in anticipation.

He grabbed my hands as he stared at me, his eyes gentle and full of adoration. "I love you. With all my heart and every fiber in my being, I am completely and madly in love with you."

Butterflies filled my stomach as my heart pounded faster in my chest. "I mean, I-I love you too but—"

"No. No buts," he cut me off. "No more excuses. Not anymore. I love you and you love me and that's all that matters. I don't ever want to spend another day without you so, if you'll have me, I want to go and be a part of Garridan with you."

My mouth opened slightly, and I inhaled loudly. "You-you want to come back to Garridan?"

"Yes."

"To live?"

"Yes."

"Forever?"

"Yes."

I swallowed around the lump in my throat as tears sprang to my eyes. "But what about your family? Your tribe? What about college? All your plans?"

"None of it matters as long as I'm with you."

"Of course it matters!" I exclaimed, pulling away from him. "What if you change your mind in a couple years? Or ten or twenty? You'll be stuck with no way out and end up resenting me."

He reached out and grabbed my shoulders, his gaze fixated on me as I tried to blink away tears.

"Robin," he said, his voice firm yet somehow still soft. "Every time I imagine my future, it's missing something. No matter how hard my head tries to come up with a positive outcome, it's like my heart is pulling in a different direction. My head is content in one place but my heart . . . It's wandering. And you want to know where it always ends up?"

"Where?" I whispered.

"With you." He pressed his lips together and shook his head then lifted one hand to my cheek, rubbing it with his thumb. "You're the destination of my wandering heart."

I tried to breath, but I was paralyzed by his words as they wound themselves through me. I tried to speak but nothing came out.

He loved me. He was choosing me. He was staying with me.

A lighthearted laugh left my lungs, and I threw myself into him. He wrapped his arms around my waist and swung me around as he matched my laughter. When my feet hit the ground again, he placed his forehead against mine. I put my hands on either side of his face, letting my lips find his.

A tingle ran up my spine as heat washed through me. His lips were soft and eager as they moved against mine, and my head grew foggy as I allowed myself to forget everything but him. Some people may not believe in soul mates—I wasn't even sure if I did—but he was the closest thing to it for me. We belonged together. We always had.

He pulled me into a hug, and I let my head rest on his chest as he held me. He was my happily ever after.

"I hate to butt into such a beautiful moment," Silas said, seeming to truly mean it, "but there's still one more hurdle to pass."

"The trial," I murmured, pulling away from Ben but keeping our hands intertwined. "I don't have any big truths, which means you do."

"Unfortunately, yes," Ben replied, looking grim. He sighed and met my gaze unhappily. "About a month after you and Matthew left Milton, Felicity and I . . . Well, we had a moment."

"A moment?" I repeated, arching one brow as I tried to suppress a smile.

"She kissed me," he explained, running his hand over the back of his neck. "And I guess I kinda kissed her back." His eyes widened and he rushed to continue. "It lasted all of five seconds, though, I swear. And we were both really embarrassed after and nothing like it ever happened again. I have no feelings for her, and she made it clear she definitely has no feelings for me."

A laugh escaped my mouth, and I threw my hand up to cover it as more threatened to come. Ben stepped back, appalled at my reaction.

"You're *laughing*?" he questioned, and I nodded as I let the giggles fly freely. He glanced over at Silas and said, "She's laughing!" as if he couldn't see that for himself.

"I'm sorry," I managed to say as I grinned from ear to ear. "It's just that's the most ridiculous thing I've ever heard. *You* and *Felicity*? No. That would never work."

"You're not mad?"

I stopped laughing and thought about it for a second. "No," I answered honestly. "I'm not."

"How?" he asked, still shocked.

"How could I be? You were both hurting and lonely and couldn't talk to anyone else about it, so I'm sure you grew close." I grabbed his hand and grinned again. "Besides, Felicity always makes inappropriate passes when she's over-ly emotional, so I'm not surprised it happened."

"So, you're not mad," Ben confirmed, "and you aren't going to hold it against me?"

"Nope. Consider it a free pass." I snuggled up to his chest again. "Besides, what kind of a hypocrite would I be if I was mad about this when you had to be okay with Alexander?" I sighed as he rubbed his hands along my back. "We're finally together again. This is our chance at a happily ever after, and I'm not going to let anything ruin it."

"I love you, Robin," he murmured as he kissed the top of my head.

"I love you too," I replied happily, then I narrowed my eyes and stuck my finger into his chest. "But if you ever do anything like that again, we're gonna have a real problem."

"Good thing you're the only person I ever want to kiss for the rest of my life."

"I better be," I muttered playfully before looking to Silas. "Did we pass?"

"With flying colors," Silas said. "But I had no doubts you would."

"So he gets to come home with me?" I asked, tears brimming in my eyes again as our future together was solidified.

Silas nodded, a coy smile lighting up his face. "But that leads us to a dilemma for me. What power shall you be granted, Benjamin?"

"I get a power?" Ben asked in surprise.

"Of course. Garridan wouldn't be very accepting of you without one. Speaking of which, I think it's time to discuss your request now, Robin."

This time, I knew exactly what I wanted from him. I knew it the second Ben said he wanted to stay with me.

"I want Ben to be able to talk to his family still. Visiting would be even better, but I won't push my luck," I told Silas.

"Done," Silas replied, and Ben did a double take.

"Just like that?" Ben asked. "How?"

"A little persuasion on the council," Silas answered.

"Like Matthew's mom?" I questioned, and he nodded. "Just how many powers do you have?"

He chortled before saying, "Enough to do what needs to be done. You'll still have to make your request to the council and validate your reasoning, but find comfort in knowing they won't refuse." He smiled at Ben. "Your family won't be out of your life anytime soon."

"Thank you," Ben replied, reaching out to shake Silas' hand. "That means more than I can say."

"It's my pleasure. Now, while we're on the topic of the council, I have some advice for you two." He stood from his seat and paced in front of us slowly. "You two are in a very unique position to bring Garridan back into the real world—to show them they don't have to hide and to teach the next generations that they don't have to fear what's outside the barrier."

Ben and I glanced at one another as he continued.

"I was part of a time where people with and without powers coexisted. We shared our lands, our resources, and our knowledge. It was a beautiful era. One in which all people thrived." Silas watched a spot over our heads as he reminisced on another time. "The day that utopia started to crack will forever be a black spot in our history because it was the start of our failure to our duties. Instead of being balanced with nature, we were out of sync with it, which meant we were also out of sync with one another. That started to cause chaos and mass destruction events that killed many." He sighed heavily. "And we still feel those affects today."

"What do you mean?" I asked.

"It was one of nature's punishments for us. Our people have to forever live with the fact that we are solely responsible for the natural disasters that strike Earth."

"You mean like tornados and earthquakes?" Ben asked.

"Yes. The Keepers of Balance are limited in ways we weren't before," Silas explained. "Even the slightest miscommunications can create strange phenomenon when trying to perform their daily tasks for the world."

"Like a tornado happening because an air Keeper of Balance is angry when working with a water Keeper of Balance," I said, finally understanding what he was saying.

"Precisely," he confirmed.

"That didn't happen before the uh—" Ben hesitated before saying the term, "the 'utopia' started to crack?"

"No, it didn't. We unintentionally created that hardship for our leaders as well as the people it affects."

"That's crazy," Ben murmured.

"It's sad," I said, trying to imagine a life without natural disasters.

"Indeed it is," Silas agreed quietly. "But it's not a reason for the people of Garridan to be naive to their surroundings. I'm not sure the normal world could ever handle knowing people with supernatural powers exist, but that shouldn't keep Garridan from venturing out anyway. The children should learn about the outside world and get to experience the things they have to offer. They should be informed instead of living in the dark."

"I couldn't agree more," I said. He spoke the words I'd been trying to say to the council for months.

"That's almost what I was trying to tell Elijah and Luna," Ben replied. "They should have some sort of knowledge just in case Garridan ever disbanded, otherwise they'd be absolutely lost."

"Which is where you two come in," Silas said, gesturing towards us. "Robin, you've already begun to make a small dent in that initiative, but it's going to take a lot more time and effort for any real change to occur. It won't happen overnight, but small steps will still get you to a goal. Having communication with Ben's family will be a leap in the right direction, but you'll both have to retain a great deal of determination to get Garridan where you want it to be."

"We can do it," I said firmly. "I know we can."

"I don't know how much the council will listen to a newly promoted outsider, but I'll do what I can of course," Ben added.

Silas smiled at him. "You're going to have a much bigger voice than you realize."

"How so?"

"Benjamin Scott Toves," Silas replied, pulling Ben's hands into his own. "You are a descendant of my twin brother, Lyle Tovert, which means you have a strong lifeline to our family's powers—air and earth. You would do well with either, but since I took away an earth element from someone today, it's only fitting I bestow it upon another to help keep the balance."

"You're—" Ben glanced at me then looked back at Silas. "You're giving me an earth element power?"

"I am."

"Are you sure?" Ben asked, his eyes wide.

"Nature is never wrong," Silas replied. "Unless you don't want it. Would you prefer something with less responsibility attached?"

"No!" Ben answered quickly. "No, of course not. I'm honored, sir. I'd like nothing less than to help Robin and the rest of the council with their duties. Even more so, I'm humbled by the chance to work alongside her to change things for the better."

"I expected nothing less. You will do our family proud, Benjamin."

"I'll try my hardest."

"Come," Silas said, pulling Ben closer to the edge of the pond.

I stayed where I was, watching as Silas closed his eyes. He clenched Ben's hands tighter, and his lips pressed together until they turned white. In the same moment, the tree illuminated a bright light. First from the trunk then from every branch and leaf that was connected to it. The pond bubbled slightly, growing just as glaring as the tree.

A low humming met my ears and my eyes widened as each tree root lit up under the translucent ground beneath my feet. Unlike a normal tree, this root system spread out as far as the eye could see and every tiny detail was exposed, as if under a microscope.

The tiny veins of roots under Ben crawled up around his ankles, latching onto him until his skin resembled what I was seeing in the ground. I was paralyzed as I looked on, mesmerized—but also terrified—by the sight. Then, just as quickly as it happened, it stopped, and everything was back to normal.

Silas let go of Ben's hands, watching him with intrigue as he tried to look himself over.

"Is that it?" Ben asked.

"That's it," Silas confirmed as I came up behind Ben and grasped his arm.

"I don't feel any different."

Silas chuckled. "Once you unlock your powers, you will."

"How do I do that?"

"I'll teach you," I spoke up. "Just like Matthew did with me. Well, except nicer."

Ben smiled at me gratefully and nodded, then his brows furrowed. "Wait. I do feel a little weird all of a sudden."

"What do you mean?" I asked in concern.

"It's like a weird, tingling creeping through me."

I suppressed a smile, remembering the feeling when Matthew first came to Milton High. "Sounds like the pull of the powers."

"The *what?*"

"I'll explain later," I replied as Silas sighed and clasped his arms together, getting our attention again.

"I'm afraid it's time for you to go home now," he said, and my heart sank a little. There was a small part of me that wasn't ready for this journey to be over. "Why so sad?"

"I guess I'm just not ready to forget all this yet," I replied.

"You won't forget everything," Silas reminded me. "Only the small details that can't leave."

I nodded, unable to speak, so Ben said, "Thank you again, Silas. For everything."

"It was my pleasure," he replied. "I look forward to seeing your lives progress and, hopefully, the start of a new era for Garridan."

No pressure or anything.

Silas held up his hands and in the blink of an eye he, along with the nature around us, disappeared. In its place sat a familiar room with familiar faces.

"You're back!" Mom cried out, running up and throwing her arms around me.

"Don't ever leave again!" Toby exclaimed as he followed suit.

"That's officially everyone," Chang said.

"Plus one," Peter said as Mom and Toby released me. "Why isn't he back home?"

"He *is* home," I replied, smiling up at him happily. "Silas granted him a gift. He's one of us now."

"Welcome to the family, son," Dad whispered, clapping him on the back as Toby grinned at him from ear to ear.

I noticed everyone else from our search party was present as well, informally lined up around the council's chambers. Matthew was smiling at the news and gave me a small wink when our eyes met.

"Oh, how wonderful!" Mom exclaimed, squeezing Ben's hands.

"Do you remember anything useful?" Peter asked, uncaring of my announcement.

I opened my mouth then shut it again as my brows furrowed together. I remembered our plane ride and the conversations our group had over the last couple days, but small pieces were missing. I remembered our surroundings, like the dense fog and the canyon, but I couldn't recall how we'd made it through those obstacles. I even remembered Silas—how he looked, how he sounded—but most of the spaces where he spoke were blank. I could see his mouth moving but couldn't hear the words.

The only thing I could clearly remember was his conversation with Ben and I after the others had been sent away. Those words were still there plain as day, but I didn't plan on telling the council about it.

"No," I finally said. "I'm sorry. I can't remember much of anything."

"Just like the others," Chang said with a sigh. "I suppose we're just not meant to have information on Silas."

Ben and I exchanged a look, and I knew he remembered the same thing I did. I held onto his arm tighter and placed my head against his shoulder. We were in this together.

"Should I ask about my family now?" Ben whispered.

"Nah," I replied quietly. "Let them stress over one thing at a time. We'll ask tomorrow."

He nodded in agreement, and I gently pecked his cheek.

"What a bust," Peter was grumbling.

"We can ask more questions tomorrow," Mom said. "For now, how about we adjourn and head home." She looked at us then to everyone else who'd come back from the journey. "You all smell like you need a good shower and look like you could use a long night's sleep."

"Nothing would make us happier," Malachi agreed, one hand on each of his son's shoulders. He looked at Ben. "And you're coming home with us as well."

"We'll figure out a more permanent solution later on," Mom said.

"No need," Malachi replied. "He'll stay with us as long as he wants."

"I appreciate it," Ben said, smiling warmly.

"Think nothing of it," Malachi insisted. "We're happy to have you."

"Hey, what's your power?" Matthew asked loudly, gaining everyone's attention.

"Earth element," he replied, causing many jaws to drop.

"They're going to have powerful babies," Dad commented, wiggling his brows as Mom shoved his shoulder.

"Elijah!" she scolded as my cheeks flushed red, and he let out a belly laugh.

"Come on, wife," he said, swinging his arm around her shoulders as she tried to squirm away from his smelly pits. "Let's go home."

"Let's go home," I repeated to Ben. The idea of his home being in Garridan made my stomach do flip flops.

"I'm already home as long as I'm with you," he replied, and Toby fake gagged.

"That was corny," he said, and I laughed as Ben caught him around the neck and ruffled his hair.

Andre and Emery followed close behind us, and I inhaled deeply as I watched everyone mess around. We were all connected in ways that could never be undone. Each and every one of them were family now and always would be. I'd lost a lot over the last year but gained twice as much, and I could honestly say I couldn't be happier. Finally.

CHAPTER THIRTY-TWO

"Are you ready for your first lesson?" I asked, coming up behind Ben and wrapping my arms around his waist.

He held onto me, and I could feel the deep breath he took as he stared at the glistening water in front of us. No one was in the park aside from him and I, allowing us to take in the serenity of the moment as the wind rustled the trees.

"I like it here," he said. "It's peaceful."

"It's my favorite place in Garridan," I replied.

"Of course it is. You've always been drawn to the water." He chuckled and shook his head. "If only we'd known the reason why."

"Still a little crazy, isn't it?" I asked and he nodded. "I never would've imagined this is how my life would turn out. Never in a million years."

"Are you saying in all our childhood days, you never imagined you and I having a future together?"

"That's not what I meant," I said with a roll of my eyes, and he grinned.

"I know."

"Ben." I opened my mouth to say more but hesitated.

He turned around so he was facing me, his brows furrowed in concern. "What's wrong?"

"Nothing. I just . . . Are you sure this is what you want?" I asked softly. "This can't be how you pictured your life turning out either."

"No, it's definitely not what I pictured," he agreed, then a small smile played at his lips. "It's much better." He cupped my cheeks between his hands. "So, please, don't do that. Don't feel guilty or think I'm unhappy. Sure, some days may be harder than others, but that would happen no matter where I ended up in life."

"You're sure?" I pressed.

"I'm positive, so don't bring it up again, okay?" His eyes were earnest but firm and I nodded. "Okay then."

He kissed my forehead, and I smiled before asking, "Ready to start training?"

"Actually I have something for you first."

He stepped back, rubbing his lips together as he slowly brought one hand up from his waistline. His forehead creased as he concentrated, and a wide smile spread over my face as a flower began to sprout from the ground. It rose higher and higher, stopping once it hit my chest level.

"How did you do that?" I asked, amazed.

"Matthew helped me last night," Ben replied, a bashful smile on his face.

"So this isn't your first lesson after all," I commented playfully, and he shook his head.

"There's more," he said. "Watch."

He twirled his fingers and a deep affection traveled through me when the pink petunia unraveled, revealing a familiar ring. He grabbed it from the newly bloomed flower and held it between us.

"This was my great grandmother's wedding ring," Ben explained softly, just as he had the first time he'd given it to me. "My great grandfather welded it for her himself. She passed it down to her son to give to his love as a promise ring, who then passed it down to my dad for my mom and now, she passed it down to me . . . For you."

"Ben," I murmured as I stared at the beautifully welded piece of jewelry.

"I know we've had our ups and downs, and you felt justified in giving this back because of them. But we'll always hit some rough spots because that's just a part of life, and no relationship is perfect." He grabbed my left hand. "So, I want you to promise you won't give this ring back to me again. Not for any reason. No matter what obstacles we run into or however many fights we may have. You can't walk away from me, from *us*, again. Can you do that, Robin? Can you promise me that?"

I blinked wildly, trying to fight back tears as I heard all the hurt layered in his voice. Choosing to walk away had been worse than being forced to walk away.

"I promise," I whispered.

"Before I put it on your finger, I have something to promise in return," he said, and I gave him my full attention as he watched me intently. "When I gave you this ring the first time, I told you it was just a promise of love. Do you remember?"

"Of course."

"While it's still a promise of that, I plan for it to mean so much more this time."

"What do you mean?" I asked.

"We've already seen what life without each other looks like and I, for one, never want to experience that again," he said, squeezing my hand. "So one day—not anytime soon but one day—I have every intention of getting down on one knee and asking you to marry me. This time, this ring symbolizes exactly what a promise ring was meant to—a promise of marriage."

My heart raced in my chest and my mouth was as dry as cotton. I reminded myself to breathe, becoming slightly lightheaded at his impassioned ambition. He was ready to commit himself to me and only me for the rest of his life.

"It's your choice, Robin," he said, his voice gentle. "If this is too much too fast, I understand. You don't have to take the ring. We'll still be okay."

I licked my lips as a tear ran down my cheek, and my voice broke as I said, "Give me the damn ring, Benjamin."

His eyes lit up as a grin encompassed his face. He pushed the object onto my finger, and I gazed at it, feeling an odd sense of completion. When I looked back up at him, he was as teary eyed as me. I wrapped my arm around his neck and kissed him, letting all the emotion travel through my lips into his so he'd know just how much he meant to me.

"I love you, Robin," he said as he leaned his forehead against mine.

"I love you too, Benjamin."

He held onto me tightly, and I sighed contentedly. Kodi and Mateo were back home with their families. Alexander was starting a new chapter in a foreign world. Emery and Andre were living at my house indefinitely, but my parents loved having them there along with Toby. Matthew was moving up ranks in the guard, finally finding where he belonged. And Ben and I were together and happy.

Everything was falling into place. For the first time in a long time, I looked forward to what the future held. I was ready to start living my life again, and that's exactly what I was going to do.

A flock of birds jabbered as they flew through the sky. I peered up at them as they flapped their wings, soaring further up and away. I may never be as free as they were, but that was okay. I was meant to be so much more than the birds I was named after. I was meant to change the world.

Well, our world at least.

EPILOGUE – FIVE YEARS LATER

I peeked around one of the flowered arches that decorated both sides of the large room. People continued filling the pews, but the front ones were already full, and my eyes danced over them. Everyone who mattered was already here, sitting and waiting for the special occasion.

On the right side, my parents sat conversing with Jeremiah and Kiona. Jeremiah patted Dad on the back, their laughter filling the space as they went on about something only funny to them—as they usually did. Mom and Kiona pointed out different details around the room, still trying to perfect things even though the event was about to start. I hoped they realized they couldn't fix anything anymore because the clock was running down.

As my eyes traveled over them, I noticed they were all starting to turn grey and was reminded how fast time goes by. It was a thief that took so much, but you never noticed until later down the road. At least it gave as much as it took.

Behind our aging parents, Malachi and Susan were in deep conversation with Felicity's parents. They always found intrigue in each other's lives, and I shook my head, once again thinking how well their families would've blended had Matthew and Felicity stayed together. But I was just happy they'd both found happiness, even if it wasn't with each other.

William and Kesha—who still only held the title of girlfriend much to her disappointment—watched as Claire and Kodi kept pulling up different articles of clothing to show off their tattoos to one another. Claire's hair had grown long, and the bottom half was dyed to match the pattern of a leopard. She still had no interest in settling down or taking on any responsibility that wouldn't have people singing her praises, but at least she did her daily job without complaint now.

Kodi's hair wasn't any tamer with each short spike a different color of the rainbow. She accentuated her milk white skin with black attire. Her travels over the last few years had done wonders for her once shy demeanor, but even all the culture in the world couldn't fix her styling problems. At least she branched out and followed her dreams though. I couldn't imagine moving every couple months, but she seemed to find joy in the learning exper-iences that came with it.

I'm sure it helped that she wasn't doing it alone. Alexander joined her in all her adventures, the two of them as thick as thieves now. Their relationship wasn't easy to under-stand, but Kodi didn't seem to mind that we ques-tioned it. None of us had spoken to Alexander since the day we found Silas, but Kodi kept me up to date on his progress and well-being, which I appreciated. He hadn't found closure yet, but I was hopeful he would, and maybe one day we'd get to see him again.

On the left side of the room, the rest of the trainees were hanging out. Andre's arm was slung over Emery as she held onto their fussy two-year-old son, Andy. Toby tried playing peekaboo to calm him down, but it wasn't working. He stood up and his girlfriend giggled at his childlike disapp-ointment. He may possess the body of a man now, but he was still as pouty and awkward as the teenager I'd met in the Cyfrin compound.

Mateo playfully pushed him aside, and I smiled at the grin that formed on his face as he knelt in front of his god-son. I could faintly hear the animal noises he'd perfected in imitating over the years and Andy giggled, immediately intrigued. Despite giving up his shape shifting powers, he still had that deep connection with animals and it showed.

The sanctuary he built was the largest in the world, and more rescues were brought in every week for rehabilitation. He was single handedly responsible for saving six endingered species, and we were all super proud of him. Going home had been the best decision for him and his future.

Emery stood to stretch, her large belly looking ready for their daughter to be born any day. Andre placed his hand over it, trying to be comforting as Emery complained. As much as she'd enjoy her time with her baby, I knew she'd be happy to get back to work.

Her research was important to our society, and she thrived on being active with her powers and in the community. Luckily, Andre was more than happy to be a stay-at-home dad, his nurturing nature perfect for the task. Plus, he had a lot of help between everyone in our family, which made his job easier.

Emery's first born, Oliver, slung his arms around Toby's neck as he picked him up. He resembled Emery in every way and loved getting to visit when Kodi did. It was a rough transition but having him in their lives fulfilled Emery in a way that never failed to amaze me. Having contact with the son she thought she'd never see again was the best thing that could've happened for her. Even if he was in an extremely obnoxious six-year-old phase with little manners.

The back doors opened and Matthew, Mahka, and Dakota strutted in looking dapper in their black suits. I said a silent prayer of thanks that Matthew's wife, Lillian, had finally convinced him to groom his wild beard. It sat nicely trimmed against his jaw instead of resembling a lumberjack without access to electricity. One of Matthew's twins saw him and stumbled down the walkway, getting closer to perfecting his movement every day. Matthew caught him before he faceplanted then threw him up in the air, making him giggle.

Lillian rushed over with their other son planted on her hip and shook her head, throwing her free hand up in exasperation. Matthew laughed then pecked her on the cheek before handing over their son so she could take them back to their seats. Malachi took one of the twins from her, ticking under his arm as he tried to squirm away again.

Matthew watched them with a smile on his face. Aside from creating his own family, he'd started a program to help rehabilitate the Cyfrin members who'd been allowed to stay in Garridan. It wasn't an easy transition for anyone, but most of them were fully accepted now, and they did their best to live up to our expectations.

Mahka playfully punched Matthew's arm, and I could tell they were going to get rowdy if someone didn't intervene. They'd gotten to be like brothers since Mahka was in Garridan so often.

Unlike Dakota—who was barely out of high school and starting college—Mahka thrived being a consultant for the two worlds. Once the council finally agreed to being taught about the outside world, he jumped at the opportunity to come here with Jeremiah. Their weekly visits turned into weekend long stays for him, and now he was here just as often as he wasn't.

I suspected he'd eventually want to find Silas so he could be granted a power, but only time would tell. For now, the council allowed him to come and go as he pleased as they slowly became more trusting of what Ben and I were trying to achieve. We'd been officially appointed to the council after we turned twenty-one but started buttering them up the day after we got back from our journey in the Amazon.

A couple of people were immediately on our side, but the vast majority were heavily against our plan to reunite Garridan with the normal world. As time passed, we'd gotten closer and closer to our goal. I guessed we still had a few more years before they'd all be on board but that was okay. Real change took time.

"Robin, it's time," Felicity said from behind me. I turned towards her, and her eyes immediately watered. She took out a tissue and dabbed at them, making sure no tears came down to ruin her makeup. "You look absolutely stunning."

"Thank you," I replied, instinctively running my hands over the white dress that sashayed around me as I moved.

"I'm so excited!" she squealed, carefully hugging me like she'd ruin something if she squeezed too hard. "I can't believe it. Can you believe it?"

"I'm just glad you were able to make it," I said, smiling gratefully.

She'd only gotten here two hours ago but still managed to get us both dolled up with hair and makeup done to perfection.

"I wouldn't miss this for the world. If I screwed up my audition because I was in a rush, all well." She shrugged. "There will be other ones."

"I'm sure you did amazing."

"Thank you!" She sighed, her eyes misting over again as she patted down my hair under the headband. "Ugh. You're getting married. I'm engaged. When did we grow up?"

"I wish I knew," I replied as she took my hands in her own, guiding me towards the front of the building. We stopped at the double doors that led into the sanctuary, and my heart hammered in my chest.

"Are you ready?" she asked gently, seeing my panicked expression.

"Uhm . . . Maybe?"

"Deep breaths. When the doors open, just focus on him. No one else is there. No one else matters."

"She's right," Dad said as he joined us, his eyes app-raising me. He pressed his lips together then sniffled.

"Dad, don't cry," I muttered, pulling at a curled piece of hair.

"I can't help it. You look beautiful, kiddo. I can't believe I'm about to walk you down the aisle."

"I can't believe it either."

"Are you sure you want to do this?" he asked, his eyes dancing playfully. "We can leave now, and I'll make you your favorite food instead."

"Dad," I groaned, then I rubbed my lips together before licking them. "Don't tempt me."

He chuckled and patted my hand as he wrapped it around his arm. "You're going to be just fine. Don't get cold feet now."

"It's not cold feet. It's the stares."

"So, again I say, just focus on him," Felicity said, smiling gently. "No one else is there."

I nodded quickly and took a few calming breaths. Music started to play, and I closed my eyes as Felicity disappeared down the aisle. A moment later, the tune changed, signaling my cue to go. I nodded once at the people waiting to open the door for my grand entrance, and they obeyed my unspoken command.

As the doors opened, everyone stood and turned to stare. I licked my lips, clinging onto Dad's arm for dear life as my knees threatened to go out. I glanced at my mom then to the trainees before my eyes landed on the front of the room.

And there he was.

Ben. My Ben.

His hands were clasped together in front of his waist, and I could tell by how white his knuckles were that he was nervous too. His hair was pulled back in a tight braid, accentuating his jawline that'd only gotten more prominent. I noticed his lips trembling at the sides as he tried to maintain his composure, and I guessed he was fighting back tears.

But it was his eyes that drew me in. The way they became awestruck when he saw me. The way they appraised me with all the love and tenderness someone could offer. The way they noticed every detail of me and the way they glossed over as I walked towards him.

I beamed as I drew closer. All the guests faded away as I focused on him. My legs still felt jittery, but as I strolled down the aisle, my confidence grew, and I became more excited. Each step was bringing me closer to the love of my life, and we were finally going to be united as one. All the struggles we'd faced in the past had led us to this moment. I couldn't imagine my life without him in it, and I was forever grateful he chose to join me in Garridan instead of going home.

As I drew closer, a strange tingling vibrated in my head, and I very faintly heard the whispered word, "Congrat-ula-tions."

My brow furrowed for just a second before I smiled widely again, knowing exactly who it was.

Silas.

Somehow, he was watching Ben and I be joined together, just as he was watching us slowly join Garridan and the normal word together. I was excited to live up to his expectations of us, and I was happy knowing we were doing exactly what he'd asked of us—creating a new era.

With each step we took, we were forging a bridge—not one of metal or brick, but one of understanding and compassion. Our worlds were being welded together, and nothing could stand in our way.

As the sun dipped below the horizon, Ben and I stood across from one another. Together, we poured a cup of colorful flowers into a bowl of water, letting them float around. We set it on a small pedestal behind us then joined hands. As we exchanged our vows, the elements seemed to whisper their blessing, declaring our union was destined by fate and blessed by nature itself.